Praise for
SMOKE ON THE WATER

"*Smoke on the Water* is a wonderful stroll down memory lane for me. It takes me back to my early Air Force days, traveling throughout Hawaii, the Philippines, and other Asian destinations. I am reminded of many of the popular haunts, as well as the divisive politics the Vietnam War evoked among us. Perhaps the most touching element of the story is the struggle of the main character trying to make his captain, shipmates and friends accept him while he struggles internally with the desire to pursue a different career path. *Smoke on the Water* will keep you wanting to turn the next page."

—RICHARD HESS, US Air Force officer (Ret.) and author of *Night of the Bear* and *High Flight: A Pilot's Journey Through Life*

"This is an engrossing account of a young officer's service on a naval vessel during the Vietnam War. Bartley takes the reader on a closely observed tour of the social world of a small ship."

—JOEL BEST, PhD, sociologist and author

"Jason Conley is fresh from his comfortable existence as a college student in suburban Philadelphia. Trained as a naval officer, he travels to Pearl Harbor on his way to Vietnam. His original assignment becomes irrelevant when he is thrust into an unexpected position as ship's engineer. His next assignment comes with its own troubles, as the captain turns out to be a mysterious and increasingly dysfunctional commander. Armed with values that often conflict with his sense of duty, Jason must reconcile this to survive. Luckily, with buddies, music and lovers, laughter is never far behind.

An authentic, thought-provoking and satisfying read."

—MAYA L. PAUL, PhD, clinical psychologist

"Jack Bartley's novel, *Smoke on the Water*, is a terrific read. As someone who lived through the Vietnam era, I really enjoyed how quickly it took me back to that fascinating time in our history. The characters are all so vivid and easily identifiable. Great characters, dialogue, and pace. I really look forward to reading more of Mr. Bartley's work."

—JASEY SCHNARZ, reader

"A great read for any former NAVFORV sailor still able to walk and chew gum at the same time. Thanks for the ride."

—RICHARD PIET, former US Navy officer

"*Smoke on the Water* is a gripping and authentic portrayal of naval service during the Vietnam War. Jack Bartley masterfully captures the tension, camaraderie, and complexity of life at sea, delivering a novel that is both immersive and thought-provoking. With vivid storytelling and an unwavering respect for those who served, this book honors the sailors who navigated war's uncertain waters. A must-read for anyone who appreciates military fiction."

—RYAN MCDERMOTT, author of
Downriver: Memoir of a Warrior Poet

SMOKE ON THE WATER

Smoke on the Water

by Jack Bartley

© Copyright 2025 Jack Bartley

ISBN 979-8-88824-637-5

All rights reserved. No part of this publication may be reproduced, stored in a retrieval system, or transmitted in any form or by any means—electronic, mechanical, photocopy, recording, or any other—except for brief quotations in printed reviews, without the prior written permission of the author.

This is a work of fiction. All incidents and dialogue, other than well-documented historical events, are products of the author's imagination and are not to be construed as real. Where real-life historical figures appear, the situations, incidents, and dialogues concerning those persons are entirely fictional and are not intended to depict actual events or to change the entirely fictional nature of the work.

Cover art and design by Lauren Sheldon

Published by

3705 Shore Drive
Virginia Beach, VA 23455
800-435-4811
www.koehlerbooks.com

SMOKE ON THE WATER

A NOVEL

JACK BARTLEY

VIRGINIA BEACH
CAPE CHARLES

Other books by Jack Bartley

Public Ed—A Novel
Hilo Dome—Book 1 of the Hilo Dome Trilogy (Summer 2025)

Dedicated to my shipmate friends and all those who served in the WestPac/Vietnam theater.

TABLE OF CONTENTS

ONE | Off the Coast of South Vietnam 5

TWO | Villanova... 12

THREE | San Diego, California............................. 22

FOUR | Oahu.. 36

FIVE | King Street, Oahu 49

SIX | Waikiki.. 55

SEVEN | Honolulu 70

EIGHT | Pearl Harbor 84

NINE | The Deck Crew...................................... 101

TEN | Subic Bay, Philippines 114

ELEVEN | Subic Bay/Olongapo/USS *Midway*................. 123

TWELVE | Gunline DMZ 140

THIRTEEN | South China Sea 151

FOURTEEN | South China Sea................................ 176

FIFTEEN | Off the Coast of South Vietnam 187

SIXTEEN | Off the Coast of Vietnam 199

SEVENTEEN | Subic Bay..................................... 205

EIGHTEEN | South China Sea 220

NINETEEN | Kaohsiung 229

TWENTY | South China Sea 245

TWENTY-ONE | South China Sea and Hong Kong 256

TWENTY-TWO | Hong Kong Liberty 264

TWENTY-THREE | South China Sea and Yokosuka 284

TWENTY-FOUR | Midway/Pearl Harbor 296

TWENTY-FIVE | Deep Water Off Kailua-Kona 305

Acknowledgments 315

About the Author 317

ONE

Off the Coast of South Vietnam

DECEMBER 1972

Fireflies. Sparking on and off on a warm, humid evening in Pennsylvania, they announced the start of another summer. However, it was not summer. It was not Pennsylvania. They were not fireflies. To Lieutenant Junior Grade Jason Conley, while standing mid-watch out on the starboard bridge wing of the destroyer escort USS *Everett*, that is what came to mind. For just one brief moment he was transported away, an illusion created by the illuminated end buoys of the fishing nets splayed out before him. The buoys bobbed in the gentle swells of the Gulf of Tonkin just off the coast of Quang Tri. They seemed to go on forever. Unfortunately, it was in the middle of this forever that Jason had to guide the ship.

The *Everett* needed to be in position that morning by five to deliver gunfire support, badly needed gunfire support; the mission was to soften up an area south of the Cua Viet River. The Army of the Republic of Vietnam (ARVN) was preparing an assault to try to regain the base at the mouth of the river. The People's Army of Vietnam (PAVN) had been occupying the base for six months; it was a strategic location for the replenishment of PAVN supplies and an area for the PAVN to launch small boats in an attempt to plant mines on the US Navy ships on the gun line. The push required both naval and air support from the United States.

Jason had reduced the speed of the *Everett* to just five knots, but even that speed would be too fast to maneuver through the maze confronting him. Lieutenant Junior Grade Ed Snyder, the *Everett*'s navigator, joined him on the bridge wing. Jason had asked him to post his best quartermasters on this mid-watch since he knew in advance that coming in this close—less than a mile off the coastline being contested with the enemy—would be tricky. Understanding the situation, Ed said he would come up to assist in any way he could.

From the bridge wing, Ed said, "I wish I had better news, but no matter how I plot a way to get to our gunfire support coordinates we have to thread that spider web in front of us."

"I was afraid you were going to say that," Jason said, shaking his head. "How long till we hit the first nets at this speed?"

"Less than ten minutes." He paused. "Look, I know you're the OOD right now. Have you notified the old man?"

"Yeah." Jason paused. "Well, sort of. I explained what our likely situation would be when I took over at midnight. He didn't seem overly concerned and didn't add anything to the standing orders for the night."

Ed stared out at the fireflies. "You know this has a lot of social implications as well as military ones."

"I know, I know." Jason followed his gaze toward the nets. *These nets are their livelihood,* he thought. *Their families depend on them. We come barging in, destroying their gear, nets that will take a long time and lots of their income to replace, not to mention that they won't be fishing during that time, and then we expect them to support our efforts to keep them from being overrun by the ARVN. These fishermen and their families live in the here and now. What might happen in the future takes a back seat.*

Jason said, "We mess up, we're the bad guys."

Ed nodded. "Yep. Hard to get a win here."

"Okay. Let me take the conn from Jack. He doesn't have any experience in these kinds of maneuvers. I just wish we had the twin screws of my old ship. Getting through these nets would be a lot easier."

Ensign Jack Culpepper was inside the bridge. Jason stepped inside and explained the situation. He announced to the bridge personnel that he had the conn and the deck.

"Set engine speed at stop."

"Aye, sir, set engine speed at stop." After a pause he heard, "Sir, engine's at stop."

Jason pulled the binoculars out of the holder attached to the bulkhead beside the bridge radar screen. The radar screen showed nothing; the buoys wouldn't be detected. As he looked out over the netted area, Jason could detect differences in the buoy placement. Many of the buoys looked to be set at the same distance apart. He assumed the area between was the location of the net. The other spaces seemed to be irregular in terms of spacing. More than likely, these spaces would be the path they would need to travel.

Jason went back out on the bridge wing and told Ed what he was thinking. Ed had his own binoculars up. Without taking them from his eyes he said, "I think you're right. It's not going to be easy, though."

Jason went back inside. "Mr. Culpepper, keep an eye on the fathometer and the radar. The last thing we need to do is run aground this close to the coast of Quang Tri province."

"Aye, sir."

"Set speed at two knots."

"Aye, sir. Engine speed to two knots."

Jason explained to the helmsman, "I'm going to be asking you to be making some drastic changes in terms of our rudder placement. We're going to try it out now to see how the ship responds at this speed. I want to know what she can do before we hit that first set of nets."

Jason gave the command. "Right full rudder."

"Aye, sir. Right full rudder." The helmsman made the adjustment. "Rudder's at right full."

Jason strained to see in the dark. While it was visually difficult to ascertain, he could actually feel the ship respond. Then, he noted a change in bearing to the nets.

"Left full rudder."

"Aye, sir, left full rudder. Rudder's at left full."

The response was better than he expected. Now, time to thread the needle. Several needles.

"Come to course two eight three."

"Aye, sir, coming to two eight three."

It was not much of a shift from their current heading, but it would aim them just to the starboard side of the closest buoy, a position he assumed was outside of the net. His plan was to treat this like a slalom course on a ski slope. Hug the gate on the left, then track to hug the next gate on the right. However, this was in slow motion, with severe consequences for more than the skier. *These subsistence fishermen deserve better*, he thought.

"Steady on course two eight three, sir," the helmsman announced.

Ed, from the bridge wing, said, "Looks good from here, Mr. Conley."

Jason again explained to the helmsman what he planned to do. "Okay, from this point forward, I'll just be giving rudder orders. I hope to maintain this speed."

To the man on the sound-powered phones, Jason said, "Tell the forward lookout to watch carefully for any movement in the lighted buoys. If they start closing in on us on both the port and starboard sides, we'll know we've snagged one. We'll have to come to engine stop to prevent the net from becoming entangled in the prop."

"Aye, sir."

Jason went out to the port bridge wing and was joined by Ed.

"Well, here we go."

Just before the port bow of the *Everett* came alongside the first buoy, Jason yelled into the helm, "Right full rudder." As the helmsman responded, Jason moved quickly from one side of the bridge to the other. They were close enough to the next set of buoys that he didn't need the binoculars. "Left full rudder."

He could feel the ship sway beneath his feet. Nothing drastic; just enough to let him know they had decent steerage. As the bow of the ship began to swing and before the next buoy came in line he ordered, "Rudder amidships." He quickly added, "How's the fathometer, Mr. Culpepper?"

"Looks good, sir. It reflects what we're seeing on the chart. However, we have what appears to be a small boat with a constant bearing and closing range one mile off the starboard side."

Jason didn't need this added distraction. "Roger that. Keep an eye on him. We're going to be making a lot of maneuvers, so the bearing should change. Let me know if it appears to be tracking us."

Ed said quietly, "This looks good, Jason. Only five or six more of these to go."

"Yeah, great." Jason could already feel the sweat beading up under his armpits. The slalom run on Upper Chief at Okemo Mountain was a lot easier than this. The next buoy was almost on the starboard bow. Even as he gave the order he was looking ahead to the next set of "gates."

"Right full rudder."

"Aye, sir. Right full rudder."

As soon as he felt the ship begin to turn and just as the helm was letting him know the rudder was set, he said, "Rudder amidships."

"Aye, sir. Rudder amidships."

After four more sets of maneuvers, Ed said, "We're just about there—recommend coming to stop."

Jason called out, "Engine stop."

"Aye, sir. Engine stop," the helmsman repeated.

Culpepper said, "We have a visual on that small boat through the binoculars. It stopped tracking us and appears to be pulled up to a set of nets."

"Thanks, Mr. Culpepper. One less thing to worry about."

The quartermasters were firing in bearings every thirty seconds through the sound-powered phones. Ed, headset on, stayed at the chart console on the bridge, plotting them just as quickly. He said to Jason, "We're still making way, but not very much. If you add a few turns in reverse, we should be perfect."

"Got it. Thanks!" Jason made the adjustment.

Jason shouted out to the bridge crew. "Excellent job, everyone! I wasn't sure we could get this done without ruining someone's life out there on the water, but we—" Jason paused. "*We* did it." Everyone on the bridge applauded.

For the last hour of the watch, Jason gave the conn back to Culpepper so he could make the minor course and speed adjustments to keep the ship in position relative to the speed and direction of the current in the Gulf of Tonkin. During that hour, Jason gave some careful thought to what his role was here on the gun line. Pretty much every day, they would get orders from the command center to move overnight to a new location off the coast and then fire rounds at coordinates supplied earlier in the day by a pilot in a spotter copter. Jason never saw the people he was killing.

Jason wondered, *Am I doing the killing? Am I pulling the trigger?*

No.

Yes.

Maybe.

I'm certainly complicit in all of this mess, he thought. It wasn't a good feeling, certainly not like one he had ever had before in his life. He remembered back to when he'd bought a bow and some arrows and taken them out to a field bordered by woods near his home to do some shooting. As he was pinning a target to an oak on the border of the field, a rabbit scooted out of the tall grass and stopped at the edge of the woods. Without really thinking, Jason stopped what he was doing, slowly picked up the bow and nocked an arrow, took aim, and let it fly. As soon as the arrow released from the bow he thought, *Holy shit! Don't let it hit the rabbit, don't let it hit the rabbit, don't let it hit the rabbit!* To his relief, it had missed. He took the weapon home and threw it in the trash, disgusted with himself. The only thing he shot after that were cans and bottles set up in the sand quarry at Blue Mountain Lake in the Adirondacks, using his friend's .22 or the artillery officer's Luger his friend's father had gotten over in Germany.

Rabbits, Jason thought. *I was upset about firing at rabbits and now people are the target.*

Jason was so deep in thought that he jumped when Ed came up beside him. He was thankful for the company at that point.

Ed said, "I might as well stay up. It's only a couple of hours before I need to do my morning star fix. Want some coffee?"

Jason smiled. "My eyeballs are already floating, but yeah, why not more coffee?"

TWO

Villanova

MAY 1971

Jason threw his packed duffel into the open trunk of his '67 Firebird. It was the same duffel he had used for his senior NROTC training cruise to Puerto Rico and the Panama Canal last summer, but this time his uniforms held all the insignia and markings of an officer, an ensign in the US Navy, not the "no-man's-land" status of a midshipman. He opened the driver's door and carefully placed the case containing his Gibson B45 twelve-string on the floor in front of the small back seat, straddling the transmission hump. The gym bag holding the clothes he would be wearing for the road trip got tucked under the top of the guitar case on the floor. He had to leave enough room for John McGinty's gear; he was picking him up in the nearby town of Ardmore, another train stop on the Main Line that ran from Philadelphia to Paoli.

As Jason admired the wax job he had done on his car, he could feel the eyes of his father on his back; he was staring out the picture window watching his son get ready to leave. At twenty-two, Jason was ready to leave home. While in college, he couldn't afford to stay on campus in a dorm, so he had spent four years commuting from the home in which he'd grown up. For much of his time at Villanova,

Jason didn't feel fully incorporated into college life. Living in the family residence was nowhere close to what he knew his college friends were experiencing living in the dorms. The small ranch house, basically a double-wide with a finished basement, isolated him from campus life. Jason spent most of the time he wasn't in class in either the library or at the campus radio station. Escapes. Refugia.

Not that it was a bad house. It was perched near the top of a sloping half-acre lot that leveled out behind the deck in the back. Three big maples shaded the front lawn, and the open back yard had once been a playing field for pickup softball and touch football games after school and on the weekends. During family parties, the field was still host to savage croquet matches. *No, no, no! You can't send me! Smack!* It was a quiet dead-end street, inhabited by kids on bikes, Simon Says, and Red Light–Green Light. The laughter, yelling, and cries of children gave way on summer nights to katydids singing to each other. Jason would miss that. Not many katydids where he was going.

Where he was going was Hawai'i, Pearl Harbor, to be exact, and his father was not ready to let him go, especially with the war in Vietnam raging. It didn't matter that Jason was going to a rescue salvage ship destined to become a deep dive habitat support vessel. It was just that it was far away, very far away. And much closer to combat.

Jason had always tried to please his parents, especially his father. His father had been an outstanding baseball player, a second baseman, so he had tried to be an outstanding baseball player—playing second base, of course. His father had played football, so he had set out to make the school football team. The problem was, although he was a good athlete and could play many different sports, Jason was simply not as good as some of the other kids in his school. The fun positions, such as quarterback or wide receiver, were already taken by guys who grew faster and had to shave before they were fifteen. These same guys could blow a fastball by him too.

So, Jason had turned to music. He could play guitar at age eleven and could read music well enough to be the guitarist in the jazz band at school. The charts were far more complex than the three-chord progressions found in most of the rock songs he loved to listen to on the radio. He formed a rock 'n' roll band with his friends and did covers of all the British Invasion tunes that were featured on WIBG (Wibbage Radio) and *The Ed Sullivan Show*. Even though his father wasn't into that kind of music, until Jason got his driver's license, he still drove Jason to his lesson every Wednesday evening after dinner, sitting in the waiting area of the music store reading the sports page of the *Evening Bulletin*. A patient, understanding, dad.

Jason had run with a large group of friends in high school. Most of them had been together in classes during junior high, and quite a few had been in elementary school with him. He attended the same school his father had gone to and had been raised in a fairly conservative, static community. Jason got good grades, but as his mother often said he never "worked up to his potential." He never could figure out how his mother knew what his "potential" was, although Jason had to admit she might really know what she was talking about; he'd gotten the same commentary from his teachers.

In his junior year in high school, Jason had decided to do things because he liked doing them or because he thought it was the right thing to do, as compared to doing the things he thought his parents would want him to do. He quit baseball and joined the newly formed soccer team. They stunk, winning two and losing eleven that first year, but they had fun. Jason had developed a much more aggressive and confident attitude playing defense in soccer. He got yellow-carded in every game, but never got a red card, and never missed a minute of play through the whole season. Because the games were after school, his father, tied up at work, never got to see him play. Jason never knew how upset this made his dad, even though he wasn't playing baseball or football, until his mother told him after he graduated.

During his sophomore year in college, he made plans with his best friends from high school to camp around the country. He had NROTC training for the first part of the summer where he discovered that he was quite adept at flying a small plane. If his vision had been better, he would have tried to become a Navy pilot. Before leaving for training, Jason plotted out driving distances and found places to camp, and then he and his friends set out after the three-day Atlantic City Pop Festival for a trip around the country: total independence. It was a far cry from living at home and commuting to school.

He had very early NROTC training after his junior year and had most of the summer off. Villanova's academic year ended in mid-May, so his training was completed by the end of June. Early in July, he went on vacation with a friend and his family up at Blue Mountain Lake in the Adirondacks. He had accompanied them many times before, and most of the people at the lodge had been "vacation friends" for years. Shortly after they arrived, a boy he had become friends with during previous visits was killed in a car accident. His friend had been working in the kitchen at the lodge; the accident also badly injured the assistant cook, who had been driving. Jason had known the owners for years, and when he overheard them talking to some other guests about how difficult it would be to keep the kitchen running, Jason told the owners he would stay for the rest of the summer and work for them. He drove seven hours home to get more clothes, his guitar, and his tape recorder-player (had to have music), then turned around and went straight back so as not to miss a day.

When his parents mildly objected to his doing this, Jason had explained the situation to them and said it was the right thing to do. Friends help out friends. Jason started washing pots and pans, an absolutely brutal job in the kitchen, but soon graduated to assistant cook. He lost his carefree summer but learned a lifelong skill. Of course, there was also the benefit of working with a lot of college-age waitresses who liked to party after the dining room closed. Drinking age was eighteen in New York. It wasn't all sacrifice and hard work.

Being in the NROTC program at college hadn't been easy, especially since Jason's sentiments concerning the war leaned toward "Give peace a chance" rather than prolonged combat. Villanova was a very conservative college, so Jason spent most of his spare time in what was probably the most liberal outpost of the school: the radio station. He was lucky to have friends there; virtually everyone at the station, except the sports jocks, were far left. An image of Captain Omega, who ran the late "underground" shift on alternating nights with Jason, immediately scrolled into his brain like an unbidden film clip from the Woodstock documentary.

Slinging a Gibson SG in a progressive rock band, The Eatanters, with some students from the very liberal Haverford College just east of Villanova down Lancaster Pike also tested his sense of social balance. Jason knew the bass player from high school, and when the Eatanters' lead guitarist graduated, Jason was asked to join the band. From the very beginning the fit was not great. Jason was the square peg to the band's round hole. Jason had to keep his hair short for NROTC while the rest of the band resembled members of Big Brother and the Holding Company. The drummer was constantly on his case about training to kill innocent children in Vietnam. Jason tried to explain his position, but eventually, even though he could play every lick from the Dead's "Cold Rain and Snow," they stopped telling him when the practices were going to be. His friend eventually told him what he already knew.

No matter what that drummer thought, Jason didn't want to set fire to villages and kill innocent people, so it was while he was in his junior year at Villanova that the plan for getting an assignment to a research vessel developed. *Keep out of the war if at all possible!* Jason was a biology major, so it seemed like a logical progression after graduation and getting his commission. As it turned out, all those ships were stationed in Pearl Harbor, Hawai'i.

Running his hand over the car's hood Jason thought, *Yes, it's definitely time to leave.* He walked back toward the house, opened the front door, and stuck his head inside.

"Okay. Guess I'm about ready."

His mother, Sheila, came out of the kitchen, wiping her hands on her apron. "Well, I'm not ready. Of course, I guess I'll never be ready." Sheila was in her late fifties and fastidious about the way she kept the house. Jason often felt like he was living in a set for a photo shoot for *Ladies' Home Journal*.

Jason stepped inside, walked quickly across the living room, and gave his mother a big hug.

"I love you, Mom, and I'll miss you. Thanks for everything you and Dad did for me. A lot of sacrifices." Sheila Conley had worked as a secretary at the high school to help the family make ends meet. Before that, she had helped at the family hardware store, but there hadn't been enough business to make it worthwhile for her to continue to work there. Jason's dad, Nick, basically ran the place by himself, trying to stay ahead of the bigger chain stores that were swallowing up his business.

He stepped back, both of them wiping away some tears. The confidence Jason had felt just a few minutes ago about leaving was starting to slip away. *It's really happening. Right now. Possibly gone forever.*

Jason crossed the room and hugged his father. "I love you, too, Dad. Just don't worry about me, okay? I'll be home after I get some leave time built up, or maybe you could come out to see me. I hear there's some great golf courses out there." Nick was almost sixty and had put on a little weight, which exacerbated his high blood pressure and angina, but he still liked to get out on the links with his good friends from the Bryn Mawr Kiwanis. Jason took a step back, looked his dad in the eye, gave him a quick pat on the shoulder, and then walked out the door toward his car. Nick followed close behind.

Jason was ready for a road trip. Comfortably dressed in Levi's, his souvenir Iron Butterfly T-shirt from when they'd played the Villanova Field House, and Converse high-tops, he climbed into the driver's seat and fired up the engine. The in-line six purred, ready to go. It didn't have the throaty rumble of the touted Pontiac V-8, but it held its own. Besides, it was all Jason could afford at the time. When he'd gotten the full ride to Villanova University through the NROTC scholarship, he'd taken out all his savings. He and his dad had gone to the local Pontiac dealership. There it was in the showroom: a red Firebird, GM's answer to the Mustang. They had just come out a month or so ago. The red glowed; it spoke to Jason. The only caveat was from his mother: no convertibles! Jason got a great deal; the dealership was owned by a friend of Nick's. Of course, Nick knew everyone in town, so that deep discount was almost a given.

He looked up at his father, gave him a smile, then stepped on the clutch, put it in first and eased out of the driveway. As he rolled slowly down the little dead-end lane, Jason looked in the rearview mirror. He could see his father standing at the end of the driveway, waving. Finally, Nick Conley slowly dropped his hand, put both hands in his pockets, lowered his head and shuffled back toward the little ranch house.

Windows down on a warm May morning, Jason drove the Firebird to Lancaster Pike. After the attendant at the Texaco topped it off, he cruised down the pike, past the university, heading for McGinty's house in Ardmore. Driving there, he had to pass through Bryn Mawr. He felt what seemed like a twinge of homesickness as he passed by Conley's Hardware just two blocks west of the firehouse. *Homesick? I just left the house ten minutes ago!* The siren drove his father crazy if he was dealing with a customer, but overall, it was a good location in town. The Main Point slid by on his right. Jason had spent many nights in the small venue listening to the best performers in folk music: Tim Hardin, Tom Rush, Joni Mitchell, Phil Ochs, Doc Watson, Jim Croce. The list of talented musicians who played there seemed endless. Then, just a few blocks down from The Point sat the old movie theater, where *The Blob* had scared the shit out of him as a young kid.

A few miles down the road he turned off Lancaster onto the street where John lived. He had been there many times, picking him up for the weekly touch football game, a basketball game at the Palestra on the Penn campus, or a double date to see The Who at the

Spectrum. John preferred to have Jason pick him up in the Firebird since his '63 Corvair's next stop was the junkyard.

As Jason pulled into John's driveway, he could see the garage door coming up in the old two-story colonial that John had lived in all his life. John, rail-thin and just over six feet tall, let the door carry itself the rest of the way open. It bounced noisily as the springs brought it to a halt. He reached down, grabbed his duffel and a small overnight case, and trundled down the drive to Jason's Firebird.

"This all gonna fit?" John peered in the back window.

"Yeah, no problem—as long as you're not planning to bring anything else."

"I wanted to bring our old spinet piano, but I guess that's out."

Jason got out of the car, opened the passenger side door, folded down the passenger seat, and with a wave of his arm declared, "There ya go. Plenty of room."

John struggled the duffel through the door and over the folded down seat. A big shove landed it on the back seat. He threw the overnight bag on top.

John looked at Jason, shaking his head. "I'm not ready for this."

Jason smiled. "You're not ready for anything that has to do with the Navy. Better get used to it; you're looking at a mandatory four years of 'Aye, aye, sirs.'"

John sighed. "Yeah, yeah, I know. I was just hoping that there'd be some kind of last-minute reprieve."

"Don't hold your breath. There's no call coming in from the governor."

John hated the Navy. Hated the routine. Hated the drills. Hated wearing uniforms. But, like Jason, he was stuck. Military discipline? Hell, John couldn't even stay in the Boy Scouts. However, with no money for college, but with aspirations to eventually get a job using his skills in math and physics, there were few options. Like Jason, he had applied for, and won, a scholarship through the NROTC program, along with his best friend from high school, Sam Alexander.

Sam was staying on the East Coast; he'd been assigned to the base in Norfolk, Virginia.

John's grades at Villanova in math and physics were strong enough to get him an invitation to apply for the nuclear power program. Admiral Rickover was the driving force behind the Navy's development of nuclear-powered ships, in particular, submarines. It was said that every sub in the fleet had to have a uniform in Rickover's size on hand in case the admiral, on a whim, wanted to do a surprise inspection—a pervasive, but never-confirmed, rumor. John had told Jason about his interview with the quirky Rickover. It didn't go well. Rickover had taken one look at John's longer than regulation hair and called in his secretary.

Rickover had stood up behind his desk, pointed at John and said, "You—stay seated." In a louder voice he said, "Miss Johnson, come in here please."

A door opened from John's right and Miss Johnson had scampered into the room.

"Yes, sir, Admiral," she said, coming to attention even though she was in smartly tailored civilian clothes.

"Turn around, look at this midshipman, and show him what he looks like."

John said he'd squirmed in his seat as this played out. Miss Johnson turned around, took a quick look at John, then bent over, bowing at him from the waist, letting her long hair cover her face. Then, she shook her head.

"That'll be all, Miss Johnson."

Still bent over, Miss Johnson said, "Yes, sir." Then, she stood up, straightened her hair as best she could, and scurried out of the room.

Admiral Rickover had then stared at John for what seemed to him like an hour. "Now, Mr. Long Hair Disrespectful McGinty, get out of my office."

Stunned, John stammered, "Y-y-y-es, sir." He stood and headed for the safety of the doorway. At the door, he turned and said, "Thank you for the op—"

"Get out!"

John's bad attitude just got a lot worse from there.

John put the passenger seat upright and climbed in. "Okay, let's get the show on the road—literally."

Jason climbed in and gave John a quick glance, then looked up at John's front door, and then gave him *Did you forget anything?* Look.

"I said my goodbyes inside. Time to get rolling."

Jason backed the car out of the drive, then headed for the Schuylkill Expressway to Philly to catch I-95 south. Jason really liked to drive, so John's job on the trip, for the most part, would be navigating and trolling for a new rock and roll radio station, as the one they had been listening to faded out as each town receded behind them.

They had several stops planned; there was plenty of time before they needed to report for duty in San Diego. John had never been out West, but Jason had seen quite a few of the sights when he was on his camping trip. On the agenda: Nashville, the Grand Canyon, and Las Vegas, with a lot of wheat and corn between Nashville and the last two stops. Just as they hit the ramp to I-95, the opening chords of "All Right Now" by Free blasted out of the radio. "Baby, it's all right now."

THREE

San Diego, California

JUNE 1971

John and Jason found an inexpensive two-bedroom apartment not too far from the Navy base. It was located on the second floor of a huge complex that resembled a very modernized Colosseum. The first floor housed offices of the complex, a couple of laundry facilities were shared by the occupants of the apartments, and there was a well-equipped fitness center, as well. The rest was open for some under-apartment parking in addition to the large lots around the outside. The apartments were on the upper three levels, and all were two-bedroom units. The open center area featured a swimming pool with a water volleyball net and a very large, heated Jacuzzi whirlpool surrounded by some beautifully landscaped tropical vegetation. There were multiple grill areas, each with wrought-iron tables shaded by umbrellas.

The majority of the apartment dwellers were young professionals and military personnel from the many Marine and Navy facilities in the San Diego area. The rest of the people living in the units were retirees, or so it seemed to Jason. He never saw any children down at the pool, and in fact, there was no play area for children even if there had been any kids around. It struck him as odd, but maybe the owners of the complex were trying to discourage young families from living there. It wasn't the best place for raising kids anyway since two bedrooms was somewhat limiting.

Many of the officers that were in training with him lived in the complex. Bob Arians and his wife were just two doors down the hall, and Bob knew three other officers and their wives in the complex that had been in his class at Officer Candidate School back in Newport, Rhode Island. All these couples had become friends during the rather intense twelve-week session that the men had endured after graduating from college to become ensigns, officers of the line in the US Navy. Now, all were to be stationed on the several rescue salvage ships that were stationed at the mouth of Pearl Harbor, just like Jason.

It was the second Saturday after their arrival, and Saturday was the time for all the officers and their wives to have a big barbeque by the pool. Jason and McGinty were invited to this one even though they didn't have spouses. As they arrived at the pool, they could see Bob and his wife, Marianne, filling up some coolers with cans of Olympia lager, a brew Jason and McGinty had never tasted, or even seen, before. Marianne was a very pretty, petite blond who looked even smaller when standing beside her tall husband.

When she saw Jason and McGinty, she stopped what she was doing and shook hands with them. "I'm so glad you two could make it. It's so nice to meet you both and I'm sure we'll see lots of each other after we all get out to Hawai'i."

"I'm afraid I won't be joining all of you out in paradise," McGinty said. "I'm assigned to a light cruiser, the *Providence*, here in San Diego. I knew Jason here," he said, poking a thumb in his direction, "in college and we rode out together. I'm glad we had his car; mine would never have made it."

Jason explained, "We've been friends all through college and in the NROTC at Villanova, and then John suggested that we room together while I'm doing my training with Bob and the other guys. I'm sure he won't have trouble finding a roommate to replace me after I leave. This is a pretty nice place."

Marianne nodded. "It sure is, and they're very good about accepting short-term rentals too. I guess it's because so many people are here just for training then moving on to some other assignment."

Ken DiMartini arrived with his wife, Carrie, and without saying a word, reached into the cooler, grabbed a beer, ripped the tab off, and took a big swig. He threw the tab in the cooler.

"Ah, nothing like a beer to start off the afternoon," he said while wiping his mouth with the back of his hand.

Carrie, tall and slender, with her long red hair pulled back in a ponytail, said, "Kenny, you could at least say hello before you start slamming them down. And here, put the tabs in this plastic cup. Someone could cut themselves reaching in the cooler for a beer."

She turned to Jason and said, "Hi, I'm Carrie." Jason shook her offered hand and had trouble looking into her beautiful green eyes, distracted by the fact she was wearing the smallest black bikini he had ever seen. Carrie was almost as tall as him, and even though she was not particularly well-endowed, she was strikingly beautiful.

"Hi. I'm Jason, and . . ." motioning to McGinty, "this is John McGinty."

"Nice to meet you, Jason and John!"

"We're in 204, just a few doors away from Bob and Marianne." Jason looked over at Ken. "Hey, Ken, thanks for inviting us to the cookout."

Ken, even though he was just a year older than Jason, was already starting to project a beer belly out over the top of his baggy swim trunks. "Good to see ya, Jason. Grab yourself a cold one. We'll get a volleyball game going when everyone else arrives."

Everyone else was Ralph Gorman and his wife, Linda, and another officer Jason knew, but not that well, Roger Griffin and his wife, Patty. Patty was carrying a big salad bowl full of fresh greens and sliced tomatoes, and Roger had a tray with slices of cheese, burger patties, and hot dogs.

Roger set the tray down on the table next to Jason and said, "Bob tells me you were a cook one summer. Are you in charge of the grill?"

"Assistant cook, actually, but yeah, I can handle the cooking duties. No problem."

After everyone grabbed a beer, they jumped in the pool and started a volleyball game. It soon became evident that most of them had no idea how to play. Bob, the tallest person in the game, easily dominated the net. Jason was glad he was playing opposite Carrie; the fact that he couldn't help staring at her was not so obvious.

When not watching Carrie, Jason did notice two other women who were in the pool observing the game. Facially, they looked a lot alike. Sisters, perhaps? The only real difference was that one had short blond hair while the other woman had long, jet black hair almost to her waist.

Jason yelled over to them. "Hey, you guys wanna join in? That is, if you don't mind playing with people who haven't a clue about how to play the game."

The blond said, "Yeah, we'd love to." She slid into the game on Jason's side and her sister, at least Jason assumed it was her sister, moved over next to Carrie. "I'm Sandy, and that's my older sister Lori. We're in 304." Sister status confirmed.

Jason said, "Hey, you're right above us." He pointed through the net, "John over there is my roommate. We moved in about a week and half ago. Of course, we didn't exactly have a lot to move in since we drove here from the East Coast. So far, we've accumulated a sofa, two mattresses, some dishes and utensils, and a stereo set. Actually, it's quadraphonic. We have more speakers than any other piece of furniture."

Laughing, Sandy said, "What more do you need? Sounds like you're all set."

"Oh, yeah. *Good Housekeeping* is going to do a photo shoot of our place on Monday."

As the so-called game started to wind down, Marianne said to Lori and Sandy, "Do you guys want a beer? You can join us for burgers too. We've got plenty. Jason's going to start grilling soon, right Jason?"

Lori and Sandy gave each other a quick look and Lori turned back to Marianne and said, "We'd love to."

Jason got out of the pool, made his way over to the grill area and checked the coals. It was time to start flipping burgers and turning hot dogs. Lori came up beside him. "Need some help? I'll get the rolls ready and get the condiments set up."

"That would be great," Jason said. He watched her as she started laying things out on a tray. Wearing a red bikini, Lori was in some ways the opposite of Carrie. Besides the inverse color pattern in hair and bathing suit, Lori was at least a full head shorter and during the game had to constantly adjust her top in order to keep things where they were supposed to be. He sighed. *Probably out of my league*, he thought. Jason had never been too confident when it came to meeting women.

They engaged in small talk as he cooked. Jason discovered that Lori had a degree in psychology and was working at a local clinic while taking a graduate course toward her masters' degree at night. Her sister was a senior biology major at the University of California San Diego. They had grown up in Flagstaff, Arizona, and Sandy had followed her sister, at Lori's invitation, to San Diego one year after Lori had enrolled in USCD. Lori was not sure what her sister's plans were going to be after she graduated in a year, but she was pretty sure she would end up at the San Diego Zoo since she had an internship there.

Jason talked about his music interests. Lori asked him if he had a guitar with him, and when he said he did, she invited him to come over before dinner the next day. "You can play for our happy hour and then stay for dinner."

"Yeah, sure. I'd really like that," he said.

After everyone had been served their first round of food, Jason and Lori grabbed some burgers for themselves and then ended up seated with Ken and Carrie. Ken was feeling no pain having downed at least a six-pack over the course of the afternoon. Carrie didn't look very happy.

"When do you report to Pearl, Ken?" Jason asked.

"I'm supposed to be there sometime next weekend. A friend lined up an apartment for us over on the windward side near Kailua. I don't think Carrie here is, shall we say, enthralled with the arrangements. We'll probably be pretty far away from everyone else. But, hell, it's what I wanted and I'm the one who's gotta put up with being on a ship like an ARS; by the way, Lori, that's pronounced *arse*."

Lori said, sarcastically, "Thanks for the clarification."

Ken, missing it entirely, said, "You're welcome." To Carrie he said, "Yo, babe, could you fetch me another beer there? You're closer to the cooler."

Carrie glared at him. "Don't you think you've had enough?"

"Look, I still have food to wash down." Ken gave Jason a look that said, *Fuckin' women*. "Never mind, I'll get it myself."

The aluminum-framed beach chair groaned as Ken heaved himself up and out to fetch his own beer from the cooler. While he was gone, Jason asked Carrie, "Is it true what I heard about Ken's ship deploying for WestPac just a week after he reports for duty?"

Carrie sighed. "That's how I understand it. He's not thrilled about that, as you might be able to tell. And I'll be stuck by myself over on the windward side."

Ken sat back down with his beer. "You guys gossiping about me?"

Carrie said, "Not really. I was just explaining about your deployment."

"Fuckin' Navy. Fuckin' sucks!" Carrie's statement about Ken being "not thrilled" may have been an understatement.

Jason and Lori finished their food, and Jason said, "I'm going to ask around if anyone wants seconds. You guys want more?"

"I'll take a dog, if there's one on the grill," Ken said.

"Okay, one dog comin' up."

Jason took a couple more orders. Lori followed him over to the grill.

"I couldn't really stay at that table anymore."

"Yeah. Kenny's a little rough around the edges and treats Carrie like shit." He looked up from the grill. "Pardon my French. I'm glad I have the cooking duties as an excuse."

A few people went back into the pool, while others sat around talking. After the cooking was done, Jason and Lori started cleaning up the grill and packing some of the food away in the coolers.

John McGinty stopped by and said, "I'm headin' up. I've actually got duty tomorrow, so my Sunday has an early start."

"Geez, John, that means you you'll hafta get up super early to catch that six a.m. mass."

"Yeah, right. Like that's gonna happen."

Even though Villanova was a Catholic university, both Jason and John were "recovering Catholics." Still, McGinty had to report in by seven. Sunday duty sucked.

As the sun set behind the apartment complex, everyone else drifted away, saying their goodbyes and calling it a night. Jason and Lori soon found themselves all alone. They decided that a nice, relaxing soak in the Jacuzzi would be a good way to end the day.

Lori said, "I have some classwork I need to finish up tonight, but I can hang out here for a little while."

This was the best thing Jason had heard all day.

They slipped into the large Jacuzzi across from three other couples who appeared to be much older than either Lori or Jason. Most of them had gray hair, except for one of the men who was totally bald.

The bald guy smiled, and said, "We're doin' our thing."

"That's nice," replied Lori. She whispered to Jason, "I have no idea what he means by that." A few minutes later, she had more than an idea.

The bald guy said, "Sorry to break up the party but we have to be getting back to our places. Early day tomorrow." As they emerged from the bubbling water, it became evident that "doin' our thing" meant skinny dippin' in the Jacuzzi. After catching an eyeful of bodies she really didn't need to see, Lori slipped entirely under the water.

Jason waved. "You all have a good night."

After the aging soakers had wrapped themselves in towels, Jason pulled Lori up to the surface. "It's safe to come up now."

"I don't think I can unsee that," she said.

"No, that sight is pretty well etched into my brain too." Jason said, laughing. "Never knew the phrase 'doin' our thing' was a warning."

At five o'clock the next afternoon, Jason found himself at the door of apartment #304 with a bag containing a bottle of chilled Lancer's rosé and a bottle of Beaujolais, the guitar case leaning against the wall next to the door. He wasn't sure what to expect for the evening. He didn't know how many of Lori's friends would be there and what they would think of him or his guitar playing. Some people weren't very enthused about hanging out with guys in the military, either, although he figured people should be used to it with the huge military presence in San Diego. Still, it was something that was always in the back of his mind.

He knocked. Jason couldn't hear anyone approaching the door due to the wall-to-wall carpeting found in most of the apartments, so he gave a start when the door suddenly swung open.

"Hi! C'mon in!" Lori was dressed in Levi's cut-offs and an untucked, plain white cotton blouse.

Jason thought, *I sure am glad she invited me to her place because I never would have had the nerve to ask her to mine.*

Lori said, "Here let me take this." She grabbed the bag from Jason's hand. "You can grab your guitar case." She turned and padded barefoot across the carpet. Jason grabbed the guitar case and stepped through the door. He took off his loafers as he entered since it seemed to be the custom in Southern California. Lori had gone around the corner of the living room to the kitchen. Her apartment seemed to be laid out exactly like his. No surprise there. "Where do you want me to play?" He heard a cork pop.

"Right there in the living room. Is the sofa okay, or should I bring out a chair from the dining area?"

"Sofa's good." Jason noticed that Lori and her sister had put a lot more effort into decorating than he and John had. Recliners. Coffee table. End tables with lamps. *Maybe when I get a place in Hawai'i,* he thought.

Lori came around the corner into the living room carrying two wine glasses, each half-filled with the rosé. She said, "I thought we could have this now since I'm making clams fra diavolo for dinner. The red will work better for that."

"Had I known we were doing Italian I would have brought a Carlo Rossi Red Mountain," Jason said. "It's got a little more heft to it, shall we say."

"Shall we say the Beaujolais is just fine," Lori said. "Grab a seat. I've got some cheese for an appetizer." She went back around the corner.

Jason yelled out to her, "Shouldn't we wait for everyone else to arrive?"

Lori peeked around the corner. "This is 'everyone else.'" She ducked back into the kitchen to grab the cheese plate.

"Um, no Sandy?"

"Nope, she has some stuff at the zoo she had to be there for tonight. Some sort of members' appreciation night thing."

Lori came back to the room and set the plate on the coffee table. She smiled as she sat down close to him on the sofa. "Just you and me."

"A toast to the two of us, then," said Jason as he raised his glass to her. They clinked glasses, and Jason leaned into her and gave her a peck on the cheek. Startled, she pulled back.

Regretting his impulsiveness, Jason said, "Um, too soon?"

Lori said, "No, not too soon." She leaned in and gave him a lingering kiss on the mouth. "There, that felt better." She smiled at Jason and said, "Now, how about some music? Is it okay if I sing along? I've been told I'm not bad."

"'Not bad' about your singing, or . . .'"

"Stop. Get the guitar out."

They spent the next hour singing together. Jason knew a lot of Joni Mitchell songs and soon discovered that Lori was better than "not bad." She knew all the words to "Clouds," "Both Sides Now," "Urge for Going," and "Woodstock." Jason was glad he was up on his folk music in addition to having played in a rock band.

"This is really fun. I can't get over how good you play," said Lori. "But someone has to make the dinner, and that someone is me."

Putting his guitar back in the case, Jason said, "Is this your way of telling me to clam up?"

Silence.

"Seriously, I'd be glad to help," he offered. "I'm not shellfish."

"Stop."

"Okay, but really, I can help."

"Only if you humor me by keeping a lid on the puns."

"You got it."

They worked together in the kitchen getting the clams ready, cooking the pasta, and warming some Italian bread to help mop up the sauce. By the time the dinner was ready, the Lancers rosé bottle was empty, creating yet another fine candle holder, and Jason popped the cork on the Beaujolais.

Over dinner, Jason learned all about Lori and her family: where she had lived, what she did in school, sports she played, family life, and what her college years had been like.

After dinner they cleaned up the pots and pans and put their plates in the dishwasher. When Jason moved into his apartment, he had never seen an under-the-counter dishwasher before, let alone used one. The only dishwasher he knew was the industrial-sized monster in the restaurant at the lodge where he had worked. In less than two weeks in his apartment, he was already spoiled. He poured them each a glass of wine, finishing the bottle. They retired to the living room sofa.

The kiss they shared before dinner progressed much further

on the sofa, and it was not long before Lori was down to wearing nothing but some very sexy lace panties. She was breathing very heavily, but managed to say, "I think we've gone far enough."

Disappointed, but respecting what she said, Jason reluctantly said, "Okay."

Lori stood up and grinned at him, still lying on the sofa. "By 'far enough' I meant far enough out here on the sofa. Suddenly Jason's enthusiasm returned. "Come with me," she said. She turned and headed for her bedroom.

"I'll follow you anywhere."

When she got through the door of the room, she slid her panties off, turned and embraced him, whispering in his ear. "Now, let's do something about *your* clothes. You won't need them for the rest of the night."

As she started to undress him, Jason closed the door.

A few weeks later, after the completion of a day's training, Jason, John, Bob Arians, and Ralph Gorman were having a beer at The Fiddler's Dream, their favorite hangout. Fiddler's Dream featured a small bar that had been lifted from a pub in Ireland and transported to the West Coast. Dark oak, faceted mirrors, brass foot rail. Small Irish bands were featured on the weekends, but the owner encouraged musicians to come by for impromptu "sessions" throughout the week. One of the regulars, an older gent named PJ Ryan, would often sit on the bar and play jigs and reels for hours on end. PJ was playing when they came in and he gave them a nod as they brought their beers over to a small table toward the back of the pub. He didn't miss a note.

"Got an update to my orders," Bob announced casually. Bob's tall, lanky frame was perched back on his chair, balanced on the two rear legs. Jason set down his pint of Guinness without even taking a taste. He leaned forward, intent on what Bob was about to say since this news would have a direct impact on his life; they were both assigned to report to the USS *Engage* (ARS 5), a rescue salvage ship scheduled for a refit to become a deep dive habitat support vessel. With just a small complement of officers on board, and San Diego being such a large town Jason thought it weird that he had just happened to meet another officer living in his apartment complex that was headed for the *Engage*. They were also both concerned about the condition of the ship. Word had reached San Diego that these World War II vintage vessels were on their last legs. *Nothing but rust buckets. Held together by the paint. Heard they're being sold off to the Turkish navy.*

"Okay, what's the skinny?" Jason asked. "You only have one more week here with Fleet Training Group before shipping out. It's about time they got around to giving us some details."

Bob brought the chair forward, looked at his beer, and then up at Jason. "I'm assigned as the ops officer and will be in charge of communications."

"Um, that's what I thought I was going to be."

"Yeah, I know. I don't get it." Ralph and John sat back in their chairs, glancing back and forth between Bob and Jason as the sound of PJ's fiddle drifted over them. Bob looked around the table, shaking his head ever so slightly. "I thought the plan was for me to be deck officer with oversight of the diving operations. When I got these orders, I put in a call to a friend already at Pearl. He says they got a surprise transfer in. Some warrant officer who requested the *Engage* specifically. Must've had some pull to make that happen. Anyway, he took the deck job I was supposed to get."

Jason took a sip of his stout. "So where does that leave me? Not many slots for ensigns on a boat just over two hundred feet in length."

"Don't know." Bob shrugged. "I guess you'll find out real soon. You're several weeks behind me since I started the training here before you, and then you had that fire-fighting school tacked on."

"Yeah. Where the hell did that add-on come from?" Ralph asked.

Jason replied, "Well, the lieutenant in charge of scheduling at the training school mentioned to me that there was an opening for the school, and since Lori and I—"

Ralph jumped in. "Wait. Who's Lori?"

"Lori? Yeah, well she's this girl who lives in the apartment complex. You met her at the barbecue."

"Oh, yeah. Long dark hair. She was helping you grill."

"Well, we've sort of hit it off, so I figured a couple more weeks here in San Diego wouldn't hurt." Jason smiled sheepishly.

"Sure. Why not?" Ralph raised his pint in a mock toast and then took a big sip.

"Okay! Okay! Anyway, I'm screwed. My training was for ops. Not a big fan of last minute surprises like this. Now I have no idea what the hell they're going to do with me on the *Engage*."

"It could be worse," said Bob. "Did you hear what happened to Ken?"

They all shook their heads.

"So, as you probably know, Ken and Carrie already left for Pearl. He was to report to the *Reliance*, except that it pulled out early and was already on its way to Nam on a WestPac deployment when they arrived on Oahu. They gave him a temp assignment at 7th Fleet Headquarters for two weeks to give them time to settle into their place in Kailua. When the *Reliance* pulled into Subic, Ken flew out to meet it, catching a seat on a C141 cargo plane."

Jason shook his head. "I hope he had an actual seat and not a cargo net like I had on a hitch back from the Panama Canal. But, yeah, I guess that beats my situation. I feel sorry for him, but it couldn't happen to a nicer guy."

John said, "Not one of your faves, huh?"

"Nah, you saw how he was at the cookout a few weeks ago."

Bob said, "He was kind of a pain at OCS training too. Still . . ."

For the next few minutes, they all drank their pints in silence, except for the sound of "St. Anne's Reel" coming from the bar. Gradually, they all started talking about what was scheduled for the following day's training, but Jason wasn't really listening. His well-conceived plan of an assignment to a research vessel was beginning to unravel before he even arrived in Hawai'i. Could something unravel before being knitted or stitched together?

No matter how he tried, he couldn't see how this was going to work out well.

FOUR

Oahu

AUGUST 1971

Jason and Bob and Marianne Arians were sitting around a Koa wood, drop-leaf table in the kitchen of Bob and Marianne's small, two-bedroom bungalow that sat on a hillside overlooking Honolulu, eating a takeout lunch from a local Chinese restaurant. The table had to be a drop-leaf because when it was fully opened it was virtually impossible to walk through the kitchen, let alone work in it. Bob and Marianne had found the rental house within a week after arriving in Pearl Harbor, located in a predominantly Japanese neighborhood just off Liliha Street. It was not too far from the base and downtown Honolulu, where Marianne worked. They still had to contend with the H-1 freeway; it was frequently jammed in both directions during the morning and afternoon rush hours. Nevertheless, they were very happy with it.

When Jason arrived in Pearl to report to the *Engage*, Bob had picked him up at the airport and driven him to the dock at the mouth of the harbor by Hickam Air Base where it was berthed. It would be several weeks before Jason's car arrived from San Diego; the Navy shipped cars for officers transferring to Pearl, but it took four to six weeks, depending on the shipping schedule. While he was waiting, he had to live on the ship, which meant he wasn't able to go out driving around looking for an apartment. On top of that, he had been appointed chief engineer by the ship's captain. Jason knew nothing about engineering. He had never even changed the oil in his car. So now he was saddled with a shitty job and stuck on a ship out on a remote pier. Typically, only the duty section stayed on board when the ship was in port. Now, it was the duty section plus Jason. Fun times.

After three days of this, Bob could tell that Jason was pretty miserable, so he had offered to rent him their spare bedroom at a very reasonable rate, with Jason pitching in for food. This worked well for a while, but with just two bedrooms, a kitchen and eating area, a small living room, and one bathroom, living conditions weren't exactly ideal. Finally, Jason had received word that his car would arrive in a week, which took some of the pressure off the situation.

It was a Saturday, and no one had to be at work. They were finishing up the last bits of rice when Marianne said, "Hey, Jason, guess who went shopping with me yesterday after work?"

Jason had no clue. "Um, Don Ho?"

"Haha! Close. Carrie DiMartini. She drove over from the windward side, and we went to the Ala Moana Shopping Center."

The Ala Moana Shopping Center was the only thing on the island that actually resembled the kind of mall they were all used to on the mainland. Back in Pennsylvania, Jason lived close to the King of Prussia Mall, supposedly the biggest one in the country. Ala Moana was much smaller, but very nice; much of it was open air, as was just about everything in Hawai'i. The mall was anchored by Sears at one end and Macy's at the other, with lots of novel Hawaiian shops in between, like Crazy Shirts, Shirokiya Department Store, Martin & MacArthur Koa Wood gifts, and Long's Drugs. Jason had yet to get there.

"So, how's Carrie doing by herself over on the windward side?" Jason asked.

Marianne frowned. "Not so good. She still doesn't really know anyone over there, so the only time she gets to talk to anyone is when the wives get together, which is not all that often."

"Well, that sucks. At least the beaches are nice over there, from what I hear."

"I don't think she needs a beach; she needs some conversation."

"What makes you say that?" asked Jason.

"Because she said so."

"Anyway, totally out of the blue, she said she'd like you to come over for dinner."

"Me?" Jason looked around as if there might be someone else in the small kitchen. "Come over for dinner? Out of the blue, huh?" Jason looked very skeptical. "Why me? Why not you?"

"Well, she knows I have Bob to talk to, and she knows you've been stuck here with us for a couple of weeks with no car, so she thought you might like a change, get out a bit, see some of the island."

"Uh, huh." Jason looked at Bob. Bob just shrugged his shoulders, then concentrated on his General Tso's Chicken as if it was saying something important to him.

Jason looked back at Marianne. "This isn't a little ploy so that you two can get a little 'alone time,' is it?"

Mariann, looking all innocent, said, "Why, no, we have had plenty of time to be, you know, 'alone.' I was just thinking of the two of you."

Jason stared at her, saying nothing.

"She said to call this afternoon."

He continued to stare.

"I have her number." She reached into the pocket of her shorts and pulled out a crumpled piece of paper with a number on it and slid it across the table.

"I don't know," Jason said hesitantly. "This just doesn't seem right."

"C'mon, it'll be fine. I mean, it's not like you don't know her. Just have some dinner and chat for a bit."

Sitting on the living room sofa an hour later, Jason decided,

What the hell. He picked up the phone on the end table and dialed the number on the scrap of paper Marianne had given him. On the second ring, a voice at the other end said, "Hello, this is Carrie."

"Hi, Carrie, it's Jason, you know, from San Diego."

"Hi, Jason. Sure, we met at the cookout."

"Right." Jason paused.

Carrie jumped in. "I was talking with Marianne yesterday, and she thought it would be fun for us to get together for dinner. You know, just hang out for a bit."

Wait, I thought Marianne said it was your idea. Jason said, "Sure. Sounds good, but it'll probably have to wait for a week or so until my car gets here since I have no way to get over there." Jason was thinking a little stalling action might get him out of it. No luck.

"No worries! I'll come over to pick you up. I already have a great restaurant picked out."

"You mean, like today?"

"Sure. Why not? You have other plans?"

"Um, no, no. Today's fine."

"Great. I'll pick you up at five. See you then. Bye." Before Jason could reply, he heard the click of the receiver. *Well, guess I'm going out to dinner.*

Carrie swung by Bob and Marianne's right at five in a dark blue '67 Mustang convertible with a white top. Jason was already walking out with Bob to meet her when she popped out of the driver's side wearing dark green short-shorts and a pale green cotton blouse. Jason noted that the green played well with her long red hair.

"Hi, Jason! Ready to roll?"

Jason was wearing khakis and a dark blue Polo pullover. "Yep. I'm ready. Wasn't sure how casual I should dress, so I shot for something between my cut-offs and dressy."

"You look great. Besides, I can't think of any place 'dressy' in Hawai'i."

He glanced over at the Mustang. "Wow! Nice car. Same year as my Firebird."

"Thanks! You wanna drive? You can drive a stick, right? We have to leave the top up because it's raining up around the tunnel of the Pali Drive."

"No problem, but yeah, I'd love to drive. You just have to give me directions 'cause I have no idea what the windward side is like."

"Okay, let's go."

Jason opened the door for Carrie, then came around and climbed into the driver's side, with Bob looking on.

Bob waved at them. "Bye now. You kids have fun. Don't do anything I wouldn't do."

Jason shot him a glare that Carrie couldn't see that almost made Bob jump. Jason put it in gear, and they headed for Liliha Street and then on to the Pali. Carrie was right; the clouds had rolled in around the peaks of the Pali Lookout, and a light drizzle was falling. Shortly after they cleared the tunnel on the other side, the rain stopped; they cleared the cloud cover and Jason got his first look at the windward side. The sheer, deeply ridged wall of the ancient volcano that is the Ko'olau Mountain Range provided a stunning backdrop to the views of Kaneohe Bay and Kailua Bay. It was difficult for Jason to keep his eyes on the road.

Carrie fed him directions to Buzz's Steakhouse across from Kailua Beach Park. Buzz's was the most well-known restaurant in the Kailua-Kaneohe-Waimanalo area; their steak and lobster dinners were legendary. They arrived before six and were able to get a table at a covered outdoor table with a view of the beach.

The waiter was at their table almost immediately, filling their water glasses, giving them menus, and taking their drink orders.

Carrie said, "I'd like a mai tai." Jason had never heard of a mai tai but having read the description of the drink on the menu, thought that it sounded good and ordered the same.

As they both looked out at the beach while waiting for their drinks, Carrie said, "That beach is where I like to come when I'm off work. During the middle of the week, it's pretty empty."

"Sounds nice." Jason paused, taking in the view, then looked over at Carrie. "So, you got a job?"

"Yeah, it was tough making ends meet since Kenny hasn't been too good about sending anything back from his paycheck. It's just three days a week over at the Kaneohe Marine Air Base Exchange. Not too difficult. The pay's not great but it's enough."

The drinks arrived, and Jason said to the waiter, "Can you give us a few minutes to look over the menu? But I do think we'd like some of the teriyaki beef skewers to share as an appetizer."

"Certainly."

Carrie raised her glass as a toast. "Here's to Hawai'i!"

Jason said, "I'll drink to that! And, to my first mai tai."

The mai tai's were big, cold, and strong. They both took long sips.

"Oh, this is great," Carrie said. "Just what I needed." She had left her sunglasses on, giving her the look of a movie star.

They looked over their menus. Carrie decided to get the lobster tail, and Jason chose a thirteen-ounce New York strip steak, medium rare. They both went with a baked potato. The waiter came back with the beef teriyaki skewers, took their dinner orders, and directed them to the salad bar, located on the other side of the restaurant behind the horseshoe-shaped bar.

As they nibbled on the tender teriyaki steak, Jason asked Carrie about what she had seen in Hawai'i since her arrival. Carrie said her favorite thing was the Polynesian Cultural Center in Laie near the North Shore. The music, dancing and luau gave her a better understanding of the origins of the Hawaiian people, although she had to admit, it was sort of like Polynesia meets Disneyland. "As an anthropology major, it was interesting to be able to talk with the islanders who worked at the 'island villages' in the center. Most of them are students from all over Polynesia and by working at the PCC they earn their tuition for the college located right in Laie."

Carrie said she was also impressed with the Bishop Museum. "Not as glitzy as the PCC, but very interesting," she said. "Much more authentic in terms of how the Hawaiian Islands came to be populated and what the Hawaiian religious beliefs were like. It's real close to Bob and Marianne's."

They finished their drinks and the steak, and Jason caught the waiter's attention. "Do you have a Mondavi dry rosé on your wine list?"

"Yes, sir, we do."

"We'd like a bottle of that with our meal, please."

"Certainly, sir. It'll be a while before your dinners are ready. Would you like another drink, and then you can get something from the salad bar."

Carrie said, "That sounds good." Holding up her empty glass. "These were terrific."

A few minutes later, the waiter returned with another round, and after a few sips, they made their way to the salad bar. It was the largest salad bar Jason had ever seen. Besides several different greens, there were olives, mushrooms, peppers, tomatoes, artichoke hearts, and chickpeas. In addition to the typical salad offerings, the bar also had sliced pineapple, mango, papaya, melon, and strawberries.

Taking it all in, Jason said to Carrie, "I guess we really didn't need the teriyaki steak."

They loaded up their plates and made their way back to the table. They were almost finished with their salads when the main courses arrived. The waiter opened the rosé and left it in a chilled wine bucket on a stand next to the table.

Looking at the wine, Jason said, "I don't know if you've had this. It's a really dark, dry rosé. Should go with my steak and your lobster."

"I'm sure it'll be fine," said Carrie. "Want me to pour?"

"Sure."

As she poured, Carrie said, "This really is a beautiful color. Much deeper than the Lancers or Mateus I usually get."

They shared bites as they ate. Everything was delicious.

Carrie said, through a mouth full of lobster, "I think this is the best meal I've ever had."

Jason had to agree; it was pretty damn good. Sheila Conley was a good baker but didn't know her way around a piece of meat. It had to be cooked *to death*, as Jason thought of it, to make sure the insidious parasites that lurked inside were as dead as the meat. He had learned to appreciate medium-rare beef while working at the lodge. Saturdays were prime rib nights, and the chef wouldn't have it any other way. If someone ordered well done, the chef would have Jason soak a slice of medium-rare meat in the au jus container on the steam table until it was colored brown. When it was served, people were amazed, saying it was the best and juiciest "well done" prime rib they had ever had. No one was ever the wiser.

They finished up the food and declined the waiter's offer of cheesecake for dessert since they were both stuffed. The waiter brought the check, and Jason snapped it up.

Carrie said, "No you don't. We're splitting this, right?"

Shaking his head, Jason said, "Nope, my treat, especially since you've had to get a job to make ends meet."

"But this was my idea."

"Didn't Marianne have something to do with this?"

Carrie grinned. "Well, maybe a little, but I don't want you to be stuck footing the bill for the whole thing."

"Don't worry," said Jason smiling. "Right now, I really don't have much to spend my paycheck on. Definitely, my treat."

It was just eight o'clock as they left the restaurant and headed for the Mustang.

Carrie said, "Hey, it's early. Would you like to see where I live? The view of Kailua Bay is pretty nice, even at night."

"Sure, I'd like that."

"Here, give me the keys. It'll be easier if I drive. It's tucked away on some back roads on the hillside."

Jason turned the keys over and climbed into the passenger side. *This is probably not a good idea*, he thought. *But then again, I thought the dinner would be a bad idea, and it wasn't. What the hell.*

It was about a ten-minute drive to Carrie's apartment, located in a small, eight-unit, horseshoe-shaped complex looking out over Kailua Bay. Carrie's was an end unit, so it had a wrap-around lanai. All the apartments were ground level, and all opened from the front out to a swimming pool, located in the center of the horseshoe. They parked and Carrie went around to the front and let them in.

The front door opened into a living room that had a glass slider on the side that faced out to the bay. There was a small dining area between the living room and the kitchen, which was surprisingly big given the overall size of the apartment. A short hall with a bathroom led into the only bedroom.

Carrie slid open the glass door, directed Jason to the lanai, and said, "Have a seat. I'll be out in a sec."

Jason sat in a black wrought-iron chair with a pad on the seat and back and looked out over the bay. The trade winds felt soft and gentle as the lights of Kailua looked back at him. Carrie came out carrying two glasses of wine.

"Here's that Lancers I mentioned at dinner. Thought you might like a glass." Carrie handed him a glass and sat down next to him.

"Thank you. Don't mind if I do."

They sat in silence for a minute looking out over the distant ocean, and then Carrie said, "I told Marianne this yesterday, and I think I should tell you. I'm leaving Kenny."

"What? I mean, what are you going to do? Stay out here? Where's home?"

"I guess you could say I'm from the Portland area since I went to high school there, but I didn't really grow up there since we moved a lot. So, I'm not sure if I want to go back there. It's kinda hard since I went away to college, met Kenny, got married, went to Rhode Island with him, and now I'm out here. It's been difficult keeping track of the few old friends I had."

"Yeah, I can see how that might be hard."

"It's just that I can't take it anymore. Even in college, Kenny drank a lot, but once he got into OCS, it got worse. I have no idea why he took that route, you know, joining the Navy. He obviously doesn't like it."

"Then, why did he do it?"

"I guess he thought it would please me. My dad was career Navy, and I talked about him a lot. Maybe he thought it would impress me." She sighed. "It didn't. I mean, when he got assigned to a ship in Hawai'i, I must admit I was pretty excited, but that wore off fast."

"It's really none of my business, but he hasn't, you know, hurt you, has he?"

"No. It's the yelling, the arguments, the slamming doors. I can show you where he punched through the wall of our bedroom in one of his fits. That was damn scary." She sighed again. "I'm sorry, I shouldn't lay all of this on you. We just had a great dinner, and I was having a wonderful time. I'm enjoying your company." She leaned over and gave him a quick kiss on the cheek.

"It's okay. Look, I'm here for you. I know you're stuck over here, but it's not that far once I get my car. You can show me that cultural center you told me about."

Carrie said, "Thanks, I really appreciate it. I'm just not sure what to do. He's gone for at least another three to four months. Do I stay here? Do I find my own place, break the lease? Go back home?" She downed the rest of her wine. "Want a refill?"

"Sure. Thanks."

She came back out with the bottle, poured each of them a glass, and plopped down in her chair. She said, "Walking back in there I realized one thing; I may not know where I'll be in a few months..." she paused and giggled, "But I *do* know that I am way too drunk to drive you home. Sorry."

Jason was not sure what to think about that. *I guess there's that sofa in the living room.* He said, "It's okay, I don't think Bob and Marianne will miss me."

"I think you're right. I think Marianne had *plans* for tonight."

"I sorta thought the same thing. I even jokingly said to her that it sounded like she was trying to get me out of the house for a bit."

"Yep. Here's to Marianne!" Carrie toasted the air with her glass and took a drink.

Jason said, "So what'll we do now? It's kinda nice just sitting out here looking out over Kailua."

Carrie looked at him and said, "Hey, we can go for a swim."

Jason said, "I'm not quite really prepared for that; no suit."

"Doesn't matter. No one is ever in the pool at night. I go skinny dipping all the time."

"You do?"

"I do." She stood up. "Here, I'll get you Ken's robe to put on just to get out to the pool. Then we can drop the robes and jump in."

Carrie disappeared inside for a while, then came back out dressed in a short, black kimono robe. She handed one to Jason. "Here ya go."

Jason took it, went inside, stripped down in the living room, and came back outside, wearing just the robe.

"Are you sure this is gonna be okay?" Jason asked.

She nodded.

They walked out to the pool, stood on the edge, and Carrie whispered, "On the count of three, we drop the robes and jump."

Jason nodded. "Okay."

"One. Two. *Three.*"

Jason did as instructed and popped back to the surface and looked around, only to find Carrie still standing on the edge of the pool with her robe on.

"Hey! What's the deal?"

"Shhh! Someone might hear you and look out here." She giggled and whispered, "I just wanted to see if you would do it." With that, she shimmied out of her robe and jumped in. She popped up beside him, threw her arms around him, and gave him a big kiss.

Jason pulled back, and smiled, "You call this swimming?"

"No, I call it *nice*."

Jason put his arms around her and let his hands drift down below her waist. "I'm not sure we should be doing this, but, yeah, it's nice."

Carrie said, "Enough talking. You can kiss me back."

So, he did.

Jason didn't sleep on the sofa that night.

The day after Carrie drove him back to Bob and Marianne's house, Jason gave Carrie a call. He had been feeling guilty about their night together, but if she was planning to leave Ken anyway, why not continue to see her. He had certainly enjoyed her company. However, there was no answer. He tried again the next day with the same result.

After a third day of trying to reach her, Jason tracked down Marianne in the kitchen. She was sitting at the table writing a letter.

"Hey, Marianne. Have you heard from Carrie lately? I've been trying to reach her."

Marianne looked up from her letter with a troubled look on her face. She stood and came over to Jason.

"Carrie called me this morning. We spoke for quite a while."

"And? Is she okay?"

"In a way, no." Marianne looked Jason in the eye. "I'm sorry, Jason, but she's decided to move back to Portland."

"What? When?"

"This afternoon. She thought it would be better if she didn't see you again, even though she said she had a great time with you. She just wants to get her life on track again without Kenny, and she just couldn't imagine still being in Hawai'i when he got back from WestPac. She said she's sorry, but she couldn't bring herself to say goodbye to you in person." Marianne paused. "She really liked you, Jason."

"Yeah. I liked her too." He looked down at the floor, then back up to Marianne. "Thanks for letting me know."

Jason went into the living room and sat down hard on the sofa. Carrie had been one of the bright moments in his otherwise bleak existence since reporting to the *Engage*.

Probably for the best, he thought. It would have really been awkward continuing to see her after Ken came back on the scene. The ARS community wasn't that big, and everybody was into everyone else's business. Besides his own feelings, he felt bad for Carrie. She had found herself in a tough situation with no real solution except to return to the stability of her hometown. Of course, Portland may not be the place for her since she had said it had been tough staying in touch with friends.

Marianne peeked out from the kitchen. "You okay?"

"Yeah. I knew this was a possible outcome. She said she was thinking about going back home."

"Can I get you anything? A beer? Glass of wine?"

"No, but thanks."

"Are you sure you're going to be okay?"

"Yeah. I just feel bad that it came to this." He looked up at Marianne. "Do you have an address for her in Portland? Do you think she'd mind if I wrote to her?"

"Yes, and I think she'd love to hear from you. For now, you'll have to write to her in care of her parents. That's where she'll be staying until she sorts things out. I'll get it for you."

"Thanks." Jason sighed. "I guess that'll have to do, for now."

FIVE

King Street, Oahu

OCTOBER 1971

Just three blocks from Jason's one bedroom cinder block apartment sat the Kuhio Grill, perched on the corner of King and University. Jason and four or five guys from the crew would meet there once a week for *pupus* and beer. That was about all the place was good for. Cockroaches? Present. One night they spotted a rat scurrying across a rafter that extended from the bar out over the seating area of the restaurant. They were all thankful it had good balance. On another night, they found a rat scrabbling around in a urinal in the men's room. *In a urinal*! No one could figure out how it could have possibly gotten in there.

The pupus were "free." All you had to do was keep ordering beer, and Millie, their waitress, would continue to bring out plates of food served family style. Depending on how many plates they went through, the guys would give Millie a tip commensurate with the amount of food consumed. The utensils were chopsticks. Jason had never used them before going to the Grill, but he learned very quickly; it was either that or starve since the rest of the guys were quite adept with them. Teriyaki steak, Portuguese sausage with cabbage, whole steamed fish, crispy fried wontons, sashimi, and steamed dumplings were just a few of the dishes that would come out of the kitchen.

The kitchen. To get to the Grill from Jason's apartment you had to walk by the door to the kitchen, which was always open. The guys had one rule; do *not* look in!

While the pupus might change from time to time, Millie was always their server. The bar was billed as a Korean restaurant, but there never seemed to be any Koreans as customers, or for that matter, anything particularly Korean about the menu. Jason was pretty sure Millie was Filipino. He would call the bar, ask for Millie, and when she would get on the phone he would say, "Hi Millie, it's Jason. You know, the *haole* guy with the beard." *Haole* means "stranger," or non-Polynesian in Hawaiian. It could also be used in a derogatory way, such as "Kill Haole Day," a not-so-official holiday in the islands.

Millie always would say, "Sure, sure. When you coming in? How many? For pupus, yeah?"

Jason would add, "And beer."

"Yeah, yeah! Beer. Sure. See you tonight."

The beer they ordered was usually Primo, the Hawaiian beer. It was light, cheap, and one could consume a lot while washing down pupus and still be able to walk back home. The company was owned by Schlitz Brewing, headquartered in Los Angeles. Rumor had it that Primo was actually brewed in LA, then shipped as a concentrate to Hawai'i to be reconstituted at the "brewery" in Aiea. Jason's description of it: twenty-four flavors in every case.

On special occasions, such as a birthday, they would order Kirin Ichiban, an excellent beer from Japan. The Kuhio Grill served it in 22.5-ounce brown bottles with raised Japanese printing around the neck. It was much better than Primo, but it was also much more expensive. A little pricey for them to be ordering on a regular basis, especially for his friends who were operating on enlisted men's salaries.

Enlisted men. Second class petty officers, to be exact. Definitely a problem for Jason since he was an officer and fraternizing was frowned upon, especially by the captain of the *Engage*. However, there weren't a lot of options open for Jason in terms of finding friends. And, what the hell. They were all about the same age and shared the same interests, especially in music. Having pupus and sharing a few drinks with them was one of the few bright spots in his otherwise frustrating life as a crew member on the *Engage*. *It's really none of the Navy's business what I do on my own time*, Jason thought.

Jason left his apartment on a warm and breezy Wednesday evening. He was dressed in Levi's and sporting his feathered warrior Crazy Shirt tee. Comfortable, worn-out loafers with no socks completed the ensemble. He walked into the restaurant area of the Grill and noticed that Sid Carper was already there, seated at the bar to the right of the front door sipping on a Primo.

Sid was in the Damage Control Division. Even though he was just a year younger than Jason, his hair was already thinning and definitely in retreat on his forehead. Jason referred to it as a "fivehead." Sid was also the best diver on the salvage ship and was notorious for upholding the diver tradition of being totally outrageous. His reputation at the Kuhio Grill was well-deserved.

One evening, just a few weeks earlier, Jason had come in and couldn't get a seat at the crowded bar. He'd stood behind Sid for a while sipping his Primo. After fifteen minutes without anyone getting up, Sid leaned back over to him and whispered, "I'll fix this." He turned back to his beer on the counter, waited a minute or two until the inevitable cockroach climbed up on the bar surface and started making his rounds. This got everyone's attention, especially Sid's. When the roach got close enough, with one quick swipe of his hand he scooped up the cockroach and popped it in his mouth. The bar emptied.

With a wave of his hand, Sid motioned for Jason to take one of the now available seats. Slowly, Jason sat down, not taking his eyes off Sid. After he got on his stool, he looked carefully at Sid and said,

"Pretty neat trick."

Sid shook his head.

"Not a trick?" Sid shook his head again and opened his mouth. The cockroach stared out at Jason. Sid spit it out onto the floor and went back to sipping his beer. The cockroach scuttled away.

"Thanks for that," said Jason. "I owe you one."

Jason was thankful that for this time they had a table to go to. He caught Millie's eye, and she motioned to a table in the back corner of the restaurant section.

"Yo, Sid," Jason called out, "Millie's got us set up over here."

Sid turned, gave Jason a big smile and sauntered over from the bar. They both sat down, and Millie brought Jason a Primo without him even asking.

"Thanks, Millie! You can hold off on the pupus until the rest of the guys show up. Should be two or three more."

As he sat down, Sid said to Jason, "The rest of the crew should be here in a few minutes. They had to take the bus since I decided to get a head start on the beer and took the car."

Sid shared a small two-bedroom apartment with Michael "Smitty" Jones, Jimmy "JJ" Johnson, and Ollie Franzen—all petty officers on the *Engage*. It was one of four apartments in a very old complex. The four units were all on the same level, elevated one-story up off the street to provide parking spaces underneath. Over the years, high rise hotels and condominiums had sprouted up all around the building, casting long shadows on it throughout the entire day. The shadows helped because there was no air conditioning.

How and why the old building still existed was a mystery; the lot itself had to be worth millions. The view through the heavily soiled, jalousie windows consisted of the back sides of these buildings and the traffic light where The Bus stopped. The windows were always open, so the noise from Paoakalani Avenue and Kuhio Avenue poured in instead of the trade wind breezes that used to cool things down when the place was built fifty years before anyone in Hawai'i knew what a high-rise was.

Being right beside the bus stop was convenient. There was regular service to Pearl and Hickam. They shared a run-down '59 Chevy Bel Air that was owned by Sid and was parked under their apartment. It worked well for transportation to and from work, but on the weekends, Sid would keep his own schedule, leaving the rest of them to fend for themselves. The other guys had plenty to keep them occupied. It was only three blocks to the beach and Kalākaua Avenue, where there were plenty of shops and restaurants, and it was just a short walk to their other favorite hangout, the International Market Place.

A few minutes after Jason and Sid sat down, JJ, Smitty, and Ollie sauntered in. They quickly spotted Jason and Sid and grabbed some wooden chairs and pulled them up to the table.

Smitty said, "Howzit?"

Jason replied, "Not bad, not bad."

Smitty looked at Sid, "So you couldn't wait for us? In a big hurry today?"

"Nah, I had shit to do over near the university and since I was in the neighborhood, I thought I'd settle in early." Sid grinned. "Hey, at least I left you a note."

"Were you picking up your guitar from the repair shop?" Ollie asked.

"Yeah, the neck needed some adjustments. Plays a lot better now."

Sid owned a Guild D35. He had bought it used, and it had seen some rough times, but it still sounded great. Smitty played a Fender bass through a Fender Bassman amp, and the three of them, Jason, Sid, and Smitty, would jam at the apartment, doing covers of Buffalo Springfield, Neil Young, and many others. They were surprisingly good.

The rest of the beers arrived, along with the first plate: whole steamed fish. Sid claimed dibs on the eyes.

JJ looked at him like he was crazy. "Why do you always bother to do that? You know that no one else here is going to touch the eyes, let alone anything else on the head of that thing."

"It's just that I have this craving for crunchy, fish-flavored buttons and I also like to get the head for myself to get at the cheek meat. You guys don't know what you're missing."

"That's okay," said Jason. "What I never knew, I never will forget." He watched as Sid grabbed the head of the fish, twisted it off the body, and put it on his plate.

JJ changed the subject. "So, what do you hear about our little jaunt down to Johnston Atoll coming up, what, in two weeks?"

Sid said, "What I hear is that there's not much to do there. A bowling alley and a ball field for something called 'mountain ball.' We get a new movie every night. Food's supposed to be great; the reef there is pristine, so snorkeling will be good. Lots of sharks, though."

Smitty said, "No women, right?"

"No women," confirmed Sid.

Jason added, "We're there to escort ships carrying some nasty ordnance from Okinawa. Could be real unstable since it's so old. Gotta carry a gas mask and an atropine injector at all times when one of those ships is in."

"Yeah, we're there to haul them off the reef if they fuck up going through the channel," said Sid. "Just where I want to be, up close and personal with a damaged ship carrying damaged deadly ordnance."

"Nerve agent, mustard gas, sarin. Lots of fun stuff is what I hear," said Smitty.

"There're two clubs on the island—officers and enlisted. At least the booze will be cheap," said Sid.

They silently toasted this news with their beers. A big plate of Portuguese sausage and cabbage arrived, and the conversation ebbed as they got into some serious eating. As he doled some of the food onto his plate, Jason was thinking, *These are the guys I like to hang with. What am I supposed to tell them? I'm an officer and I can't do stuff with you off the ship? Like I'm too good for them?* He took another sip of his Primo. Silently he said, "Fuck the Navy." Then he thought, *Shit, I'm beginning to sound like Kenny.*

SIX

Waikiki

DECEMBER 1971

Jason pulled his red '67 Firebird into the parking space next to Sid Carper's '59 Bel Air on a warm Friday evening. Their apartment had two spaces allotted to it, but since Sid was the only one with a car, the extra space was almost always open. Parking in Waikiki was a hassle, but having Sid's extra space made it easy. Jason was meeting Sid to go grab a bite to eat and a beer (or two) down at the International Market Place, with a jam session to follow back at the apartment. The Dagger Bar had good local food, and the beer was relatively cheap given it was downtown Waikiki. Sid came down the stairs from the apartment and they walked the eight blocks down to the Market Place.

The International Market Place on Kalākaua Avenue was a hodgepodge of shops, bars, restaurants, and kiosks that were supposed to create the atmosphere of being in Korea, Japan, China, or the South Seas all at the same time. It succeeded in creating the atmosphere of being in a tourist trap. The buildings and shops were centered around a giant banyan tree. Up in the branches at a height equivalent to the second floor, was the location of the office and home of Donn Beach, the Market Place's creator and manager. A nifty tree house. Most of the kiosks featured costume jewelry that could be purchased just about anywhere but had the cachet of being a souvenir from Waikiki. T-shirts and flip-flops were available at any number of places, as were gaudy Hawaiian shirts. There were some nice establishments, upscale shops with high-end, name brand clothing, and the Don the Beachcomber Restaurant and Tiki Bar that featured well-known entertainers over the years like Don Ho and Martin Denny. The clientele in the open-air market was a real mix of locals and tourists, which made for excellent people watching. Tahitian-style dancers and torches scattered around between the shops completed the tiki scene.

Jason and Sid found seats at the bar and ordered food and a couple of Primos. Jason got the Kalua pig platter and Sid had the Korean barbeque. Both came with a scoop of rice and a scoop of macaroni salad. Jason could never figure out how macaroni salad had become so common in Hawaiian dishes, like the plate lunch specials at the L & L or Rainbow drive-ins. While they ate, Sid spent most of the time complaining about a girl Ollie had picked up in The Dagger and brought home one night a week or so ago that had never left.

Jason asked, "So, she doesn't chip in for food or contribute anything?"

"Oh, she contributes, all right," Sid smirked. "Just not in the way you might expect. You'll see; you'll meet her tonight."

The conversation ended when their attention was drawn to an impromptu performance by a mai tai–infused forty-something tourist doing her rendition of "Aloha 'Oe."

Jason watched in amusement, shaking his head slightly. "Sorry, Queen Lili'uokalani."

Sid added, "This place never disappoints."

When she encored with "Tiny Bubbles," Jason and Sid thought it was a good time to leave.

Back under the apartment, Sid pulled a small cooler filled with Primo out of the trunk of Jason's Firebird while Jason grabbed his guitar. Jason had left the cooler in his car rather than taking it inside when he arrived knowing most of the beer would have been gone by the time they got back from the Dagger. They climbed the stairs to Sid's apartment. A small wisp of sweet smoke drifted out through the top of the screen door.

Jason opened the door. "Looks like someone's got a head start," he announced. "And I do mean *head*."

Smitty, JJ, and Ollie had pulled kitchen chairs into the living room area. Smitty had his bass out and was trying out a few runs. Ollie and JJ were passing a joint back and forth. Hearing Jason, Smitty looked to the door, "All right! Beer's here." Smitty stopped playing and leaned his bass against the wall, something that always made Jason cringe. He could just see someone knocking into it and having the bass hit the floor, busting off its headstock.

Jason set his guitar case down and JJ offered him the joint. "Wanna hit?"

"Sure. Looks like Sid and I have some catching up to do." He took a draw on the joint and passed it to Sid. "Good stuff. From Maui?"

"Yeah, a guy I know brought it in last week on a sailboat. He's docked at the Ala Wai."

Jason opened the cooler, got a church key, opened some beers, and passed them around. He then grabbed another chair from the kitchen and dragged it in so that it faced the chair Smitty was using. Ollie grabbed his beer and relinquished his chair to Sid. Sid had already opened his case and pulled out his Guild D35. Jason got his Gibson twelve-string, and they all tuned up their instruments. Smitty already seemed pretty tuned himself.

Sid asked, "Where's our guest?"

Ollie said, "Sparrow's taking a nap in my bedroom. I'm sure the music will wake her up."

Smitty asked, "Whaddaya wanna play? Some Buffalo Springfield?

Neil Young? Crosby, Stills, and Nash?"

Jason suggested, "Let's start with one we all know really well to warm up, and then tackle some new ones. 'Heart of Gold?' Key of A minor?" Sid started the opening notes, with Jason and Smitty coming in. Jason did the lead vocals. While they were playing, Sparrow strolled out of the bedroom. She was wearing an open red satin kimono and nothing else. She walked over to the sofa and plopped down next to Ollie, who had just lit up another joint.

"Can I get a hit off that?" she asked sleepily.

"Sure."

It was hard for Jason to concentrate on the lyrics and his playing, but they got through the song without any problem. It was the first song they had ever played together and was still a favorite. Sid turned to Sparrow and said, "Sparrow, this is Jason. He's an officer on the ship with us."

"Ooohh, an officer. Nice to meet you, Jason."

"Nice to meet you, Sparrow. Can I get you a beer?"

"Sure. Thanks." She looked at the others. "An officer *and* a gentleman. Nice."

Besides being virtually naked, Sparrow was a petite blond, with long, straight hair down to her waist and a slightly pouty mouth under beautiful blue eyes. Jason thought, *She looks like she could be sixteen, but she came home with Ollie from the Dagger, so I guess she's at least twenty-one.*

Jason brought the opened beer over to Sparrow, trying to look into her eyes as he did so. It was difficult. "Any songs you'd like to hear?"

Sparrow crossed her legs and brought her hand up to her chin as though she was thinking it over. "Do you know 'For What It's Worth?'"

"Um, sure. One of my favorites." He went over, picked up his guitar, and they began to play, with Jason singing, once again. Sparrow drank her beer, watching and listening intently.

When they finished the song, Sparrow said, "That was great. Want me to roll another joint?" She didn't wait for an answer. She stood up, went to the glass coffee table, and set up shop there, sitting cross-legged on the rug.

They played for several hours, with Sparrow fetching beers for them and rolling joints. Jason, Sid, and Smitty finally decided it was a little late to continue with the music, and JJ and Ollie had already crashed in one of the bedrooms, so they sat around drinking and talking about new songs they might try. Sparrow listened in. Jason was pushing for "Broken Arrow," a Neil Young song from Buffalo Springfield, but Sid had some doubts about it. Tricky timing and chords. "We'd definitely have to lower the key," Sid said. "None of us can sing those high notes that Neil hits on that song."

Sparrow asked, "Do you guys know any Dead?"

"I used to do 'Cold Rain and Snow' in my old band but I'm not sure we could pull it off acoustically. We should give it a try, I guess."

"Another one that you guys could nail is 'Ripple.'"

Jason agreed. "Yeah, that's a real possibility. Good suggestion."

They continued the discussion for a few more minutes. In a highly unusual move, Sid got a piece of paper and actually wrote some of the ideas down.

Changing the subject, Jason asked, "Hey, are we still on for that afternoon job at the *Y* next weekend?"

Sid said, "Yep. Two hours. They're providing the sound equipment, microphones, EV speakers, and I think they even have a Crown amp."

Jason said, "It's good they have it because we sure don't. Maybe someday."

"I'll see if they can give us some rehearsal space so Eddie can get his drum kit over there. We don't have many chances to play with him since his drums won't fit in the apartment." Eddie Santos was another petty officer on their ship and could play the hell out of the drums. He wouldn't need much time to learn their sets.

Jason looked around and whispered, "Where'd Sparrow go?"

Sid whispered back, "I think she hit the head."

Still in a whisper, Jason asked, "Is she always so, shall we say, open?"

Sid and Smitty nodded, keeping quiet as Sparrow rejoined them. "More beers, guys?"

They all had another round, and Sid said to Jason, "I think you better not drive back tonight. You can crash on the sofa bed here."

Jason nodded. "I believe you're probably right. Wouldn't be the first time."

Sid and Smitty downed the rest of their beers and took turns hitting the head. Sid came out of his bedroom with some sheets and a pillow and threw them on the couch.

"You know the drill."

Jason opened up the bed, fitted the sheets to it, and went into the bathroom. No toothbrush, so he "borrowed" someone's mouthwash, swirled it around and thought, *That'll have to do.* When he came out of the bathroom, he could see Sparrow had collected all the bottles and was puttering around in the kitchen, cleaning up. *So, she does do something.* It was usually difficult to tell the interior of the apartment from a dumpster.

He was stoned, slightly drunk, and beat. He kicked off his loafers, got undressed, and climbed naked into bed. He didn't think the pokey springs of the old, worn-out sofa bed mattress would give him any problems in terms of falling asleep. In fact, he was out like a light before he even finished that thought.

Even though the sun had risen over Waimanalo Bay on the windward side quite some time ago, it took a while for it to peek over the Koʻolau Mountain Range and penetrate through the high rises in downtown Waikiki. It wasn't so much the light as it was the morning traffic noise on the streets just outside the apartment's living room windows that caused Jason to stir. He was thinking, *After last night, I probably should feel worse.* He looked at the watch on his wrist: just after seven. It was then that he realized that he wasn't alone in the bed.

He could make out Sparrow's long hair splayed out over one of the throw pillows from the sofa. She was breathing softly, evenly, but he couldn't tell if she was awake or not, so he wiggled closer to her and gently shook her shoulder. She was awake. He could tell because she rolled over and threw her right arm around his waist, drawing him even closer to her, as if she had been waiting for him to move so she could spring her trap. The kimono was gone. She slid her right leg in between his legs and slowly brought her knee up close to his crotch.

She whispered, "So, last night you were an officer and a gentleman. Are you planning to be a gentleman now?"

Jason's body was already telling him the answer to that question. "I can be gentle and a man—does that sound okay to you?"

"As long as we don't wake anyone, it sounds perfect."

Jason listened. The snoring from the bedrooms was almost as loud as the traffic noise. "I don't think there'll be a problem with that."

After they made love, they lay still in the bed for a few minutes. Sparrow whispered, "Let's go get a shower before anyone wakes up."

"You're full of good ideas."

Jason got out of bed, offered his hand to pull her up out of the bed, and they padded into the bathroom and shut the door. *Save water; shower with a friend.* Jason thought that was an odd phrase since whenever he showered with a "friend," the shower lasted a long time, typically longer than two consecutive regular showers. After they were done, they climbed out of the tub, dried each other off, and shared a long kiss.

Sparrow said, "So, what are you up to the rest of the day?"

"Not sure I'll be *up* for a while."

She smacked his arm. "Not what I meant."

"Oh. Don't know. No plans."

"Well, let's do something together."

"Are you a good swimmer? We could go to Hanauma Bay and go snorkeling. We can rent you some gear at the Frog Man Dive Shop on Kalākaua, then swing by my place to get my suit and gear, and then head out to the bay. Have you been there?"

"No, but I've heard it's awesome."

"Get your suit on and maybe bring some other clothes in case we want to go out to eat later."

"Be right back." Sparrow went into Ollie's room and in less than a minute she was back out, still naked, but carrying a large, denim-covered overnight bag. "All my stuff's in here."

"All of it?"

"Everything except my toothbrush and a few other toiletries in the bathroom." Sparrow opened the case, rummaged around for a bit, and pulled out a bright blue bikini. "This'll work." She shimmied into the suit, then pulled out a pair of denim shorts and a white blouse to wear over the bathing suit.

"Okay. All set."

"Don't you think you better tell Ollie where you're going?"

"Last night after you crashed, I told him it was time for me to be moving on. He knew I was planning to leave soon, so it really wasn't much of a surprise. Ollie knew my real reason for coming here, to Oahu, was to move to a commune, a farm, out on the North Shore."

Jason was a little surprised by this, but given what he knew about Sparrow so far, it made some sense. "Oh, okay. Then get your stuff out of the bathroom and we can throw the bag in my car."

Sparrow collected everything from the bathroom, threw it in the bag and zipped it up. "Okay, let's go."

Jason grabbed his guitar case and looked at the cooler. "I'll get that later. I have another small one we can take to Hanauma."

At this point, Sid wandered out of his bedroom wearing a pair of striped boxers. "Hey, what's up?"

Jason said, "We're going to Hanauma. Wanna come along?"

"Nah. I told some guys I'd meet them down on the beach to do a little surfing. Conditions are supposed to be decent today." He looked at Sparrow, then at her bag, then back to Sparrow. "So, is this goodbye?"

"Yeah, Sid, I'm gonna make my way up to the North Shore. It's about time. You're probably sick of me hanging around. Thanks for letting me crash here for so long. I really appreciate it. You guys are great."

"No problem. Welcome anytime."

"Thanks." Sparrow looked at Jason. "Okay, now we can go."

They went down the stairs to Jason's car, put Sparrow's bag on the back seat and Jason's guitar in the trunk, and walked down Paoakalani toward the beach. When they got to Kalākaua Avenue, Jason looked out at the ocean and saw that Sid probably would have a good day of surfing. The waves were nice and steady. Not huge like at the North Shore this time of year, but they had a nice regular pattern to them.

Frog Man Dive Shop was just a few doors up the street. Inside, Sparrow got fitted for a mask and snorkel, tried on size six fins, then traded up half a size when they proved to be too tight.

Jason said, "Tight is usually better than too loose, but those probably would have cut off all circulation to your toes."

They packed everything in a mesh bag and headed back to the car. Jason backed the car out from under the apartments and headed over to his own place.

As he made his way over to King Street, Jason glanced over at Sparrow. "So, I'm guessing that Sparrow isn't your real name."

Sparrow smiled, "No, my real name's Olivia. Olivia Gatling."

"You mean like the gun?"

"Yep. A distant relation, but that's my family."

"Where'd the 'Sparrow' come from?"

"Before I came over to Hawai'i, I had been living in San Francisco for a couple of years. I had been at Stanford but dropped out and joined the hippie scene. Lived in a big house near Haight with a lot of people that came and went, had a few waitressing jobs, spent *a lot* of time at the Fillmore. When I was around the house, I used to sing to myself a lot. Not sure when, exactly, but they all started calling me Sparrow, and it stuck."

"Stanford, huh?"

"Yeah. I was doing pretty well, but once I got drawn into the whole 'sex, drugs, and rock and roll' thing, I didn't feel like keeping up with my studies." She looked at Jason. "My parents were pissed!"

"I bet. I don't think I could have pulled that off."

"Well, San Fran's where I heard about this commune. My parents know I'm in Hawai'i, but they don't know what I'm planning to do. I'm twenty-one but they still get on my case about stuff."

"Yeah, that never stops."

They arrived at Jason's apartment and went upstairs. Jason put on a pair of black bathing trunks and gathered up his snorkeling gear. Sparrow wandered around the apartment while he made some ham and cheese sandwiches.

"Not much in the way of furniture," she commented.

"No. Pretty basic. A sofa and chair. Kitchen table and chairs. A king-size mattress on the floor in the bedroom, my stereo, and a lot of records."

"Ya got the basics."

"Yep. Let's head out."

Hanauma Bay is an ancient, extinct, volcano crater that flooded with seawater when the ocean-side wall collapsed. Over the years, a coral reef formed across the front third of the crater floor, cradled by a crescent-shaped sandy beach. Parking is at the top of the crater, and access to the water is down a steep, gently curving driveway. During the walk down, the spectacular view reveals the pale coral formations framed in shades of pale to deep turquoise in the shallows and a beautiful lapis blue out toward the ocean. Sparrow stopped several times on the way down to absorb the sight. Speechless, she would look at Jason, shake her head in disbelief, and then go on.

Hanauma Bay was one of Jason's favorite places. The *Engage* was often on "tropical hours," so the men had to be in early, by six o'clock, but they were off duty by two, sometimes earlier. Jason liked to spend the late afternoon snorkeling and reading on the beach. He was glad he was able to share this special place with Sparrow.

They spread large beach towels out on the sand, unpacked their gear and headed for the water. When they got to the water's edge, Jason put down his fins, looked down to the inside of his mask, and spit on each lens. Sparrow looked on as he rubbed the spit around.

"What the fuck are you doing? That's gross."

"Keeps the lenses from fogging up." Jason held up her mask. "We've already swapped spit, so will it be my spit or yours?"

She snatched the mask away from him. "Even so, I think I'll use my own spit. Doesn't seem quite the same, somehow. I mean, this sits on my face, not in my mouth." She paused and thought about what she had just said. "Don't even go there." Another hesitation. "Well, maybe later."

"Have you done it before?"

"Snorkeled or . . ."

"Snorkeled."

"Only in someone's pool. It seemed pretty easy."

They rinsed their masks, put on their gear, and swam out in the shallows. The visibility was not particularly good at first, but the farther away from the shoreline they got, the better things looked. Parrotfish, butterflyfish, and convict tangs were everywhere. Jason noted that Sparrow was a good, confident swimmer, so he led them out between a set of buoys into the deeper water where bluefin trevally raced past, a blur of silver and neon blue.

Back on the shore, they flopped onto the beach towels, exhausted.

"That was wonderful," Sparrow gushed. "Never did or saw anything like that before."

Jason stood up and tossed her a bottle of suntan lotion. "Here, we better put some of this on. Sun's pretty intense midday."

"Can you do my back?"

"I can do your front too."

"Not here."

Jason sighed. "Okay. Turn around."

As they sat on the beach eating their sandwiches, Sparrow asked

Jason about his guitar playing.

"I took lessons starting when I was eleven. It was with an old Italian guy who smoked what looked like dog turds—hand-rolled dog turds from Italy, mind you. There was so much smoke in the studio I could barely see the music. I use the term *studio* loosely. Picture a large walk-in closet. But he was good, really good. On occasion, he played with the Philly Orchestra. He would write out musical scores for songs he wanted me to learn right off the top of his head. Never saw anything like it. Everything I've been able to do musically since then was because of him. I even played in the jazz band in high school. There were plenty of guitar players in my school, but no one else could read the charts."

"I could tell you were really good last night."

"Thank you. But what did you think of my guitar playing?'"

"Stop." Sparrow gave him a look. "Anyway, I sure heard a lot of guitarists while I was in San Francisco—seemed like everybody played—and you're as good or better than any of them. Did you ever think about trying to make it out there?"

"I was too caught up in middle-American suburban life, focused on getting a degree at college, and knowing the only way I could pay for it was through some kind of scholarship. In some ways, it was always about not disappointing my parents and doing what all my friends were doing. Very conforming. Not very original—or exciting."

"That's where the Navy came in. The scholarship?"

"That's where the Navy came in, right."

"I could see how moving to the West Coast would have been difficult, but did you ever think about trying to make it in music in the Philly area somehow?"

"I've been in so many bands I can't remember all the names of them. One band, The After Sixers, was sponsored by the After Six formal wear company. They got us some great jobs; even got us booked to play a dance show on TV. That was in high school. No matter what band it was, there was always 'the dream.' You know, have your band 'discovered' by some producer, then signed to a label. But there wasn't much chance of that happening on the East Coast, especially in Philly. The band I had in college was good. A couple of guys I knew from jazz band in high school were still in the area, so we added them to the group, going for an Electric Flag or Ten Wheel Drive sound. We had one gig where we had some producers show up. Since we were based in the Philly area, I think they were looking for more of a 'blue-eyed soul' sound. And we were still doing covers. No originals."

"So, no go?"

"Yeah, they passed."

They soaked up the sun for a bit, did another dive, and then decided to head back to Jason's apartment.

They made love in the shower and then sat on the sofa in the living room, Sparrow cradled in Jason's arms in her kimono and Jason in his underwear. Jason put on *Every Picture Tells a Story*, Rod Stewart's album that he played to death. As they sat and listened, Sparrow hummed along. The album ended, and Jason got up to pick up the tone arm on his AR turntable.

"Hey, want to go see Mark-Almond tonight at the Blaisdell Arena? I'm sure it's not gonna sell out."

"They're really good. I saw them when they were with John Mayall at the Fillmore. But, no, can we just stay here?"

"Sure. I can go get us some Chinese takeout. There's a good place within walking distance."

"That's perfect."

Jason fished a takeout menu out of a drawer in the kitchen and they decided on orange beef and kung pao chicken. Jason phoned in the order. He got dressed and headed out to pick it up.

They ate with chopsticks at the kitchen table, washing down the food with a bottle of Mondavi rosé, then went back to the sofa to listen to more music. Simon and Garfunkel's "Bridge Over Troubled Water" got played twice. While it was playing, Jason told Sparrow about his camping trip around the country with his friends after the Atlantic City Pop Festival.

"We were at a campground in Big Sur. Riverside Campground. We were playing music across the campground from where our tents were pitched. Someone came up and said, 'Simon and Garfunkel are camped over on the other side of the campground.' We ignored it since that's where we were and hadn't seen anyone famous over there. When the second person came by and said the same thing, we had to go check it out."

"And they were there?" Sparrow asked.

Jason nodded. "They were there. So, we got to sit around a campfire and sing songs with Simon and Garfunkel. It was mostly oldies; a lot of Everly Brothers and Buddy Holly. In fact, the only song of their own that they sang was 'The Boxer.'" Jason paused. "I should say that Paul Simon sang. Garfunkel was so stoned he mainly sat on a log and stared at the fire."

"Well, that's pretty damn cool, Jason Conley."

The next morning, after some scrambled eggs and toast, Jason offered to drive Sparrow out to the commune on the North Shore. His heart was not in it, though. In the morning, after they had made love, he had asked her to stay with him for a while. She hesitated but finally said that she wanted to see her plan through.

They didn't talk much as they drove past Pearl Harbor, out through the pineapple and sugar cane fields in the central part of Oahu, past Schofield Barracks, and finally to the old Dillingham Airfield on the North Shore. The farm commune was located across the street between the road and the ocean. Jason parked in front of a dirt driveway that had a hand-painted sign marking the entrance: *The Farm*.

Jason opened the trunk and got out Sparrow's overnight bag. She was standing by the sign.

"Are you sure you want to do this?" he asked.

Sparrow nodded and looked down. "I do have to be more honest with you. I'm actually meeting a guy here I knew in San Francisco. He's the one who got us into this place. He should be here already." Sparrow looked back up at Jason, her eyes were misting over. "I had a wonderful time with you, Jason. It was too short."

"Doesn't have to be."

"We'll see. I just need to give this a try. Please just kiss me and say goodbye."

Jason gave her a passionate kiss, knowing it wasn't going to change her mind.

"Goodbye, Sparrow. You have my number. You know where I live. Call me if you need anything. Anything."

"I will." Tears were running down Sparrow's face as she turned and trudged down the dirt drive.

Jason got in his Firebird. The drive back to Waikiki seemed to take a lot longer than the drive out to The Farm. He thought about the fact that since arriving in Hawai'i he'd had, basically, two one-night stands, and in each case, the woman departed soon after. Not the best track record. Not even a good track record. In fact, it pretty much sucked.

As he thought about it, it was probably pretty unrealistic that he was stuck in the military and expected, well, hoped, that a hippie from San Francisco would really find him appealing. *At least she looked me in the eye and seemed a bit sad to be leaving.*

His discussion with her about her dropping out of Stanford for a life of 'sex, drugs, and rock 'n' roll' had stirred something inside him. It was the first time he had really admitted to anyone that he had been going through life doing things because he thought that's what others expected of him. His parents. His friends. Conforming. Really? Conformance in 1971 was definitely not part of popular culture. *What am I missing here?*

Jason shook his head as he drove down H1 to his apartment. *I'm twenty-two and basically trapped in a lifestyle that doesn't really fit who I want to be.*

Sparrow had guessed the truth. He did like playing music more than just about anything. He *did* want to be in a successful rock band. There was just one problem.

He didn't have the guts to follow through on it.

SEVEN

Honolulu

AUGUST 1972

The parents were coming. How the hell was Jason going to explain the disaster that had been his first tour of duty, a very shortened tour of duty, on the *Engage*? He was personally disheartened because he felt like it was the first time in his life that he had truly failed at anything. There was not a lot he could do about it, though; he simply was not cut out to be a chief engineer. No training. No aptitude. And as he admitted to himself, no desire. By the time the *Engage* returned from its brief second deployment at Johnston Atoll, it was obvious to everyone that Jason's time on board the ship was coming to an end.

Oh well, like I told Sparrow, at least I didn't conform.

In June, Lt. Cmdr. Hardy had called him into his stateroom, sat him down, and said, "You're being transferred to the USS *Everett*, a destroyer escort. You'll have two weeks of training in San Diego for your new post and then it is my understanding that the *Everett* will deploy on a WestPac/Vietnam tour, probably for nine or ten months."

Jason's mind was racing. WestPac? Vietnam? And his parents. They were coming for a visit, a visit that would begin when he returned from his San Diego training and end pretty close to the time he was due to report to his new ship. The only good thing that clicked in his head was that he was going back to San Diego for two weeks. He would have the chance to see Lori again, but that would be it. He couldn't really ask her to follow him back out to Hawai'i and then have to tell her, "Oh, by the way, I'm getting on a ship that's leaving for Vietnam for ten months." Jason remembered what had happened to Kenny.

So, this is what I get for being a fuckup, he thought.

After getting an official copy of his orders, Jason was able to figure out a timeline that would get him to San Diego for his training, then back to Pearl Harbor the day before his parents arrived. He requested and was granted a week's leave between his return from San Diego and the day he was due to report on board for duty. This was also the same day the *Everett* was due to deploy. It was not ideal. His new command was putting pressure on him to report aboard the ship immediately upon his return from San Diego, but he had accrued leave and his parents' trip had already been booked.

Jason's parents arrived on TWA Flight #1 from St. Louis. He knew they would be pretty gassed after a long day of travel, so he had left the plans for the evening up in the air so they could decide how much they would like to do. He arrived in plenty of time to buy a couple of purple and white dendrobium orchid leis from one of the stands scattered around the airport. When they came through the gate, Jason almost did a double-take. Almost. He knew his parents well enough to know that they took flying as a serious business, and as such, they dressed appropriately. Nick Conley was wearing a blue blazer with a red and blue striped tie, and gray slacks. His mother, Sheila, wore a nicely tailored yellow dress with a string of pearls. Donna Reed could not have pulled it off any better.

"Mom! Dad! Over here." His wave caught their attention, and they exchanged some quick welcoming hugs, he draped the leis around their necks, and then they headed for the baggage claim. Jason had warned them to travel light. Every place in Hawai'i was very informal, and there was not a lot of room in his Firebird to accommodate a lot of bulky luggage. It was twenty minutes before any bags from their flight began to appear. A screeching buzzer and flashing light on top of the carousel announced their arrival. Jason told his dad he would grab the bag for him.

As they waited for the bag, Sheila looked at Jason and said, "So what's up with your face?" She reached over and gave his beard a tug.

Jason had been wondering how long it would take. "You're allowed to have beards in the Navy, so I thought I'd give it a try."

His mom was shaking her head. "Well, I don't know about—"

Jason turned to his father. "So, Dad, what does your bag look like?" Jason asked, changing the subject.

"A gray Tourister."

Jason looked at the array of gray Touristers being presented in baggage claim and thought, *Well, this might take a while.* After checking just five address tags on the bags, he found the correct one. It weighed a ton.

"What did you bring with you? All the pots and pans from the kitchen? Some of the power tools from your work bench?"

"Now, Jason," his mother started, "You know I don't want to be doing any laundry while we're out here."

"You do realize that the hotel can take care of that for you, right?"

Nick said, "Why spend money when you don't have to."

Jason shrugged. "Good point, Dad." With a hernia-inducing tug, Jason grabbed the bag and headed for the parking lot.

"I booked you into a very nice..." and with a look at his dad, "and inexpensive hotel right across the street from the beach and next to the zoo. The Park Shores."

His mother wrinkled her nose. "The zoo? It isn't going to stink, is it?"

"No, it isn't going to stink," Jason said with a sigh. *Seven days, huh?* He made something up to appease her. "The trade winds carry all the odors straight out to sea."

Jason drove them through the industrial harbor area rather than on the H1 Freeway. It was a more interesting drive, and in the late afternoon the freeway was basically a parking lot. He pointed out various points of interest as they drove down Nimitz Highway. "I'll take you shopping at the Ala Moana Shopping Center. It's nothing like the King of Prussia shopping center. Mostly open air and they have a hula show every afternoon."

He turned on to Kalākaua Avenue, the main drag through Waikiki. His mother pointed out the Royal Hawaiian Hotel. "That pink hotel was here when your uncle Frank served here during World War II. There were only two hotels on Waikiki Beach then, and that was one of them." She turned to Nick, who was sitting in the back. "If it's that old, I bet it's all musty."

Jason rolled his eyes. It was one of the most exclusive hotels on the strip, but he didn't feel like bringing that up. *Let it ride.* When they reached the corner of Kalākaua and Kapahulu avenues where the Park Shores Hotel was planted, the view opened up to large banyan trees growing around the zoo with a vista of Diamond Head as a backdrop.

His father exclaimed, "Look at those trees! Could've made you a great tree house if we had something like that back home."

Jason turned the corner and parked on the street directly across from the hotel. "Here we are. You should have a great view of Diamond Head or the ocean, or maybe both." He wrestled the Tourister out of the Firebird's tiny trunk and carried it over to the front desk. His parents followed close behind, taking it all in.

Jason said, "I have a room reserved under the name of Conley." He motioned with his head. "My parents will be staying for a week."

"Ah, yes, Mr. Conley. They are all set. Seven nights in a nice room on the seventeenth floor."

They took the elevator up. Sheila said, "Jason, this place is gorgeous."

"They have a small, but very nice, restaurant on the ground floor, perfect for breakfast, a quick lunch, or drinks and pupus."

Sheila started shaking her head. "I don't think I could eat anything named *pupu*. Could you, Nick?"

"I'll try anything they put in front of me," he said. *Good for you, Dad*, Jason thought.

Jason was grinning. "Mom, pupus are snacks, appetizers." As he opened the door, "Don't poo-poo the pupus." He opened the luggage stand and put their bag on it.

"Okay. You'll have to decide how tired you are from traveling and the jet lag. It's already past nine your time. I wouldn't recommend taking a nap. The best way to handle jet lag flying east to west is to stay up as long as you can. If you make it past nine our time, you'll be in good shape tomorrow. You'll wake up around five, but you'll be ready for a day of sightseeing." He looked from one parent to the other. "Why don't you unpack, maybe get a shower, and then you can decide. I'll wander around the beach for a half hour or so and then come back to the room. Okay?"

"Sounds like a plan," Nick said.

Jason left his parents, took the elevator down, crossed Kalākaua, and took a leisurely stroll south on Waikiki Beach. The sun was pretty low on the horizon already, but there were still surfers out there trying to catch just a few more waves. Some of the clouds that had escaped the grasp of the Koʻolau mountains were drifting out over the ocean. *Could make for an interesting sunset*, he thought. *I wonder what Lori's doing now*. His two-week training session in San Diego had raced by, and with his deployment coming up, Jason and Lori hadn't made any plans for her to join him in Hawaiʻi. *I guess we'll see what happens after I get back from my deployment.*

Jason checked back in on his parents after an hour had passed. Lost in his thoughts, the time had sort of slipped by him. They decided to get something light to eat since they'd had a meal on the plane. When they said this, Jason said, "So, pupus it is." Nick and Sheila gave each other skeptical looks, but in the end, went along with the suggestion. They caught the elevator down to the hotel restaurant and settled in at a table. A waitress came by and gave them specialty cocktail menus and said she would be back in just a minute.

Nick scanned the menu quickly and then asked Jason, "Do you think I could just get a beer here?"

"Of course. What were you thinking of?"

"Miller."

"Um, no, not a good idea. You're in a new place, try a new beer. My two favorites are Kirin, from Japan, and good ole Primo from right here in Hawai'i. It's probably more like Miller than the Kirin."

"Primo it is, then."

"What are you thinking of having, Mom?"

"This Chi Chi drink sounds very tropical. Coconut and pineapple with vodka. I'll get that."

The waitress came back to take their drink orders. Jason ordered a Kirin for himself so his dad could taste it. She left food menus for them to consider while she placed the drink order.

"So, how adventurous do you feel? I can order some things I think you'll like, and maybe one or two that might push you a bit," Jason said.

Nick said, "Okay. I think we can handle it."

"Just no octopus," Sheila added.

"Hadn't planned on it," Jason said.

The waitress returned with the drinks, and Jason ordered Filipino lumpia, yakitori, teriyaki beef skewers, crispy fried shrimp wonton, steamed pork pot stickers, and sashimi. He figured he would end up eating all the sashimi.

Sheila asked, "What's lumpy yah?"

"Lum-pee-ya. It's basically a Filipino egg roll."

Nick said, "Yeah, I remember something like that from when I was in the Philippines during the war. It was pretty good." Nick had bounced back and forth between Australia and the Philippines as a member of the Seabees, the engineering corps for the Navy and Marine Corps.

"And sashimi?"

"Thinly sliced raw ahi."

"Ahi?"

"Tuna."

"You mean like from a can?"

"No, I mean like from a fish."

"I'll pass."

"Thought you might."

The food arrived, and everybody sampled everything, with the exception of the sashimi. That was okay by Jason. While they ate, they made plans for the coming week. Of course, Nick and Sheila wanted to see Pearl Harbor and the Arizona Memorial. Beaches would include Hanauma Bay, Waimanalo Bay, and the North Shore, even though the big waves were not in during the summer. A few cultural things would include the Bishop Museum and the Polynesian Cultural Center. Jason wanted to get a golf game in with his dad, preferably the one at Wheeler Air Base while his mom could do some shopping on Kalākaua Avenue or the Ala Moana Shopping Center. Going out for dinner would be a night at the Officers' Club and a trip to Kailua for Buzz's Steak House. Jason hadn't been back since his dinner there with Carrie.

Sheila asked, "What about work? Don't you have to go in to work on your boat?"

"No, no 'boat' work for me. I took leave for the time you guys were going to be here. Look, I haven't seen you for a year. One week of leave is the least I could do. Besides, I'll give you time to be on your own. We don't have to rush around to try to do and see as much as possible. It's a vacation. Besides, after you tour here and then do Maui, you'll definitely want to come back. Guaranteed."

By the time they were finishing the pupus, Sheila was halfway through her third Chi Chi. She looked a little droopy.

Jason said, "You know there's vodka in those drinks, don't you, Mom?"

"Can't taste it. Can't be much." She looked at her watch. "I think I need to wind this. It says it's only eight thirty."

"No, that's right, Mom. Maybe you guys should call it a night; it's two thirty a.m. your time. We can get an early start by going to

Pearl Harbor tomorrow. It's best to get there early. We can follow it up with the Bishop Museum. After that you can grab some lunch and then relax, maybe catch some late afternoon rays on Waikiki Beach."

Jason asked the waitress for the check, which he deftly snatched up before his father could nab it. His father glared at him. "I was going to pay for that. You shouldn't have grabbed that so quickly."

"I learned from the best."

"Okay. But I'll leave the tip."

"As long as it's not 'buy low, sell high.'"

His father grinned. "You're right. You learned from the best."

Jason gave his parents a hug goodbye, walked with them over to the elevator, and then walked out into the breezy, warm air of a Waikiki evening. *Not a bad start*, he thought. *At least discussions about my job didn't come up very much.*

Jason picked up his parents at the Park Shores at seven the next morning. They had already been up for two hours, had breakfast, and had taken a long walk on the beach. He drove them on the H1 to the main entrance of Hickam Air Base, flashed his ID at the guard, and drove to where his now former ship was docked. *Might as well get this part over with*, he thought.

It was easy to see the ARS docks from the parking area. He could see that the *Engage* was out to sea, probably towing targets for the day. That made it easier; no one was there to recognize him.

Nick's father was shaking his head as he surveyed the ships. "That's what you're on? Kinda small, aren't they?"

"Yeah, they're small, old, rusty, and don't ride the waves very well." Jason paused. "Also, I'm not on one of those anymore. Just thought you'd like to see what they're like."

Sheila looked surprised. "Not on one anymore? What's that mean?"

"It means I got transferred. I got assigned to a position on the ARS that I had no training for, and they—'they' being the captain—decided to get someone on board who was qualified."

Nick looked concerned. "So, you got a demotion?"

"No, just a transfer. In fact, I was in training in San Diego for my new assignment for two weeks and got back here the day before you arrived. Part of my job will be as an air controller for ASW operations. Antisubmarine warfare. I'll also be in charge of First Division: deck officer. The training was great." Jason looked at his worried parents. "Don't worry; it's a better fit. And the ship's twice as big. C'mon, we'll drive over and take a look at her."

They got in the Firebird and drove over to the main section of the base where the destroyers, light cruisers, and tenders were located.

Nick asked, "So, what's the ship like? What are the other officers like?"

"Don't know. Haven't been on board yet. I report the day after you guys leave for Maui." He neglected to mention that the ship also was departing on a WestPac/Vietnam tour of duty that day. An easy lie of omission.

Jason pulled up to the parking area at the end of the pier where the *Everett* was docked. "That's the ship. Looks a little more formidable, doesn't it? It's only been about three years since it was commissioned."

Sheila said, "Well, Jason, as long as you're all right with this transfer . . ." She let it tail off.

"It's fine, Mom. No worries." Actually, he had *tons* of worries, but they were of no concern to his parents, as long as they didn't know about them.

They drove out of the main base, and then back into the part of the base that housed the ticketing area and museum rooms associated with the Arizona Memorial. After they were issued their free tickets, they wandered through the historical section that had details of how the whole Pacific campaign had played out. Nick's father was totally engrossed in this aspect of the base and spent a lot of time pointing out where and when he had been engaged during the war. Jason could see his mom tearing up a bit. He didn't think that what his father had done had ever been presented so graphically to her before.

They viewed a short film before boarding the launch that takes people over to the actual memorial. Coming out of the small theater, Jason could see that it had deeply affected both of his parents. The film contained actual footage of the December 7 attack with the Japanese fighters and torpedo bombers totally destroying the ships as they sat idle on a Sunday morning. It moved Jason, but he knew his parents were a lot closer to the events that unfolded on the screen than he was. It hit them personally; the war had kept them away from each other for four tortuous years.

The memorial itself actually straddles the sunken hull of the USS *Arizona*. The names of all the men who were lost that day are posted on the front wall. It was noted that many of the men were never recovered from the ship, so that in effect, the hull had become their tomb, a tomb that still leaked small amounts of oil that spread across the surface of the water in a shimmering display that slowly drifted away. The tears of the *Arizona*. Viewing ports enabled the visitors to look down on to the actual deck and gun turret of the ship and to look out at the markers that showed where the rest of the fleet had come to rest on battleship row at the hands of the Japanese.

No one spoke.

After twenty minutes, the shuttle returned and deposited a new group and then boarded Jason and his parents and the rest of the people who had come across the harbor with them. It was a quiet car ride from the memorial to the Bishop Museum, their next stop for the day.

The beautiful koa wood display cases, woodwork, and staircases fascinated Jason's father and helped to dissipate the somber mood that had sailed with them from the Navy base. The museum was home to artifacts from all over Polynesia, describing how the Hawaiian Islands came to be populated, how the royal Hawai'i family of the Kamehameha lineage came to rule the islands, how the Hawaiians interacted with nature and the environment as part of their everyday life, and how Hawaiian religion was deeply intertwined with nature, humans, and the gods. The museum visit was topped off with a true Hawaiian plate lunch at the cafeteria. Kalua pork, chicken long rice, *lomi lomi* salmon, and a scoop of rice or macaroni salad were all hits. The *lau lau*—fatty pork and salted butterfish wrapped and steamed in *lu'au* and *ti* leaves—not so much. Jason explained, "It's an acquired taste."

It was midafternoon when he dropped them off at the Park Shores. "Get some beach time. I'll be back around six to pick you up for dinner. Dress casual."

The rest of the week went very smoothly. At first, they probed a bit.

"So, are we going to get to meet your friends?"

"No, I think they're out at sea. Remember, the *Engage* wasn't in when we drove out there."

"Are we going to get the chance to see your apartment?"

"No. It might scare you to see me living in such squalor."

"Is there anyone special you're seeing?"

"Yes. You guys. Right now."

"Don't be a smart ass. You know what we mean."

"No. No one special. There is someone in San Diego but the ocean sorta gets in the way."

His parents really enjoyed the pageantry of the Polynesian Cultural Center and the luau that was part of the package Jason had booked for them. Buzz's Steakhouse was a hit the following night, especially the expansive salad bar. Jason had warned them ahead of time to skip the pupus and head straight for the greens and fruit. The highlight of the meals was the Officers' Club dinner. Jason picked the night of the prime rib special where a huge slab of meat was wheeled from table to table on a cart and then sliced to order. It also gave Jason's parents a chance to dress up a little.

Although Jason had wanted to take his father to the Wheeler Air Force base for a round of golf, due to time constraints they settled on the Hickam course. It was flat, not as scenic, and even with the trades blowing, it was pretty hot. Nick didn't seem to mind. They had dropped Sheila off at the Ala Moana Shopping Center, where she planned to buy a few gifts to take home to their friends and get some lunch. When Jason and Nick arrived at the Hickam clubhouse, Jason said to his father, "Better buy at least a dozen balls. I'll get a dozen too."

His father said, "I can see why *you* might need a dozen, but not me."

Jason smiled. "Well, you're right. I'm not a very good golfer. But the roughs here are brutal. Just off the fairway, the grass stops and the hardened lava starts. It's a jagged surface filled with nooks and crannies, so that if your ball goes in there, it bounces around like it's in a pinball machine, then disappears down a hole, just like on the last hole at a minigolf course."

"The ball just disappears?"

"It just disappears."

Nick rented a nice set of clubs while Jason used his basic set. They were his father's old clubs.

While they were on the tenth green, Nick said, "You know, your mother's not too keen on that beard."

"How do you know that?"

"Because she said, 'I'm not too keen on that beard.'"

"Not surprised."

End of discussion.

At the end of the round, Jason had three balls left, his father, five. Nick said, "You were right. That's a dog of a course."

"Dog of a course?"

"Yeah, it's a rough rough."

"Let's go get Mom."

For their last night in Waikiki, Jason treated his parents to dinner and a show at the Outrigger. His father was wearing an extremely tacky Hawaiian shirt, a black background covered with large pink flamingos. Jason didn't have the heart to tell him the only flamingos in Hawai'i were right across the street from their hotel at the zoo. His mother wore a very tasteful sarong-type dress that featured yellow hibiscus flowers, the state flower of Hawai'i. He complimented her on how she looked and on the authenticity of the dress design.

Nick said, "How come you didn't say anything about mine?"

Jason smiled and said, "Didn't need to; your shirt speaks for itself."

The show featured the Society of Seven, a group of singers and multi-instrumentalists who also wove comedy routines throughout the act. He knew his parents would eat it up. They did. They couldn't stop raving about it as they walked along the beach to the Park Shores.

Early the next afternoon, Jason picked them up and drove them to the airport for their short hop over to Maui on Aloha Airlines. The conversation in the car was a replay of all that they had done, as well as tips from Jason about what they should do on Maui. He had booked them at the Pioneer Inn. He first became aware of it when the *Engage* was in the harbor conducting training over an old World War II submarine that had been intentionally sunk in the deep water just outside of the Lahaina harbor. He and his friends had enjoyed a few drinks there after taking a shuttle boat ashore when the training had been completed. A month or so later, he had booked it for when Lori had come to visit. His parents didn't need to know how he knew about how comfortable the rooms were.

At the gate, he gave his dad a hug, and his mother a hug with a kiss on the cheek. She teared up, just a bit.

"Don't worry; you'll be back for another visit, right? I'm here for a while."

Sheila nodded and Nick said, "You can bet on it."

He waved as they disappeared through the gate, then headed for his car. He had to drop off a set of keys for the Firebird at Sid's apartment. Sid was going to pick it up at a parking lot on the base near where the *Everett* was docked and take care of it for Jason while he was gone. Unbeknownst to his parents, while they were getting ready for the next leg of their vacation, he had vacated his apartment, placed his meager belongings in storage, and checked into a hotel close to the base for his last night on Oahu.

Now, as Jason drove to the hotel, a deep sense of foreboding crept through him. Having to step on board the *Everett* the next day was the inevitable conclusion to a series of events over which he had no control. Not feeling hungry, he parked the car in the hotel parking lot and braced himself for what he figured to be a sleepless night.

EIGHT

Pearl Harbor

AUGUST 1972

Jason trudged down the pier, a packed duffel slung over his left shoulder and the guitar case protecting his twelve-string Gibson in his right hand. The early morning sky was overcast, the gray clouds contributing to the growing sense of doom that had taken root in Jason's stomach. Heading down a pier in Pearl Harbor to a new ship just one year after he had been assigned to his first tour of duty was the last thing he expected.

It just wasn't supposed to turn out this way, he thought. But Jason now found himself ready to embark on a US Navy, Knox-class destroyer escort, the USS *Everett*, bound for a WestPac tour that would transport him to Yankee Station and the "gun line" off the coast of Vietnam. The ship was due to depart in just a few hours, and Jason knew virtually nothing about the vessel that loomed over him at the pier or what the people were like who were already on board.

Even though it was just nearing seven, Jason set down his load, took off his cap, which he hated wearing, and wiped the beads of moisture that had formed on his forehead. Humidity? Nerves? Probably a bit of both. He put his cover back on over his thick, sandy blond hair, picked up the duffel and guitar, and walked deliberately toward the gangway. Some of the events that led up to this situation played out in his head yet again, adding to his sense of dread. Ever since he had reported to the *Engage*, it felt like he had bought a ticket for a train that would take him to the destination of his own choosing, but now it was a total runaway with no way for him to get off, and the Navy could switch the tracks as they saw fit. He could hear Keith Relf from the Yardbirds singing, "Train kept a rollin' all night long, train kept a rollin' all night long."

As Jason walked up the gangplank, he noticed two men watching him from the quarterdeck. He stopped in front of them.

The j.g. in front of Jason said, "You must be our new guy."

Jason set down his duffel and guitar and saluted the ensign on the stern. The man in front of him then returned his salute while Jason said, "Yes, Ensign Conley, reporting for duty."

"Lieutenant Junior Grade Joe DiLorenzo, officer of the deck. Welcome aboard. This is Petty Officer Second Class Liston. Are we going to have a musical sendoff for our deployment?"

Petty Officer Liston said, "I don't think we're getting the music, sir, unless he has some kind of amplification equipment stuffed in that duffel. It would be nice, though."

Petty Officer Liston picked up the duffel and guitar. "Let me get these, sir. I'll just set them over here out of the way of quarterdeck traffic." He picked them up and moved them aside while Joe shook Jason's outstretched hand.

"I head up the Damage Control division on the ship. And, unless the XO has other plans I don't know about, you'll be our deck officer and bunking with me." He turned to Liston, "Liston, could you ring up the XO and let him know Ensign Conley is aboard?"

"Will do, sir!"

Jason went over to his duffel and fished out a leather portfolio. He opened it up and pulled out some official looking papers. He passed them over to Joe and said, "Here's a copy of my orders, just to make everything official."

DiLorenzo glanced at them and then handed them back. "Thanks. I'm sure they're in order. They already have a copy down in the ship's office, from what I understand. I guess we can just hang here until the XO shows up and makes what I just told you official."

Liston caught Jason's attention. "Excuse me sir, but what do you have in the case?"

Jason looked at Joe, then back to Liston. "A guitar."

Joe smiled.

"Um, yes, sir, I kinda figured that. But if you don't mind me asking sir, what *kind* of guitar?"

"It's a Gibson B45 twelve-string. It goes everywhere with me. Bought it new in '65."

"Very cool, sir. Some of the guys will be interested to hear this. A few of them play, and there's a couple of guitars down below. Freddie, one of our quartermasters, is planning to buy a set of drums while we're deployed."

Jason looked puzzled. "Where is he going to put a set of drums?"

"We're going to be using the hangar bay as a souvenir storage area," Joe said. "The DASH chopper's not going with us; won't be needing it for what we're going to be doing—no sub hunting on the South China Sea. So much for your ASW training." He smiled again, shaking his head slightly. "You won't believe what people will be buying overseas. Furniture, stereo equipment, dinnerware, pianos, cameras, and even motorcycles."

"That's right, sir," Liston added. "I hear that Ensign Culpepper is set on getting a pretty big Yamaha. We're all hoping the exchange rates, especially on the yen, stay pretty good."

Jason smiled. "That's good info. I wouldn't mind picking up a Nikon, a few lenses, and a quadraphonic set up. A friend of mine in San Diego had one and it was pretty awesome. You haven't heard 'Sunshine of Your Love' until you've heard it in quadraphonic."

"Yes, sir! And by the way, sir, I like your taste in music."

Joe said, "I see the XO heading our way. Let's see what he has to say, get you squared away in a stateroom, and then we'll figure out where you should be as we get underway; it'll probably be up on the bridge so you can see how it all works here."

As Joe predicted, Jason was assigned to Joe's stateroom and was designated to be the first lieutenant or deck officer, duties he would begin to become acquainted with once the ship cleared the harbor. Jason began unpacking his duffel in his newly appointed quarters. A small space, it was filled by a dull gray bunk bed positioned against the forward bulkhead and two gray metal desks up against the adjoining two bulkheads; there was really only enough room for one person to be in there comfortably. He thought about his first look at Joe on the quarterdeck: taller than he was, rather heavy-set with thinning hair, it would definitely be a tight fit. He and Joe would share a head out in the passageway with two other officers he had yet to meet. Their space was across a short passageway in front of the head. There wasn't room in there to stow toiletries, so he found a place near the entrance to the stateroom to put his dopp kit.

The XO, Lieutenant Commander Archie Burns, a tall Black man with an incredibly bushy mustache, had given him a whirlwind tour of the wardroom, ship's office, and a quick walk around the deck, pointing out the 5-inch/54 caliber Mark 42 gun turret on the forecastle, and the ASROC antisubmarine missile launchers. After showing him the stateroom, he apologized for the rush and excused himself to the bridge to begin preparation for getting underway.

Jason said, "No need to apologize, sir. It's really me who should be apologizing for arriving so close to getting underway."

"We'll talk about that later, Mr. Conley. I guess it couldn't be helped. Don't worry about it." He turned to go up to the bridge but then looked back into the stateroom. "I'll look forward to seeing you on the bridge. It'll be a lot different from the one you're used to."

Jason listened as the XO's footsteps retreated quickly down the passageway. Regret for not being on board sooner washed over him. He hoped that this wouldn't dog him for the rest of his time on board.

He wondered how many times he was going to hear, "Couldn't you have been here sooner?" throughout the course of the day. He had just finished stowing all his gear and finding a secure place for his guitar when he heard over the ship's loudspeakers, "Station the sea and anchor detail. Station the sea and anchor detail!"

A little shiver of apprehension ran through him. *Well, I guess it's show time.* Jason stepped out of the stateroom into the passageway and headed for the bridge.

The preparations for getting underway are extensive, and yet most Navy vessels make it look effortless. Years of institutional knowledge come into play to orchestrate getting the ship to step onto the dance floor that is the harbor. The ship shivers with anticipation as the 1,200 psi steam plant is fired up. All ties with its land partner are discarded: phone lines, electricity, gangway, and finally the lines that bound the ship to land. A tug floats in waiting, should there be a need, a stumble to be aided if called upon.

Jason, standing on the portside wing of the bridge, noted that Lt. David Barnaby, operations officer, delivered the commands and received information with a total air of confidence. Of course, he'd done this before. Many times. Maneuvering a 438-foot ship endowed with but a single screw, however, was no easy task. Jason thought about how he'd handled these duties on the *Engage*. At just over half the length, with a responsive diesel-electric power plant—and most of all, twin screws—getting an ARS underway was more like backing his Firebird out of a garage as compared to backing up an eighteen-wheeler. Since the *Engage* was docked at the mouth of Pearl Harbor, there was very little inner harbor congestion and traffic to get in the way or become a distraction. Back it out, throw it in first, and step on the gas. The USS *Everett* was a much different beast.

"Engine back one-third."

"Back one-third," echoed the helm response.

Barnaby watched as the pier started to drift by. His aviator Ray

Bans hid any nerves that might be expressed through his eyes, but Jason doubted there was much to reveal.

"Right full rudder."

"Aye, sir, right full rudder," the helmsman responded. "Rudder's at right full."

The stern swung toward the open water of the main part of the harbor. Lights flashed from other ships as signalmen engaged in their own form of conversation. *Goodbye. Good luck. Don't worry about your girlfriend, I'll take care of her.*

"Midships."

"Aye, sir, midships," the helmsman echoed. "Rudder's amidships."

The *Everett* glided gracefully over the smooth harbor surface. The stern just cleared the last pier.

"Left full rudder."

"Aye, sir left full rudder," came the response. "Rudder's at left full."

Jason watched, taking it all in. Anticipation was the key, he realized. Like a chess game, moves needed to be thought out several steps in advance. The ship couldn't turn on a dime. It didn't stop by itself, either, having no brakes other than the engine. The quartermasters on the bridge wings, each manning a pelorus, fed a steady stream of sightings to the navigator, Lieutenant Junior Grade Ed Snyder, who plotted the ship's location and tracked its progress into the main channel.

Ed looked up from his chart. "Recommend engine stop."

Barnaby gave Ed a quick glance and said to the helm, "Engine stop."

"Aye, sir. Engine stop."

After a short pause, Barnaby gave the command, "Engine ahead one-third. Come right to two zero five."

"Aye, sir. Coming right to two zero five," the helmsman repeated. "Steady on two zero five."

The verbal dance continued as the main part of the harbor receded. Helm orders, bearings, and lookout reports of small boats in the harbor all fed to the man with the conn, Lt. Barnaby. He had the final say, except for the captain, as to what the ship would be doing. Jason notes that the captain was not even on the bridge. He was directly above him on the flying bridge with the XO. Obviously, he could take control at any time from his position, but he seemed content to pace back and forth, taking in the view.

Jason was unfamiliar with this inner part of Pearl since the *Engage* was stationed at the mouth of the harbor. He was quietly taking it all in, staying out of the way of the people intent on performing their duties, when he realized they were approaching the open ocean. To port, he could see four of the six rescue salvage ships stationed in Pearl docked at the pier that was, in fact, attached to Hickam Air Base. While stationed on the *Engage,* Jason had driven through Hickam to get to the pier, past several of the buildings that still had bullet holes in the exterior walls from the Japanese attack on December 7, 1941. The attack that had drawn his father into the war.

As the *Everett* passed the docks, he could see some of the men he had served with working on the aft deck, guys he still considered to be friends. Some, fellow musicians. None of them seemed to take notice as the destroyer glided past. Just another workday at the mouth of the harbor. He missed the men, but not the ship or its captain. Good riddance. Lt. Cmdr. Hardy had made Jason's life miserable for an entire year.

At the harbor entrance, Jason knew a familiar odor would greet him. Just as ships hit the first rollers coming in from the open water, a sickly-sweet smell from the Dole pineapple cannery in Honolulu, carried by the trade winds, would sweep across their decks. Jason always described it as smelling like someone took one hundred pineapple upside-down cakes and shoved them as far back into your sinuses as they could go. The ship's rolling movement and the almost visible odor had cost many novice sailors their breakfast.

Clear of the harbor, Jason figured it was time to track down his new boss, Lieutenant Doug Kimos, head of the Weapons Department on the *Everett.* Jason found him in his stateroom just as the rainiest spot in the world, the island of Kauai, came into view off the starboard bow. Lt. Kimos was a bit shorter than Jason but weighed considerably more. He had already been in the service long enough to have been through one long sea-duty tour out of San Diego, a quick shore-duty stint in the same location, and then destroyer school, a training for line officers back on the East Coast at Newport, Rhode Island. Kimos, having grown up in Florida, was missing the warm weather after his winter training along the cold North Atlantic, and had asked his detailer for a posting in a warmer climate. With ships deploying to WestPac from Hawai'i on a regular basis, a DE out of Pearl was the perfect fit.

As a department head, Kimos had a stateroom all to himself, located just forward of the officer's wardroom on the main deck level. The door was slightly ajar. Jason hesitated a moment, then knocked lightly.

"Enter!"

Jason pushed the door open and found Kimos seated at his desk, working on some forms. He stood and extended his hand.

"Welcome aboard, Mr. Conley," he said while shaking his hand. "I'm assuming you don't mind if I call you Jason."

"Not at all, sir."

"Oh, and by the way, when we're just sitting around shootin' the shit, you can skip the 'sir' stuff." His slight Southern drawl made this opening sound welcoming and friendly. First names and no 'sir' stuff sounded good to Jason.

Kimos said, "Have a seat," as he motioned to a metal chair that sat beside his desk.

"Now, from what I understand, you were chief engineer on your last ship." He paused and gave Jason a slight smile. "How in the hell did that ever happen?"

Jason smiled back. "Well, how much time do you have? I can give a long or a short version."

"Let's keep it relatively short; lunch is coming up soon."

Jason explained about the switch-up in orders.

Kimos shook his head slightly throughout the explanation. "So, let me get this straight. You had no training in engineering prior to your arrival, and they expected you to take over the whole department. Did you have a chief under you?"

"Actually, I had two chief petty officers; one for the engine room and one in damage control. He was also the dive master. It probably would have worked out okay, except for the fact that they hated each other and spent most of the time sabotaging each other or stabbing each other in the back whenever they got the chance, especially if they were in conversation with Lt. Cmdr. Hardy." Jason shook his head. "In Hardy's eyes, I was a total incompetent since I couldn't keep the two of them in line." He paused. "I guess, in a way, I was."

"So, this Hardy expected an ensign right out of college to keep two lifers in line and run an entire department he'd never had any training for."

"That's pretty much it. The other problem was that I have absolutely no aptitude for any kind of mechanical procedures. I've never even changed the oil in my own car. You know all those aptitude tests they give you before getting into an NROTC program?"

Kimos nodded.

"Engineering—dead last."

Kimos picked some forms up from his desk. Jason could see what they were. Fitness reports. "Given all that, I'm surprised that your fitness reports are as good as they are." He looked down at them, then back at Jason. "I mean, they're not great, by any means, but they're not bad, either."

A bit of uneasiness crept through Jason at these remarks. He knew his fitness ratings were not good enough for him to get the promotions he needed to advance toward a career in the service. Not that he wanted a Navy career. Jason just wanted people to recognize that he was capable of doing a good job.

Jason said, "The reason those reports are at least decent is due to the men who actually did the work in the department. The men under the two chiefs respected me and tried their best to keep things running smoothly. I think, in part, it was because I was closer to their age and that I could relate to them. In fact, and I'll tell you this up front, off the ship, many of them were my friends; they were the guys I'd go to the beach with, hang out in Waikiki with, play music with, and go to the Islanders games with. Was I fraternizing with the enlisted men? Yeah, I guess I was. And I'm sure Hardy knew of this, but he never said anything about it. It all helped to keep me on his shit list, though."

Kimos nodded slightly. "How many officers were on board?"

"Besides the captain and the XO, just three. Besides me, there was someone in charge of ops and an officer who handled deck operations, salvage ops, and weapons. The ops officer, Bob Arians, is married, and the deck officer was a warrant officer. He kept pretty much to himself."

Kimos asked, "You're not married, right?"

Jason shook his head. "No, just a 'kind of' girlfriend back in San Diego. She was getting ready to move out to Hawai'i, at least I think she was." He paused. "Or maybe I was just hoping that would be the case. I mean, we're not engaged or anything. Anyway, that's right about when I received my orders to the *Everett*. There wasn't much point in her coming over if I wasn't going to be here."

Kimos was looking at the fitness reports. "Yeah, that makes sense." He looked up at Jason. "Sorry about that. Deployments can wreak havoc on relationships."

Jason nodded.

Kimos went on. "Well, you'll have a fresh start here. I'm sure you've heard that you'll be heading up our deck division. And you have a good crew to work with. We'd like to have a chief head up the division, but Petty Officer First Class Bennie Clarke knows his stuff and knows how to handle the men. He's an excellent boatswain's mate. You'll get to meet him after lunch. Speaking of which, it's about that time. Let's head back to the wardroom and see what's cooking. The grub's pretty good on board." As they stood up to leave, Kimos said, "After lunch, you and I can have a little sit down with Captain

Zhao; he's probably taking lunch in his stateroom. Then, we can meet the rest of your crew up on the forecastle."

Jason followed Kimos the short distance back to the mess thinking, *Much better start than on the previous ship. This could be okay.*

The wardroom was just forward of amidships and stretched almost from the starboard exterior bulkhead to the port. A long table covered with a white tablecloth and set with fourteen place settings awaited them as they entered the room. Two stewards, older looking Filipinos, bustled about making last minute adjustments to the settings and putting out serving utensils. Another Filipino, a much younger looking man, was manning the galley. He looked out into the dining area through a wide opening on the forward side of the galley and spoke to the other two stewards softly in Tagalog. They nodded in response. All was ready. Time for the officers to take their seats.

Jason was stunned at the formality. There was nothing at all like this on the ARS where everyone ate together, enlisted and officers. The only concession made for rank was a table reserved for the officers and a table for the chief petty officers. No linens. No place settings. Chow was served cafeteria style on metal trays, and everyone got the same thing. The food was good. The atmosphere, not so much.

Apparently, there were assigned seats, and Jason's was located about two-thirds of the way down the table from the captain's end. There was an empty place setting on his left that belonged to Joe DiLorenzo, who had relieved Barnaby just before noon as OOD. On his right sat Lieutenant Junior Grade Norm Shapiro, supply officer. Doug Kimos sat opposite him, while the XO pulled out a chair on the right side of where the captain would normally be seated, at the head of the table. David Barnaby sat opposite him. Jason noted two other ensigns at the table: Jack Culpepper, communications officer, and Frank Gallagher who was in charge of the gunfire control technicians. A j.g. in a Coast Guard uniform sat at the end of the table opposite where the captain normally would be. Ed Snyder was part of an officer exchange program between the Navy and the Coast Guard and served as the ship's navigator. The thickest, reddish brown beard Jason had ever seen enveloped his face. In addition to the captain's and Joe's, one other place setting remained empty, belonging to the officer who had gone up with Joe to be his junior officer of the deck on the bridge. The XO introduced Jason to everyone at the table and then asked everyone to introduce themselves as the stewards brought out bowls of tomato soup.

Ed caught Jason's attention. "Yo, Jason! It's good to have another beard on board."

Jason said, "Compared to yours, I'm not sure I can even call this a beard. I could probably shave it off and no one would notice."

Jack Culpepper chimed in. "Three of us had beards when Ed came on board. One look at his and we all shaved ours off." Culpepper had grown his mustache back, but it looked very strange in combination with his flat-top haircut.

Ed laughed. "When I noticed they had shaved theirs, I shaved mine too. I thought the captain had delivered some sort of edict about being clean-shaven."

Norm Shapiro said, "Yeah, but once he found out there wasn't any rule about it, he let it grow back. In three days—and I'm not exaggerating—in just three days it looked just the way it does now."

Culpepper added, "Truth!"

The stewards cleared the bowls and began to serve the next round: grilled cheese sandwiches.

As they served, Jason looked around the table and remarked, "Wow, just like I was back in junior high school. What's for dessert? One of those bricks of Neapolitan ice cream?"

Everyone looked at each other. Doug Kimos laughed and said, "How the hell did he know?"

"Really? I was just kidding," Jason said. "Anyway, this was my favorite lunch back then. Or maybe it was just that lunch was my favorite part of the day."

"Just a little comfort food to get us on our way," said the XO.

Norm said, "You know why it's called Neapolitan? Back when

there was a huge influx of Italian immigrants, they brought—"

Ed, intentionally interrupting Norm said, "So anyway, Norm bunks with me across from the stateroom you're in with Joe." He directed his next comment to Shapiro. "I guess the 01 level is going downhill if they're letting an ensign move in."

Shapiro smiled. "Yeah, I may be better off sleeping on the flight deck than staying up there with you guys." Shapiro was tall and thin with jet black hair, slicked back and kept rather long, even for the rather relaxed standards found in Pearl. Some commander would have been on his ass about it if they were based back in Norfolk, VA. "No-fuck" as it was known in the Pacific. "No-Fuck, Vagina."

Frank Gallagher chimed in. "Don't pay any attention to them, Jason. Norm doesn't even stand watches, one of the perks of being laundry officer." To Jason, Gallagher looked far too young to be an officer. He looked a bit like Beaver Cleaver, an appearance some braces in his teen years might have helped.

"That's supply officer to you, *Ensign*. Let's see how your uniforms look the next time they come back to your stateroom . . . *if* they make it back to your stateroom."

Ed said, "Yeah, be careful Frank. Extra starch in the shorts? Not a good thing."

Frank pointed at his crotch. "Yo, Norm, I got your starch right here."

Norm said, "I can believe that. You probably need the starch."

The XO looked down the table at Jason with a grin on his face. "As you can see, everyone on board is very mature. It's hard to believe they all work so well together."

The rest of the lunch conversation centered on quizzing Jason about life on an ARS. There was a lot to explain since the *Engage* had gone from being a salvage ship to being a support vessel for the deep dive habitat located just off the coast from Kailua.

Jason said, "There's a lot more. I'll save those stories for some boring mid-watches."

Doug stood up, pushing his chair back from the table. "If you'll excuse us, *gentlemen*," looking directly at Frank, "Jason and I have an appointment for him to meet the captain."

"Now? So soon after having a meal?" quipped Frank.

This drew a slight frown from the XO.

Frank backpedaled. "I mean, um, you know, like going in the water after eating. Um, never mind. Sorry XO."

Archie Burns good naturedly waved him off. "See you at dinner, Frank."

Doug turned to Jason. "Ready? Need to hit the head?"

"No, I'm good."

"Okay, then. Let's do this thing."

Doug and Jason made their way to Captain Zhao's stateroom located directly below the bridge. Zhao, as was his custom, took lunch by himself. In fact, he typically took all his meals in his stateroom. It was unusual to see him out and about on the ship. The XO and Ed Snyder were the two officers who had the most contact with him. Burns would have a brief conversation with him in the morning to review the day's upcoming activities, and Ed would have to see him every evening to go over the standing orders for the night watches on the bridge.

Zhao's reclusiveness was not limited to the ship. He had been on Oahu for over five years. After a brief shore duty assignment attached to the US Pacific Fleet Command, he assumed command of the *Everett*. Except for deployments, he never left the island of Oahu and as far as anyone could tell, didn't engage in many social activities. When in port, his daily routine consisted of driving from his house on base to the ship, and then back home again in the afternoon.

His Chinese accent was still very pronounced, even though his family had left Shanghai shortly after he turned three years old. They'd settled in the Los Angeles area, where Zhao attended high school. In his senior year, he won an appointment to attend the US Naval Academy in Annapolis. In spite of suffering a nervous breakdown in his junior year, he graduated with honors, majoring in physics.

Zhao took command of the *Everett* shortly before its first WestPac deployment, a brief six-month trip as a rescue support ship during carrier operations mixed in with a few gunfire support missions. The majority of that crew was still on board for the current deployment. Even so, Zhao remained an enigma. The bond that typically forms between captain and crew during combat situations never materialized.

Before taking the ladder up to the captain's stateroom level, Doug turned and said in an almost whisper, "So, have you heard anything about Captain Zhao since you've been on board?"

"Not really. Seemed sort of strange that he wasn't at lunch with us, just getting underway and all for this deployment."

"Yeah, well, get used to it." Doug looked up the ladder, almost as if he expected Zhao to be listening in. "Besides meeting him now, the person to check in with if you want to know more about him would be Ed, since he has to deal with him every night. Ed prepares the standing night orders for his signature."

Doug headed up the ladder with Jason close behind. When he reached the door to the stateroom, he knocked lightly, just a few raps. "Captain Zhao. It's Doug Kimos with our new ensign, Jason Conley." After a moment, Doug looked back at Jason and shrugged. He turned back and spoke to the door. "You said this would be a good time for an introduction."

The door opened slightly, and Captain Zhao's face appeared framed in the opening. He looked at Kimos, then at Jason, then back to Kimos.

"Okay, okay. I guess this is as good a time as any. Come in, come in."

His face disappeared but the door did not open any further. Doug pushed the door open and walked in with Jason following. Jason was surprised at how short Zhao was. Very slightly built, it was almost like his uniform was a size or two too big. Zhao moved around his desk and sat down, motioning to Kimos and Jason.

"Sit! Sit!" Kimos and Jason sat in wood-framed, leather fronted chairs facing the captain.

Zhao looked at Jason for a few seconds, then said, "So, you're Ensign Conley." Nothing followed.

Jason said, "Yes, sir. It's a pleasure to be aboard the *Everett*."

Zhao stared at him. "Pleasure? Really? It's a pleasure to be on this ship? Wait until we're out at sea for a month; you'll see how pleasurable it is."

Jason was taken aback but tried not to show it. The big problem was, what to say next?

Doug to the rescue. "Jason here was on board an ARS prior to getting his orders for the *Everett*. Not exactly the best 'ship of the line' experience, really. From our conversations so far, I think he's going to enjoy the company of his fellow officers, something he never got to experience on the *Engage*."

Jason agreed, "Yes, sir, Lieutenant Kimos has that right. Having lunch with everyone before coming up here was ten times better than how things would go on the *Engage*."

"Grilled cheese, right? You like grilled cheese?"

"Um, yes, sir, I actually like it a lot. It brought back memories of my junior high school lunches."

Zhao paused, then said, "Well, this isn't junior high. Just keep that in mind."

Jason looked at Kimos, then back to Captain Zhao. "Uh, yes, sir. I'll do that." Searching for a way to continue, Jason said, "Leaving port today went really smoothly. It was quite impressive."

Zhao said, "Mr. Barnaby's quite good, isn't he? Pretty calm, excellent skills. You think you can ever do it that well?"

"Yes, sir. It'll take a lot of practice getting used to how this ship handles, but I already have a lot of experience being the OOD on a ship."

"Yes, well, we'll see about that. An ARS isn't exactly a destroyer, is it?"

"No, sir, it's not."

"Well, I'm sure you have things to see to, just coming on board."

Kimos said, "Yes, sir. He's on his way to meet his deck crew now."

Zhao said, "Well, I'm sure that will be a 'pleasure,' too, won't it Mr. Conley? Nice meeting you. Welcome aboard and all that. Dismissed." Zhao stood up, nodded at each of them, and then went into the head.

Quietly, Kimos said to Jason. "I think it's time to leave."

After they made their way down the ladder to head to the forecastle, Jason said, sarcastically, "Well, I thought that went rather well."

Kimos said, "Actually, from what I've seen before, that wasn't bad." He grinned. "Anyway, shake it off, it was nothing personal. He's that way with everyone. Now, let's go meet your crew."

As they made their way forward, Jason wondered what this crew would be like compared to guys he knew on the *Engage*. There was already a different dynamic going on with the officers here on the *Everett*. It felt good. Comfortable. Probably be best not to get in too tight with the enlisted guys here. That hadn't played too well the last time around.

NINE

The Deck Crew

AUGUST 1972

Kimos and Jason climbed down a deck and made their way forward after leaving the captain's stateroom. Inwardly, Jason was still shaking his head over his initial encounter with Captain Zhao. However, he was looking forward to meeting the men of his division. He had been thinking a lot about the crew from the *Engage*, his friends, and was wondering what the crew would be like on this much larger warship. He thought the comparison might prove interesting.

Petty Officer First Class Bennie Clarke, a tall Black man who looked far too young to be leading a large division on a warship, had assembled the men on the forecastle, aft of the gun mount and forward of the ASROC launcher. He was facing the men, but turned when he heard Kimos and Jason approaching, delivering a crisp salute upon their arrival. The officers returned the salute.

Kimos said, "Petty Officer Clarke, your men did a great job getting underway."

Jason added, "I was very impressed. Coming from an ARS, I can see there's a lot more going on here to coordinate."

"Thank you, sirs. I was very proud of the way First Division conducted itself," Clarke responded. "We've just finished stowing all the line and we're ready to start some routine maintenance on the bulkheads."

As Clarke spoke, Jason looked over the men standing at attention. Men? His first thought was, *These guys look so young, much younger than the guys on the* Engage. Of course, then he realized that his friends from his former ship were all petty officers, so they had been in for several years and had a rate; most of the men he was looking at now were seaman recruits or seaman apprentices, most of them not too long out of high school. Many newly enlisted men get assigned to First Division as they work through what rating they plan to strike for when they put in enough time to qualify. At twenty-three years of age, Jason felt like an old man.

Jason said, "At ease, men. I just wanted to introduce myself since I'll be your new division officer. I'm Ensign Jason Conley and served on the *Engage*, an ARS you may have seen on our port side as we left the mouth of the harbor this morning. I was in engineering there. I'm from Pennsylvania and went to Villanova University, a small college you might know from our basketball and track programs." He noticed a few of the men nodding at that. "I'm looking forward to working with Petty Officer Clarke here; I've heard great things about him."

Clarke smiled. "Thank you, sir. May I ask a question, sir?"

"Of course."

"Well, as we were getting squared away after departure, some of the men said that you brought a guitar on board and that you were really into music."

Jason smiled. "Man, the scuttlebutt really moves fast on this ship, but yeah, I have a guitar with me. I've been in bands and had my own radio show in college."

Clarke looked over his shoulder, back at his men, then back to Jason. "So, on our last deployment, we wanted to have some 'breakaway' music, you know, something that would make a statement about us as a ship."

"Breakaway music? I'm afraid I'm not following."

"You know, sir. For underway replenishment."

"You've got me there, Petty Officer Clarke. We never did underway replenishment on the *Engage* while I was on board."

Kimos stepped in. "It's become sort of a tradition for each ship to have its own sorta theme song for when it breaks away after replenishing from an oiler or supply ship."

Clarke nodded. "That's right, sir. But, on our last deployment, we didn't have one."

Jason looked puzzled. "Why not?"

Kimos said, "Let's just say the captain wasn't too keen on the idea." Then, to Clarke, "Are you sure you want to get our brand-new ensign caught up in this? He hasn't even been on board a full day yet."

"No, sir. You're probably right sir. But just in case you want to give it some thought, it should be a song that represents the way we kick ass over there on the gun line doing gunfire support." The men behind him were all nodding in agreement.

Jason smiled and thought for a moment. "Okay, a song idea just popped into my head, but why don't we throw it open to the men? Please put the men at ease so we can have a little discussion."

"Yes, sir!" Clarke turned to the men. "At ease. As you were." The men relaxed and Jason stepped forward.

"Okay. You heard our discussion. You want a song that kicks ass, a song that represents this ship. Any ideas?"

A voice from the back said, "One Toke Over the Line."

Jason turned to Clarke and Kimos. "Always a joker in the crowd." Then, smiling broadly, he turned back to the men. "Ha, ha! Good one." He paused, then said, "No, for obvious reasons."

Another volunteer said, "Light My Fire."

Jason nodded. "Not bad! At six minutes and fifty seconds it would give us plenty of time to come alongside or breakaway. And, it has 'fire' in it."

A seaman apprentice said, "Excuse me, sir, but how do you know exactly how long the song is?"

"I was a late-night DJ for a couple of years in college. There would be no one else in the studio to watch the equipment, so if you needed to take a piss you'd put on 'Light My Fire,' dash down the hall to the men's room, take a piss, and then get back to the studio before the song was over." This drew some laughter from the men.

"Any other ideas?"

"'Born to Be Wild.'"

"'Riders on the Storm.'"

"'Bad Moon Rising.'"

"'Jumpin' Jack Flash.'"

There were nods of agreement on all the suggestions, and some dissent, as well. Jason said, "Well, I like all those, though some more than others. Do you mind if I suggest one?"

Petty Officer Clarke said, "Go for it, sir."

"'Smoke on the Water.' It's on Deep Purple's new album *Machine Head*."

Several of the men yelled out, "Yeah! Perfect. That song kicks ass, just like us."

Clarke turned back to Jason. "Excuse me, sir, but do I have the right song in my head? Isn't that song about some asshole firing off a flare gun that sets fire to a club and recording studio by a lake in Europe somewhere."

"That's it. I'm actually impressed that you knew that since no one can understand the lyrics except for the 'Smoke on the water, fire in the sky' chorus. Anyway, that's the part people will remember, and played over the ship's 1MC, it's probably the only thing that will be understood by the ship we're alongside. A ship's PA system isn't exactly high-fidelity." Jason paused, and a big grin spread across his face. "Plus, it's got one of the *best* guitar riffs in all of rock and roll."

Clarke addressed the men. "Whaddya think? Show of hands, all in favor?"

Most of the men raised their hands and Clarke said to Jason, "They like it, sir. I guess now it's up to you to run with it."

"Thanks, Clarke. What do you think, Mr. Kimos?"

Kimos said, "Perfect song, but I'm just not sure you should get into it with the old man on your first day."

Jason said, "I'm assuming it'll be quite some time before we do any underway replenishment. We're going into Subic before we head out on the gun line, right? Maybe *we* can subtly bring up the topic. You know, ease him into the idea."

Kimos gave him a look. "What do you mean 'we'?" They both looked over at the men, who were totally absorbed in their discussion. All of them were grinning.

Kimos said to Clarke, "Okay, we're not going to solve this here. Get the men back to work and let us . . ." He looked over at Jason, "let *us* work on it."

"On behalf of the men, thank you, sirs!" Clarke said.

Jason said to Clarke, "Okay. Dismissed. You and I can talk more after quarters tomorrow."

"Yes, sir! Thank you, sir!"

As Kimos and Jason headed back to the wardroom, Kimos said, "I'm not sure you know what you've gotten yourself into."

"Me? I thought I heard an 'us' back there."

Kimos let out a small sigh and kept on walking.

Kimos and Jason had First Watch from eight o'clock until midnight. In terms of getting sleep, it's the best of the night watches, far better than the brutal mid-watch, the one that followed theirs. However, since watches rotate, everyone gets their turn at missing sleep, and when certain day-ops, such as underway replenishment, call for an all-hands effort, no one has a chance to catch up on missed rack time.

It had been several months since Jason had been out to sea at night; he never got tired of seeing the stars as they can only be seen from the middle of the ocean. Even when he camped in the desert, the Milky Way paled in comparison to what stretched overhead now, a creamy swath across a jet-black sky.

Underway in the middle of the Pacific is often a time for reflection since there's not a lot going on. Now far past the Northwest Islands, there was very little in the way of boat traffic. Jason had the conn, but there were no course or speed changes to make. It was often a time for some quiet conversation out on the bridge wing against the stellar backdrop of the night sky.

Jason talked with Kimos about Lori. He had stayed with her in San Diego while he was doing two weeks of antisubmarine warfare training just before he reported to the *Everett*. Before that, she had been to Hawai'i for a two week visit in February. She seemed to be having a wonderful time, even given the less than luxurious accommodation of Jason's apartment on King Street. The four-day trip over to Maui had been the highlight of her stay.

"Have you ever been over to Maui?" Jason asked Kimos.

"No, but my wife and I have been to the Big Island. We stayed at Volcano House, right on the rim of the Kilauea Crater."

"Sounds dangerous."

"It sounds dangerous, but it's really quite safe. I think it's been there since, what, 1917?" Kimos paused, thinking about it, then asked Jason, "So, what's Maui like?"

Lori and Jason only needed to pack one bag between them since they would only be in Maui for four nights. They threw the suitcase in the trunk of Jason's Firebird, along with a bag holding two sets of snorkel gear, and headed for the airport. They boarded a Hawaiian Airlines DC-9 and less than forty minutes after takeoff, they were touching down at Kahului, Maui.

Jason had found a military discount deal through Island Dreams Rental Car Company. When the person at the desk handed him the keys and pointed out the car, Jason realized why it was a discount, and that it was no dream. More like a nightmare. *Oh, well*, he thought, *it's cheap*.

Lori kept glancing at Jason as they walked over to the car, a bright yellow AMC Gremlin.

"Are you sure this is our car?"

"Well, we'll find out as soon as I try to open the hatch for our bags." Jason inserted the key and turned it. The hatch popped open. He gave Lori a resigned look. "It's ours."

He threw the bag and snorkel gear in, went around to the passenger side door, and with a great flourish said, "Your chariot awaits, milady."

In a fake English accent, Lori said, "Why thank you, kind sir."

Jason explained that he was familiar with the Gremlin model.

"When I worked at the lodge up in the Adirondacks, all the staff would meet in the bar after the dining room shut down. The last diners were usually out by eight thirty. They were all people staying in the cabins and most got up early to fish before breakfast. Thank God I didn't work breakfasts."

"Not an early riser, huh?"

"Only if there's something to get *up* for."

"Stop."

"Anyway, one of the waitresses, Betsy, had a brand new Gremlin and wanted to drive it, so after a round at our own little bar, six or seven of us would pile in and head off to do a road trip to all the local bars. The closest one was in Indian Lake about nine miles away. Every place we would hit was at least ten miles from the last spot."

"You fit that many people in a car this big?"

"Yeah. Not too safe, right, but we all survived. It was kinda nice being crammed in the back with all those girls." He grinned. "Good thing Betsy didn't like to drink."

Jason told Lori more stories about life as an assistant cook at Blue Mountain Lake as they made their way through the valley in the middle of the island to the little historic whaling town of Lahaina on the west coast of Maui. Jason pulled the Gremlin into the parking lot of the Pioneer Inn on Wharf Street, a plantation-style hotel that looked out over Lahaina Bay,

Lori said, "Oh, my God, Jason, it's beautiful."

"Our room's on the second floor. We'll be able to sit out on the wrap-around deck and check out the humpback whales in the bay. I brought some binoculars."

They settled in, did a little whale watching, then took a drive before dinner over to the Iao Needle, back toward the airport in the center of the island. They hiked around the historic park centered around an unusual geologic structure that jutted up in the center like the island was giving the rest of the world the finger. Jason explained that this was where Kamehameha the Great had defeated the army of Maui, thus taking control of the island.

When they got back, they had dinner in the Bar and Grille, a restaurant located on the first floor of the hotel, and were greeted at the door by an old wooden statue of a whaling ship captain.

They both got the mahi mahi "grilled to perfection" as the menu described.

Jason said, "Why do people write stuff like 'grilled to perfection' on a menu. What else would they do, grill it until it wasn't perfect, burned to a crisp? 'Hey, order this, it tastes like shit.'"

Lori looked at him across the table. "Do you have a lot of these little peeves?"

"No, no, I just think it's a little odd, that's all."

Lori laughed, "I know what's a 'little odd' around here, and it's not the menu."

Over dinner, they made a plan for the next day, which was the famous, or infamous, depending how one looked at it, "Road to Hana," a fifty-two-mile trip featuring over six hundred hairpin turns, one lane bridges, and beautiful waterfalls. Lori said she would drive to avoid getting car sick. Jason had no problem with that since the ride wouldn't bother him; you really couldn't be on an ARS if you got seasick. After dinner, they went upstairs to their double bed. The bed was a little small, but they didn't notice.

The next day, Lori did an amazing job negotiating all the tricky turns. Jason felt a little bad about having her drive since it was difficult to take in the scenery and keep your eyes on the road. The road was carved into the lower side of Haleakala, surrounded by tropical rain forest the entire distance. Heliconia, bird-of-paradise, and hibiscus were just a few of the many tropical plants that were easy to see from the car. After more than two hours and several stops to take in the waterfalls, they arrived at Hasegawa's General Store, family owned for sixty years. They were hungry and thirsty, but the general store easily took care of those needs. Jason bought an "I Survived the Road to Hana" sticker for his guitar case.

After leaving the store, they explored the trails of 'Ohe'o Gulch, also known as the Seven Sacred Pools and waterfalls. The trails were lined with towering bamboo stalks and spreading banyan trees. Neither of them had ever seen anything quite like it. Before heading back to Lahaina, they glimpsed the Red Sand beach on the opposite side of Hana Bay. Lori declined Jason's offer to make the hike out to the beach for some nude swimming.

On the way back, Jason drove the last half of the trip, so Lori got the chance to see some of the views. By the time they reached Kahului, she was feeling just a bit queasy, so they stopped and watched some of the surfers at a nearby beach until she felt better. Finding a good shave ice stand helped quite a bit.

As Jason said, they had to get up the next day at oh-dark-thirty to be able to get to the top of Haleakala to see the sunrise. It was worth it. The sun was visible just briefly as it peeked up over the horizon. They hugged each other to keep warm as a cloud bank moved in to produce some amazing reds, pinks, and oranges in its wispy cotton candy-like fringes. Standing on the rim of the crater, they were so high that the cloud bank was actually below them and moving their way. The sun outraced the clouds, coming up over the top of them to illuminate the alien surface of Haleakala, home of the Hawaiian goddess Pele. The crater had a beauty all its own, dotted with cinder cones in pastel hues of brown, gray, and ocher.

"Surreal," said Lori. "So beautiful." She reached for Jason's hand and gave it a squeeze.

When the cloud hit the eastern edge of the crater, it sought out a notch in the wall and then seeped through like cream being poured into coffee from a small pitcher. Hypnotized, they watched for twenty minutes as the crater bowl filled.

They finally pulled themselves away and explored the crater rim, in awe of the unusual silver sword plants, a particular species endemic to Haleakala. They went back to the Gremlin and drove slowly down the road, stopping every so often to take in the spectacular views.

Back at the Pioneer Inn, they sat out on the lanai and had breakfast and Bloody Marys as they looked out over the bay; easily, the best Bloody Mary Jason had ever had. Jason convinced Lori to try the Portuguese sausage as a side to her scrambled eggs. She was pleasantly surprised. The sun out on the lanai felt good after the chill of the early morning. The clouds had been captured by Pele and stored in her crater. They spent the rest of the day wandering around the town being typical tourists.

That evening they went back out to a bar they found in their wanderings earlier in the day that had live music. The Mongoose was just a step above being a dive bar, with a small stage on the right as they entered. Scattered wooden tables and chairs created a maze-like path to the huge, mirrored bar that occupied almost the entire back wall.

Lori and Jason found a table about halfway across the room from the stage and ordered a couple of Primos, checking out the place until the music started. It was not long before Willie and Joe Chambers took the stage with a couple of acoustic guitars. Jason was simply blown away.

"I saw these guys as part of the Chambers Brothers at the 1st Quaker City Rock Festival in 1968 at the Spectrum in Philly," he gushed. "Moby Grape, Buddy Guy, Big Brother and the Holding Company, the Chambers Brothers, and Vanilla Fudge all for four bucks. Vanilla Fudge came on at about one a.m. and played to a half-empty arena. Most people were fried by then. The smoke was thick that night."

On the stage in Lahaina, the two brothers did a mixed set of blues, gospel, and covers, and as they were putting their guitars away after the first set, Jason approached them at the stage.

Jason said, "It's really great seeing you guys. Enjoyed the set. I saw you a few years ago at the Spectrum in Philly. The 1st Quaker City Rock Festival."

Joe said, "Yeah, yeah, we was there."

Willie added, "I wasn't too sure we'd be able to follow Janis, but we did okay."

"Shit, it was more than okay," said Jason. "Blew me and the entire crowd away. Can I buy you guys a beer while you're on break? I'm at a table over there with my girlfriend."

"Hell, yes," said Willie.

Jason headed back to the table with Willie and Joe Chambers in tow. When they arrived, Jason introduced them.

"Willie. Joe. This is Lori Feretti."

Lori said, "So nice to meet you. Jason was just telling me about the concert he heard back in Philly with you guys. I must admit, I love 'Time Has Come Today,' but I like your version of 'People Get Ready' even more."

Willie said to Joe, "Hey! She knows our stuff!" Jason was impressed at her comment, as well.

Joe said, "Well, as a family, we started off singing gospel, so that tune kinda comes natural to us."

The beers arrived, and they sat and talked about music just like they were old friends. At the end of their break, Joe and Willie thanked Lori and Jason and carried their beers back with them, toasting the two of them from the stage.

Jason and Lori stayed for another set, then waved goodbye as they left the bar. They wandered back to the Pioneer Inn, arm in arm.

"You know," said Lori, "I was a little concerned when I saw you head up to the stage to talk with them, but they were really nice. Just regular guys. I really enjoyed talking with them, even if it was a short conversation."

"Glad you liked it. Just don't expect me to bring celebrities to our table every night."

The final day in Maui was spent snorkeling at Kaanapali Beach at Black Rock in front of the Sheraton. Jason had been snorkeling a lot at Hanauma Bay since moving to Oahu, and he had snorkeled in the Keys and Eleuthera. Lori had never done anything like it. It took her a while to get used to breathing with a snorkel. The first time she stuck her head under water, her breathing accelerated like a steam engine leaving a station.

She popped her head up out of the water and Jason said, "Relax. Relax. Breathe easy. I know it's a weird feeling at first. It's just that you're not used to breathing through your mouth instead of your nose."

"Now that you mention it, you're right. Mouth breathing's not the norm." She took a deep breath. "Okay, let's try this again. I'll get it."

She did get it and was rewarded with a spectacular array of fish: Moorish idols, giant turquoise parrot fish, more species of butterfly fish than she could keep track of, a very large moray eel, and the highlight, she was actually swimming with a green sea turtle. After almost an hour, they headed for the beach and then sat in the shallow water removing their fins. She stood up and pulled off her mask and snorkel, absolutely beaming.

"That. Was. The. Best!" She was still breathing heavily. "But I need a rest!"

They stretched out on their beach towels for an hour, got some sandwiches at a local restaurant that was perched on the edge of the beach, then went back out for more.

"Out of all that we've done these past four days, this was the highlight." She threw her arms around Jason and planted a big kiss on him, right there on the beach. They had dinner out in town and spent one final evening in their little double bed.

As they drifted off to sleep after making love, Jason said, "I love you, Lori."

"I love you, too, Jason."

They flew back to Honolulu the next morning. Lori only had one more day before she had to return to San Diego. It had been magical, but in the end, nothing was settled in terms of her coming back to Hawai'i, and Jason wondered if that was his fault. Should he have made a commitment to her at that time rather than keeping things loose? True, they both said they loved each other, but should he have taken it further? They exchanged letters over the next few months, often mentioning ways to visit each other. The orders to the *Everett* decided everything for them. When they said goodbye at the airport, Jason didn't know yet that the Navy would give him an opportunity to see Lori again, this time in San Diego just weeks before whisking him away on the *Everett* for a WestPac/Vietnam tour.

Nine to ten months at sea is not a good time to try to start a new life with someone who has been left behind, especially if the someone had to come to a place where she had no friends and no promise of a job. Jason was not sure, but he feared fate had taken away any chance he had to be with Lori on a more permanent basis.

TEN

Subic Bay, Philippines

SEPTEMBER 1972

The six-day transit from Pearl Harbor to Guam gave Jason a chance to ease into the daily routine of a destroyer escort, as well as to get to know his men. When on the bridge, he was the junior officer of the deck (JOOD) and had the conn for most of those times, although there were usually no speed or course changes to be concerned with on the open ocean. He did, however, have the conn when they did a man overboard drill. He timed his turnaround perfectly and came right up alongside "Oscar," the dummy they used in the drill. Executive Officer Archie Burns nodded his approval.

The *Everett* spent a few days in Guam replenishing supplies and fuel. Jason had become good friends with his bunk mate, Joe DiLorenzo, and Ed Snyder, the navigator who bunked across the passageway from him. They went on liberty together and decided to seek out a restaurant they had heard about off base. A cab picked them up at the gate. Joe and Ed climbed in the back, which left Jason up front in the passenger seat, or what later became known as "The Seat of Death." Leaving the gate, the cabbie accelerated so quickly that Jason was pushed back in his seat the way an astronaut gets crushed on takeoff. The cab ripped through narrow streets in small villages, scattering squawking chickens everywhere and narrowly missing mothers with small children in tow, leaving a cloud of dust in its wake—or so it seemed to Jason. Apparently, there were no brakes in the cab since the driver used the horn to clear the way without ever slowing down. A couple of drinks before dinner soothed their rattled nerves. They were pretty much in agreement they had already faced death before they even entered the war zone.

Five days after getting underway from Guam, they steamed through Luzon Strait just north of the Philippines into the South China Sea. The sea was rough, and sheets of rain pelted the windows on the bridge. So much water was breaking over the bow that they had to pull the forward lookout. Visibility was down to one hundred yards, so pulling the man didn't make much difference in terms of the ship's safety. They would have to rely on the surface search radar.

As they headed south, the rain began to slacken, and by staying close to the shoreline the seas became relatively calm; they were able to repost the lookout. The quartermaster on the port pelorus was even able to get fixes from navigation points on land. They skirted Capones Island, then Silanguin Island, keeping both well to port. Lieutenant Barnaby was the OOD and had the conn once again for maneuvering the ship into port, and by the time he guided the *Everett* into the mouth of Subic Bay, with Grande Island off the starboard side, the rain was a soft drizzle.

Jason was the JOOD and paid close attention to what Barnaby was doing. He was not yet ready to have the conn under these circumstances, but it wouldn't be long until he would be in Barnaby's position. They received orders to berth outboard of two other destroyer escorts, the *Whipple* and the *Rathburne*, both in for repairs after spending a month on the gunline. The *Everett* would be in for just a few days before it would make its presence known on Yankee Station.

As they made their approach, he could see Third Class Petty Officer Hernandez on the forecastle getting ready to heave a monkey fist—a large woven knot that serves as a weight on a line—over to the men on the *Whipple*. The toss was perfect, and the men on the *Whipple* quickly pulled the thin line across, followed by the much thicker main line that would secure the bow of the *Everett* to theirs. A similar set of actions followed at the stern. A set of heavy-duty marine fenders kept the ships from making contact with each other as the lines were tightened.

It was just after one o'clock and the rain had stopped, for now. It was getting toward the end of monsoon season, but the rains were far from finished. However, the men were ready for some liberty, and nothing could dampen their spirits. Before that could happen, the ship needed to be squared away, orders for food and other goods needed to be confirmed, and schedules for delivery had to be established. Only then could the men be turned loose onto the streets of Olongapo City, one of the wildest liberty towns in the world.

"Now hear this, liberty is granted to sections two, three, and four, to expire on board at twenty-four hundred hours, September 9. Now liberty."

Now Liberty—the sweetest words any sailor can hear. It applied to officers too. Jason, Joe, Ed, and several other officers had made plans to head into Olongapo for some drinks, food, and entertainment, but torrential rains had returned by the time liberty was declared. They decided instead to head for the Subic Bay O' Club for some drinks and dinner and hope for a better day tomorrow.

Dressed in civvies and rain jackets, they departed the *Everett*, showing their IDs and requesting permission to cross over at the quarterdecks of the *Whipple* and *Rathburne*. Jason had grabbed a tarp from one of the deck lockers, and once on the pier, they spread it out over their heads, each person holding an edge, in an attempt to keep dry as they made their way across the base to the club. It was somewhat effective, but even so, everyone was soaked from the knees down by the time they got through the door of the club.

En route to the club, they had to pass through part of the shipyard. The giant cranes rode on rails as wide as those found on regular railways. They were walking parallel to one of the rails when Ed said, "Whoa! What's that thing sitting on the rail up ahead? A rat, maybe?"

As one under the tarp, they crept up on the mysterious creature.

"Holy shit!" Joe exclaimed. "That's no rat. It's a cockroach!"

Again, as one under the tarp, they quickly moved away from the largest insect any of them had ever seen.

It was just after five o'clock, and the club was relatively empty thanks to the weather. The club itself was a very large open room with two bars, one near the stage against a long wall with no windows, and another that sat in front of a broad expanse of windows that looked out over the harbor. The rain was so heavy that the view was diminished to the point of being nonexistent. There were tables and booths that spread out from a small dance floor that was laid out in front of the stage. They easily found a rectangular table big enough for the eight of them to be seated.

Jason was seated at one end of the table, with Joe to his right and Ed to his left. Directly across from him was David Barnaby, with Frank Gallagher, Norm Shapiro, Doug Kimos, and Jack Culpepper in the other seats. A Filipino waiter in a white server's jacket, black bow tie, and black pants came over to take their orders.

"Will you gentlemen be having dinner with us tonight?"

Ed quipped, "I guess that leaves Norm out."

Jason said, "Yes, but I'm sure everyone would like a drink or two—"

"Or three," Ed inserted.

"—before we order."

"Certainly, sir. What would you like?"

Jason ordered a Tom Collins, as did Joe, David, and Jack. Everyone else ordered Black Russians, except for Norm.

Norm said, "I'd like a Grasshopper."

"He's your roommate," Jason said to Ed.

Ed just shook his head and said, "I hope he doesn't get smashed on those; they'd look nasty coming back up."

"Don't you worry," Norm said. "I can hold my booze."

"Yeah, but that's not really booze," said Joe. "'Booze' isn't that shade of green. A Grasshopper looks more like some kind of antifreeze."

"How would you know?" Norm asked.

Joe quipped, "Your mom drinks them."

"Leave him alone," said Doug. "It's okay if he can't handle the hard stuff."

"Easy for you to say. It's not your stateroom that he's going to hurl in later tonight," said Ed.

The waiter returned with the drinks. He returned with drinks two more times before Jason said, "I think we're ready to order dinner."

David Barnaby said to everyone at the table, "The prime rib here is legendary, and you probably won't be seeing that on your plate out at sea."

Everyone took him up on that suggestion. It came with a baked potato and an iceberg lettuce wedge salad. When the waiter had finished asking everyone how they would like their prime ribs done, he turned to Jason and asked, "Will you be having wine with dinner?"

Jason looked around the table. Everyone was nodding.

He said to the waiter, "Looks like we will. I think some Beaujolais will go nicely with the prime rib."

Ed said, "Ah, Blue Jay Haze, my favorite."

"Excellent choice, sir. How many bottles?"

"Well, there's eight of us, so that means we need eight bottles."

"Very good, sir." Jason smirked at the waiter's eye-roll as he turned to place their order with the kitchen.

A Filipino band had started playing while they had been ordering their dinner. They were doing covers of Creedence Clearwater Revival songs, and Jason swore that if he was listening to a CCR recording at the same time, he wouldn't be able to tell the difference between the band and the record.

Jason said, "That's really some good stuff they're playing. I love CCR. My band in college was actually named after one of their songs, 'Fortunate Son.'"

Joe said, "Why don't you ask if you can sit in on a tune."

"Nah, they're really—."

"Never mind. I'll ask."

Before Jason could stop him, Joe jumped up from the table, heading for the stage.

Jason could see Joe talking to one of the guitarists, who began nodding his head. Joe turned and waved him up.

Under his breath, Jason said, "Shit." He got up and reluctantly headed for the stage.

When he got there, the guitarist invited him up, took off his guitar and handed it to Jason. It was a beautiful Gibson SG with a cherry red finish, just like he had seen Clapton playing the first time he saw Cream. Inspired after seeing Clapton, Jason had gone out and bought one for himself.

"Wow, nice axe," he said to the guitarist. "Got one just like it back home."

He strapped it on and looked over at the rest of the band. "You guys know how to play 'Who'll Stop the Rain?' Kinda works for what's going on out there." They all knew it, and everyone agreed on the key of C.

Jason started the opening guitar riff, stepped up to the microphone and started singing. "Long as I remember, rain's been coming down . . ."

The club had filled up by this point, and the chatter in the club stopped when they began to realize there was someone new up on stage, one of their own. Jason ended the song on the final instrumental riff and watched as everyone in the club applauded, with his table standing as they clapped and hollered. He handed the guitar back to the band guitarist, thanking him profusely and telling him how much he'd enjoyed playing with them. As he made his way back to the table, many people came over to him, patting him on the back, telling him, "Great job."

Jason sat down, looked around smiling, then looked at Joe and said, kiddingly, "Don't ever do that again. I thought I was going to shit a brick up there."

"Well, you didn't." He paused. "Wait, did you check your pants?"

Their waiter brought their dinners to the table with the help of another server. The portions almost hung over the edge of the plates. Bowls of sour cream were placed out on the table, along with bowls of blue cheese dressing and Russian dressing for the iceberg wedges. Additional bowls arrived with extra crumbles of blue cheese for the salads. And, of course, wine was served.

Jason raised his glass in a toast. "Here's to David's recommendation. This looks absolutely awesome!" Everyone clinked glasses and dug in.

As they were finishing their meal, Joe leaned over to Jason and said, "Do you know that guy over at the end of the bar by the stage? He keeps looking over this way, and I think specifically at you."

Without looking over, Jason said, "Probably just a fan, haha."

After a minute, Jason glanced over toward the bar. "Holy shit, yeah, I know him. That's Ken DiMartini; he was in San Diego with me and went to one of the other rescue salvage ships in Pearl, the *Reliance*. It was already on a WestPac deployment when he caught up with it, so this is his second go 'round out here. Not one of my favorite guys in the world and I'm not sure he cares for me much either."

"Why's that?"

Jason didn't really want to get into the details with Joe, so he said, "Let's just say he was a real jerk at this cookout we had at the apartment complex where we both lived. Treated his wife like shit. Even so, I guess I should go over and say hi. I'll be right back."

Jason got up from the table, just a little unsteady from all the wine and drinks, and made his way across the bar until he came up right behind the guy.

"Hey, Ken, Fancy runnin' into you out here."

Ken turned around slowly. He was nursing what looked like a large whiskey and was obviously drunk. "Well, if it isn't ole Jason. Caught your act. Not bad. What am I doin' here? Fightin' for my country, right? I can't believe we're back out here again. No sooner we get to Nam then we got pulled back in here to Subic to haul in some tin can that got clipped in the ass by some piece of crap Filipino boat out near the mouth of the harbor. Fucked up her screw; couldn't make it back."

"How long are you guys here for?"

"We're outta here tomorrow. Back to Da Nang."

"Guess you know Olongapo pretty well. We just got in and we'll probably head over there tomorrow."

Ken, ruefully, shook his head. "Oh yeah, I been there. Sampled the 'wares' many times, shall we say. Some real cuties. How many times do ya gotta hear, 'Hey, Joe, buy me drink.' Hell, I bought more than a drink, if you know what I mean. Helped me get over it."

"Get over it? Get over what?"

Ken looked carefully at Jason for a moment. "Get over the 'Carrie-gram' I got the first time I was here. It was waitin' for me when we got our mail delivered when we got sent here for maintenance after doin' some work near the rivers. Been celebratin' ever since."

Jason had known what the "problem" was, but he certainly wasn't going to let on to Ken how he knew that. He let Ken go on.

"She left me, Jason. Carrie went home to Portland, and she ain't comin' back."

"Um, I'm sorry to hear that, Ken. Did she say why?" Jason was *really* hoping that Carrie hadn't gone into too many details in her "Carrie-gram."

"She basically said she was tired of my bullshit, plain and simple." Ken paused, obviously trying to think about something. "Hey, that was about the time you were staying with Bob and Marianne, right?"

Jason nodded.

"I think that little bitch Marianne had something to do with it; she and Carrie were pretty tight." He looked at Jason again. "You know anything about that? You were there."

"No, I don't know about that. I can't believe Marianne would put something like that in Carrie's head, if that's what you're implying."

Ken was getting a little too close to the truth, and in a way, Jason was part of that truth.

"I'm sorry that all went down, Ken. I really am."

"Thanks. Don't know what I'll do when we get back. *If* we get back. We're yanking boats right off the beaches in real shallow water. If we scrape bottom in that ole rust bucket I'm on, we're goin' down." Ken looked unsteadily at Jason. "You doin' okay?"

Jason nodded. "Yeah, doin' fine. Seems like a good ship and good crew. In fact, I should be gettin' back to my buddies over there. I think we're gettin' ready to head back. You take care, Ken."

"Yeah, I'll do that. I'll do that. Maybe we'll get together back in Pearl."

"Sure, yeah, let's do that." Jason hesitated, then turned to head back to his table.

Ken swiveled back to his drink, downed what was left, and staggered off his stool. "Gotta hit the head," he announced to no one in particular as he headed away from the bar.

Jason walked slowly back to his friends at the table. Ken was the last person he had wanted to see. But it could have been worse.

It could have been a *lot* worse.

ELEVEN

Subic Bay/Olongapo/USS *Midway*

SEPTEMBER 1972

At liberty call the next day, Joe and Jason made their way over to the Subic Bay Exchange. The exchange in the Philippines was well known for doing more business than any other exchange in the world, and Jason knew exactly what he was looking to buy. The exchange was so big and diverse, if you really weren't sure what you were looking for, it was easy to get sidetracked or lost.

Both men were looking to buy cameras and audio equipment. Jason already owned some high-end audio gear: a belt drive AR turntable and AR 3a speakers. He had an old Wollensak portable tape recorder that his parents had given him for Christmas when he was in high school. It did double track recordings, and he had used it to record some of the jam sessions he and the guys from the *Engage* had in their apartment in Waikiki. It did a serviceable job. Now, he was looking for something a little better.

Joe was looking for a turntable and found a nice Sony model. While in the Sony "section," Jason found a TC-377 slant front reel-to-reel tape recorder that did sound-on-sound and had three possible recording speeds. This was just what he needed. They made their purchases and had the salesperson keep them behind the counter for them while they looked at cameras.

Joe bought a Canon. Jason was tempted because it was a really good price, but he had his heart set on a Nikon. They had a Nikkormat for sale with through-the-lens monitoring for shutter speed and aperture, but when the salesperson showed him the Nikon Photomic FTN with a 50mm Nikkor lens, he knew that was what he wanted. Happy with what they bought, they carried them back to the ship to stow and pick up Ed for a night out in Olongapo.

The walk to the main gate heading out to Olongapo was a short one from where they were docked. They knew they were getting close to the bridge that crossed over into Olongapo just by the smell. The bridge spanned what essentially was a drainage ditch or canal known as "Shit River." It was aptly named since that was what was in it.

They flashed their IDs at the marine stationed at the gate and he waved them through, along with many other Navy men looking for fun. As they walked across the bridge, they could see children standing on the banks or in small boats, yelling up to the people crossing over.

"Hey, sailor, throw me money."

"Hey, Joe, how about a quarter."

"You throw. I dive."

Several of the sailors tossed nickels and dimes, intentionally missing their targets, the outstretched hands of the kids, the baskets they held, or the boats they stood in, so the children *had* to dive into the water to retrieve the coins. The men got a big laugh out of it. To Jason, it was an absolutely disgusting thing for these guys to be doing. He'd had a microbiology and a parasitology course at Villanova and couldn't imagine what sorts of diseases and infections these kids were contracting just for a few cents. Jason was beginning to understand how the term "ugly American" had come to be and couldn't wait to get across.

At the far side, Magsaysay Drive picked up and went straight through the middle of town. It was a dirt road that had turned into a river of mud from the torrential rains. It was so bad, even the jeepneys were confined to the side streets. There were concrete sidewalks, and a concrete median strip in the middle of the so-called road. Jason wasn't sure who had done it—store owners, bar owners, hotel staff, or city workers—but someone had laid out broad wooden planks to span the mud so that people could cross from one side of the street to the other. Good for business. Jason was also amused to see that some revelers were already so drunk they failed to negotiate the wooden "sobriety test." Some were totally coated in mud. It looked especially bad for those who had decided to go ashore in their dress whites rather than in civvies. Typically, guys go ashore in uniform to impress the girls, something that wasn't really necessary in Olongapo. Regardless, they were, in fact, making quite an impression.

They changed dollars into pesos at the money exchange and made their way into town on the sidewalk.

As they looked into the bars and shops, Ed said, "You know, since you've got your guitar with you on the ship, I was thinking about buying one over here. I used to play, but it's been a couple of years since I picked one up. There's what looks like a music shop across the street. I can see guitars hanging in the window."

Jason said, "I'd be glad to help you pick one out. Let's see what they've got."

The three of them negotiated the planks, going one at a time so as not to have the board sag into the mud from the weight of all three being on at the same time. As they peered into the window, Jason shook his head and said, "Something's not right here. Let's go in for a closer look."

As they came in, the proprietor came up to them and said, "You want guitar? Have many guitar here. Many Gibson."

Jason took a look at the instruments hanging from the ceiling and on the walls. There were "many guitar here" all right. All different body shapes and headstocks. They did have one thing in common—the Gibson logo was stamped on every headstock. There was one problem: none of them were Gibsons. Jason whispered to Ed, "You know, I think we might want to look in the Subic Exchange, just to see what they have."

They started to leave the store, and the proprietor said, "I give you good price. Not what on sticker. Good price!"

Jason turned and said, "Fine. Thank you. We might be back." *But we won't.*

When they got out of the store, Jason said, "Wow. Just learned a good lesson. Buyer beware. Every one of those guitars was a knock off. Junk."

Joe said, "Hey, here's a jewelry store. I bet we can buy a 'Rodex' for cheap."

"Yeah, I'll bet we can," said Ed. "But what we need now is a place to buy some cheap beer."

Jason looked around. Every other store front was a bar or a casino. "I think we just might be able to find that."

They walked a block or so and heard Motown music drifting out of one of the clubs. The sign that identified The Zanzibar Club looked like it could use more than a touch-up and was perched on the small overhang that shaded the entrance. As soon as they went in, a beautiful young woman in red short-shorts and a white blouse greeted them and said, "You want table? I seat you. Get you beer. Yes?"

Joe said, "Yes to all of that, thanks."

The club was pretty dark except for the professionally lit stage. A full Motown review group with horns and all the dance moves made famous by groups like the Four Tops and the Miracles was up there doing perfect renditions of all the big hits.

The woman showed them to a table large enough to seat six people in the center of the room. "I'm Carol. I take care of you. San Miguel?"

Jason said, "Sure, three San Miguels." Jason had never had a San Miguel, but he had heard it was a nice, light Filipino beer. Besides, the water was undrinkable, so you had no choice but to drink beer. Mixed drinks were not really an option, either; the ice was contaminated too.

When Carol left, Joe said, "She doesn't get paid by the club. She makes a commission on each beer she sells and, of course, tips. Even with all these people here, it doesn't add up to much."

Carol returned with the beers and said, "You pay now. I come back for another round."

They each gave her five pesos, which amounted to a US quarter apiece. It was way too much; the bar would take 2.5 of those pesos and give her back 0.5 pesos, so the tip was generous, but they would get excellent service.

They were on their third round and thoroughly enjoying the show. As far as rhythm and blues acts went, Jason had only seen Sam and Dave in concert, and they weren't really a Motown act since they recorded on Stax records out of Memphis. The only true Motown acts he had seen had been on *The Ed Sullivan Show*. While watching this Filipino group, he began to think he had missed out on something.

Carol came back. "You want girls, yes?"

Ed said, "No, just another round, thanks."

"You sure?"

"Yes, we're sure."

She looked disappointed but went to get another round. They were sure she got a commission on that kind of transaction too.

As time passed, the noise in the crowd became louder, fueled by the drinks. Arguments were breaking out at tables all around them. One table near the front was particularly rowdy. One of the guys at the table, dressed in jeans and a brown Polo shirt, had been yelling at the band. "Play some Stones! We want the Stones!"

The lead singer tried to be polite. "Sorry, sir. Only Motown. We are Uptown Motown Review."

"I don't give a shit what you are. I want to hear some fuckin' Stones. Now!"

He stood up, making to lunge for the stage, but one of his buddies pulled him back, causing him to sit back down in his chair. He didn't hit it squarely, which caused the chair to tip over sideways, sending him sprawling. He kicked out to try to catch his balance but only succeeded in hitting the underside of the table with his foot so hard that all the beer bottles went flying, shattering all over the floor.

He pushed himself up off the floor, badly cutting his hand in the process. He turned on the guy who had grabbed him, yelling, "You stupid son of a bitch." He shoved him back into some other tables. He focused his wrath back to the band on the stage, "Now I'm coming for you, you fuckin' Filipino asshole."

The stage was basically just a set of risers elevating the band about three feet off the floor. As the guy put his hands on the edge to try to climb up, the singer grabbed a microphone stand with a heavy metal base. Swinging it like a golf club, he caught his attacker right under his chin, sending him flying back onto the floor. He didn't get up. The guys at his table went over to him, lying in the broken glass and spilled beer.

It was then that the Shore Patrol showed up, one a first class petty officer, the other a second class.

"Just in the nick of time," Jason said.

The first class told the downed man's buddies to step back, which they wisely did.

"What's his name?"

"Greg."

"Greg what?"

"Greg Farnsworth."

"Navy?"

"Yeah. We're on the *Whipple*."

"Then I'd advise the rest of you to get back on the *Whipple*. Now!" The first class was obviously pissed.

"What about him?" One of his buddies pointed at the attacker on the ground who was starting to moan and roll his head back and forth in the beer. Blood was trickling from his mouth where he had bitten his tongue.

"We'll be taking care of him. Now, beat it."

The men left, and after a few minutes the SPs got Greg to his feet. They each grabbed an arm and drag-walked him out of the club.

The band began to play again as if nothing had happened. Joe said, "Nice floor show."

Jason said, "Yeah, never saw anything like that on Ed Sullivan."

They finished the last round and decided they'd had enough excitement for one evening. Walking back to the base along Magsaysay Drive, Jason said, "I don't know about you guys, but I'm fucking starving."

Ed said, "Me too. I remember seeing a couple of stands on our way in. They looked kinda like hot dog stands, but they were grilling something. Maybe some barbeque?"

Joe said, "I could definitely go for some barbeque."

They found a stand not too far from the entrance gate to the base. A man in the stand was grilling some meat on skewers, but they couldn't tell exactly what it was.

"Teriyaki beef?" Jason ventured.

"Not sure there's a lot of beef around here," said Joe, doubtfully.

The man, dressed in baggy khakis and a yellow-flowered shirt heavily stained with grease said, "You hungry? You want monkey meat? Five pesos."

Joe, his face scrunched in disgust, said, "Monkey meat? Man, I'm hungry, but I don't think I'm *that* hungry."

Jason noticed two men standing off to the side of the stand eating meat off the skewers and went over to them.

He motioned at the skewers in their hands. "How is it?"

One guy in what used to be white pants and a blue cotton shirt who seemed barely able to stand up said, "Monkey meat! Best fuckin' monkey meat I ever had!"

Jason looked dubious. "How many times have you eaten monkey meat?"

The guy looked at the skewer and then looked back up at Jason. "First time."

"What's it taste like?"

"Whaddya think? Monkey!" He laughed at his own joke. "No, really, it's sorta beefy."

"Okay, thanks for the review." Jason went back to the stand.

"Guy says it's sorta 'beefy.' His word."

Ed said, "Why don't you get a couple of skewers, try one, and if you don't puke, we'll join you."

"What's in it for me?" Jason asked.

"I'll buy them for you."

"Whoa, big spender. Ten pesos." Jason grinned, "Sure. Why not? As long as you're buying."

Ed paid the vendor and handed the skewers over to Jason. Jason looked at the skewers, then at Joe and Ed who were watching him intently. And while still watching them, brought the skewer up to his mouth and pulled a piece off with his teeth.

After a moment, he said, "Kinda chewy, but it tastes all right."

Joe said, "Swallow. We wanna see ya swallow."

Jason swallowed. "Really. Not bad. In fact, highly recommended."

They all bought skewers, three apiece, and ate them as they walked back to the *Everett*.

When they got back to the ship, they headed for the wardroom and found the Filipino stewards getting mid-rats ready; chili over rice, one of Jason's favorites. He was a little sorry he had stopped for the monkey meat.

Jason leaned into the galley and said to the man preparing food, "Yo, Bautista! We just had monkey meat in town."

Bautista got a big grin on his face. "Monkey meat, huh? I don't think so."

"Why do you say that?"

He laughed. "Can't be."

"Why not?"

"Us Filipinos *ate* all the monkeys." Bautista laughed some more.

Joe and Ed had been watching this exchange, along with another steward named Cruz.

Ed asked, "So, what *did* we eat?"

"Dog," Cruz volunteered.

Joe paled a bit. "Dog? As in Lassie?"

"Yep. Very common here."

Jason said, "Boy, were we ever barking up the wrong tree."

Ed started laughing, and through his laughing got out, "Oh my God, that's so wrong, so wrong. We could have been standing there looking at the skewers saying 'Who's a good boy? Who's a good boy?'"

Jason said to Bautista, "I think we'll need some of that chili as a chaser."

"Yes, sir. Want to know what the chili's made with?"

"Just serve it up, Bautista." He turned to Ed and Joe. "Everyone's a comedian."

The next morning, Joe and Jason walked into the wardroom for a hastily called officers' meeting at 1000 hours. Ed was already there, with Jack Culpepper and Norm Shapiro.

"So, what's this all about?" Jason asked.

Ed directed his thumb at Norm. "Norm here thinks we're getting underway a day early. At least that's the scuttlebutt he's hearing."

Norm was nodding his head. "Word has it that a typhoon is bearing down on us, and Subic is expected to take a direct hit."

They all stood as the XO entered the wardroom.

"Seats, gentlemen." The lieutenant commander didn't look happy.

"We have received orders to get underway at sixteen hundred hours this afternoon to rendezvous with the carrier *Midway* in the South China Sea. We'll be in formation with her, the light cruiser *Providence*, and three other tin cans like us. I'm assuming *Whipple* and *Rathburne* will be right on our stern as we head out. No idea about the third destroyer; probably the escort ship already with the *Midway* working flight ops support. When you're dismissed, get the word out to your divisions to secure this ship for heavy seas. It should only last for two days or so, but it looks like it will be a serious storm.

We'll set sea and anchor detail at fifteen hundred hours. Sorry to cut our time here a little short. I know that every section didn't get equal liberty time; tell the men we'll make it up next trip in. We'll be here a lot."

The XO looked over at Ed. "I'll get more detailed information for you to prepare the captain's standing orders for tonight as soon as I get them. The only thing I know for certain is that we'll be steaming in a hexagonal formation, and we'll be directly astern of the Midway."

"Yes, sir."

"One other thing. Some of you haven't experienced seas like this before, and neither have many of the men on board. Make sure all the racks and bunks have straps to secure them when they try to get some sleep. Note the word 'try.' It can get pretty harrowing out there; sleep won't come easy. And we don't want guys thrown out of their racks onto the deck, especially from an upper bunk. They'll probably be getting a few bruises just trying to stay upright during their watches as it is."

The XO looked around the table. "Any questions?" He paused. No one spoke. "Dismissed."

Jason sat on the edge of his bunk in his stateroom after getting the word out to Petty Officer First Class Clarke and the rest of the men of First Division. Joe and Ed were seated on the chairs by the desks.

"Ever been through one of these?" Jason asked.

Joe said, "Yeah, we went through one about halfway through the last WestPac. It makes things pretty miserable for everyone for a couple of days. We'll get through it. I'm just disappointed we didn't get back out to Olongapo. I was ready to hit some of the casinos out there; shoot a little craps."

Ed said, "The cutter I was on was based on the West Coast, so we never really experienced anything like a typhoon." He looked over at Joe. "How does betting on craps work, anyway. Seems complicated."

"Nah. Not really. We'll go out next time we're in and I'll show you how it works."

Jason said, "I'm with Ed. Black Jack's about all I can handle. Thank God I never experienced heavy seas on the *Engage*. That old tub bobbed like a cork even in relatively smooth water. I guess some of the worst seas we encountered were just off the coast of Oahu in the Molokai Channel."

"Heard that can get pretty rough," Joe said.

Jason nodded. "We were towing a deep dive habitat to be lowered down to two hundred feet off the coast of Kailua. With the habitat in tow, the ship couldn't ride the waves normally, so the bow was heaving up and then plowing into the next swell like it was trying to imitate a fuckin' porpoise. I had the deck *and the conn* for eleven straight hours for that transit. I was beat. Not really looking forward to two or more days of it here."

The *Midway* was already out in the South China Sea just south of Manila with the escort destroyer *Kilgorn*. The predicted track of the typhoon had the eye of the storm passing through the southern islands of the Philippines, so the plan was to rendezvous off the west coast of Luzon then head through the Luzon Strait for the open ocean east of Taiwan.

As they got underway, sustained winds of at least 45 mph were being felt in Subic, and the rain had started to pick up from the drizzle that had been present all through the morning hours. Maneuvering the ships out of the harbor with poor visibility and high winds was a dangerous proposition but remaining in port was even more so. By the time they cleared Grande Island at the mouth of the harbor, everyone who was out on deck during special sea and anchor detail was soaked regardless of the type of rain gear that was worn.

Jason had been out on deck with his men and had to go back to his stateroom to change out of his wet uniform. As he started to strip off his wet clothes, he could feel the pitching motion of the ship begin to intensify, as well as the roll. *It's only going to get worse*, he thought. *Dinner's going to be fun.*

The destroyer escorts *Rathburne*, *Whipple*, and *Everett* steamed in a linear formation to the rendezvous, with *Everett* in the lead position. Captain Zhao was the most senior of the ships' captains, so until they reached the *Midway*, he was in command of the formation. David Barnaby remained as the OOD and Frank Gallagher had the conn. They were to be relieved by Jason and Joe at 2000 hours.

By 1800 hours, most of the junior officers were seated in the wardroom. The forward door opened and as Lieutenant Commander Archie Burns entered, he announced, "Attention. Captain is in the wardroom."

Everyone came to attention and remained so until the captain took his seat at the head of the table. As he took his seat, a few officers exchanged discreet glances as if to say, "What the hell is this all about?"

"Be seated, gentlemen."

By this time, the ship had taken on a rather dramatic, but rhythmic, pitch. The rolling motion, however, was seemingly random, with the furthest point of the roll punctuated by a stuttering vibration, as if the ship couldn't decide if it wanted to right itself, or not. Since the long part of the wardroom table was aligned from port to starboard, the motion from one end of the table to the other was quite dramatic, like a rather sophisticated, but unpredictable, playground see-saw.

Jason looked over at Ed, who as the navigator, was seated directly across the table from Captain Zhao. He turned his head to follow Ed's gaze to the galley, where the stewards were preparing to serve the first course: soup. Jason looked back at Ed, shaking his head ever so slightly and mouthing the words, "Not good."

Ed nodded.

Steward Cruz brought the first bowl from the galley, and as is the custom, began to serve the captain first. Just as he was about to set the bowl on the table, the ship rolled violently to port, causing Cruz to lose his balance and dump most of the contents of the bowl onto the captain's lap. Everyone looked on, horrified, as Captain Zhao leaped to his feet, wiping at his pants and shirt with his napkin in a vain attempt to clean the creamy potato leek soup off his uniform.

Zhao turned on Cruz, who had ended up catching himself on the arm of the wardroom couch. "You stupid incompetent fool! Look what you've done! I'll have you up at captain's mast for this!" His face had turned deep red and was contorted with rage. He yelled into Bautista inside the galley. "Send food to my stateroom. Solid food, or you'll be at mast with him!"

When Zhao had stood, everyone at the table had come to attention. They were still at attention when Zhao stormed out of the wardroom, slamming the door as he left.

As the XO tried to assure Cruz that he would not, in fact, be going to captain's mast, Jason turned to Doug Kimos, and as he started to open his mouth, Doug said, "Do. Not. Say. A. Word."

The XO turned away from Cruz, and very quietly said to Bautista in the galley, "I think we can skip the soup."

Jason had already relieved Frank Gallagher of his JOOD duties by the time Joe and Ed got to the bridge. Ed had a copy of the standing orders and had the quartermaster log them in. Joe took the deck from David Barnaby.

Ed said to Barnaby, "If you're heading for the wardroom, don't get the soup."

Barnaby looked at him quizzically. "I'll explain later," said Ed.

After Barnaby left the bridge, Jason asked Ed, "So, how was it?"

"Come over here by the radar screen." The three of them moved over to the bridge radar and stared as the sweep across the scope revealed the two blips that were the *Rathburne* and *Whipple* astern of them.

Very quietly, Ed said, "So, I knocked on the door and said I was ready to pick up the standing orders." He paused. "Nothing. No response. So, I knocked again, and I could sort of hear him moving in his stateroom. After what seemed like several minutes, he opened the door. He was just standing there in his bathrobe. At first, he didn't seem to acknowledge that I was there. He looked a little bleary-eyed, as if he had been asleep."

"That doesn't sound good," said Jason.

"No, he didn't look good. He motioned me to grab a chair that was lying on its side by his desk; apparently it hadn't yet been strapped down for heavy seas. I picked it up and sat down. He sat behind his desk and mumbled a few things about the rendezvous, and then he said, 'That'll be all.'"

"Really not good."

"Right. I've done this enough, so I knew what to write even though I couldn't understand half of what he was saying. I hurried to complete it sitting there in front of him so I didn't have to come back later for his signature. So, when he dismissed me, I was ready to have him sign off." Ed was shaking his head. "He did it, but it didn't look much like his normal signature. I thanked him and left, after securing the chair for him."

Ed kept staring at the radar screen, then looked at Joe and Jason. "I think he was on something. I mean, I've been around enough people doing pot and 'shrooms to know that look. I think he took some kind of sedative, or something. I hope he's okay enough to strap himself in his bunk."

By this time, everyone on the bridge was holding onto something just to stay upright. The bow was plowing into the swells; the forward lookout had been pulled during Barnaby's watch. No one could be out on deck as wave after wave swept down the length of the ship. Jason glanced at the roll gauge mounted on the bulkhead behind the helmsman to see if what he was feeling was what the ship was actually doing. It was. He decided not to look at the gauge again.

They found the *Midway* and her escort ship soon after they left the Luzon Strait. Technically, Joe should have informed Captain Zhao of their maneuvers, but given the circumstances, he felt it was better not to try to contact him. Under orders from *Midway*'s captain, they took their place one thousand yards astern while the other four ships were spaced equidistant from each other on the points of a hexagon. Due to the sheets of rain hitting the bridge windows, visuals were virtually impossible. Philippine typhoons had been known to deliver over ten to twelve inches of rain in one day with winds well over 110 miles per hour.

At first, keeping track of the other ships on surface search radar was relatively easy. Distances and bearings could be tracked on the bridge and in CIC, the Combat Information Center. The men in CIC were in contact with the bridge via sound-powered phones. However, after several hours, the blips began to wink on and off with each sweep. Joe and Jason realized that the ocean swells had grown so large that when they were in the trough of a wave, the surface search radar was unable to detect ships that were in another trough at the same time. Losing something as large as an aircraft carrier on radar meant that the swells were at least forty feet in height from trough to crest. The only good thing was that due to its size, the blip of the *Midway* was much more consistently displayed than the other ships in the formation, and since each ship took its position relative to the *Midway*, they theoretically should all be safe as they endured the typhoon. Theoretically.

As the watch progressed, Jason noted that no one was seasick. Apparently, concentrating on doing one's job and simply struggling to stay upright was enough to take your mind off being sick, lending some credence to the theory that motion sickness was mainly mental. He also couldn't imagine going through a storm like this on a ship like his previous one, the *Engage*. He wasn't sure the metal that made up the hull could take this kind of pounding.

The watch seemed to go on forever, but at 2345 hours, both Joe and Jason were relieved of their bridge duties by Doug Kimos and Jack Culpepper. They had both been in the wardroom for mid-rats, and Kimos said, "Unfortunately for you guys, we ate all the soup. Sorry."

Jason said, "Haha! Funny. Really, worth stopping down there?"

Culpepper said, "Only if you have a craving for turkey and cheese sandwiches. Nothing special tonight. It's probably pretty rough trying to work in the galley. I did manage to stay upright and balanced enough to get some coffee in me." He looked around the bridge. "Although, given these conditions, I probably won't have any problem staying awake."

Joe and Jason decided to skip mid-rats; not worth the trouble. They braced themselves against the bulkheads as they made their way aft to the staterooms. It wasn't easy.

As they went to enter their stateroom, Jason said, "I'm guessing Ed won't have to get up to do a star shoot tomorrow morning."

"You got that right," Joe said. "If I was him, I'd just stay strapped in my rack for the whole day."

Jason got undressed, climbed in his bunk, found the straps, and pulled them tight. He figured he wouldn't be tossing and turning much during the night. The ship would do that for him.

He never fell into a deep sleep even though he was exhausted from just remaining upright during his watch. It felt more like a state of semiconsciousness throughout the whole night. And the next day promised to be more of the same.

After two days, the rain let up and the seas became calm enough to carry out normal ship operations. The other ships peeled away, returning to Subic, leaving the *Everett* to follow the *Midway* to Yankee Station off the coast of Vietnam to assist with flight ops. The *Everett*'s job was to be the rescue pick up ship if any of the pilots had to bail out of their F4 Phantoms for any reason. Typically, if a jet missed the arresting cable, it could power up enough to, in effect, do a touch-and-go. The Phantoms certainly had enough power to do that. They could stand on their tail and shoot straight up in the sky like a rocket, if needed. They weren't the most maneuverable planes, but they were good enough for the Navy Blue Angels precision flight team.

At first, Jason thought watching the flight operations was fascinating, and he got lots of good pictures from the *Everett*'s perfect vantage point. At least he thought they were good. He would have to wait to see how they came out after getting them developed back at the Subic Bay Base Exchange. But, after two weeks, even the miracle of landing a plane on a postage stamp in the middle of the ocean became blasé. Everyone was glad when they were relieved of their duty on Yankee Station and could begin gunfire support operations.

TWELVE

Gunline DMZ

SEPTEMBER–OCTOBER 1972

Jason watched from the starboard bridge wing as the small spotter copter buzzed across the bow of the *Everett* with the grace of a giant dragonfly. It banked hard to its right and skimmed low over the water of the South China Sea and headed south, probably to Da Nang for refueling. Every day the copters would fly high over the DMZ to locate targets, send the locations to Task Force 77 command, and then take flight from the land to relative safety over the open water. Soon, Ensign Jack Culpepper's communications team in CIC would receive the coordinates of a target and the *Everett* would be directed to break ranks from the gunline to do a night steam to put that designated target in range of its 5-inch gun. Sometimes it would be a solo mission, but on other occasions it might be in tandem with other ships, such as the guided missile destroyer *Goldsborough* or the light cruiser *Providence*, John McGinty's ship.

It had been a week since they'd broken away from the *Midway* and Jason had to admit to himself that the gunline was a more interesting assignment. There was something different going on each day. He was feeling a bit nervous about what he was facing that afternoon; they were breaking away from the line to have an UNREP/VERTREP with a Military Sealift Command fast combat supply ship and he had been tapped to have the conn. Lieutenant David Barnaby would be the OOD. It would be necessary to come alongside the AOE-1 *Sacramento* at a distance of about thirty yards and then maintain that position for as long as the replenishment took.

The *Everett* broke away from the gunline and headed for the rendezvous point with the *Sacramento*. An hour later they had the AOE both visually and on the surface search radar. Barnaby called the captain to the bridge. The *Sacramento* had set a course to minimize the effects of ocean swells and set a speed of twelve knots. It was up to the *Everett* to overtake it and get into position.

"Captain on the bridge!" rang out from the quartermaster.

Captain Zhao walked across the bridge to where Barnaby and Jason were standing.

Jason said, "Good afternoon, Captain. We are at fifteen knots and just one mile astern of the *Sacramento*. Request permission to take position for underway replenishment with the *Sacramento* on our port side, sir."

Zhao nodded. "Permission granted." He walked out to the port bridge wing. "It looks like we have a calm day for this operation, a welcome change from our typhoon encounter."

Jason noted that Zhao was smiling. *Looks like he's in a good mood*, he thought. *Perhaps this is a good time to approach him about the breakaway music.*

Jason joined him on the bridge wing. He was more nervous about this than bringing the ship alongside the *Sacramento*. "Excuse me, Captain, I've been having some conversations with the men of my division, and they would like to do something that gives our ship an identity, something that speaks to our role here in gunfire support, something that tells the replenishment ship something about us."

"And what is it they are proposing, Mr. Conley?"

"Sir, a breakaway song."

Zhao looked puzzled. "What kind of song?"

"Breakaway song, sir. Something they can identify with. Something the crew of a replenishment ship would recognize."

Zhao turned away and looked out to sea. "I don't know, Mr. Conley. Doesn't sound very professional."

Jason was about to say, "But all the other ships are doing it," but then he thought about his mother saying, "Just because all the other kids are doing it doesn't make it right." He withheld that comment, substituting, "It's actually become common throughout the Navy now, sir, like a tradition. It embellishes a ship's reputation; as I said, it gives us an identity. We're not just any old destroyer escort; we're the *Everett*—and we kick ass."

Zhao turned and looked pointedly at Jason. "Kick ass, huh?" He continued to stare at Jason, but it was hard to judge what he was thinking since he had on his Ray Bans. Finally, he said, "How does it work?"

Jason thought, *This is promising.* He then said, "Actually it's quite easy, sir. I have a recording of the song cued up on my reel-to-reel tape recorder. As we break away, one of the men on the bridge hits the play button and broadcasts it over the 1MC."

Zhao looked back out at the ocean, shaking his head slightly. "So, Mr. Conley, you say this is becoming a tradition in the Navy."

"Yes, sir."

Zhao turned back to him. "What's the song?"

"It's a new one called 'Smoke on the Water.'"

"'Smoke on the Water?'" He paused. "Rock and roll, I suppose."

"Yes, sir. It's for the men, sir. They really like it."

Zhao didn't answer for about a minute, then finally said, "Okay, we can try it. I don't suppose you have this already set up for today, do you?"

"As a matter of fact, sir, I have my old Wollensak all set up and ready to go here on the bridge."

"You're mighty sure of yourself, aren't you, Mr. Conley."

"It's not about me, sir. I just knew you'd try to do right by our crew."

"Very well," Zhao said with a sigh. Then he added, sarcastically, "I can't wait."

The replenishment went very well. Jason maintained the *Everett*'s position by adding or subtracting turns of the screw, rather than by giving orders in knots. Although the course had been set by the *Sacramento*, minute adjustments in bearing had to be made through the helmsman due to the unusual hydrodynamic forces caused by the two ships steaming so close to each other. The water rushing between them tended to draw the ships together, and the way in which the ship hit certain swells would have the opposite effect. It was not physically challenging, but the mental strain was exhausting.

As the *Everett* took on fuel, a VERTREP was conducted by helicopter, with refrigerated goods and other stores on pallets being delivered to the flight deck. Conducting an operation such as this was literally an "all hands on deck" affair. Many of the men had just come off watch, while some would have to go on watch as soon as the replenishment ended. Replenishment interfered with the normal watch-rest-eat cycle, but it was necessary to keep the ship on station.

As the time to breakaway approached, Jason felt proud that he had only needed to get Barnaby's advice a few times. Having the conn during an UNREP was one of the major steps to being able to assume the duties of an OOD, and Jason thought it went well. He was also coming up for promotion to lieutenant junior grade. Mastering the underway maneuvers would look good.

Jason received word through the sound-powered phone that the VERTREP was complete, and all the stores were secured in the hangar bay for transfer to the mess decks. The oil line probe had been withdrawn from the *Everett*'s receiving bell and was being retracted over to the AOE, along with the communications line.

It was show time!

Captain Zhao had been talking with Barnaby. He glanced over at Jason and then came over to him. "Well done, Mr. Conley. I was just having some discussions with Mr. Barnaby concerning your readiness to assume the duties of OOD. It's his opinion that you are ready. That, and the fact you've already been OOD on your previous ship. I agree with Mr. Barnaby. Congratulations."

"Thank you, sir."

Jason had already shown the quartermaster where to hold the mic near the speaker on the Wollensak. As the *Sacramento* slacked the tensioning line for release from the *Everett*, he gave the signal to hit the play button. As the opening chords to "Smoke on the Water" rang out, the men on the forecastle started cheering. The men on the bridge all had big grins on their faces. Barnaby gave Jason a thumbs-up.

Captain Zhao looked at Jason and said, rather loudly, "What is that noise?"

"It's the song, sir. 'Smoke on the Water.'"

Zhao threw his hands in the air, started shaking his head, and walked off the bridge.

The quartermaster announced, "Captain's left the bridge."

Jason looked at Barnaby and said, "Well, that went rather well."

The man on sound-powered phones said, "Sir, the line to the *Sacramento* is clear of our ship. Also, we're getting a message from the *Sacramento* by signal lamp. 'You guys rock!'"

With a big grin on his face, Jason commanded the helmsman, "Right full rudder. Steady on course two nine zero."

"Aye, sir. Rudder's right full coming to two nine zero."

"Steady on two nine zero."

Jason thanked all the men on the bridge for a job well done and brought the ship up to twenty knots to return to the gunline. He stepped out onto the port bridge wing to enjoy the rest of the afternoon.

Back on the gunline, and after lunch the next day, a motor whale boat from the USS *Hoel* DDG-13 came alongside. It was their turn in the gunline rotation to send in a boat to Da Nang to pick up mail for the other ships on the gunline and to rotate movies between the ships. Movies were shown nightly in wardrooms and the mess decks, conditions permitting. They were 16mm versions, some highly edited, of relatively new feature films.

Petty Officer First Class Bennie Clarke was on the fantail with several other men from First Division to haul the mailbags aboard and offload the movies that had already been screened on the *Everett*. It had been several weeks since the *Everett* had mail call since they had been well off the coast as they performed plane guard duty for the *Midway*. The mail was just catching up to them now, and the men were very excited to get some news from home. They were also tired of seeing the same movies over and over.

Clarke yelled down to the men from the *Hoel*. "Whaddaya got for movies?"

One of the mates on the whaleboat sorted through the movie bags. He held up a bag. "This one has *Easy Rider, Dirty Dozen, Butch Cassidy*, and *Clockwork Orange*." He held up a second bag "This one's got *Green Berets, Planet of the Apes, Odd Couple*, and *Rosemary's Baby*."

Clarke turned to the other men around him. "Whaddya think? First bag?" They all agreed to the first bag and hauled it aboard.

He yelled down to the boat. "See ya in a few days—that's when we're the delivery boat." They took the bags down below to sort the mail and deliver them to the mess decks, the chiefs in the goat locker, and the wardroom.

Jason, Ed, and Joe went down to the wardroom and picked up their mail. Jason had six letters, four from Lori, one from his parents, and one from an old girlfriend from Villanova that he still kept in touch with. Ed had some letters from his girlfriend, Chelsea, with whom he shared a house in Waimanalo. He also got a package from her, wrapped in paper that looked like it was repurposed from old grocery bags.

"That's my Chelsea. Never waste anything."

Jason and Joe were eyeing the box. Ed noticed them staring. "What?"

Simultaneously, they asked, "Aren't you going to open it?"

Ed reddened slightly. "No, I think I better open it in my stateroom. I never know what she'll send me. One time, when I was on the cutter, I opened a package from her in the wardroom and it was a pair of her lace panties and a bra scented with patchouli oil. Got lots of questions on that one."

Jason gave him a look. "Patchouli oil, huh?"

"Yeah, she's kind of counterculture, you might say. My own little resident hippie. She's a trip. Wait'll you meet her."

"Reminds me of someone I met in Waikiki." Jason's thoughts drifted back to when he left Sparrow at the driveway of the commune.

They went back to their staterooms to read their letters and for Ed to open his mystery box. Later that evening as they left the wardroom after dinner, Ed whispered to Jason, "Brownies. She made me brownies. I was afraid they'd be stale, but she had them triple-wrapped in plastic wrap. I'll share them later."

The sea was very calm that night, and the oppressive afternoon heat had dissipated. Ed and Jason were scheduled for mid-watch later. After watching *Easy Rider* in the wardroom, Ed suggested that they go out and sit on the flight deck and have some dessert. "Bring your guitar; let's have some music."

Around 2200 hours, they found themselves sitting on the edge of the flight deck. Jason was playing some quiet instrumentals, and they were talking about the mail they had received while munching on Chelsea's brownies.

"So, what did Lori have to say?" Ed asked as he chewed on a brownie.

"You know, the usual: 'miss you,' 'wish I could be with you,' 'I hope you're safe.' It's kind of ironic that the movie was *Easy Rider* tonight. That was the last movie we sorta saw at the drive-in before I left."

"The drive-in, huh. So, I guess this is the first time you actually saw most of the movie."

"Well, yeah, but it's not what you think."

"Never is."

Jason stopped playing. "No, no, I mean the drive-in. We weren't actually at the drive-in in my car."

"Explain, please."

"Okay. Lori and her sister discovered that you could get up to the roof of the apartment complex through a door at the top of the stairwell. It was never locked, for some reason. If you walked about halfway around the roof, you could look out at the screen of the drive-in movie theater that was right across the street."

"Oh, that's pretty cool. You could add your own dialogue."

"Yeah, well, that's one activity. I remember the first time she told me about it. She had said to me, 'Let's go to the drive-in tonight. I'll make some food, like for a picnic. Maybe a bottle of wine. Whaddya think?' I thought it was a good idea, of course. My group of friends from high school used to go to the drive-in in Devon on Lancaster Pike all the time. Around eight thirty that night, I went to her apartment to pick her up. She answers the door with an actual picnic basket, a blanket, and some pillows. She says, 'Here, carry these,' and hands me the pillows and blanket. She closes the door and heads for the stairwell, but instead of going down the stairs to the parking lot, she goes up. I'm standing there on the landing looking like a dummy and she says, 'C'mon. This way.' She opens the door, and we walk around the roof until we can see the drive-in screen. Only then did it sink in what she had in mind. She had me spread out the blanket, she arranged the pillows and opened the basket. She had a baguette, cheese, some pepperoni, two wine glasses, and a bottle of Beaujolais."

"Yeah! Can't go wrong with Blue Jay Haze!"

"She pulled out a corkscrew, handed me the bottle and said, 'You can have the honors.' So, we ate, drank, watched the movie, for as long as we were eating, anyway. After that, we didn't see much of Peter Fonda and Dennis Hopper."

"I'm guessing what you were doing was more interesting than the film."

"You got that right." Jason nibbled at his brownie. "These are really good. So, what's Chelsea like? How did you meet?"

"Believe it or not, it was a blind date a friend of mine set up for us when I was in San Diego on the cutter *Whitetip*. We double dated to see the Byrds in concert—"

"Wait. Was this the summer before last? Lori and I were there. They did like a twenty minute jam-intro to '8 Miles High.'"

"Yep, that's the one."

"Small world."

"It's a small world after all."

"Don't go there. I'll have to tell you about my encounter with that in Disneyland sometime." Jason paused. "Shit. Fuck you. Now the damn song's stuck in my head."

"Sorry." He looked at Jason. "Not really. Anyway, we really hit it off even though she was kind of leery about me being in the military. She's very much a peacenik flower child. When she realized I was Coast Guard and not shooting things up over in Vietnam, she warmed up to me. Anyway, we dated some more, and eventually we moved in together. Then when I got the officer exchange assignment to the *Everett*, she moved with me out to Hawai'i. She already had friends on the North Shore who had been bugging her to come out, so she was really up for the move."

"Even though you were going to a destroyer escort?"

"Well, she's still not happy about that. She's getting used to it, and she really likes the little cottage we have in Waimanalo. Suits her just fine."

"I guess we should think about getting some coffee to wash down these brownies before we go on watch," Jason said as he started to put his twelve-string back in the case. "Hey, how did you end up with this watch anyway?"

"Barnaby asked if I could spell him. Not feeling well, for some reason."

Ed wrapped the remaining brownies in the plastic wrap and was putting the lid back on when he said, "We knocked off the top layer of the box. Four down, eight to go. Hey! There's a note taped to the top of the lid."

He opened it and read it to Jason. "Dear Ed, I hope you enjoy these *special* brownies I made for you. Love, Chelsea." He looked up at Jason. "Uh-oh."

"Whaddya mean, 'uh-oh?'"

"The word *special* is in quotes."

"Well, they were pretty . . ." Jason paused. "Ohhh. You mean *special* special."

"Knowing Chelsea, yeah, special special."

"Fuck. Now what. We go on watch in forty-five minutes."

"Well, let's not worry about it. Maybe it's not strong stuff. Let's go get some coffee."

Jason dropped his guitar off in his stateroom and met up with Ed in the wardroom. Not needing anything more to eat, they sat on the wardroom couch and sipped their coffees.

Jason looked at Ed. "Anything?"

"Nothing yet."

"Maybe we're in the clear."

"Yeah, maybe."

After a few more sips, they simultaneously lowered their mugs, looked at each other and said, "Whooooaaa," as the wave washed over them.

"Uh, what do you want to do?"

Ed shrugged. "Well, I think I can function just fine. I say we ride it out."

"Okay. Let's do this."

They made their way up to the bridge and relieved Joe and Jack Culpepper.

Joe said, "It's been very quiet tonight. No radio chatter."

Ed said, "Quiet. Quiet is good. I like quiet. Let's hope it stays that way." He giggled slightly.

Joe gave him a funny look. "You okay?"

"Yeah. Fine. Go get some mid-rats. Chili tonight."

"Okay. See ya tomorrow."

Joe and Jack left the bridge. For now, all that Ed and Jason had to do was maintain position on the gunline, a pretty easy task.

Ed took out a tube from his pocket and pulled out a cigar. "I got another one. Want it? Dominican Republic." Mid-watch cigars had become a regular feature. Everyone was looking forward to their planned visit to Hong Kong where they could buy Cuban cigars. Totally illegal, but all the evidence would go up in smoke.

"Yeah. Don't mind if I do. Thanks." They lit up the cigars and walked out to the port bridge wing. They could see some lights in the distance along the Vietnam shoreline, as well as some lighted marker buoys for fishing nets set close to the mouth of the river.

Ed said, "Let's just hope we don't have to do any intricate maneuvers to get in position later tonight."

Jason agreed. "Yeah, if it stays like this, we'll be fine." Jason was thinking, *It's not like this is the first time I've had a good buzz on. We almost always passed around joints of Maui's finest during our jam sessions at the apartment on Paoakalani Avenue and we still sounded good.*

He paused in his thinking.

Or at least we thought we did.

THIRTEEN

South China Sea

OCTOBER 1972

For nearly two weeks the *Everett* fired on targets around the DMZ. With only one 5-inch gun, maintenance on the gun and fire control electronics had to take place when the gun was inactive, which was not frequent. Lt. Doug Kimos was the weapons officer, and it was his responsibility to make sure all the work was carried out. But the man who made it all happen was Chief Gunner's Mate Harold Younger, an ex-Navy SEAL who knew the workings of the 5-inch/54-caliber gun better than anyone. Younger was a well-muscled, aggressive looking Black man, with a buzz haircut and perpetual scowl on his face when at work. It was said that the men who had to go wake him from his sleep to go stand a watch would poke him with yardstick so as not to be close enough to be the target of his karate chop, a waking reflex response conditioned from being in extremely hostile situations. Off duty, however, he was a fun-loving goofball who loved performing as an amateur magician.

Chief Younger was talking with Joe and Jason on the helicopter flight deck. Jason wasn't really involved in the conversation since they were primarily talking about strategy at a craps table. He was half listening to the conversation while watching one of the small spotter copters circling just off the starboard bow of the *Everett*, one of his mechanical dragonflies. Jason was startled to see a huge splash erupt from the ocean, about twenty to thirty feet high, almost directly under the copter.

Jason interrupted their conversation. "Yo, guys, look over here and check this out. I'm watching this copter off our starboard bow when suddenly this big splash erupts almost directly under it. It was almost like the copter dropped something in the water, but it couldn't possibly be carrying anything big enough to make a splash like that. Even if the chopper itself went in, it wouldn't make a splash as big as the one I saw."

Joe and Younger looked to the area where Jason had said the splash occurred. While they were watching, another splash went up, closer to the ship, but the copter was nowhere near it.

"Shit! We're taking mortar or rocket fire from the shore," Younger yelled. "Take cover."

The only cover near the flight deck was the hangar bay, but the big sliding door to the hangar was down and locked. The hatch beside the door, however, was open. The three men sprinted for the hatch, and all three hit it simultaneously. It looked like the Three Stooges trying to get through a door at the same time. If one of them had done a Curly imitation, "Whoop, whoop, whoop," it would have completed the scene. In the end, Younger easily pushed aside Joe and Jason. When they finally all got inside, they looked at each other and broke up laughing. Sometimes people have odd reactions when under stress.

Jason, looking at Younger, said, "Hey, Chief, whatever happened to 'officers proceed through an opening first' protocol?"

Younger grinned. "Well, sir, I believe there's another expression, 'All's fair in love and war' that trumps that."

Jason stared at him for a few seconds. "Okay. Ya got me there."

Joe was looking concerned. "Have either of you felt the engine kick in? Standing orders are for us to get the hell out of here as soon as possible if we take on enemy fire."

Jason asked, "Who's OOD?"

"I think Barnaby's up there," Joe said.

An announcement came over the 1MC. "Captain to the bridge."

"What the hell? He doesn't need to call the captain for this. Just get us the hell out of here." Joe was looking agitated at this point.

Younger nodded his head in agreement. "Yeah, we can't stay here and duke it out with anybody." He looked around the hangar bay. "This whole superstructure is just thin aluminum. A shell could easily penetrate it, and if it's an incendiary round, it might even set it on fire."

Jason said, "Well, fuck, it's a good thing we all got in here then."

Finally, they could feel the deck under their feet start to vibrate as the engine kicked in and the *Everett* began to move out of harm's way. As they did, Jason couldn't reconcile what he was feeling. First time being shot at, and there was definitely a huge adrenaline rush. But surprisingly, he'd felt no fear, except for the reflexive act of trying to take cover. In the back of his mind, he knew that the fire from the shore was extremely inaccurate. They were basically lobbing ordnance out at them; it wasn't at all like being on the ground in face-to-face jungle combat. Still, they'd been shot at. Would the idea of someone trying to kill him catch up with him later? At the moment, he wasn't sure.

The following afternoon was special for many of the men on board the *Everett*, including Jason. Promotion ceremonies were held on the bridge with Captain Zhao presiding. Zhao seemed to be alert and in unusually good spirits.

There were many men from all divisions who were leaving the "seaman" designation behind, having successfully completed all the requirements for promotion to third class petty officer. Jason was losing his "butter bars," the collar insignia for the rank of ensign. His work on the bridge and as head of First Division had basically erased the mediocre fitness reports he'd accrued on the *Engage*. His boss, Doug Kimos, along with David Barnaby and the XO, Archie Burns, had all contributed glowing appraisals to his fitness reports that had led to his promotion to lieutenant junior grade, with silver replacing the gold. His ability to assume the duties of OOD also became official, and he was to stand his first watch in this capacity on the mid-watch.

Captain Zhao also revealed that after more than a month at sea, the *Everett* was due for some R&R in Kaohsiung. They were scheduled to leave the gunline as soon as the promotion ceremonies were concluded. The port of Kaohsiung was known for its bars, hotels, restaurants, and shops. It was all a lot classier than what was found in Subic and Olongapo. The news was well-received throughout the ship.

A ship's party was to be scheduled at the Harbor Hotel, and Ed was designated as the chief liaison, negotiating the pricing for a dance hall and band, open bar, and fees for rooms for those who had overnight liberty and wanted to take advantage of the opportunity to spend a night off the ship and in the company of one of the many ladies who would be present. Ed took this responsibility very seriously.

Ed caught up with Jason after the promotion. "Congratulations on the promotion. I don't suppose you'd like to come ashore with me when we arrive to help in the negotiations with the Harbor Hotel mama-san. We'll need the motor whale boat to cross the harbor. I think you can arrange that, right? Chief Younger will go with us to represent the enlisted men."

"Sure thing. I'll let Clarke know that we'll need the boat and crew members to man it. I'm betting he'll want to go."

Getting to Kaohsiung was not going to be easy. Another typhoon was brewing, and this one was expected to turn north as it hit the Philippines. The *Everett* planned to ride it out in the South China Sea enroute to Kaohsiung. This time they'd be steaming alone.

Jason relieved Joe as OOD for the mid-watch, his first in that capacity. For mid-rats he had grabbed a banana since trying to eat anything else with the swells that had developed was just about impossible. His JOOD was Frank Gallagher. The helmsman was Petty Officer Second Class Liston, the same man he had met on the quarterdeck when he first reported to the *Everett*. Jason was glad to see he was graced with a highly qualified man at the helm, someone experienced with the high seas they expected throughout the watch.

Heavy rains began to lash the bridge around two in the morning, halfway through Jason's watch. Gallagher had the conn, while Jason paid close attention to the surface search radar. It was hard to tell without any points of reference, but by the time the torrential rain hit them, the swells seemed to be as deep as the last typhoon when they had lost the *Midway* on the scope—at least forty feet. He had already pulled the forward lookout.

As Jason watched the radar screen, he noticed what looked like electrical interference of some kind skitter across the image. Suddenly, about one-third of the scope went dark. He turned to the man on the sound-powered phones.

"Get a hold of CIC and ask them if they've got something weird happening on their radar."

"Aye, sir."

As he was waiting to hear back, yet another third of the scope went dark, so that the sweep was now illuminating just one-third of the screen.

"Sir, CIC reports they are missing part of the picture on their scope."

As he processed that bit of information, Jason said to the helm, "I know you can't see the swells, Liston, just do your best to keep us on our heading."

"Aye, sir. These swells are causing quite a bit of swing as we ride through them." The words were barely out of Liston's mouth when the bow of the *Everett* nosed into a particularly heavy wave, making it feel as though the ship had been stopped in its tracks. A deep shudder seemed to ripple from bow to stern, like a dog shaking off water after a plunge in a lake. As Jason watched the radar screen, it winked off.

"Shit," Jason whispered to himself.

"Sir, I have a report that we lost the radar."

"Tell CIC we have the same situation up here. Our screen is dead," Jason replied.

"No, sir. I mean we lost our radar. That report was from the lookout strapped down on the fantail, not CIC. He said he heard the radar dish bounce on the flight deck. It then landed on the safety lines just five feet away from his location, balanced on the top line for a bit, then flipped into the ocean."

Jason stared at the man who had just delivered the report, then said, "Well, holy shit. That changes things. Is our lookout okay, other than being tied onto the fantail in a torrential downpour."

"He says he's fine, sir, other than what you already mentioned. Also, if I may add, sir, he had a few more, shall we say, 'descriptors' to go along with that."

Jason laughed. "I'll bet he did! Tell him to make his way forward and get below decks."

"Aye, sir."

Jason grabbed the phone that was the direct line to the captain's quarters. He could hear it ringing, but Captain Zhao did not respond. He hung up and gave it another try. Nothing. Jason turned to Seaman Metters, who was serving as messenger on the watch.

"Metters, have you been paying attention to our situation here?"

"Yes, sir."

"I need you to go down below and wake Lt. Cmdr. Burns. Tell him he's needed on the bridge."

"Yes, sir."

Jason, with one hand on the bulkhead, walked over to where Gallagher was standing.

"Frank, we have a problem," he said quietly. "I can't raise Captain Zhao on the phone, so I've sent for the XO."

"Seems like the right thing to do. This is a helluva way for you to start as an OOD."

A few minutes later, the XO came up the ladder and onto the bridge, looking surprisingly awake. Jason went over to him. "Sorry for disturbing you at this time of the night, sir, but we have a situation."

"No problem, Mr. Conley. I wasn't really sleeping anyway."

Jason explained about the radar, and then not being able to reach the captain. Burns nodded through the whole explanation, and when Jason was finished, he said, "You know what this means, right?"

Jason nodded. "Yeah, I'm guessing we're going to come about and head for Subic."

"Yep."

"Sir, might I suggest we just reduce our speed for now until it gets light, and then we can get a visual on these swells. Coming about in the dark might be tricky; we don't want to get broadsided down in a trough as we try to do a one-eighty."

"Makes sense, Mr. Conley. Meanwhile, I'll see if I can rouse the captain. You can contact me if anything else comes up."

"Yes, sir. Thank you, sir."

The XO left the bridge, and Jason told Gallagher to reduce the speed of the *Everett* so that they could ride the swells as safely as possible and still maintain proper steerage. Gallagher and Liston worked together to achieve this. The rain was still coming down in sheets when Doug Kimos and Jack Culpepper arrived to relieve them.

Subic Bay. Again. Morale was at an all-time low as word spread throughout the crew that repairs would probably take two weeks. No Kaohsiung. No ship's party. No hotel. No Chinese girls. Just more crossings of "Shit River" into Olongapo.

The *Everett* was the first ship back in port after the typhoon passed and was tied up directly along the pier for the repairs. One by one, a few of the destroyers and destroyer escorts that had been in formation with the *Midway* once again, slipped back into the harbor.

Two of them, the *Spieth* and the *Corrigan*, tied up outboard of the *Everett*. They didn't expect to be in port more than a couple of days since none of the work they needed was that extensive.

Lt. Cmdr. Archie Burns was in a difficult position. He knew that word had spread among the officers that Jason had been unable to rouse the captain when the radar dish was torn off its mounting, the cause of their return to Subic. He called for an officers' meeting for nine o'clock on the first morning back, shortly after the men were dismissed from quarters. As far as he knew, Captain Zhao's absence on the bridge was not a matter of discussion in the enlisted ranks. Jason hadn't made an issue of it and had handled it as discreetly as possible; for that Burns was grateful. However, he had no idea what he was actually going to say to the officers in the meeting. Since all but Norm Shapiro would be standing watch while underway, they had a right to know what they might be facing, especially late at night during an emergency.

Burns had been able to rouse the captain by pounding on his door for several minutes. When Zhao finally did respond, he was bleary-eyed and fairly incoherent. He didn't appear to be drunk and mumbled something to Burns about having to take some medication. With the captain incapacitated, Burns finalized the decision to return to Subic through Task Force 77 command and made arrangements for the repairs to begin as soon as they were docked. He was okay doing these things, but the uncertainty of something like Zhao being incapacitated during the next emergency was worrisome.

Captain Zhao had made a brief appearance on the flying bridge as the *Everett* had entered the harbor and docked but had not engaged in any conversations with any of the officers except the XO. Their exchange wasn't exactly what could be called a conversation. It was merely a reaffirmation that what Burns had arranged was correct, with no further discussion of the incident, and certainly no apology from Zhao.

As the last officer took his seat at the table in the wardroom, Burns stood up at the end of the table. All the side conversations ceased.

"Gentlemen, I'm assuming that most of you know why I called this meeting. En route to Kaohsiung, during the mid-watch and in heavy seas, we lost our surface search radar, literally. It was an event that Mr. Conley thought was serious enough that it warranted a call to Captain Zhao. In that, he was absolutely correct. There is no way this ship can operate safely without a surface search scan, especially entering a port as busy as Kaohsiung and without any prospect of getting repairs done there. As you also know, Mr. Conley was unable to rouse the captain at zero two hundred hours and sent a messenger to let me know I was needed on the bridge. Again, the correct decision. When it was deemed safe, we came about and made for Subic. And"—Burns paused, looking around at the officers seated at the table—"here we are. Please let the men know that we are making plans to visit Kaohsiung at a later date, and that our visit will include a ship's party. I know when people awoke in the morning expecting to see us on an approach to Kaohsiung but instead found us enroute to Subic, there was a lot of disappointment. I totally sympathize."

Burns paused for a moment, then continued. "From Captain Zhao's actions and what he said to me, it appears that he was heavily medicated. I don't know what the medications are or what they are for. I do know that we can't be sure that this sort of situation won't happen again. As I just described concerning the events of last night, Mr. Conley did the right things, and if you find yourself in a similar situation, you are to contact me in the same manner. Any questions?" The XO paused and looked around at the officers. "Yes, Mr. Barnaby?"

"Sir, is this a matter that should be reported at the Task Force level? Not having a commanding officer who can respond during a combat or dangerous situation seems a bit risky."

"For now, I don't plan to report this. Since I made the arrangements to return to Subic through Task Force 77, they are aware that something unusual went down. As it stands, it's a one-time incident. That decision might come back to bite me in the ass. However, if there is a recurrence, I will certainly consider that kind of action."

Barnaby nodded.

"Mr. Snyder?"

"Sir, what should I do about the standing night orders?"

"If you go to Captain Zhao's cabin and can't get him to respond, bring them to me, and I'll sign off on them. Then, I'll try to ascertain the captain's condition and go from there. Yes, Mr. Conley."

"Sir, is the two-week estimate for repairs still realistic?"

"Yes, unfortunately it is. So, there's plenty of other work to be done. Mr. Kimos has already made me aware that some much-needed maintenance on the gun and gunfire control will be taking place, and there's plenty of jobs for engineering and the deck crew to work on. Let's take advantage of this bad situation." He smiled. "And, of course, make use of the base facilities and the hospitality found in Olongapo." Burns looked around. "By the way, I want to congratulate all of you. Our deployment to date has been exactly what the Task Force wanted. We've accomplished everything they've thrown at us. Let's keep up the good work. Please pass that along to your men. Dismissed."

As everyone started to leave the wardroom, Jason said to Joe and Ed, "I'm going over to the Exchange after I have a word with Clarke. Wanna come along?"

"I'm in," said Ed.

"I'm stuck on the quarterdeck starting at noon," Joe said, "I'll make it another time."

Jason returned to the *Everett* after buying another lens for his Nikon at the exchange. He found that being out at sea with nothing to spend paychecks on made it easier to justify an upgrade to his camera. The Nikon had come with a 50mm lens when he bought it, but the one he really wanted, probably the best Nikkor lens made, was the 105mm portrait lens. It probably wouldn't be the last lens he would buy while on WestPac. He still had visits to Hong Kong and Japan waiting in the wings. He went to his stateroom to stash away his purchase.

After leaving his stateroom, he headed forward to the forecastle to see what Clarke had First Division working on. He knew painting was needed on the gun mount and ASROC launcher, so he figured they would be somewhere up near the bow. He found Clarke near the gun mount supervising the men, but he was distracted by the activity occurring outboard of them. It appeared that the *Spieth* was casting off its lines with the *Corcoran*. They were getting underway and seemed to be in a hurry to do so.

"Yo, Clarke, I thought they were supposed to be here for at least another day or two."

"That's what I thought, too, sir, but the way they're hustling to get underway makes me think something's up."

The last line was barely on deck when the *Spieth* pulled away from the *Corcoran*.

As the Spieth made its way toward Grande Island, Jason said, "That was fast. Hope they didn't leave anyone behind."

As they watched, an announcement came over the 1MC.

"Lt.j.g. Conley, please report to the quarterdeck."

Jason wondered, as he made his way astern to the quarterdeck, *Why is Joe calling me to the quarterdeck?*

Joe intercepted Jason just before he arrived at the quarterdeck, dangling what looked like a key attached by a small chain to a metal tag. When Jason got close, Joe whispered, "We got ourselves a jeep."

"What the hell are you talking about?"

"You saw the *Spieth* pull out, right? Apparently, they got emergency orders to the gunline because the *Whipple*'s gun went down, and they're headed back in for repairs."

"So?"

"They didn't have time to return their ship's vehicle to the motor pool, so since we're the inboard ship, they left the key with me and asked me to return it for them."

"Sooo . . ."

"So, I'll get it to the motor pool." Joe paused. "Eventually."

"Small problem. Won't the motor pool be expecting it?"

"No. When they gave me the key, they said they were in such a hurry to get underway, they disconnected the phone line to the pier before anyone thought about the jeep. The motor pool has no idea they've left." Joe had a big grin on his face. He pointed over toward the pier. "It's right over there, parked next to ours and the *Corcoran*'s."

"Well, it should make getting over to the Cubi Pt. O' club a lot easier. Of course, getting back to the ship after a night at the club might be another matter."

Only three people knew about the jeep: Joe, Jason, and Ed. It had to stay that way or things would definitely become "complicated." The good thing was, all the jeeps looked alike, so if anyone spotted them driving away in a vehicle, there was no way to tell if the jeep they were in belonged to the *Everett* or not.

After liberty call the afternoon that Joe emancipated the *Spieth*'s jeep, the three of them left the ship and headed for the parking area. They did the best they could to make sure no one was coming off the ship directly behind them, although that was difficult given the number of men heading for Olongapo. Finally, there was a break in the stream coming down the gangway and they jumped into the jeep, Joe behind the wheel and Jason ensconced in one of the rear seats. Ed rode shotgun.

Joe announced, "Cubi Point, here we come!"

The Cubi Point O' Club had two distinct phases; one when an aircraft carrier was in, and one when there was no carrier present. With a carrier in port, the club was total mayhem. There were two floors to the place; the bottom floor had a mechanical catapult that could slingshot a jet cockpit replica named "Red Horse One" at high speed toward a pool of water. Riding on rails and powered by compressed air, the only way to stay dry was to catch the arresting cable by dropping Red Horse One's hook, similar to landing on a carrier's deck, before entering the water. The timing was so tricky that only the best of the jet jocks could do it, usually early in the evening before the alcohol diminished their reflexes. Of course, that didn't stop anyone and everyone from attempting the impossible, including some high-ranking dignitaries making the rounds. Under Secretary of the Navy John Warner, someone Jason had met while serving on the *Engage*, had given it a try once and failed miserably. Being a good sport, Warner thought it was great. He spent the whole rest of the night having some drinks with the pilots in a soaking wet flight suit.

The second floor had slot machines with better odds of winning than in Olongapo, a nice bar, wooden tables with white tablecloths for dining, a stage for local bands to deliver perfect covers of the current tunes, and of course, beautiful servers. The upper floor offered a panoramic view of Subic Bay, looking directly over the air station and Leyte Pier, where the carriers docked, and all the way across to the naval base where the "black shoes" manned their ships. There was not a lot of crossover in personnel between the Cubi Point and the Subic Naval Base clubs, partly due to the distance between them. Having a jeep solved that difficulty.

Jason, Joe, and Ed drove the winding road up through the Philippine jungle to the club perched high atop Upper Cubi. They parked the jeep and went in through the bottom floor and made their way upstairs to the bar and dining area. Jason and Ed each ordered a Tom Collins while Joe got a 7&7. As they waited for their drinks, they noticed that very few people were in the club. They didn't have to look out the window to the bay to know that there was no carrier berthed down below.

They made their way over to the slots and tried their luck for a while. After an hour, Joe was five dollars richer while Ed and Jason each lost a little over a dollar. A server in a tight-fitting black satin dress came over to them as they were playing.

"You need another round?"

Jason said, "Yes, thank you, and so do my friends here." Jason pointed at Joe. "He's ahead. He's buying."

Joe frowned, "Hey, why should I be penalized for my skill at slots."

"Yeah, skill," Ed scoffed. "Pulling that lever the right way; it's all in the wrist."

Jason said, "From what I understand, his wrist is very talented."

"Is your understanding first-hand?"

"No, our bunking situation is strictly platonic."

A few minutes later, the server returned with their drinks. "You pay now or run tab?"

Jason said, "He'll run a tab."

Ed added, "Thanks, Joe."

The server looked at Joe. "You name really Joe?" She giggled. "So, when you go in Olongapo and girls say, 'Hey, Joe, buy me drink,' it like they really know you?"

"Yeah, they really know me, all right."

"Okay, Joe. I run tab for you." She left to serve other customers.

Joe looked at his two friends. "Good thing it doesn't cost much here. You two should be buying *me* drinks. I'm the one who procured the jeep."

Jason, imitating the server, said, "No, Joe, don't be mad. I buy you drink next time. Right, Joe?"

Joe stared back at Jason. "Okay. Fuck it. No big deal. Let's get some food. Just can the imitation."

Jason, using the same voice, "Whatever you say, Joe."

They grabbed a table with a view of Subic Bay. Their server stopped by with menus, which they perused as they finished their drinks. Ed kept looking at Jason, who kept looking down at his menu then glancing over the top of it. After seeing him do this several times, he swiveled in his chair to see what was getting his friend's attention.

At a table close by, and in Jason's line of sight, sat three women, two brunettes and a blond. Ed looked back at Jason. "I was wondering what was more interesting than the menu."

"Yeah, they definitely caught my eye." Now, Joe turned to look. "Try not to be so obvious." Ed and Joe turned back.

Ed said, "Wonder what they're doing here."

Jason said, sarcastically, "Hmm, hard to tell, but it looks to me like they're having some drinks."

"No shit, Sherlock." Ed took another furtive glance. "I just didn't think women had been invented over here yet."

Joe and Jason looked at each other, and simultaneously said, "Invented?"

Jason added, "In case you hadn't noticed, our slinky server is definitely a woman."

Joe added, "I think Ed's been out at sea too long."

Ed was shaking his head. "No, no, I meant non-Asian women. Wonder where they're from."

Jason said, "Probably the States."

"You're full of wisdom this evening."

"Thanks. I try."

At that moment the server came by. "You ready to order?" She noticed them looking over at the table with the women. With a giggle she said, "You want girl, Joe?"

Joe shook his head. "Everyone's a comedian tonight."

"I go ask."

"No go ask. Just get food. And wine."

They ordered New York strip steaks, baked potatoes, and lettuce wedge salads. And, of course, three bottles of Beaujolais. Joe said, "I think we're in a rut."

Ed said, "Gotta have that Blue Jay Haze."

"I meant the steak, potato, salad routine."

Jason said, "So, have them bring up one of their famous 'Cubi Dogs' from downstairs."

"No, I don't think so."

The waitress came back with three wine glasses and three bottles of wine. She looked at Joe. "Open bottles?"

"Yes. Please. Open bottles."

She deftly opened all three bottles and then said she was going to check on their orders. But, instead of going back to the kitchen, she went over to the table with the three women.

Joe noticed. "Wonder what she's doing over there."

Ed said, "Could just possibly be taking their food orders. Just a guess."

Jason said, "No, get girl for Joe."

The server left their table and went back to the kitchen. Jason could see the three women talking, leaning over the table as though conspiring to do something. He sipped his wine without taking his eyes off them. He was surprised when all three women stood up, picked up their drinks, and headed for his table.

He whispered to his friends, "Look like Joe get girl."

As they arrived at Jason's table, he stood to greet them, quickly followed by Ed and Joe. Jason smiled and said, "Good evening, ladies."

The blond, dressed in a dark blue skirt and pale blue blouse asked, "Are you guys going to be drinking all that wine yourselves?"

Jason said, "Well, it is our custom, but we would not be beyond sharing."

Ed added, "Right. Sharing."

Jason said, "Um, would you care to join us? It's a big table and we can grab a few more chairs."

One of the brunettes, dressed in a maroon skirt and white blouse said, "I think we'd like that. We wouldn't be cramping your style, would we?"

"No, these guys have no style," Jason said. Ed and Joe shot him a look, then scrambled to get three chairs.

When they were all seated, Joe said, "Hi, I'm Joe, and this is Ed Snyder and Jason Conley."

The blond said, "Nice to meet you. I'm Judy Syndergard." She looked at the brunette in the maroon skirt and said, "This is Pam Quigley and sitting next to Jason is Sharon Hanley." Sharon was wearing a short green skirt and pale yellow short-sleeved knit pullover. Jason had definitely noticed the skirt, or more accurately, the long legs inside the skirt.

Sharon said, "We couldn't help but notice that you guys were drinking wine instead of the usual shots and beers the fly guys usually have. Also, why aren't you downstairs playing in your little airplane?"

Ed said, "Well, to start with, as far as the wine is concerned, we're highly sophisticated."

Joe nearly did a spit take.

"Secondly, we're not 'fly guys.' We're also not big on chowing down while we're soaking wet, which we would be if we were playing in the Cat Room," Ed added.

"So, what are you? Supply guys?" Pam asked.

"No, we're on a ship, the *Everett*, docked across the bay," Jason said. "We're in for repairs since we lost our guidance."

Judy laughed. "That sounds naughty."

Joe said, "Well, that's us."

"So, we usually don't see many sailor-types over here. It's not as easy to get to Cubi Point as the Naval Station O' Club."

Joe hesitated. "Well, uh, we have our own jeep."

The women all looked at each other. "Well, that sounds like fun," Pam said.

"It is," said Ed. "I'd love to take you for a ride."

"I bet you would," said Pam.

"In the jeep. I meant in the jeep."

"Sure, you did. Still sounds like fun."

The server in black satin along with another satin-wearing server, this one in blue, interrupted the banter with the dinners. They had the dinners for the women, too, as if they had anticipated this eventuality. As the server in black placed Joe's steak in front of him, she whispered, "See. Joe get girl."

After the servers left. Jason asked, "So, what are nice girls like you doing in a place like this?"

Pam laughed. "Wow, that's original."

Ignoring the remark, Jason said, "Wait, let me guess. Aviation mechanics."

Sharon said, "Close. We're nurses at the hospital and dispensary."

"I knew that. I just didn't want you to think I was stereotyping you."

"So, you don't think I could be an aviation mechanic?"

"No, I think you'd make an excellent mechanic. I'd let you handle my dipstick."

Pam and Judy both snickered, and Sharon blushed. The server brought over three more wine glasses and Joe passed around one of the bottles, which was quickly emptied so they started into another. While they were eating, a five-man band set up on stage and started playing covers of early Beatles tunes. After they finished eating, they all got up and danced on the small dance floor in front of the stage.

Jason was paired with Sharon. "It's been a long time since I danced," he apologized. "I'm usually on stage in the band playing for others to dance."

Sharon smiled. "You're doing fine. What do you play?"

"Guitar. Some of the stuff these guys are playing plus songs you might hear on what's called 'underground radio.' Never made much money at it, but I've always been in a band, ever since junior high school."

Sharon said, "I played in marching band in high school. Flute."

"Do you like Jethro Tull? I got to see them back home in Philly at the Spectrum."

"I love Tull. I don't know how Ian Anderson perches on one leg and plays the way he does. Certainly not like marching band. Back in Philly, huh? I grew up in what you guys call 'down the shore.' Sea Isle City. But I know Philly pretty well since I did my nursing program at Hahnemann."

Jason smiled. "I dated a girl I met in Sea Isle for a while, and a nurse from Hahnemann. Nothing came of either relationship, though. My family always went down the shore for our vacations. Usually Ocean City."

"Yeah, a real family town. No booze."

The band's cover of the Beatles' version of "Twist and Shout" ended and Jason and Sharon went back to the table. Jason ordered two more bottles of wine. The six of them sipped wine as they got to know each other, looking out at the lights of the harbor.

Pam said, "We better be catching the shuttle back. The three of us have an early shift tomorrow."

"Too bad you have to work on a Saturday. We're planning on going snorkeling off the beach over on Grande Island," Joe said. "Also, you don't have to catch the shuttle. We can drive you back."

Judy looked doubtful. "Six in a jeep? How would we manage that?"

Ed smiled. "Laps. No problem."

"When does your shift end tomorrow?" Jason asked. "We could hold off going if you want to come."

Sharon said, "We're done at noon, and that sounds like fun."

Judy and Pam nodded their agreement.

"Okay, then, let's get you guys back to the BOQ."

They settled up their bill, with Joe paying most of it. The jeep was a tight fit. Joe drove with Ed riding shotgun. Pam sat in his lap. Jason climbed into one of the jump seats in the back and Judy sat across from him. Sharon climbed on to Jason's lap, giving him a quick kiss as she did so. The ride down from Upper Cubi seemed more precarious in the dark than when they'd come up the hill in late afternoon. The wine might have had something to do with it. Nonetheless, they arrived safely at the bachelor officer's quarters and the guys escorted the nurses to the front door. Jason and Sharon slid off to the side of the building for a little privacy in the shadows. Sharon threw her arms around Jason and gave him a very passionate kiss. She pulled away and said, "It's too bad you guys have a midnight curfew on your ship. We could make this last a little longer."

"You can sneak guys up to your room?"

"It's not a girls' dorm, for God's sake. Yes, we can 'sneak' people into our rooms."

"I'll have to remember that for after our little beach outing tomorrow." Jason gave her a quick kiss. "See you tomorrow at twelve thirty, okay?"

"It's a date." Sharon smiled, turned away, and went inside.

Jason was looking forward to the Grande Island excursion for two reasons. First, he had heard that snorkeling in the Philippines was outstanding, with two to three times more species of fish than could be found in Hawai'i. Then, of course, there was Sharon. He hoped his luck with her would be better than his recent record of experiencing two "one and done" relationships back in Hawai'i. He was thinking that calling them "relationships" was a bit of an exaggeration; they were more like one-night stands. Of course, falling for someone in a war zone really didn't have success written all over it. And on top of that, though promising, he had no idea how things would work out with Lori.

Joe, Ed, and Jason skipped lunch in the wardroom the next day. They planned to have burgers and fries over at the snack bar on the island with the girls. Just after noon they left the ship, snuck into their jeep, and headed for the BOQ. They parked the jeep, went inside, and spoke with the sailor on duty at the main desk. He rang up Lt. Syndergard, Lt. Hanley, and Lt. Quigley to inform them that they had guests.

Sharon was the first one down. She immediately went over to Jason and gave him a quick kiss. She was wearing a blue-and-white striped beach cover-up and sandals. She had several beach towels tucked under her arm.

"I am ready for the beach," she said. "I might just sleep most of the afternoon after getting up at five to start the morning shift."

"We'll have to see if there's an equipment rental shack over there in case you want to go snorkeling," Jason said.

"I'm pretty sure there is. A couple of the nurses have been over there, and I know they snorkeled. I don't think they have their own stuff."

Pam and Judy came down at the same time. "I've got some

Coppertone," Judy said. "We're going to need it. Not a cloud in the sky."

They piled into the jeep with the same seating arrangements as the previous night. It was a short ride over to the pier to catch the Grande Island boat shuttle. The shuttle was basically the same kind of motor whaleboat that Jason was in charge of on the *Everett*. It was being run by a couple of second class petty officer boatswain mates, who helped the ladies into the boat. Jason and his friends were the first to board and were followed by several others carrying snorkeling gear and towels. The petty officers cast off and they headed out to the island at the mouth of the harbor.

After docking at the Grande Island pier, they made their way to the snack bar, ordered burgers, fries, and San Miguel beers, then ate them at a picnic table on a patio close to the beach. When they were finished, Jason found the equipment rental shack and got Sharon outfitted with some gear. Judy and Pam decided they were just going to rest on the sand and do some reading, with maybe a little bit of swimming thrown in here and there.

The girls shed their beach cover-ups. Sharon was wearing a strapless, one-piece electric blue suit, high cut so that it accentuated her long legs. Pam and Judy were in bikinis, Judy's a tiger print pattern and Pam's a deep blue.

Jason, Sharon, Ed, and Joe went to the water's edge and geared up. They didn't have to go out very far before they encountered the edge of a coral reef. Jason was blown away. What he had heard was true—the reef was teeming with a dazzling array of fish, anemones, urchins with long black spines, sea fans, and corals. He found a pocket in the reef with a sandy bottom. The four snorkelers swam to the middle of it and then let themselves drift as they took in the view. Every so often, they would find another nook in the coral and spend some float time there.

In the fourth sandy pocket, Jason could see Ed dive down to the bottom, reach his hand to the surface of the coral, and pull out something green. *He's going to get himself stuck with urchin spines doing that,* Jason thought. Ed swam over to Sharon and Jason and showed them what he had found: an American five-dollar bill.

Treading water, Ed took out his snorkel and said, "Pretty cool! The fish are great, and we get paid to look at them." Imitating a pirate, he said, "Aaarrgghh! There's treasure to be had in Subic, me lads and lassie!"

They went back to their drifting reef observations. Joe suddenly dove to the bottom and came up with a ten-dollar bill. As soon as he surfaced, Jason and Sharon both dove and returned to the surface with more bills. They continued this routine for fifteen minutes, collecting all the bounty the reef had to offer. After ten minutes passed with no more money appearing, they headed for the beach. They walked up the sand to where Judy and Pam were sunbathing and showed them their booty. They began laying the bills out on Pam's blanket, counting as they did so.

"One hundred and ten dollars," Ed exclaimed. "Our little beach excursion suddenly became very profitable."

"Where do you think it could have come from?" Pam asked.

Joe said, "No idea. Never seen anything like it."

"I guess someone could have dropped their wallet over the side while they were on the whaleboat coming or going," Ed said. "I guess we should check at the snack bar to see if anyone has reported a lost wallet."

Jason and Ed went over to the snack bar, ordered some more San Miguels, and asked the attendant if anyone had lost a wallet. They came back with the beers, and Ed said, "No one."

Jason added, "Looks like it's ours."

Sharon said, "This calls for a celebration. Lobster and champagne tonight at the O' Club."

"Sounds like a plan," Jason agreed.

They spread out the money on a towel to dry. Jason and Sharon took turns rubbing Coppertone on each other's backs and shoulders, then settled down to soak up some sun. After an hour or so they climbed back aboard the harbor shuttle and returned to the main base.

Joe and Ed dropped off Pam, Judy, Sharon, and Jason at the BOQ. As he got out of the jeep, Jason said quietly to Joe, "When you come pick us up for dinner, can you bring me a change of clothes?"

Joe looked confused at first, and then said, "Oooh. Sure, sure thing. Will do. You two kids have fun."

Ed, noting Jason was not getting back in the jeep, said, "Wait. What? Where's he going?"

Jason gave him a little wave, turned, and walked with Sharon into the BOQ. They all eventually had their lobster and champagne at the O' Club, but not before Sharon showed Jason that she could, indeed, "sneak" people up to her quarters.

It had been a week and a half since they met the nurses at the Cubi Point O' Club. Every late afternoon or night when they didn't have duty, they would take the jeep to one of the clubs or the movie theater. Depending on who could make it, it might be just one couple, a double date, or as in the first time they used it, all six. Inevitably, the jeep ran low on gas. They couldn't take the jeep to the motor pool to fill it up since the attendant would make an imprint of the metal tag attached to the key to charge the ship's account for the fuel. Since the jeep had been *appropriated*, a term Joe preferred to *stolen*, someone might begin to question why this jeep was running around ten days after the ship it had been assigned to had left port.

Shortly after ten o'clock, in the shadows to the side of the maintenance building where the jeeps were parked, three figures moved furtively along the side of the building, then crouched down beside the *Everett's* jeep.

"Did you get all the stuff?" Ed asked.

"Yeah. I packed it all in this duffel down in engineering," Joe said. "No one will miss it."

"I filled the tank of our ship's jeep an hour ago," Jason said.

Ed looked around. "Good. Then I guess we're all set. Anyone ever done this before?"

Jason shook his head. "Closest I've come to this was siphoning my fish tanks when I needed to change out the water. The trick is getting a draw on the liquid without actually inhaling it into your lungs."

"Well, in that case, you're the sucker."

"I guess if I go through with it, I really am a sucker."

"That's what she said."

Jason snickered. "Ever wonder why it's called a blow job? Birthday candles get blown."

Joe said, "You need good embouchure." Jason and Ed stared at him. "I mean, that's what I've heard."

Jason said, "Hey, what did the girl say when she walked into the sperm bank?"

Joe said, "Yeah, yeah." Then tilted his head back as if he was gargling. "I'd like to make a deposit."

"Okay, okay, let's get on with this," said Ed.

Joe pulled out a five-gallon jerry can, a length of tubing, and a funnel with a long spout out of the duffel, while Jason twisted off the cap to the jeep's gas tank. He then inserted the tubing into the tank until he felt it hit bottom, then using a utility knife, he cut the tubing to a length that extended several inches into the jerry can. Now, the difficult part. If he inhaled gas fumes he could end up with chemically induced pneumonia. Tough to explain, and even tougher to recover from. All for having a little fun driving around with nurses to the clubs and the BOQ.

Jason took one last look around and said, "Okay. It's showtime." He placed his lips on the tube, and using mainly his cheeks, took a quick draw on it. He had his hand on the tube right where it entered the gas tank, so he could actually feel when the liquid was over the top. He took the tube out of his mouth and plunged it into the jerry can. The gas flowed.

"Lookin' good," said Ed.

They topped off the jerry can and placed the gas cap back on the ship's jeep. Staying low, they shifted their clandestine operation over to their jeep. Joe held the funnel in place and Ed poured the gas. "We could be a pit crew at a NASCAR race," Joe said.

When they finished, Joe stowed the can and the funnel back in the duffel and threw the tubing into a trash can that was alongside the building. Mission accomplished and ready to roll.

Jason and Sharon had a few more evenings together before the repairs were complete on the *Everett*. Jason prolonged his departure each night from the BOQ until the last minute, racing through the base to get back to the ship before the midnight curfew. It reminded him of when he'd had his "Cinderella license" in high school that required him to be home by midnight. He'd take his girlfriend to the movies, then for some eats at Minella's Diner, and then engage in a torrid make-out session on the front bench seat of the '65 Ford Galaxy he'd borrowed from his parents, parked along the side of a country road. In fact, the song "Let's Get Lost on a Country Road" by the Kit Kats became "their song." *Sure, I can make it from her house in Wayne to my place in Villanova in five minutes. It's only a little over six miles. Good thing Conestoga Road is empty that time of night*, he'd reason. That Galaxy could move.

Sharon couldn't come to see Jason's ship get underway. She was on duty at the hospital. Jason was glad, in a way. He preferred to have the image of her standing naked by the bed as he'd kissed her goodbye the previous night lodged in his head. They assured each other they would write, and Jason said there was no doubt in his mind that the *Everett* would be back in port several times before the WestPac was complete. This was not a final goodbye.

FOURTEEN

South China Sea

NOVEMBER 1972

It was a week before Thanksgiving, with not much to give thanks for—except for the fact they were on a ship and not in the jungle on land. Jason was grateful and feeling a little bit guilty that Subic and Olongapo provided some respite from the gunfire, monsoons, tedious watches, and underway replenishments. The guys in country didn't have that.

The men of the *Everett*, in the weeks following their unscheduled visit to Subic Bay, had fallen into a fairly predictable routine providing gunfire support along with other destroyers and light cruisers on the gun line—late afternoon or early evening orders, steaming to a location while threading through Vietnamese fishing nets, and then firing on the designated targets the following day made up their days.

Every so often the ship didn't receive any orders. The whole day would be spent maintaining a fixed position by matching the speed and direction of the current. The mid-watches were brutally boring. It was inevitable that certain activities or "contests" developed to help pass the time. Some were better than others.

The idea of a dance contest had a very short life span. In fact, only one dance contest was held, orchestrated by Joe. None of the "contestants" would have been invited to be on American Bandstand. However, they did their best, and as the bridge crew "tripped the light fantastic," each guy trying to out-do the moves of the man before him, the wooden deck gratings on the bridge did their own tap dance on the metal deck plate beneath them. Unfortunately, the metal deck also served as Captain Zhao's ceiling.

The phone on the bridge rang. The direct line from Zhao's stateroom. Joe waved his arms for everyone to stand still and then picked up the phone.

"Bridge. Lt.j.g. DiLorenzo."

"Mr. DiLorenzo, what the fuck is going on up there?" It was obvious the captain was irate; after all, it was past two in the morning. "There's so much noise coming through my ceiling, it sounds like..." Zhao hesitated to catch his breath. "It sounds like people dancing up there!"

Joe had to cover the mouthpiece as he stifled a laugh. "Um, no, Captain. Since it was a quiet watch, I thought the crew could clean the metal decking, so we had to move the wooden deck gratings around to get to it. Sorry. Didn't think we were making that much noise."

Zhao had yelled, "Well you are. Knock it the fuck off," and slammed down his receiver.

Joe said to Jason and Ed later, "I figured Zhao was probably so narked up he won't remember it in the morning. Must've been pretty loud to break him out of his nighttime stupor."

Jason and a few others had a quieter activity: the cigar ash contest. The rules were simple. Everyone participating would light up identical cigars at the same time. The person who could smoke the cigar for the longest time without the ash falling off was the winner. Toward the end of the contest, everyone would have their heads tilted back so that the cigar and its ash was straight in the air. It looked like a group limbo contest without a crossbar. They never got a call from Captain Zhao.

A new ensign had come aboard while they were in Subic. Billy Weston was a storyteller. More specifically, he would spin "shaggy dog" tales that had the most stupid, surprising, or gruesome endings possible. It was not so much a contest as it was being entertained while on watch. He claimed that he made them up and told them to his three young children. Jason thought that Billy's kids were going to be in need of some serious therapy later in life.

One night when Jason was on mid-watch, he realized that there was a huge helium tank tucked away just aft of the bridge. The *Everett* had been designated as the weather ship for a month. Periodically, they would launch helium-filled weather balloons and receive radio transmissions recording the data that was collected. Ed was in charge of those operations, so Jason hadn't paid much attention to the fact that the tank was there. Around three o'clock one morning, Jason had a brilliant idea, or so he thought. First, he told his JOOD, Jack Culpepper, what he was going to do. Then, he went out on the bridge wing, found the tank, opened the valve, and took a couple of deep breaths from the nozzle. Jason came back inside the bridge and started giving orders.

"Right full rudder! All ahead full! Left full rudder!" He startled everyone because he sounded just like Alvin from Alvin and the Chipmunks. It got some good laughs out of the men and broke up a rather boring night. Also, no call from the captain.

Captain Zhao, however, became the target of one bizarrely creative crew member: the mad shitter.

Every ship has one at one time or another. Jason had been hearing about the mad shitter over the past few weeks. Joe said, "The guy left a big pile on the decking in main engineering, a particularly steamy pile since the deck plates get well over a hundred and ten degrees in the main compartment. Yet another dump was found in the passageway leading to the mess decks. Still another load was found in front of the goat locker. The guy must have a death wish. I wouldn't want to piss off our chief gunner's mate. Or maybe that would be 'shit off.'"

Jason said, "Yeah, this guy's routine gives a whole new meaning to 'dropping the load.'" "Dropping the load" was an engineering expression for when the engines accidentally trip off-line.

Joe said, "Well you are *not* going to believe the latest location chosen by our tricky turdster." He paused.

"What? Am I supposed to guess?" Jason said.

"You can guess all you want, but you won't get it right."

"Okay. Where?"

"Captain Zhao's desk in his stateroom."

"You've got to be shittin' me."

"No, but be careful. Someone else might."

"How the fuck did he get in there? Zhao hardly ever leaves the place. Wasn't the door locked?" Jason thought for a minute. "He must've had a shit fit."

"Haha! Oh, he had one all right. I heard all this from the stewards because one of them had to go in and capture the elusive corn carp. The whole time he was wrapping things up, shall we say, Captain Zhao was yelling at him in Chinese."

"What balls that guy has. Can you imagine if Zhao walked in on him while he was preparing his *pupu* platter? What could you possibly say? 'Oh, my God! Am I sleepwalking again? I thought this was the head!'"

Joe asked, "Have we run out of different names for shit yet? Anyway, it'll be interesting to see if the shitter strikes again. I somehow doubt it. How could you possibly top laying one out in the captain's stateroom, on his *desk*."

"Has he assigned anyone to try to get to the bottom of this?"

Joe laughed. "Yeah, I think he's got a rear admiral on it."

The daily gunline routine was about to be interrupted by an UNREP. The *Everett* was running low on shells. Chief Gunner's Mate Harold

Younger's expertise had kept the single 5-inch gun in top shape and word had reached the *Everett* that their gun had fired more rounds per day than any other single barrel on the gunline. Smoke on the water, indeed.

Jason was not on the bridge for this underway replenishment. He was stationed on the forecastle to oversee the delivery of the pallets of shells that were being sent over by the munitions ship, and the return of the retrograde—spent shell casings—that had accumulated from all the gunline activity. The casings were ready for transfer, stored in huge net bags that were secured against the forward bulkhead of the superstructure just aft of the ASROC launcher. Jason had some misgivings about the planned operation. The *Everett* was plowing through heavy seas, and even though there was no typhoon, the ship was taking water over the bow; it was not a safe situation for the men handling the munitions and retrograde.

Jason's boss, Lt. Doug Kimos, was the OOD, and Jason sent word up to the bridge through the sound-powered phones that he believed the UNREP should be postponed until conditions calmed down. Kimos relayed word that he would bring his concerns up with Captain Zhao and then get back to him.

Jason could see them closing in on the USS *Flint* steaming about one thousand yards ahead of them. Not only would conditions be bad on the forecastle, but Jason also knew Kimos would have a difficult time maintaining position alongside the huge ammo ship while connected by the transfer cable. The VERTREP on the flight deck would be troublesome, as well. Having a chopper set down a pallet of shells, or anything for that matter, on a heaving flight deck would be no picnic.

The man on the sound-powered phones said, "Excuse me, sir. Lt. Kimos wants to speak with you directly. Here's the headset."

Jason knew this meant bad news. He slipped the headset on and spoke into the mic. "Conley here."

"Hey, Jason, I gave it a shot, but Zhao is in a snit about something and says that we're going through with this no matter what." Jason looked up to the bridge wing and saw Kimos looking down at him. "I tried pressing him on it, but no go. If it means anything to you, the XO agrees with your assessment of the situation."

"Okay, Doug, thanks for trying. I know it had to be tough sticking your neck out to try to change Zhao's mind."

"Don't worry about me. Just do your best to keep you and your men safe. Getting ready to approach. Kimos out."

Jason watched Kimos head into the bridge as he took the headset off. He handed it back to the sailor who had been assigned that duty for the UNREP. He made his way over to Petty Officer First Class Clarke and explained the situation. It was obvious to Jason that Clarke agreed with him concerning the danger they were facing. He was shaking his head ever so slightly as they discussed what was about to happen.

The receiving rig was set up just aft of the gun turret and forward of the ASROC launcher. As they steadied in position alongside the *Flint*, the man on the phones said to fire the messenger line over. Clarke fired the compressed air powered rifle that launched the line over from the *Everett's* port side. The men on the *Flint* retrieved it, secured the cable and pulley assembly to it, and the men on the *Everett* heaved it across over the turbulent water. The movement of the ship made it difficult to stand upright, let alone heave a line, but they managed to get it on board as the salt spray whipped around them, stinging their eyes. The rig was secured to the king post and the first pallet of shells began to make its way across. At the same time, Jason could see the chopper from the *Flint* heading toward the flight deck with a large canvas bag dangling underneath it.

Just as the pallet on the forecastle was lowered down to the deck, the bow of the *Everett* plunged into a swell causing the whole ship to shudder. Sea water washed over the decking and one of Jason's men lost his footing and fell on the pallet. He rushed over to him and helped him up.

"It's okay, sir. I'm fine."

Jason glared up at the windows on the bridge and expressed his frustration by pointing at the pallet and the man who had just fallen, to no avail.

"Okay, Clarke, let's send the pulley back with a bag of retrograde. Looks like we're not getting a reprieve."

The operation was repeated three more times with great difficulty. The salt spray and water on the deck made conditions extremely hazardous. Jason was wondering how Kimos and the helmsman were able to maintain position. As the fourth pallet started across, the *Everett* once again plowed into a huge swell. The ship lurched violently to starboard as a wall of green water swept over the deck. Jason felt the wave pick him up and felt his ribs compress as it smashed him into the netting holding the retrograde against the bulkhead. The casings were a poor excuse for a cushion, but better than the bulkhead itself. Several bags came loose, and shell casings scattered across the deck and rolled over the side.

Jason regained his footing and took a deep breath. His chest was sore, but he needed to check on his men. Clarke was clinging to a lifeline on the starboard side, his legs dangling over the side of the ship. The sound-powered phone man had one arm wrapped around the ladder of the gun turret, while two other men hunkered down in the shelter of the gun turret itself. Jason helped Clarke get back on deck and then headed for the aft side of the gun mount where his men had sought shelter.

When the wave hit, Jason had heard a loud snap and twang like a giant guitar string had been plucked. From his days on the *Engage*, he knew what that was. He didn't have to look up at the receiving rig on the king post to know that the cable with the pulley assembly had snapped and was gone. After it broke, the release of the tension caused the cable to twist as it whipped around. Luckily, this took place out over the water and not on the deck. He had heard of towing cables snapping and taking men's legs off. Unfortunately, the cable and the pulley assembly became entangled in the harness carrying the pallet of shells. The broken tail of the cable with its explosive cargo was now dragging through the rough waves causing the pallet to smash repeatedly against the side of the munitions ship. Jason knew the shells needed to be primed to go off, but something about a pallet of 5-inch shells pounding against the side of a loaded ammunition ship didn't sit well with him. As he and his men looked on sheltered behind the gun mount, they could see two men on the *Flint* scramble up their rig with an acetylene torch to cut away the broken cable with its dangerous cargo. They were all relieved when the cable, pallet, and shells slipped away below the water.

Jason said to Clarke, "Let's resecure this retrograde and get the hell off the forecastle as fast as we can."

"Aye, sir."

The man on the phones said, "Sir, the bridge says to secure from the UNREP detail."

"What? So soon?" The sarcasm was not lost on the phone man. "Let them know we're all okay down here. Just a little soggy."

"Aye, sir."

The captain of the *Flint* ordered a breakaway and a halt to both the UNREP and VERTREP. As the retrograde cleanup continued, Jason could see members of the bridge crew staring down at them. He gave them a little wave and then went back to helping his men.

It felt good to be back in a dry uniform and seated at the wardroom table waiting for dinner. Jason hadn't had the chance to really talk much about his experience; they had fully secured from the UNREP just an hour before. He didn't expect Captain Zhao to be at the meal, but he wondered where the XO was. It was unusual for Lt. Cmdr. Archie Burns to be late. Norm Shapiro caught his attention.

"I understand you went surfing this afternoon."

"Yeah. I had quite a spectacular wipeout. Should've bailed on the wave earlier."

"I was back on the flight deck for the VERTREP. It was bad enough back there. Can't imagine what you guys up forward went through. The chopper pilot was actually asking us if we wanted to call it off. We told him it wasn't our decision to make."

Doug Kimos leaned in. "Yeah. Jason asked me to ask the captain to postpone the UNREP, but Zhao wasn't backing off. And Jason wasn't the only one questioning the situation. The captain of the *Flint* asked us several times if we thought it was safe on our end to go through with it. Technically, it was his call, but he was leaving it up to Zhao's judgment. At the end of the op you could tell even over the radio that he was pissed about how things went. I'm betting some commander at 7th Fleet is catching an earful even as we sit here."

Burns came in the wardroom just as Kimos was ending his part of the conversation. "Catch an earful about what, Doug?"

"The debacle that was supposed to be an UNREP today, sir."

"To say that it didn't go well would be a dramatic understatement." Burns looked over at Jason. "You okay, Conley? You and your guys caught the brunt of it."

"Yes, sir. We're all fine. Just a little shaken up. It's not until well after it's over that you begin to think about what could have happened. What if Clarke had missed grabbing the lifeline and gone over the side? It would have been really hard to do a man overboard maneuver while trying to break away from the *Flint*. The high seas wouldn't have helped, either. A bit scary, in retrospect." He was quiet for a moment. "We probably would've lost him."

Burns was nodding his head. "You're right, Conley. It would have been tough. And, by the way, Doug, you're right about Fleet getting an 'earful.'" Burns looked around to make sure the stewards were not within earshot. "I received a message from the captain of the *Flint* that he was filing a report on the incident."

Kimos asked, "*You* got a message, sir?"

"Yes, me, not Captain Zhao. Read into it what you want." He let it hang there. At this point, the stewards came out of the galley with dinner: roast chicken, string beans, and mashed potatoes. As Jason dug in, he was thinking that maybe he didn't want to be in the center of this. His experience of being on the wrong side of a ship's captain hadn't fared so well the last time. He was also still shaken about almost losing Clarke. There were a lot of different ways to get killed over here.

The day before Thanksgiving, the *Everett* and *Flint* got a replay and conducted a successful UNREP/VERTREP, and then the *Everett* returned to its duties on the gunline. The following day, the officers found themselves back in the wardroom, but this time for a Thanksgiving feast. Jason wondered if some of the goodies for the meal were some of the items that had made it over during the VERTREP. It wasn't exactly like "mom" used to make, but it was a worthy attempt. Turkey, of course, with stuffing, cranberry sauce, a string bean mushroom soup casserole, carrots, mashed potatoes, and pumpkin pie was all served family style to make it feel more like home.

Jason said, "This looks really good. However, to make it seem more like home, I think we should have set up a 'kid's table' for the ensigns."

Weston said, "Weren't you just promoted, Conley?"

"Yep. That's why I'd get to sit with the grown-ups."

The XO said, "Anyone want to say grace?"

Several people said, "Grace."

The XO sighed and began carving the turkey.

As they all began to eat, Jason was thinking that just a year earlier he had been on the *Engage* for Thanksgiving, just off the coast of Kailua tending to a deep-dive habitat. He'd been unable to hang out with his enlisted friends while underway and had felt so lonely. Plus the captain had made it clear by then that he was displeased with Jason's performance. Maybe he did have something to be thankful for this year, after all.

As he looked around the *Everett's* wardroom, he realized that in a very short time, he had made some very good friends. Even though it seemed a bit maudlin, he raised his glass in a toast.

Everyone looked up and then raised their glasses.

"Here's to friends!"

"Here, here!"

"There, there!" chimed in Ed and Joe. Jason knew he could count on them to say the right thing.

The XO was shaking his head. "Can't you guys ever be serious?"

FIFTEEN

Off the Coast of South Vietnam

EARLY DECEMBER 1972

Mail call. Jason was glad that he didn't have to be out in the motor whaleboat making deliveries; that task on this very rainy day belonged to the crew of the *Providence*, McGinty's ship. Jason knew his friend wouldn't be in the boat, so he didn't bother to greet it; he knew they would never turn a comm officer loose in a small boat out on the open water, especially in bad weather.

Jason was glad to receive several letters from Lori, two from his parents, two from Sharon, and a surprise letter from Sparrow. From the tone of their letters, his parents still seemed to be upset with him for not telling them about his WestPac/Vietnam orders to the *Everett*. Of course, there were many things Jason had never told his parents, and never would, starting from back in junior high school.

Jason and his friends used to have a model-making club, mainly with Revell plastic ships and planes. As they built the models, they would preload them with firecrackers, cherry bombs, and M80s acquired on various family vacations, smuggled in from Canada or surreptitiously purchased at South of the Border Resort, a South Carolina motel and tourist trap. Then, ironically, using the flammable glue that they had used to build them, they would set them on fire and float them out on

Bobby Fahey's pond. Even more dangerous were the firecracker fights with one team defending the tree house and the other team trying to deafen them by throwing explosives through the "windows," again at Bobby's. Fun Times. More than once, Jason had wondered where the hell Bobby's parents were during all this. Blowing up models and firecracker fights weren't exactly quiet activities.

As he got older, the clandestine activities took on a different, more mature tone: make-out sessions with dates in his parents' Ford Galaxy (bench seats were great), having sex with his girlfriend for the first time after a Christmas party during their senior year of high school (again in the Ford), the crazy bar hopping at Blue Mountain Lake, and the incredible nighttime parties out on Rock Island in the middle of Blue Mountain Lake fueled by cases of Boone's Farm apple wine.

Then there were the innumerable parties he attended in college that were slightly out of control. There was one NROTC prom (drinking and dancing party, in that order) held at the Bellevue Strafford Hotel in Philadelphia where the entire group, chaperones and all, were thrown out of the hotel just before midnight. The place had been booked until one. It was probably the dancing on the tabletops, with two of them collapsing, that had pushed that one over the edge. *Come to think of it*, Jason thought, *Olongapo's not that much different.*

Did all this previous history justify not telling his parents he was going to Vietnam? Yes. That and he hadn't wanted to spoil their vacation in Hawai'i by worrying about him, a vacation for which they had been saving up for a long time.

Joe said, "Yo, Earth to Jason. What the hell are you lost in?"

"Oh, just got these letters that made me drift back to over a year ago when I got my orders to the *Everett*. It was pretty hectic. I left the *Engage* and was sent to Anti-Submarine Warfare School in San Diego for two weeks. The day after I got back to Hawai'i, my parents arrived for a week on Oahu before going over to Maui. The day after they left, I reported to the *Everett* and I was gone, gone, gone."

"So that's why you didn't report earlier. You had leave arranged to be with your parents."

"Yep. Guess I never really explained that."

"Everything okay back home and with Lori?"

"Yeah. The letters just sorta sent me back in time, I guess. Especially to those three weeks before coming aboard. The two weeks in San Diego were great."

Lori had picked Jason up at the San Diego airport. She was waiting at the gate and when Jason came through the door in his uniform, she ran up to him and gave him a big hug and a kiss. This drew smiles from the other people waiting to greet friends and relatives, thinking, perhaps, that he was returning from a Vietnam tour. Jason had traveled in uniform since he was on orders to the ASW school and oftentimes the airlines would bump soldiers and sailors in uniform up to first class, which they had for him this time around. He was glad Lori was there to meet him for more than one reason. He had really missed her after their wonderful time in Lahaina and it was hard to pass up the free drinks the stewardesses plied him with on the plane. Driving would have been problematic.

Lori said in Jason's ear, "I guess we should cut this short; people are staring."

"I don't mind."

"No one's home back at my apartment. My sister's at work at the zoo."

"I guess we should cut this short; people are staring."

"I knew you'd see it my way."

They drove back to the apartment complex where Lori lived and where Jason had shared an apartment with his friend, John McGinty. They took the elevator up to the third floor and carried Jason's bags to her apartment. Lori unlocked the door and stepped in. Sandy was sitting on the sofa with a book.

"Hi, Lori! Home early from work," said Sandy. She glanced over at Jason's crestfallen face. "Glad to see you, too, Jason."

"Oh, no, no, not what you think. I'm glad to see you, too, Sandy. I was just thinking about something else when I walked in."

Lori shot him a look.

"C'mon, let's get your bags in my room and you can get out of that uniform."

Jason glanced sideways at Sandy. She returned his look with a toothy, shit-eatin' grin. Sandy knew full well what the plan had been. Jason picked up his bag and carry-on and Lori followed him into her bedroom. She said, "Well, what do you want to do now on this quiet Sunday afternoon?"

Jason thought for a minute. "We could go to a matinee at the drive-in."

Lori looked confused. "Matinee. Drive-in. I'm missing something here." Then, a smile began to creep across her face. "Ooooh. Got it. Um, but what do we tell Sandy?"

"We can tell her we're going on a little picnic. We'll have the blanket, pillows, basket of food, wine. Sounds like a picnic to me."

"Broad daylight, huh? This is really naughty."

"Thank you."

"Get changed. I'll get the stuff."

Lori headed for the kitchen to get some food together for the "picnic" while Jason shed his uniform for some more suitable attire. When he came out of the bedroom, Lori had everything ready.

Sandy was watching all this quite skeptically. "So, what are you two up to? Looks like a picnic."

"Always knew you were on top of things," Jason said.

"I guess the two of you just need some time to catch up on things, right?"

"Exactly."

"Okay, then. Well, off you go. Home for dinner?"

Jason looked over at Lori who said, "Yeah, there's some salmon in the fridge, enough for all of us. We'll be back well before dinnertime." They gathered up their food, wine, blankets, and pillows and escaped out the apartment door.

As they went up the stairs, Jason asked, "Do you think Sandy is suspicious?"

"I know my sister. I'm *sure* she's suspicious."

It was hot on the roof, and it got even hotter. It being Sunday was probably a good thing. No maintenance work would be happening to interrupt the "movie."

The next day, Jason reported to ASW school. He was there to be trained as an air controller, working with up to three aircraft at a time. The two primary aircraft were the SH-3 Sea King helicopter and the fixed-wing, four-engine turboprop P3 Orion. An ASW officer can control three aircraft at once: three copters, two copters and a fixed-wing, or one copter and two fixed-wing—but not three fixed-wing aircraft. While the copters were highly maneuverable, the P3 could stay in the air for long periods of time and travel at relatively high rates of speed, well over four hundred miles per hour. The tail of the Orion housed a MAD "stinger," a magnetic anomaly detection device that could pick out the magnetic signature of a submerged submarine from the background magnetic field of the Earth. The Sea Kings had the capability of hovering to lower sonar booms that could operate either actively or passively. With three copters, it was possible to use triangulation to zero in on a sub's position.

During the first week, Jason learned about ASW tactics and the flight characteristics of the aircraft. He also became comfortable speaking through a headset to the aircraft "crews," people running the electronic simulations of the copters and planes. Another one of the trainers "piloted" the submarine on a course known only to him. It was basically an extremely complex electronic version of the game Battleship, except in this simulation, all the parts were moving simultaneously.

In the evening, back at Lori's, it was a little frustrating since much of what he was learning was classified, including the electronics used for training. All he could tell her was that it was one of the most fascinating things he had ever done. Not as fascinating as doing acrobatics flying a T-38, single-prop training plane, or doing barrel rolls in an F-9 jet during his NROTC summer flight training in Corpus Christi, Texas, but pretty damn close.

Thursday evening, they made plans to meet up with John McGinty and go out for some drinks and dinner at Fiddler's Green, just for old times' sake. John drove them in his used 1968 Toyota Corolla that, with three people in it, could barely get out of its own way. The Corolla had a fine patina reminiscent of a fridge that might be found in a Sears scratch-and-dent appliance warehouse. They walked into the bar and were greeted by the fiddle playing of PJ Ryan. Jason remarked, "Some things never change."

They found a corner table; a waitress brought them menus and took their drink orders. They really didn't need the menus; the dishes never changed. Jason remarked, "I'm ready for a Guinness. A good pour is tough to come by out in Hawai'i."

The drinks arrived and John said, "We're getting ready to deploy. Looks like we'll be over there at the same time as your new ship."

"Yeah, should be interesting. Hopefully, at some point, we'll end up in Subic together."

"Weekend's coming up. You and Lori have any plans?"

Lori said, "Sunday, Sandy's giving us a behind-the-scenes tour of the San Diego Zoo."

"I'm *really* looking forward to that," Jason added.

"I don't suppose I could tag along."

"Don't see why not," Lori said. "I'll double-check with Sandy and get back to you."

"Hey, why don't you guys go to Disneyland on Saturday? Have you ever been?" John suggested.

Jason shook his head. "That's just for kids, isn't it?"

Lori disagreed. "No, I think there's a lot there for everybody.

Anyway, we can be kids for a day, right?"

John said, "I've been there a couple of times. Lots of good rides, like Space Mountain." He looked at Jason. "Remember when we'd all go up to Willow Grove Amusement Park outside of Philly? We used to have a blast there. Disneyland is like an advanced version of that. Very advanced."

Jason looked at Lori. "I'm game, if you are."

Jason and Lori left early on Saturday to get up to Disneyland by midmorning. They arrived to find the closest parking lot jammed, and had to go to a remote lot and take a shuttle in. Jason said, "I have a little bit of a foreboding feeling here. Not a big fan of crowds or waiting in lines."

Once inside the park, it became obvious that Jason was not going to be a Disneyland fan. However, he tried to maintain a positive attitude so as not to spoil it for Lori, who seemed to be taking it all in with a great deal of enthusiasm.

"Were you a Disney fan growing up?" Lori asked.

"Yeah, the whole family was. We'd all watch *Disney's Wonderful World of Color* and when I was little, I was totally into *Zorro* and *Davy Crockett*. They were probably my two favorite Halloween costumes, ever."

Lori laughed, "Got any pictures of that? I'd love to see you dressed up as Zorro."

"I'm sure my mom has some."

"I loved all their productions of *Sleeping Beauty*, *Cinderella*, *Peter Pan*, and *Lady and the Tramp*."

"Yeah, the movies were great. My favorite was *Fantasia*. In fact, me and my friends just saw it a few months ago at the theater down by the Kuhio Grill. It is *truly* spectacular if you see it stoned, which we were. Thinking about it afterward, we all agreed that the cartoonists that worked on it could *not* have been totally straight when they came up with all that."

"Yeah, you might be right."

"One thing I never got was Mickey Mouse and the rest of the cartoon characters. Just not funny, especially when compared to Looney Tunes. Tasmanian Devil, the Martian, Bugs, and of course, Road Runner and Wile E. Coyote. Now that's funny stuff."

"Yeah, nothing like getting crushed by an ACME anvil."

"C'mon, cartoon slapstick is great. Of course, being a girl, you probably didn't like the Three Stooges, either."

"What do you mean, 'being a girl'?"

"It's a scientific fact that you feminine types don't like the sophisticated humor of Moe, Larry, and Curly, who, by the way, were the best. You can keep Shemp and Curly Joe."

"Ah, a Stooges connoisseur. I knew there was something special about you."

"Nyuck, nyuck, nyuck!"

While they were having this esoteric discussion, they walked around the park, becoming more and more disheartened about getting on any kind of ride. The lines were ridiculous.

Jason said, "Let's see, you wait in line for an hour to get on a ride that lasts five minutes. Not good."

Lori stopped, grabbed his arm, and pointed. "Look. A ride with no line."

"What? Can't be good then."

"Well, it's got to be better than walking around talking about the Stooges."

Imitating Curly, Jason exclaimed, "Hey! I resemble that remark."

"C'mon. What've we got to lose?"

They entered the building that housed the ride and boarded a small car that was supposed to look like a boat on the water but was actually being pulled by a cable on a set of rails that were hidden from view.

"What is this? A Tunnel of Love of some sort?" Jason asked.

"No, it's called It's a Small World."

With a slight jerk, the ride started. The boat rounded a curve, and they were confronted by a scene that Jason found almost nightmarish. There were little dancing dolls all singing an absolutely irritating song in sing-song little girl voices.

It's a world of laughter, a world of tears,
It's a world of hopes and a world of fears,
There's so much that we share,
That it's time we're aware,
It's a small world after all!
It's a small world after all,
It's a small world after all,
It's a small world after all,
It's a small, small world!
It's a small world after all
It's a small world after all,
It's a small, small world!

And it continued. On and on. Scene after scene. It seemed to never end. At one point, Jason thought he might have screamed. Quite suddenly, in the middle of the ride, the boat lurched to a stop.

"Wait. What?" Jason was panicking. "Why did we stop? The music didn't stop. The dolls haven't stopped. Why did *we* stop!"

"It's a small world after all."

Lori said, "Calm down. I'm sure we'll start moving soon. Just relax and enjoy it."

"It's a small world after all."

"Enjoy it? When we get back to your place, I'm going to find a Stooges marathon on TV and force you to watch it."

"It's a small, small world."

Twenty horrifying minutes later, the boat jerked forward and headed for the exit.

"They better damn well have psychiatrists waiting for us at the end of this ride, because this is one hell of a traumatic experience," Jason said. "It's . . . it's . . . it's life changing and not in a good way!"

When the ride finally came to rest, they clambered out of the boat and headed back into the park. Jason was looking around. "I need a beer."

Lori looked at him. "I hate to tell you this; there's no booze in Disneyland."

"What! That's freakin' un-American." Jason stopped. "Wait. I can still hear them! Inside my head!"

"It's a small world after all."

After the wonderful world of Disney and an absolutely incredible behind-the-scenes tour of the San Diego Zoo, Jason had to return to the harsh reality of ASW. Well, not really reality since all the training sessions were done electronically. The second week was spent refining his technique. The timing sequence of the P3 Orion torpedo drop was not a mechanized process. It required the air controller to have a "feel" for the course and speed of the target sub and the flight path and speed of the turbo-prop aircraft. The trick was to get the drop so that the torpedo landed slightly forward of the sub just off the port bow. The search sequence of the torpedo started with a circular course in a clockwise motion. If perfectly placed, the sub would basically run into the torpedo right on its bow. Evading it would be nearly impossible.

Watching his radar screen, Jason would track the plane and track the sub by marking the glass with colored grease pencils. When he had the plane coming in on the right intercept course, he would tell the person who would actually drop the "fish" to drop it, "Now . . . now . . . now." On the third "now," the torpedo would be released. At the end of each exercise, the run was analyzed by everyone involved by watching an electronic playback on what looked like a movie screen. The track of the sub was a dotted red line. The choppers were dotted blue lines, and the Orion was a smooth green tracer. Once in the water, the torpedo was a yellow dotted line. Each phase or step in the operation could be paused, at which point feedback was given. By the end of the week, Jason was nailing the sub on virtually every run. He worked best with two choppers using sonar and having the P3 make the torpedo drop. At the end of the week, he was awarded his ASW air-controller certificate.

That evening, Lori and Jason enjoyed one last drive-in movie. Even though he enjoyed Lori's company, it was difficult not to think about what was coming up. He was going to be heading to WestPac/Vietnam the moment he set foot on the *Everett*. But before that, he had to entertain his parents for a week on their visit to the islands before they headed off to Maui for a few more days. He wasn't sure which task would be more difficult.

Lori drove Jason to the airport the next morning. Their conversation seemed a bit stilted to Jason, partly because being trapped in a nasty situation, he really had no idea what to say. As she walked him to his gate, he told Lori that he would like her to move out to Hawai'i after his WestPac tour was completed. She kissed him long and hard at the gate and whispered, "I love you, Jason," as he held her. However, she said nothing about a possible move. They parted, and Jason headed for the plane while Lori turned toward the exit. Both looked back before they lost sight of each other, straining for one last glimpse through the throng of air travelers who couldn't care less about their situation.

Jason had a lot to think about on the plane back to Honolulu. Not surprisingly, his thoughts centered on the idea that Lori might be the person he would like to spend the rest of his life with, but that they would be separated from each other for at least the next nine or ten months. Hard to take. He dwelled on the fact that Lori had not committed to coming over to Hawai'i after his return from the deployment. She had said, "I love you," but the unsuccessful long-distance relationships he had been in before haunted him. Their relationship would be reduced to exchanging letters, letters that had to be sent halfway around the world, delayed by weeks as the mailbag pursued the ship as it fulfilled its missions. Of course, he hadn't proposed. That was on him. A ring would have made his intentions clearer than an offer to come shack up with him on the islands. He simply was not ready to take that step.

His sigh must have been louder than he thought. A stewardess leaned over him and said, "Is there anything wrong, Mr. Conley?"

"Um, no, just thinking about the girl I just left in San Diego."

The stewardess smiled. "Would another gin and tonic help?"

"Probably not, but then again, why not give it a try?"

SIXTEEN

Off the Coast of Vietnam

DECEMBER 1972

Jason had to go on watch in an hour. He and Billy Weston had the shift from eight o'clock to midnight. It was probably Jason's favorite watch. Cruising orders came in frequently during this time, and the *Everett* would start making way to their appointed station. He hadn't had much of an opportunity to be on watch with Weston, so he was curious as to how comfortable the new ensign was with having the conn.

He thought about the letters he had received at the last mail call. He was pleased that Sharon had written so soon after their departure from Subic. Not once, but twice.

The departure had gone smoothly. Not as far as Sharon was concerned; she couldn't be there. However, there was the small matter of the "appropriated" jeep. Joe had volunteered to have the quarterdeck watch as the *Everett* made preparations to get underway, knowing full well that he had to orchestrate a clean getaway. He had directed one of the men from the *Everett* to return their ship's jeep and catch the shuttle back from the motor pool. No problems there. Then, at the very last minute, just before the telephone cable was to be disconnected and sent back over to the pier, he used the quarterdeck phone to call the motor pool.

"Motor pool. Chief Norquist."

"Hi, Chief. This is the *Everett*. We just noticed that there's been a jeep parked next to ours while we were in port. There's no ship outboard of us and we are about to get underway. We turned our jeep in a half hour ago. You might want to send someone out to check it out."

"Who is this?"

"Like I said, I'm on the *Everett* and we're getting underway, ready to cast off. I wanted to let you know about this be—" Joe jiggled the phone's cradle disconnecting the call.

The *Everett* slipped away.

At the time, Jason had no idea what Joe had done, but as the ship pulled away from the pier, Jason was paying more attention to the abandoned jeep and the road leading from the motor pool than he was to the work his men were doing on the forecastle. When Grande Island drifted by on their portside, he sighed and returned his attention to the work of securing from sea and anchor detail. The jeep had been fun.

Now Jason made sure he had a couple of cigars before he made his way up to the bridge for his time on watch. Upon arrival, he relieved Lt. Barnaby of his OOD duties and watched as Weston assumed the conn. For the moment, they were simply to maintain their position while awaiting further assignment.

Jason's mind drifted back to the surprise letter from Sparrow Gatling. He assumed she had gotten his address from Sid somehow. He still couldn't believe the flighty hippie was related to the machine gun family. In the letter, Jason felt he could sense some sadness creeping in. Perhaps the commune was not all she thought it would be. Perhaps the guy she met out there turned out to be a jerk and she was stuck with him out on The Farm. She had talked about their remote location, and how it took a while to feel accepted. Many of the members had been there for several years, she said. Well, there wasn't a lot he could do for her from Vietnam. She would have to either ride it out or possibly move back to San Francisco. He had enjoyed her company, even if it had been for just a day.

The man on the sound-powered phones broke Jason away from his thoughts.

"Sir, this is from CIC. We've received orders to proceed to these coordinates." He wrote them down as he was speaking and handed them to Jason. "I think it's off Quang Tri, sir."

Jason looked at the paper and said, "You're probably right. It's been a real hot spot for us lately."

He handed the coordinates to Weston. "Plot out a course to get us here. No hurry, we won't be seeing any action until morning. I'll ring the captain and fill him in."

Jason picked up the direct line to Captain Zhao's stateroom, and not surprisingly, received no response. He told the messenger of the watch, "Let the XO know that we're to proceed to a station off Quang Tri province for some gunfire support in the a.m. Getting underway shortly."

"Aye, sir."

He walked over to the chart table to see how Weston was doing with setting his course. He had it all laid out and was ready to ask permission to proceed.

The messenger arrived back on the bridge with the XO's approval.

"Okay, Mr. Weston. Let's do this."

They had been cruising at ten knots through a relatively calm South China Sea for about an hour when the quartermaster on duty announced, "Captain on the bridge!"

Jason wheeled around in surprise as Captain Zhao stepped through the hatch.

"What is going on here, Mr. Conley?" The bridge was dark, but Jason could hear the anger in Zhao's voice.

"Captain, we received orders about an hour ago to proceed toward a position off Quang Tri to be ready for a gunfire support mission tomorrow morning."

"Why am I just hearing about this now?"

"I called your stateroom as soon as the orders came in but didn't get a response. I then informed the XO and got permission to proceed."

"Is that how we do things on this ship, Mr. Conley? Wait. Don't answer. Let me tell you." He leaned in close, looking up into Jason's face. "It's not."

"With all due respect, sir, this is the way we've been conducting operations for a couple of months now." Jason glanced over at Weston and noticed he was talking with the bridge messenger.

"Well, Mr. Conley . . ." Zhao poked Jason in the chest with each of the next words. "It's. Not. The. Right. Way."

"Sir—"

"Consider yourself relieved of duty. You will confine yourself to your stateroom." He walked over to stand in front of the helm.

Jason turned to the quartermaster and said quietly, "Make sure you log all this."

"This is Captain Zhao. I have the deck and the conn."

Jason came over to Zhao and said quietly, "Sir, it is my opinion that you aren't fit to take on those duties at this time."

"Your *opinion* is irrelevant. I believe I gave you orders to leave the bridge."

"I cannot leave the bridge under these circumstances, sir."

"Where is my bridge messenger? I need the master at arms here on the double."

At that moment the messenger stepped through the hatch with the XO one step behind.

The XO said, "Belay that. Captain, bridge wing please."

Zhao glared at the XO but followed him out on the starboard bridge wing anyway while Jason and Weston waited near the helm. After five minutes of what appeared to be an animated discussion, the XO stuck his head in through the starboard hatch, "Resume your duties, Mr. Conley. You, too, Mr. Weston."

"Yes, sir. Thank you, sir. This is Mr. Conley. I have the deck. Mr. Weston has the conn."

Jason went out to the starboard bridge wing in time to see the XO disappearing down the aft ladder to the deck below, escorting Zhao back to his stateroom without the spectacle of going back through the bridge.

The next morning, Lt. Cmdr. Archie Burns called an officers' meeting in the wardroom. Only Joe and Culpepper were missing since they had the bridge watch and were awaiting further orders for the gunfire support mission. Jason had said nothing about the incident that occurred the previous evening and had told Weston to do the same. However, word had spread through the enlisted ranks, so the scuttlebutt about Zhao's bridge appearance had made its way throughout the *Everett*.

"Gentlemen." The XO paused and looked at the men seated before him. "Last evening on Mr. Conley's watch, Captain Zhao, in a state of medical distress, tried to commandeer control of the ship. He was upset that he had not been informed of our orders to proceed to our current location. Mr. Conley had tried to do just that, but the captain was unresponsive. So, as we have been doing for some time now, I was informed of the orders and gave permission to proceed." He paused again. "I had to escort Captain Zhao back to his stateroom. I then radioed Seventh Fleet Command and filled them in on the incident. They were already aware of some previous difficulties associated with Captain Zhao and his medications, such as our munitions UNREP that went sideways. As a result of our exchange of messages, Captain Zhao is now on medical leave, and I am temporarily assigned as acting captain of the *Everett*. Captain Zhao will remain in his stateroom until we reach our next port of call, Subic Bay. We will be there for a short time, perhaps just a couple of days. It's likely that Captain Zhao will leave the *Everett* at that time and a new captain will come aboard. Until that time, I am assuming all the duties normally handled by Commander Zhao."

Jason noted the subtle change from "Captain Zhao" to "Commander Zhao." It would now be "Captain Burns." At least for the foreseeable future.

"Any questions, gentlemen?" Burns looked around, and seeing no questions forthcoming said, "Dismissed."

Everyone stood as he left the wardroom. They then clustered around Jason and Weston, peppering them with questions as to what had gone on during their watch the previous night. Jason gave them an abbreviated version of the events, noting that he had been shaking like a leaf during the whole exchange with Zhao. He thanked Weston for his quick thinking in sending the messenger to fetch the XO.

"I think Billy here may have saved my ass."

Everyone drifted out of the wardroom and Jason went up to his stateroom to write a letter to Sharon, letting her know that he would be back in Subic sooner rather than later. Given the mail system, he might even beat the letter there. When he finished, he took it down to the ship's office to make sure it got into the next mailbag that left the ship.

Sharon got the letter three weeks later. In San Diego.

SEVENTEEN

Subic Bay

DECEMBER 1972

Jason had Christmas dinner in the Subic Bay O' Club with Joe, Ed, and his old college friend and roommate from San Diego, John McGinty. It was definitely not what Jason had in mind when he'd heard the XO, now Captain Burns, say they would be going back to Subic for a short stay. Sharon was gone.

When they had pulled in and secured the ship, he made a call to the BOQ where Sharon and her friends had been living. He was informed that many of the nurses that had been stationed in Subic had been transferred stateside to San Diego, including Lt. Hanley. So, instead of a nice dinner with Sharon followed by "unwrapping" his present—Sharon—Jason was stuck with his *Everett* buddies and his friend from home. All in all, it could be worse; he could be in country in Vietnam. However, it could have been a lot better. A whole lot better.

The *Providence*, McGinty's ship, had already been in Subic for over a week for repairs. The *Providence*, along with three other ships that had heavily armored superstructures, had steamed into Haiphong Harbor and had a shootout with the shore batteries there, like a bunch of gunslingers at the OK Corral. McGinty said the bullets hitting the bulkhead of CIC sounded like a heavy hailstorm. After shooting the harbor up, the ships retreated, but as they retreated, they mined the harbor. What was interesting, McGinty said, was that the *Providence* had sent messages to as many civilian ships docked in the harbor as possible, warning them to get out safely while they could. In other words, they had let the North Vietnamese in Haiphong know what was coming down the pike, defying them to do something about it.

"By the way, you guys are getting a helluva great new captain."

Ed looked at him quizzically. "What are you talking about? We don't even know who it is or when he's reporting."

Jason said, "Wait. You know something?"

"Well, as comm officer, I see messages come and go, and I don't think these orders are classified. Sooo . . ."

"Spill it."

"Your new commanding officer is our current XO, Commander Ernest R. Zeigler. Coming your way two days from now."

Ed said, "Okay. What's he like?"

John paused as the first round of cocktails arrived. He took a sip of his Tom Collins, drawing out the suspense.

"C'mon. C'mon," Ed spurred him.

"All right. He's fantastic. I'm really sad that we're going to lose him. Hell, he even plays on our basketball team. And he's good!"

Jason, Joe, and Ed looked at each other and clinked glasses in a silent toast.

John continued. "He really looks out for the men—officers and enlisted alike. Very personable."

Joe said, "This sounds like the exact opposite of what we have now. Or should I say, what we used to have."

"Well, my loss is your gain," John said. "I think you'll be very pleased."

Dinner was served after the second round of cocktails—an incredible prime rib dinner, with each person commandeering their own bottle of Beaujolais.

Jason raised his glass, "A toast! A toast to my old friend John McGinty for surviving the shootout without shitting himself."

John said, "Wait, not so fast on the latter part."

The whole table burst into laughter, then drank their wine.

"Okay, just kidding. But I gotta tell you, when that noise started it *was* scary as hell. I was more concerned about the ships with us. They had some good armor, but not as thick as what we have on the *Providence*."

Ed said, "Our superstructure is aluminum. Our ship would have looked like Swiss cheese if we had gone in there."

Jason said, "Well, we're all here now. I must admit, you aren't the company I thought I'd be keeping, but I guess you'll have to do. You're just not as, shall we say, attractive, as a nurse."

John looked around at them. "So, you were expecting to be here with some nurses? How would that have come about?"

The three officers from the *Everett* began to tell John about the jeep, Cubi Point, and the snorkeling money expedition. John kept shaking his head as the tale unfolded.

"So, you guys stole a jeep?"

Jason was shaking his head, "No, no, according to Joe here, we 'appropriated' a jeep. 'Stole' has too much of a criminal overtone to it."

"So, you guys stole a jeep." It was not a question this time around. "And siphoned gas."

Joe said, "Well, yeah, just a little. We made a lot of trips to Cubi Point and sometimes had six people on board."

John, grinning broadly and shaking his head said, "Ya gotta love it." He looked at Jason. "I'm getting shot at while you're banging a nurse." He raised his glass. "Gotta hand it to ya, excellent work!"

The prime rib was followed by dessert, some excellent New York-style cheesecake. Then over some after-dinner bourbons, Joe and Ed grilled John about what Jason was like in college.

Ed asked, "So, we already know that he can play guitar. What was he doing with that in college?"

"For a while, he gave guitar lessons at a music store in Wayne, and he played in a Grateful Dead cover band with some guys from Haverford College. But then after he started at the radio station, he formed a band with a couple of the guys from there and a few of his friends who were still around after high school. They were pretty good. Had a lot of local gigs, especially dances. Of course, when they played twenty-minute jam versions of 'Crossroads' or 'Spoonful' some of the dancing sorta petered out."

Jason added, "It was tough balancing the dance tunes with the more progressive rock songs. We managed. We had fun."

Joe looked at Jason. "He seems to be quite the successful ladies' man, at least with a certain nurse that used to be here. How was he in college?"

Jason said, "You don't have to answer that."

John grinned, "Sure I do. Just one example. Throughout the summer leading into his senior year, he was dating three different girls simultaneously, all named 'Emily.' That continued throughout that first semester too."

"Very clever, Jason," Joe said. "No way to slip up with a wrong name."

John said, "It was fun hearing him on the radio. He'd feature a solid hour of a group, play album sides, and was one of the regular hosts of the 'Cryptic Comedy Circus,' a sort of improv thing the station ran on Friday night. They even had a small live audience in the studio."

"Jason abandoned the NROTC intramural teams to play on the radio station teams, mainly flag football and softball. Plus, just about every weekend we had a pickup touch-football game. On Thanksgiving weekend, it was a full-on tackle game. Four games, four broken bones. We were lucky it was only one per game."

Jason was laughing. "There was a reason for that. As soon as someone broke a bone, we'd have to quit the game to get them to the emergency room at Bryn Mawr Hospital."

"We'd play on a practice field at one of the local high schools. We even kicked field goals. Jason was the best kicker out there."

"Okay, enough of this crap." Jason looked down at his empty glass. "Another round to celebrate getting Zhao off the ship?"

Everyone agreed. Why not?

The bourbons arrived, served in solid, heavy-based whiskey tumblers. After a sip or two, Jason looked at his watch. "Holy shit! Look at the time. We need to get out of here to get back before curfew."

John protested. "But we just got these bourbons."

Joe looked at his glass, "What the hell. Let's just take them as 'travelers.'"

Jason said, "Sounds good to me."

The four of them quite discreetly spirited their spirits out of the club. On unsteady legs they made their way back toward the pier where the *Everett* was docked. The *Providence* was the next pier over. They stopped along the water's edge to look out over the harbor and to finish their drinks.

"Here's to our new captain," Jason raised his glass. "May he be as good as John says he is. It will be a more than welcome change." They all raised their glasses and drank.

Joe said, "We probably shouldn't bring these back on board. Whaddaya wanna do with them?" He was slurring his words ever so slightly.

"We could heave them in the harbor," Ed said.

John looked at Jason. "Why don't you show off your place-kicking skills with that glass?"

Jason looked dubious. "Kick a glass?" He paused. "Okay. I'll do it if we make it a contest."

Ed said, "I'm in."

They all lined their glasses up on the edge of the grass adjoining the wooden bulkhead that rimmed the harbor.

John said, "I'll go first; Jason goes last."

John took a three step drop off the glass, then with a rapid approach and a swing of his left leg, launched his glass into the harbor. It didn't go far.

He chided himself, "Didn't get all of that."

Joe lined up his kick similar to the way John did, except that on his kick his left leg slid out from under him, and he landed hard on his butt. His right foot grazed the glass, which rolled off the grass, over the top of the bulkhead and plopped into the water.

John looked down at him. "I think I've got you on distance *and* style points."

Joe looked up. "Shut it."

Ed was next and managed to launch his glass a couple of yards farther than John's attempt.

"Looks like we have a new name atop the leaderboard," he announced. "Okay, Bigfoot. You're up."

Jason, upon his approach, actually looked as though he knew what he was doing. He kicked it hard with a nice follow-through and sent it at least ten yards beyond Ed's attempt.

"Woo-hoo! We have a winner. Wait. What do I win?"

"I'll show you how to play craps tomorrow night when we go into town," Joe volunteered.

"I'll buy you a beer," said Ed.

"Oh wow. Big spender. San Miguel's a quarter in town."

"Take it or leave it."

"I'll take it."

They made it to the gangway, said goodbye to John, and went up to check in through the quarterdeck. As he stepped on the ship, Jason felt something odd in his right shoe. It didn't hurt; it just felt funny. He made it up to his state room and collapsed in his bunk full clothed. He was out before Joe made it back from his visit to the head.

The next morning, Jason had no recollection of falling asleep. Passing out was probably a more fitting term. Slowly, very slowly he sat up in his bunk and assessed the situation. Fully dressed. Check.

Shoes still on. Check. Spinning sensation. Check.

He swung his legs over the edge of the bunk and bent over to unlace his shoes. It felt like the ship was underway, in a typhoon. He remained motionless for a minute until the seas settled. Jason unlaced his right shoe and tried to take it off, but it hurt like hell. What the fuck? He finally pried the shoe off and gingerly peeled off the sock to reveal a second toe in all its multicolored glory, but primarily purple.

Jason stared at it as the memory of the previous evening's place-kicking contest washed over him.

"Looks broken to me."

He looked up to see Joe peering over the edge of the upper bunk.

"Yeah. I came to the same conclusion."

"I don't think there's much you can do for that except tape it to the adjoining middle toe."

"Yeah. I came to the same conclusion. However, first I need to get a shower and then some coffee, in that order, so I can actually function at quarters this morning."

"You and me both."

Jason got his shower and found some adhesive tape in one of the drawers of his desk. He managed to get a few loops around the toes and was surprised that it didn't hurt more. That is, until he tried to jam it into his shoe. Once in, however, the shoe acted like a splint, so he was able to walk down the passageway to the wardroom almost normally. Coffee was calling. The greasy looking sausage and scrambled eggs, not so much. Joe, Ed, and Jason got two mugs of coffee in each of them and made it to quarters.

After quarters, Jason went over to the base dispensary where they said, "Yep, looks like it's broken. Here's some better tape."

Later that day, Archie Burns came into the wardroom looking to get a cup of coffee. Before he got his coffee, his attention was diverted to the side of the wardroom where the sofa and large end table were located. Joe, Ed, and Jason were gathered around the table setting up

Jason's tape recorder, Joe's turntable, some small bookshelf speakers, and a receiver/amplifier Ed had picked up.

"What's going on, guys?"

Ed looked up from the wiring he was working on. "Oh. Hi, Captain. We're about to do some recording."

"Recording? What's getting recorded?"

Jason said, "We bought a bunch of bootleg albums in town. They were all less than fifty cents each. They're pressed on really cheap vinyl with flimsy covers. If we play an album once, it gets all the crap out of the grooves from the cheap production. Then, we play it three or four more times and record it each time on to the reel-to-reel. After that, the fidelity of the soft vinyl is shot, and then we toss the album. We can fit at least three albums on each reel."

Burns came over to take a closer look. He picked up the small stack of records sitting beside the recorder.

"Joplin's *Pearl* album, Allman's *Fillmore East*, The Who's *Who's Next*, and Traffic's *Low Spark*. Pretty good stuff. Not familiar with these guys, though: Spirit and Quicksilver Messenger Service."

Jason said, "Quicksilver's a San Francisco band that's kind of in the shadows of Jefferson Airplane and the Dead. Spirit's also from California. In fact, the lead guitar player's name is Randy California."

Captain Burns shuffled through the albums. "You know, customs might give you a hard time about bringing these back to the US because of copyright problems."

Ed said, "We don't plan to bring them back. That's what the recording sessions are for. We leave the stuff set up here, and each time one of the guys does a recording, they mark the cover. After four marks, the album gets tossed, like Jason said. Anyone who wants to use it is welcome to do so."

"Okay. Just letting you know. Let me get my coffee. I'd like to hear either the Quicksilver or Spirit record, if you don't mind."

Jason said, "Sure thing, Captain. We're ready to tape right now."

After playing *What About Me*, Quicksilver's album, Burns said,

"Have you got any Marvin Gaye, like 'What's Goin' On?' I've got a tape deck of my own."

Joe said, "I saw that record in the store. We'll pick it up for you next trip in. Give us a reel of tape and we'll put something together for you."

Archie Burns smiled and said, "I'll look forward to hearing what you put together. Thanks!"

It was a low-key dinner at the O' Club that evening. Cheeseburgers, fries, and beers. Jason, Joe, and Ed didn't want to get too juiced before heading into Olongapo for some music and gambling. They crossed Shit River and headed for The Eclipse, one of their favorite clubs. There was a big bar and stage downstairs and a casino upstairs. The bands that played on the stage usually specialized in British Invasion music and as always, did near perfect covers.

They found a table in the middle of the room and a Filipino waitress in a slinky yellow faux-satin dress slit way up the side came over to take their orders.

"You want drink, Joe?" She said this while looking at Jason.

"Actually, I'm Joe," said Joe.

"And I'm Jason."

Turning to Joe, she said, "Wait. You really Joe?"

"Yep."

"Oh! It your lucky night. Every Joe come in get San Miguel for twenty-five cent."

Ed joined in. "That's quite a deal. That's what I paid for it last time I was in here."

"Oh, you Joe, too?"

Ed shrugged. "Yeah, why not?"

"Too bad, Jason. You not Joe."

Ed said, "Ah, but I lost a bet with Jason last night and said I'd buy him a beer. So, I'll have two San Miguels."

Joe said, "I'll just have the one, for now."

"Okay. I no tell anyone Jason gets special price too." She left to get their beers.

"What the hell was that all about?" Joe asked.

Jason said, "Not sure, but I think you sorta started it."

The five-piece band on stage started into "Ferry Cross the Mersey" just as their beers arrived. The tables were starting to fill up with sailors and their "dates." The waitress looked around. "Many sailor here with girls. You want girls? I know girls."

"Nah. We're good. We're going up to do some gambling soon."

"You can take girl up there."

"That's okay."

The waitress shrugged and left. Halfway through the song, the door to the street was flung open and a shirtless man wearing Levi's burst through the door and fired a pistol into the ceiling. Waving the gun over his head, he ran across the small dance floor in front of the stage as he continued to fire the pistol.

Jason, Joe, and Ed dove under the table and stayed there until the gunfire stopped. The band had stopped playing and were huddled at the back of the stage. Just as Jason peeked up over the edge of the table, the shore patrol came through the front door with their .45 automatics drawn.

One of them saw the band at the back of the stage and yelled, "Did you see where the gunman went?"

Half the men in the band pointed toward the swinging doors that went into the kitchen. The shore patrol took off in pursuit.

Emerging from under the table like prairie dogs coming out of their holes after a golden eagle flyover, Joe, Ed, and Jason slipped back into their chairs.

Jason said, "I didn't know the band had a floor show."

"They need to work on it more. The act didn't mesh very well with the music," Ed said.

"Yeah, and we didn't get to see the end of the chase scene."

Joe said, "I think it's time for the casino. Let's head up."

They grabbed their beers and headed for the stairway near the front door that was the entrance to the upstairs facility.

The top of the stairs opened to a large room that was home to a bar at the far end and gambling tables clustered by the particular way in which men could be separated from their money. On the far right, where there should have been windows looking to the street, was a solid row of slot machines. Almost every machine was engaged. There were four tables for blackjack, then four tables for craps, and two roulette wheels close to each end of the bar. They picked up fresh San Miguels at the bar and made their way to a space at one of the craps tables.

Joe said, "Until I become the shooter, we'll start with some simple bets using the Pass Line and Come Line."

Jason said, "The 'Come Line'?"

"Yeah, the 'Come Line,'" Joe said, "There's also a 'Don't Come Line.'"

Jason laughed. "I know that one. It's 'Is it in yet?'"

They made several bets as the dice rotated from shooter to shooter. When it was Jason's turn, he passed to Joe. By that time, they were all still about even in terms of money lost or won. However, Jason was still confused as to what strategy he should be following under certain roll conditions. Plus, since they had to stand the whole time; his toe was starting to bother him.

"I'm heading over to grab a seat at the blackjack table. At least I'll feel like I know what I'm doing, and I can get my weight off my foot." Jason picked up his chips and went over to an empty seat.

He sat down. The man to his right, wearing Levi's and a white cotton shirt with the sleeves rolled part way up, had an anchor tattooed on the inside of his right, heavily muscled forearm. Sitting next to the tattoo was a Filipino girl in a tight blue miniskirt and a frilly, pale-blue blouse. She was playing using the man's money and both were drinking what looked like whiskey sours. Jason couldn't help but notice that she was also stroking the guy's crotch in a very provocative manner. He wondered how the man could concentrate on his cards. As the cards were dealt, it appeared he really couldn't concentrate, as he took a "hit" while showing seventeen. Jason had a ten of hearts and a jack of clubs. He felt secure in holding. The dealer ran up to nineteen. Jason won; Levi's lost.

Well, he lost the hand on top of the table but was getting quite a deal with the hand under the table, Jason thought.

The man downed what was left of his sour and placed his hand on the girl's thigh right at the hemline of her skirt. Both of them, for the most part, kept their eyes on the dealer. Jason noticed the man's hand as it started to make its move up her thigh and under the dress. Just about when Jason thought he should have reached "the promised land," the man stood up so abruptly his chair fell back to the floor. He grabbed the girl by the shoulders and pulled her backward so hard that the chair flipped over with the girl in it. Except, it was then revealed as her skirt rode up to her hips and in the absence of underwear that she was not, in fact, a girl.

"Son of a bitch," Levi's screamed. "You're a fuckin' Benny Boy."

He went to kick 'Benny' in the crotch, but as he swung his foot, Benny grabbed it, and with a twisting motion, brought the man down. As soon as he hit the floor, Benny was on him, raining blows down on his face.

However, Benny wasn't very big, and the punches were so wild that Levi's was able to roll him off and gain his footing. They were now facing each other, Benny with his back to the stairway. Levi's advanced on him, but as he pulled his arm back to throw a punch, Benny kicked him in the solar plexus. Apparently, he knew a little karate.

Jason was standing back from all this, and most of the people at the tables closest to where the fight was now had stopped their games to watch the action. One of the bartenders was on the phone.

Levi's was almost doubled over from the kick, gasping for air and Benny took a step closer to deliver a kick to his face. But from his crouching position, Levi's bull-rushed Benny and tackled him, driving him back into the wall at the top of the stairs. Both men now had their arms around each other in a clinch, and as they danced to maneuver to gain an advantage, Levi's' right foot slipped off the top step. Still embracing each other, both men somersaulted down the narrow stairwell, landing at the bottom in an awkward sprawl. Benny was motionless. Levi's' right leg was bent sideways at the knee and the lower part of his left arm had a joint in it where there shouldn't have been one. A shard of white bone protruded through a bloody gash.

People from the first floor came over and tried to move the two to where they could be better examined and treated, but Levi's was writhing in such pain that he was difficult to approach. Finally, the shore patrol arrived, again, along with the local police to sort things out. The two shore patrol officers grabbed Levi's under the armpits and dragged him screaming out into the middle of the small dance floor. The police were still working to revive Benny. Sirens in the distance sounded the arrival of an ambulance. After stabilizing Levi's' leg and arm, he and an unconscious Benny were placed on stretchers and taken away, Benny escorted by the police and Levi's by the shore patrol unit.

Jason wandered over to the craps table and said to Joe and Ed, "Yet another unsuccessful floor show."

Ed said, "Yeah, but this one covered two floors."

"So, what do you guys want to do?"

Joe said, "If we can hang until I get to be shooter again, I'll be fine to head back after that."

Jason nodded. "I'll go back and play a few more hands, then. Good luck."

The next morning at ten o'clock, all the officers were assembled in the wardroom to meet the new captain. Jason, Joe, and Ed had leaked a bit of the news to a few of the others, but some were still unaware of the new captain's arrival. The wardroom door opened, and Lt. Cmdr. Burns came into the room and announced, "Attention on deck!"

Cmdr. Ernest R. Zeigler followed close behind and then took his position standing at the head of the table. "Be seated, gentlemen."

Cmdr. Zeigler was tall, even taller than Archie Burns. He had thick black hair, graying at the temples, and wore rectangular gold-framed glasses. He also looked like he worked out quite a bit. He looked around at the seated officers.

"Okay, let's get to it." He smiled. "I'm as surprised as you are." He waited until the laughter stopped. "I knew I was coming up for a command assignment, but I never thought it would happen in the middle of a WestPac deployment. It might take me a little while to get the hang of this ship as compared to the *Providence*, so I'm going to be leaning on you for some help. It's a little strange not having the chance to get acclimated in port."

Jason raised his hand. "Permission to speak, sir."

"Permission granted, Mr. . . ."

"Conley, sir. Jason Conley."

"Oh, yeah, your buddy Mr. McGinty said I should keep an eye on you."

"Um, well, I'm not sure what he—"

"Just kidding. He did say you were friends—went to school together and shared an apartment for a short time in San Diego."

"Yes, sir. I also wanted to say that I fully understand how you feel. The day I set foot on board the ship left for this WestPac deployment. So, we're—"

"In the same boat, so to speak." Ziegler finished Jason's sentence for him, which got some laughs and a grin from Jason.

Off to a good start, he thought. *Certainly more personable than Zhao.*

Ziegler said, "I appreciate everything Lt. Cmdr. Burns has done to keep this operation running smoothly, and he will be invaluable in getting me up to speed. Speaking of which, we'll be getting up to speed tomorrow. We get underway at zero eight hundred. We'll be heading back to the gun line doing the same kind of ops as you did before. Then, we will be getting an R & R visit to Kaohsiung. I understand you got screwed out of your visit earlier in this deployment. We'll make it a delayed New Year's party." He paused. "So, for now, start making preparations for getting underway, hit the clubs in Olongapo one more time, but just be ready to sail at zero eight hundred. I'll be touring the ship with Lt. Cmdr. Burns, so let your men know about our plans and that they have a new captain on board." He paused, again. "Any questions?"

Joe raised his hand. "Joe DiLorenzo, sir. Is it true you're a good basketball player?"

Ziegler smiled. "How did that get out over here? Let's just say I like sports: basketball, softball, flag football, and especially volleyball. I hear there's a good intramural program back in Pearl and at Barber's Point Naval Air Station. I'd like to play, if the teams will have me."

"Count yourself in, sir."

"Anything else? Okay, then let's get to work."

As he stood to leave, Burns announced, "Attention on deck."

Ziegler and Burns left the wardroom.

When the door closed, everyone began talking at once. The overall gist of their conversations was, "This looks way better than before. We caught a break."

EIGHTEEN

South China Sea

NEW YEAR'S DAY 1973

Just one week into his tenure as captain of the *Everett*, Ziegler seemed to have found his niche. He spent most of his time on the bridge, but engineering, CIC, and the deck crews didn't escape his attention. All the men enjoyed talking with him. Unlike his predecessor, Ziegler seemed to be genuinely interested in what they had to say and understood how they felt being pulled away from their homes and families for such an extended period of time. One major thing the officers noticed: meals. He was almost always present. Having the chance to simply converse about matters other than the ship's business was refreshing.

There were two other men who were becoming conditioned to life on board the *Everett* who had come on board just about the same time as Cmdr. Ziegler. Jordan Kleiser and Sam Lee had been working with the gunfire control technicians for the short time the *Everett* was in Subic and were now continuing their work out at sea. Kleiser was a short, stocky, balding man with wisps of reddish hair that he tried to maintain as a comb-over but found this an almost impossible task in a twelve-knot wind while underway. Sam Lee was much younger with straight black hair that always looked as though there was a static electricity field around it. Both were employees of Houston Electronics, a firm known more for its work in the field of handheld calculators than for warfare electronics.

Kleiser and Lee took their meals with the officers and talked about the work they were doing with a great deal of reticence. They stressed that the actual electronics involved were highly classified and the devices being tested would remain as a series of "black boxes" for the duration of their stay. They also said that even though the officers and men would not fully understand how the instruments worked, they would get to see the results of their black box installations in a very graphic manner.

Kleiser and Lee had installed a TV monitor on the bridge that was connected to the devices that were now employed by the gunfire control techs on the ship. What they were able to tell the crew was that they now had the use of a laser-ranging sensor for the ship's gunfire control that was accurate to within one yard at a distance of one mile. They had also installed an infrared sensor that projected an image on the bridge-mounted TV. This was specifically meant to be used as an engine heat detection device during night ops. The *Everett* had been chosen as a test vessel due to its highly active tours of duty on the gunline and for its reputation in maintaining its 5-inch gun.

All this new technology was there to address two of the problems facing the South Vietnamese forces and their US military support groups. One, the North Vietnamese Army was supplying the Viet Cong south of the DMZ by running supply trucks down the beach south of the Bến Hải River at night. Ships at sea were unable to detect their movements in the dark and the South Vietnamese Army was unable to penetrate close enough to conduct an intervention. Second, when US ships were stationed off the mouth of the Bến Hải River at night in preparation for gunfire support, small boats would come out of the river and deploy divers in an attempt to attach mines to the undersides of the hulls of the ships. They hadn't been successful, so far, but it was only a matter of time before one would slip through. Houston Electronics had won the contract to supply the Navy with a way to combat these difficulties.

While the supply truck movement was suspected to be an almost nightly occurrence, the small boats with divers seemed to be more infrequent, occurring primarily under the darkness of a new moon. With the infrared sensor on board, the crew of the *Everett* was poised to find out what was actually happening and had the authority to take interdictive measures. The first test was to be on Jason's mid-watch.

Jason was OOD and Jack Culpepper had the conn. The sky was lit only by the stars and Jason thought it to be a perfect scenario for small boats to be cloaked in darkness to make a stealth attack on the ship. At one o'clock in the morning, the bridge became almost uncomfortably crowded as Captain Ziegler, the XO, Kleiser, Lee, and Doug Kimos piled in to see how the first test would go. Ziegler suggested that those not involved in directly running the ship move outside to the bridge wing. Jason was thankful for that. He was about to suggest that very thing but really couldn't see himself giving Ziegler and the XO an order, even as a suggestion.

Culpepper was giving orders to make minuscule changes in speed and course to maintain position, while Jason kept his eye on the monitor. Most of the time, he was focused on the beach area, but at 1:35 a.m. he noticed four small blips making their way out of the mouth of the Bến Hải River. He stuck his head out the hatch to the bridge wing.

"Captain. XO. I think we have something."

Everyone piled back into the bridge and found a spot with a clear view of the monitor.

Ziegler turned to Jason. "Well, what do you make of this, Mr. Conley."

"A couple of things, sir. First, since this is an infrared image, we're probably looking at the heat signatures of small outboard motors on the sterns of something like a sampan. Second, I know that many times this motor and boat configuration is used by fishermen, so we can't really do anything until we can ascertain their intent."

"How do you plan to do that?"

"We haven't seen evidence of any fishing nets deployed in this area either south or north of the river mouth. And there are definitely none in our immediate vicinity. If they maintain a constant heading toward us, I would have to assume they are not friendlies."

"Would you hail them? Give them a warning?"

"We could do that, sir, but I doubt that they would hear it over the noise of the outboard motors. I've spent my whole life around small boats and it's almost impossible to hear the people next to you in the same boat. Even if they could hear it, they probably wouldn't understand us and we don't have anyone on board who speaks Vietnamese."

Meanwhile, the four boats had formed a line and were continuing on track toward the *Everett*.

Kleiser said, "From a technical perspective, this image looks good. It's working as planned."

Doug Kimos donned the headset for the sound-powered phone and was now in direct contact with both gunfire control and CIC. "Do you have a range and bearing on the first of the small boats?"

From both units he heard, "Aye, sir."

"Stand by. Keep tracking it."

"Aye, sir."

After a few minutes, Jason turned to Ziegler. "Captain, I don't believe they're coming out here to greet us with leis and pineapples."

"I agree, Mr. Conley." He paused and watched the progress of the small boats. They had slowed considerably, but now less than a mile of ocean separated the *Everett* from the boats. "Looks like they're trying to keep the engine noise down."

Jason nodded in agreement.

"You have permission to fire. It'll be on your orders, Mr. Conley."

"Aye, Captain." He looked toward Kimos, then back at the monitor, and then to Kimos again.

Kimos said, "Anything wrong, Mr. Conley?"

"No, sir." He paused. "Fire one round at the lead boat."

Kimos repeated it into the phones.

The 5-inch gun barrel was almost parallel to the surface of the ocean at this point. The roar of the gun broke the silence of the night. Everyone's eyes were fixed on the screen. The front blip flared just ever so slightly. Then, it was gone.

As everyone continued to watch, the three remaining blips became motionless on the screen.

Ziegler said, "I think we have their attention."

Jason nodded. "Fire on what is now the lead boat." Kimos relayed the order. The result was exactly like the first. The last two blips now started to move, the first one ninety degrees to the port of what its former course was, and the rear boat ninety degrees to starboard.

Jason said, "They're splitting up. Fire at the boat now at the approximate bearing of two one zero."

Again, Kimos relayed the order, and again, the blip disappeared.

The last boat had now come about and was heading back toward the river mouth. Jason said to Kimos, "If it was me in that boat and I just saw three boats taken out with three shots, I'd be shitting myself."

Kimos said, "I'd lock the motor in place to run straight and jump over the side. Take my chances with the sharks."

Jason nodded, sighed, and said, "Fire on the final boat."

The gun roared but the blip continued on its track.

Lee said, "Son of a bitch! We missed."

Jason looked at Lee. "No one's perfect. Fire again." The screen went blank.

Jason turned to Ziegler. "Sir, mission complete. Personally, I'll take four out of five."

Ziegler said, "I'd like to have a foul-shooting average that high." He turned to Kleiser and Lee. "That was excellent work by you, gentlemen."

They said simultaneously, "Thank you, sir."

Kleiser added, "Your crew executed things perfectly."

Ziegler said, "I'm going below. Mr. Conley, contact me if other targets appear. I'd like to be on deck for any of the action that involves the testing of this equipment. Also, well done."

"Yes, sir. Thank you, sir."

Ziegler made his way around the helm and headed for the hatch that led to the ladder going below. The quartermaster announced, "The captain has left the bridge."

The XO followed close behind, giving Jason a pat on the back as he departed.

Kimos said to Jason, "Well, that couldn't have gone any better."

"I was glad you were up here to talk to CIC and gunfire control."

"No problem. Wouldn't have missed it. I have this watch tomorrow night. Could be interesting." He took off the headphones and made his way below.

Alone on the bridge wing, Jason thought he had just witnessed a whole new way that combat was going to be conducted in the future. The long-distance shelling that they had been doing had already made him feel guilty in a disconnected way. It certainly wasn't like facing your enemy in a trench just hundreds of yards distant. The whole idea of war following rules, whether by agreed-upon conventions or simply through some moral principles held by an individual human combatant, seemed almost bizarre. *It's okay to kill someone this way, but no, not that way.* Now, watching the action on a TV screen put a whole new twist on it. Yes, it's an electronic blip. But that blip represents a person or persons. Sure, those people were out to do some killing of their own, but this new technology combined parts of old-style, in-your-face warfare and parts of the long-distance warfare of shelling distant targets. You still didn't actually see the enemy, but you did see something that represented their presence. In some ways, it reminded him of the playback he saw during his ASW training. The difference was the playback was 100 percent electronic. There were no people. On the screen he just watched, the blips had been people. Jason found it disquieting. Reality on a TV screen.

Jason caught up with Doug Kimos at lunch in the wardroom the day after Kimos had been on mid-watch.

"So, any action last night?"

"Ha! That's normally a question you might get in port after a night in Olongapo. But, yeah, we detected a truck on the beach. It was pretty bizarre and just a little different from the boats on your watch."

"How so?"

"So, just after zero two hundred hours, I see an image on the screen moving from right to left."

"In other words, north to south on the beach."

"Right. But this time it was an actual image, not a blip. You could actually see a dim outline of a truck with a very bright spot in the area where the hood would be."

"Not just a blip."

"Not just blip. This infrared sensor must be pretty sensitive and I'm sure the truck engine radiates more heat than an outboard." Kimos paused. "So, I call up the captain; he shows up followed by the XO and the Houston Electronics guys. We watch the image for a while, and we know it's not a friendly just from where it is relative to where the South Vietnamese are. Finally, Captain Ziegler says to take it out."

Kimos took a sip of his coffee.

"We were about a mile and a half out, and gunfire control had a lock on it, so I gave the order to fire."

"Last night, the blips just disappeared," Jason said. Was this different?"

"Yep. First, we missed on the first shot. You could actually see a light flare up where the shell exploded just a few yards in front of the truck. The image of the truck stopped moving. Then, in a jerky motion, it started backing up."

"The jerky motion was probably from the driver having a shit fit and not handling the clutch too well as he tried to accelerate too fast in reverse."

"Probably right. Next shot, missed again but even closer right behind it. I'm betting the range was dead on for both shots, so now the driver is probably thinking, 'one in front, one in back . . .'"

"'I'm fucked.'"

"Exactly. And he was. Next shot and the image disappeared."

Jason was nodding his head. "Do you find this kind of weird? You know, being able to see an image of your target but not the people you're killing? It feels different from the long-range targets we shoot at that are miles away, that we can't even see. They are *targets*, not images of what represents a person or people."

Kimos nodded. "I hear you. But you know deep down that when you shoot at a target, a target designated by the coordinates we receive, you are probably killing people."

Jason nodded. "Yeah. It's the *probably* that makes it different. The coordinates we get are for a munitions depot or a supply center, you know, *objects, locations*."

"Objects and locations where there are people. People working to kill other people. I mean, I know none of us has experienced it, but it would be like seeing a radar blip of any enemy ship out at sea on the radar screen or the sonar detection of an enemy sub, like you were trained to do at ASW school. We would fire on it even if we couldn't see it."

Jason was looking down at the tablecloth. "Yeah. Yeah. I get it. I experienced it to a degree with the ASW stuff. It was like a game, although it really shouldn't have felt that way." He looked up at Kimos. "But it does *feel* different. Objectively, it shouldn't. In reality, it does."

Kimos sighed and said, "Well, we're stuck here, and these are the cards we've been dealt."

Jason smiled, "Cards I understand. This feels more like watching Joe play craps in Olongapo. Nothing seems logical and it's tough understanding the rules."

"I hear you, Jason. Just hang in there. In a few more months we're out of this. Back home."

"That'll be good. Hope this feeling doesn't follow me." But he suspected that it would. Not just back home, but for the rest of his life.

NINETEEN

Kaohsiung

JANUARY 1973

Ed stuck his head into Jason and Joe's stateroom. "You ready to meet the mama-san and do some wheelin' and dealin'?"

Jason said, "Yeah, I'll be right there. Meet you in the wardroom."

The *Everett* was docked in Kaohsiung harbor but on the opposite side of the broad bay from where the main part of the town was located. They came into the harbor just two days after New Year's Day. After being at sea for New Year's Eve, the crew was ready for some serious R & R and Ed, Jason, and Chief Gunner's Mate Harold Younger were going ashore in the motor whaleboat to make preparations with the mama-san of the Harbor Hotel for a delayed celebration.

Ed and Jason left the wardroom and stopped by the goat locker to pick up Younger. The three of them made their way to the davits holding the whale boat. Boatswain's Mate First Class Clarke and Boatswain's Mate Third Class Stainton were already there, getting the boat ready for departure. It was easier and faster to take the boat than to circumnavigate the streets around the harbor in a cab. And from the reputation the cabbies had and from what Jason had experienced in Guam, it would be a lot safer.

The boat was lowered, and Stainton released it from the davit hooks when it settled in the water. Clarke, at the helm, wheeled the boat smartly away from the ship. They proceeded slowly because to say the harbor was busy would have been an understatement. Sampans, small motor craft, sailboats, and large freighters all seemed to be moving in random directions vying for space on the glassy surface of the harbor. The noise of trucks, cars, and the shipyard cranes carried across the water of the busy bay and mingled with the odor of diesel fumes and Asian cooking. The whole town was alive and deeply engaged in the day's business.

Jason sat near the bow and studied the face of his helmsman. "Do you know where you're going, Clarke?"

Clarke grinned. "Yes, sir, I checked it all out on a chart before we left. Although I must admit, it's a lot more confusing than it appeared on the chart. More variables in play here."

"I'll say! I've never seen anything quite like this."

"Me neither, sir. First time here."

As they approached the dock on the far side of the harbor, they could see the Harbor Hotel standing just a block inland on a busy street filled with cars, bicycles, scooters, and colorful pedicabs. From Jason's perspective on the boat, the density of people and machines looked impossible to navigate, even for just a block.

As soon as they tied up at the pier and climbed out of the boat, they were surrounded by children of all ages with their hands out asking for money or candy.

Younger said to the group, "As we walk over to the hotel, always know where your wallet and watch are."

Clarke said, "I think it's obvious that Stainton and I need to stay with the boat."

"You got that right," Jason agreed.

The three-man delegation made their way to the hotel with their youthful entourage in tow. The kids didn't give up until the *Everett*'s men were safely inside.

They found themselves in a large waiting room with a check-in desk at the back facing the entrance from the street. The man behind the desk had slicked-back hair and was wearing a gray tailored suit with a black necktie.

"Ah, you are here for Hazel Chen?"

"That's right," Ed replied.

"You follow me, please."

He led them down a short corridor that opened to a huge, two-tiered ballroom. At the far end, across an expansive dance floor, was a large stage. Dead center over the floor, about at the same level as the second tier, hung a classic faceted mirror ball. They were standing beside a mirrored bar that spanned the entire back of the ballroom. Round tables that could hold six to eight people lined the walls under the balcony that made up the second tier. As they walked out to the center of the dance floor, they could see that the second floor was laid out just like the first floor, but the area above the stage held more tables and chairs. Another bar spanned the back wall of the second tier directly above the bar on the first floor.

Ed said, "It looks like they should be able to handle anything we can throw at them."

Jason agreed. "Yeah. This is definitely more than adequate."

As they gazed up at the second-floor bar, a voice behind them said, "Gentlemen. Welcome to the Harbor Hotel."

They turned to find themselves looking at a woman in her forties or fifties, not more than five feet tall, with long hair piled neatly into a bun on the top of her head. She was wearing a simple black dress and a thin gold necklace.

"I am Hazel Chen. I am glad you want to do business here."

Ed said, "Nice to meet you. I'm Ed Snyder, and this is Jason Conley and Harold Younger." As Ed said their names, she bowed ever so slightly towards them.

"Nice to meet you all. You like our ballroom?"

"Very much," said Harold. "I think our crew will like it too."

"We host many parties here."

Jason nodded. "So we've heard. You have a great reputation throughout the fleet."

"That is good to know. Would you like to sit and discuss terms? Would you like a beer?"

"Please. Yes, to both," Ed said.

After Hazel placed an order for their beers with the bartender, they sat at a round wooden table just to the right of the first-floor bar. She folded her hands in front of her on the table and said, "Here is what we offer. Party from eight o'clock to midnight. Six-piece dance band plays rock and roll: four sets. Open bar entire time, beer, mixed drinks, wine. Finger food served by waiters from our kitchen. Hostesses for"—she paused—"companionship and dancing from eight to midnight."

Ed was nodding as she recited this. "That sounds perfect." He turned to Jason and Harold. "What do you guys think?"

Harold said, "Sounds good to me."

Jason nodded.

Ed turned to Hazel. "So, what's the fee?"

"How many men?"

"Around two hundred."

"Eighteen hundred American dollar."

"I've got nine hundred American dollars."

Hazel Chen shook her head. "Then you not have party."

The beers arrived and everyone took a sip. A pause in the negotiations.

Ed said, "Okay, I can do one thousand."

Hazel shook her head.

"C'mon, that's just over four dollars per person. Each person would have to drink more than a half case of beer to use that up."

"Ambience," said Hazel.

Ed looked around. "Ambience," he repeated. "Okay, twelve hundred American dollars, half now and half after the party ends."

Hazel did not shake her head this time. She took a sip of her beer. "Fifteen."

Ed sighed and looked at Jason and Harold. "Okay, split the difference: thirteen hundred and fifty American dollars."

Hazel nodded, raised her glass in a toast, and said, "Deal."

Ed echoed, tapping her glass with his. "Deal."

"Now, I have special bonus for negotiators." She looked around at the three men. "Each negotiator get room and girl for night."

Jason almost spit his beer out. "Night? Like in all night?"

Hazel Chen shook her head. "Room. All night. Girl, for party. After that, up to you. But she be special girl for you. I pick."

Jason said, "Well, that's a nice offer but—" He felt Harold kick him under the table.

"We'll take it," Ed cut in.

They all toasted the finalized deal. Hazel said, "The night of January 5, right?"

"Right."

"Then, seven hundred now and we are good, yes?"

"Yes." Ed pulled out a roll of money, peeled off seven Benjamins, and handed them to Hazel.

"Pleasure doing business, gentlemen. Excuse, please. Must get back to work. Please stay to enjoy your beers." They all stood, and Hazel walked down the corridor toward the front desk.

Ed, Jason, and Harold sat back down. Jason looked at Ed and said in a low voice, "So, where did all that money come from?"

"Norm Shapiro said it all comes from Geedunk sales."

"That's a lot of Hershey bars and Paydays."

Harold said, "A lot of that is from the soda machine. You do know that every time the machine gets reloaded several Olympia beer cans find their way into the machine at random. That way, whenever one of the men goes for a soda, they stand a small chance of getting a beer."

Jason nodded. "So, it's like playing a soda slot machine, except that you get an Oly instead of three cherries and a cash payout."

"Sometimes, the man who pulls the beer does better if he sells it rather than if he drinks it. Quite an auction can happen below decks."

Jason said, "That's pretty cool."

Harold agreed. "Yeah, it's safe too. Even if someone bought out the whole machine, there aren't enough beers in there to get even the smallest sailor buzzed."

Jason looked back at Ed. "So, what were you prepared to spend?"

"What she asked for the first time. I didn't want to spend that much, but I would have gone that high. We can always use the extra cash to do stuff like buy some beers for everybody at one of the pickup softball games back in Subic."

"So, we did all right?" Jason said.

"We did all right," agreed Ed.

That evening, Jason, Ed, and Joe found an interesting little restaurant within walking distance of the pier where the *Everett* was docked. Although the cuisine was primarily Chinese, there was an eclectic mix of European dishes on the menu, such as raclette and tripe stew, and non-Asian desserts, like baked Alaska. Jason was not even sure he knew exactly what baked Alaska was, but he wasn't very interested in dessert, anyway. He was prepared to try something a little more authentic and adventurous.

For a Chinese restaurant, the setting seemed rather formal. The tables were covered with white linen tablecloths and the waiters wore short black dinner jackets over formal white shirts and black bow ties. The place settings appeared to be fine porcelain, and the chopsticks were faux ivory. At least, Jason hoped they were fake. He didn't want to be eating his food with elephant tusk.

They were seated and ordered Taiwan Beer Original before placing their food orders. As they waited for the beers to arrive, they took the time to look around at the other patrons. They were the only Caucasians present. The waiter brought out the brown bottles and some glasses. He opened the bottles in front of them and poured a small amount of beer into Jason's glass, similar to a sommelier presenting wine for tasting and approval. Jason took a sip, nodded, and the waiter poured beer into everyone's glasses. He gave a small bow and took their orders for the first course.

After the waiter left, Joe said to Jason, "Really? Octopus stew?"

"Yeah. Why not?"

"I'm sticking with something more familiar—pork pot stickers."

Ed said, "I was tempted by the jellyfish and cucumbers but played it safe with crispy wontons."

Jason said, "Jellyfish and cucumbers? Right, Ed. Anyway, I'm willing to share."

"Nah, it's all yours."

The waiter returned after a short time with their food. An oddly shaped soup spoon accompanied Jason's stew. He could see large pieces of octopus tentacles swimming in a dark brown broth with green onions and tofu.

"Check out the suckers on these tentacles! A dish that'll really stick to your ribs. And throat. And roof of your mouth."

"Hah! Just like at communion when the priest would give you the host and before you could get back to your pew it was stuck to the roof of your mouth," Joe said.

"The host?" Ed looked puzzled.

Jason explained. "Yeah, it is a dried, very thin wafer that represents the body of Christ. It has been blessed by the priest and only he is allowed to touch it."

Joe said, "Everyone taking communion comes up to the rail in front of the altar and as the priest comes by, you open your mouth and sort of stick out your tongue. He places the host on it and mumbles 'Body of Christ.' You close your mouth and, voilà, there it is, stuck up there like a second skin."

"And since you aren't supposed to touch it, even though it is touching you, you can't poke your finger up there to get it loose." Jason was laughing. "You have to sit in the pew trying to push it loose with your tongue or, God forbid, use your tongue to create a suction on it to pull it loose. That usually just results in clucking noises and dirty looks from your dad."

Ed said, "I had no idea. I'm Presbyterian and we just have what looks like good Italian bread and grape juice."

Jason plucked a tentacle piece out of the stew and tasted it. He discovered it had a very mild fish flavor and was just slightly chewy. The broth was briny with hints of garlic. Delicious. Best of all, it didn't stick to the roof of his mouth.

"You guys missed out. This is great."

The waiter returned. "Is good?"

Jason said, "Yes, is good."

"I take order. More food?"

Joe nodded and said, "We'd like an order of the pineapple spareribs with sweet and sour sauce, an order of orange beef, and prawns with snow peas."

"Very good." He gave a little bow and was off.

Jason had finished his stew and was watching a table of four seated next to them. All were of Asian descent and were conversing in Chinese. *No eavesdropping here*, he thought. As he watched, two waiters wheeled out a brass cart carrying what he assumed was their baked Alaska. It looked large enough to serve four, and from his perspective, appeared to be a huge mountain of browned meringue. One of the waiters was warming cognac in a small copper pan over a Sterno burner while the other was inserting a shot glass at the very peak of the meringue, making it appear to be a dessert volcano.

Jason whispered to Joe and Ed, "Ya gotta check this out."

The waiter with the small copper pan ignited it with a lighter, then began to drizzle it slowly into the shot glass, allowing it to overflow, creating what appeared to be lava. Unfortunately, his hand was not steady enough and accidentally drizzled too much flaming cognac directly onto the meringue, causing it to disintegrate around the shot glass. The glass tilted, then rolled down the mountainside, spewing flaming cognac out of the dish and onto the tablecloth.

The people at the table stood up and screamed. The waiters screamed. Everyone was yelling in panicked Chinese and one of the waiters was fanning the flames with a napkin in a misguided attempt to put it out.

Jason noticed the table next to the conflagration had not yet been set, so he jumped up, pulled the tablecloth off, and draped it over the flaming table. The fire was out.

Stunned into silence, the waiters and customers looked at Jason, then at the table, and then back to him. They started clapping.

"Ahhhh! Yes! Yes! Very good, very good!" The waiters were patting him on the back. Jason held his hands up to indicate, "it's nothing," then put them together as if to pray, gave a little bow, and sat back down with his friends.

He said to Joe and Ed, "Looks like I finally got to use that fire school training."

Their waiter brought out their dishes and set them down for them to eat family style. He looked at the mess at the table beside them, then turned to Jason and gave him a thumbs-up.

The food was delicious and was gone in no time. They decided to pass on dessert but ordered some cognacs. Jason said, "In brandy snifters, please, not on meringue or on fire." The waiter smiled and returned with three cognacs.

After they finished their drinks, Jason asked for the check and the waiter said, "No. No pay. All good."

Jason protested. "No. No, really, we should pay—"

The waiter stopped him. "No. No pay. All good. Have good night." He bowed slightly and disappeared into the kitchen.

Joe looked at Jason. "Thanks, Jason. We always knew you were good for something. Plus, now I have something to write home about."

They left their waiter a huge tip.

A surprise mail delivery caught up with the *Everett* the afternoon of the ship's party at the Harbor Hotel. Jason got several letters from his parents, two from Sparrow, and one from Lori. He sat on the edge of his bunk and opened his parents' letters first, and, as always, caught up on all the news that was happening back home. In other words, not much. Sparrow sounded like she was in a better place, because she was in a better place. She had left the commune and gotten a job at a sandwich shop that had just opened around the corner from the Kuhio Grill. *They sell some sort of Italian sandwich called a* hoagie. *It's crazy here; the college kids can't get enough of them. Ever hear of a* hoagie? Jason smiled to himself. A hoagie? In college he'd eat at least two a week that he'd get from Tony's Deli in Garrett Hill to have for dinner at the radio station on the nights of his show. He was not surprised that she left the commune, but he was surprised that she stayed in Hawai'i, and even more surprised when in the second letter she said she got an apartment in his old building, right next to his old apartment. She was also going back to school part-time at the University of Hawai'i for marine studies. *Good for her.*

He opened Lori's letter and immediately got a bad feeling when he saw it was only one page. She usually wrote missives approaching a novella in length.

Dear Jason,

I don't really quite know how to tell you this, but I won't be coming out to Hawai'i. My old boyfriend from high school is a contractor at the Navy base here in San Diego. I didn't know he was here, but as it turns out, he had rented an apartment in my building. I was at the pool one day and, well, there he was. We just sort of fell back into it, our relationship. I guess I never really stopped having feelings for him. I love you, Jason, but something about this rekindling feels right. I'm sorry, so, so, sorry. Who knew he'd end up here and we'd find each other again. It's a small world . . .

Love,
Lori

Jason was crushed. *It's a small world.* He did *not* need to read that. Was he surprised? No. There was always that feeling in the back of his head that things were never going to work out between them, especially when the WestPac orders had come in. But there was also the feeling that, yeah, why not? This just might work. It had been the most serious relationship he had ever been in with anyone, including his girlfriend from high school. That had been a young love, a first love, a time of discovery for both of them. He smiled as he thought back to that senior year in high school. Magical. Jason sighed and read the letter again. It didn't take long. The letter was short and bittersweet. *Should I write back? What would I say?* There was nothing to say. He could feel his eyes tearing up as he thought about them in Maui, the "drive-in movies," even "It's a Small World." Fuck. Just fuck.

The door to the stateroom opened and Ed stuck his head in.

"Hey."

"Hey."

"You don't look too good. Things okay at home?"

"Yeah. No problems at home. But . . ." Jason wasn't sure he could say it without crying.

Ed stepped into the stateroom. "But, what?"

"I just got a 'Dear Jason' letter from Lori."

"Oh, fuck no."

"Fuck, yes."

"I am so sorry, man."

"Yeah. Me too."

"Anything I can do? I know it's sort of useless for me to say since we're halfway around the world from—"

"Yeah, from her. Nah. I'll be all right . . . in a bit." Jason looked up from the letter at Ed. "We got a party to go to tonight, right?"

"Right."

"Open bar, right?"

"Right."

"Well, then, we better get ready. I'll see if I can self-medicate myself back into a better mood."

Jason, Ed, and Harold Younger caught the first shuttle from the *Everett* over to the Harbor Hotel. Before disembarking, Jason double-checked with Clarke to make sure the schedule was in place for boatswain's mates to be available for shuttle service throughout the night. He assured Clarke that his men would be compensated with extra time off in the final two ports of call the *Everett* was scheduled to visit before returning to Pearl: Hong Kong and Yokosuka, Japan.

They met Hazel Chen at the front desk after shedding the entourage of begging children once again. She gave them each a key to a room, Jason 609, Ed in 610, and Harold in 611.

"Come, we meet your girls." They followed Hazel through the corridor to the ballroom.

Waiting by the bar in the ballroom were three Asian girls, one much taller than the other two. In fact, Jason thought she may have been the tallest Asian he had seen on this trip. She was wearing a black miniskirt with a red blouse and had her hair cut straight across so that it just touched her shoulders. She was beautiful, as were the other two women. Hazel introduced her as Lola; she bowed slightly as her name was said.

Lola had eyes only for Harold Younger and announced, "I want big Black man, okay?"

Harold nodded enthusiastically.

Jason said to Ed, "Chief's always had a way with words."

Lola came over to Harold, took him by the hand and said, "You get me drink?"

Harold, still nodding, said, "Me get you drink," and they moved over to where the bartender was standing behind the bar.

Hazel looked at the remaining girls, then over to Ed and Jason.

"Meet Susie and Cathy."

Susie had long black hair down to her waist and was wearing a form-hugging white satin dress with a slit halfway up her left thigh. Cathy had her hair tied back in a long ponytail and was wearing a dark blue miniskirt with a black blouse. Susie came over to Jason and put her arms around his waist.

"We have fun tonight, yes?"

Jason, smiling, said, "Yes, I think we will. Let's start with a drink." They walked over to the bartender with Jason's arm around Susie's shoulders.

Ed looked at Cathy. "Guess it's you and me, Cathy."

"Sound good to me."

As they headed to the bar, Ed said, "Thanks, Hazel."

"You welcome, Ed."

The band was setting up, doing sound checks, and getting the lighting in place. Several Fender guitars were on stands in front of large Ampeg amplifiers lined across the stage, and the drummer was testing the mic position on his double-bass drum Ludwig kit. Jason thought they at least *looked* ready to unleash some serious rock and roll.

Jason and Susie found some seats at a table halfway between the bar and the stage but facing the stage so Jason could watch the set up that was going on.

Susie said, "What's your name?"

"Jason."

"Jason? Unusual name, yes?"

"Somewhat. Not as common as 'Joe.'"

Susie playfully slapped him on the shoulder. "Oh, you funny guy. Everybody 'Joe' to us until we get to know you."

"Can I take a guess that Susie is not your real name?"

"Why you say that?"

"Just a guess."

"Well, you smart man. My real name is Li."

"That's pretty, why not use that?"

"Hazel Chen thinks sailors want taste of home. Use American names."

"Does 'Li' have any special meaning in Chinese?"

"It means 'pretty' or 'beautiful.'"

"Well, your parents sure got that right."

Susie turned away slightly, blushing. "Thank you, Jason."

The Harbor Hotel ballroom was starting to fill up as the shuttle continued its service and some of the men grabbed cabs to come around from the far side of the harbor. Jason was wondering how many would spend the night at the hotel with no curfew as there was in Olongapo. He was guessing quite a few.

Jack Culpepper, with a "date" in tow, arrived at the table and said, "Mind if we join you? This is Sandra." Sandra was wearing a satiny blue dress with a dragon embroidered on the side from her shoulder to the hemline.

Jason said, "Sure." And as they sat, he looked at Jack and said, "You moved quickly."

Jack grinned. "No time to waste!"

The band cranked up a version of "Proud Mary" and soon the dance floor was filled with gyrating bodies, men ready to let loose after being away at sea and on the gunline for months on end.

Jason and Li had another drink, Jason with a whiskey sour again, and he figured Li was being served ginger ale with a maraschino cherry. Whatever. He was having fun and forgetting, almost, the letter he'd received earlier in the day. As the first notes of Percy Sledge's "When A Man Loves A Woman" started, he grabbed Li's hand and said, "C'mon. This is my favorite slow dance. I can't believe they're playing it."

Jason held her close as they swayed to the rhythm and sighed.

Li looked up. "Why sigh? You okay?"

"Yeah, I'm good. I'm okay."

After the dance, they found Ed and Cathy. "You guys having a good time?"

Ed smiled. "You bet. This was worth every penny."

Jason said, "The band is fucking awesome." He looked at Li, "Pardon my French."

"That not French."

Jason laughed. "Yeah, you got me there."

A waiter came around with plates of crispy fried wonton and mini egg rolls. Jason said, "Just what I need to soak up some of this whiskey."

Ed agreed. "Yeah. I hear ya. They make a good drink here." He took a drink as Cathy and Li sipped their ginger ales.

The drinking, eating, and dancing continued for several hours. At some point, Jason excused himself to use the head. He pushed open the swinging door and looked at the row of sinks lining the right side of the bathroom. Half of them were filled with vomit. One was in the process of being filled by a sailor he recognized as one of his deck crew. As the man was retching, his glasses slid off his face and plopped into the bowl. The man fished them out, wiped them off on his shirttails and put them back on his face. Shaking his head, Jason moved to the other side and found a reasonably clean urinal to use. Even there, it seemed as though any porcelain receptacle was a target for barf. As he zipped up, Jason thought, *Well, at least they're having a good time, for now. The morning might be a different story.*

Around eleven Jason said to Li, "I think I've had enough for one night. I'm ready to turn in. I have a room here."

Li said, "You want me to stay?"

Jason said, "Yes, I would like you to stay. Very much."

"Okay. We go upstairs."

They said their farewells to Ed and Cathy. Ed said, "Right behind you."

They found the elevator in the lobby and punched in button number 6. On the way up Jason hugged Li and gave her a kiss. Li smiled. Walking down the hallway, Jason could feel the whiskey at work, but found room 609 without a problem, and even opened the door without fumbling around with the key.

The room was small with a metal-frame queen size bed, a small chest of drawers, and a small bathroom with a sink, toilet, and open shower with a drain in the floor. Pretty rudimentary, but, after all, it was free.

Jason faced Li. "Okay, I've never had this sort of arrangement. How does it work?"

"You give me twenty dollar and I stay the night."

"That simple?"

Li nodded.

"Okay." Jason fished out a twenty dollar bill from his back pocket and Li slipped it into a small purse she had placed on the chest. He placed his arms around her, found the zipper at the back of her dress and slowly pulled it down. The dress slipped quietly off Li's shoulders and fell around her feet. He was surprised to discover she was totally naked. *I guess she came ready for action*, he thought.

Jason unbuttoned his polo shirt and pulled it over his head. Li said, "You get undressed and in bed. I need to get ready." She grabbed her purse and went into the bathroom and shut the door. Jason did as he was instructed. Naked, he climbed under the covers to wait for Li to come out of the bathroom.

And, promptly passed out.

TWENTY

South China Sea

ONE WEEK AFTER KAOHSIUNG

Jason and Ed stood on the bridge as the sun was setting, the horizon a mix of crimson and orange fading up to a deep blue. Admiring the scenery was not the primary reason Ed and Jason were up on the bridge wing, although it was quite stunning. Ed had Jason along with him to take his evening fix, shooting the stars with a sextant. Jason had expressed an interest in learning how to use it, so Ed had taught him how to sight a star, use the index arm to bring the star's image in the mirror down to the horizon, and then take the resulting angle reading into the chart room behind the main part of the bridge to use the huge book of tables to plot the ship's location. At first, the precise "three-point fix" was a little elusive, but with practice, Jason was soon matching Ed's fixes.

After they plotted the location for that evening, Ed said, "You know, when we get back to port, I'm due to return to the Coast Guard. My exchange program is done. Have you thought about becoming the ship's navigator? I mean, there's more to it than doing a star fix, but they have a good school back in Pearl out on Ford Island that you can go to. It's a good job to have on a ship. Also, in general, the quartermaster crew is great to work with."

"Yeah, I can see that, and that sounds like something I'd like to do."

"Okay. Let me bring it up to Captain Ziegler and we'll set this thing in motion. You don't want to be deck officer forever."

"Got that right. I mean, it's not a bad job, but your position is infinitely more interesting. And if I'm going to be on here for at least another year after we get back, I'd rather do it as navigator."

They left the red-lit chart room and stepped back onto the bridge, now encased in the black of night. A new moon this evening. The red light of the chart room kept their eyes adapted to the dark, so they were still able to see everything clearly on the darkened bridge. They stayed just long enough to log the fix and then headed down to the wardroom to catch whatever movie was being shown for the night. One disadvantage as navigator was that you almost always missed at least the first half hour of the film. Of course, since the films were not new releases, it was probably something you had already seen.

As they were walking down the passageway to the wardroom, they could hear the distinctive music from Sergio Leone's *The Good, the Bad, and the Ugly*. They stopped, looked at each other, and said, "Seen it," simultaneously.

Ed said, "Let's go up on the flight deck and play some music."

"Sounds good. Got any more brownies? No watch to stand tonight."

"Sorry. My supplier's getting to be a bit unreliable. Maybe it's because I told her that sometimes they might put some sniffer dogs on the mail bags."

"I think that's more likely for the mail heading home. There's a fair amount of quality stuff being sold in Vietnam."

Jason grabbed his Gibson and Ed picked up his inexpensive-but-playable Yamaha that he'd bought at the Subic Exchange, and they headed for the flight deck. They sat on the edge of the deck and played a few Buffalo Springfield tunes that Jason had taught Ed.

"You know what you said up on the bridge wing about getting transferred back to the Coast Guard after we get back from WestPac?"

"Yeah."

"Well, you're not the only one who's departing. I think the XO's leaving, Joe will be outta here, Barnaby will be gone. It's gonna be a whole new wardroom."

"Yeah. Pretty much."

"Do you know yet where you're going?"

"Probably back to the West Coast. They might keep me in Hawai'i, but that's not likely. I did stop them from doing one thing."

"What was that?"

"They were going to send me to the Coast Guard station on Johnston Atoll; it's an unaccompanied tour. The only bennie is that you get an extra month's leave after doing a year there." Ed shook his head. "I killed that idea *mucho pronto*." He looked at Jason. "Wait. You've been there, right?"

"Yeah, twice for a total of six weeks. That's about as much as I could take of it." Jason was shaking his head. "But a whole year? There's two ways I'd do that—"

"No way and no fuckin' way." Ed finished his sentence for him.

"Right."

"So, what was it like?"

"Well, I don't know what the Coast Guard does there. There's certainly not a lot of coast to guard. But for us, we were there to escort munitions ships through the channels between the formations of table coral as they brought loads of toxic weapons from Okinawa to be buried deep into the coral of the main island below the base. It was called Operation Red Hat and basically it was to get rid of some really nasty stuff. Whenever a ship was in, we had to carry a gas mask around with us and be ready to use a pressure-activated atropine needle to counteract the effects of an accidental release of nerve or mustard gas."

"Sounds pleasant."

"The first day in, we had to take a class on chemical warfare weapons. Saw some lovely photos and film of what chemical agents can do to a human. Then, we had to prove that we would stick ourselves with the needle if necessary. After seeing the pictures, I didn't have any qualms about sticking myself with a needle. That would have been the least of my worries."

"How'd they make sure you'd go through with the needle stick?"

"So, they passed around these needle cartridges. The needle was spring loaded and attached to a vial of atropine. At least, that's what the real deal had. There were about thirty of us in the class. One of the cartridges was loaded with saline; the others were dummies, wouldn't fire the needle. On the count of three, everyone had to slam the cartridge down on their thigh. 'One, two, three!' I brought mine down quickly and didn't feel a thing. However, the guy next to me screams out like someone just cut off his foot; the needle went right through his pant leg."

"That was close."

"Yeah. One away." Jason paused. "Other than that, they did their best to try to keep you entertained while you were there. In fact, it's funny that *The Good, the Bad, and the Ugly* is playing tonight in the wardroom. I saw it twice there, once on each visit. They had a big outdoor screen set up to show a movie every night after dinner. Sorta like a drive-in without the cars."

Ed said, "Or the girls."

"Right, no women on the island. Except a female seal."

"You mean like a circus-balancing-a-ball-on-the-nose seal, not a Navy SEAL."

"Yeah. The seal was kinda scary. They had Sailfish and Sunfish sailboats there that you could take out. As soon as you launched off the ramp, caught the wind and really got underway, the seal would slip into the water and start to follow you around, like it was waiting for you to tip over so it could bite you. Having the seal behind me made me a better sailor. I mean, it never bit anyone." Jason started laughing. "Well, no one except this crazy guy named Sanders."

"How did he get nailed?"

"So, the seal always seemed to be on the boat ramp."

"To keep an eye out for the guys taking the sailboats out."

"That's what we all figured. Seals are pretty smart. It's also where she slept every night. One night we were coming back from the enlisted men's club and one of the guys was dead drunk. Not unusual. We had to walk by the ramp to get back to the ship, and as we passed by, Sanders, who happened to be the drunk of the night, says, 'I'm gonna pet the seal.' We tried to talk him out of it—told him he was drunk and to leave the fuckin' seal alone. But he insisted, 'No, no, it wants to be petted. It's lonely.' So, before we could stop him, he goes over and pets the seal. Gotta give him credit; he actually did it."

"What did the seal do?"

"It wakes up, whips around so fast we could barely see what was happening, chomps down on Sanders' hand and shakes it as hard as she can, like a dog going after a stuffed toy. She lets go and starts 'arfing' at him. He falls down and does his best to back away while he's sitting on his ass. He was a mess. Blood everywhere—on him, on the ramp. We grab him under the armpits, keeping a close eye on the seal, who has now settled back down after teaching Sanders a lesson, and pull him up and away. We got him over to the dispensary, where it takes twenty stitches to sew him up. They wrapped a bandage around his hand that was so big it looked like a white first baseman's mitt."

Ed said, "Ah, the wonders of alcohol. It gives you courage. Stupid courage, but courage, nonetheless."

"There was certainly no shortage of alcohol. Besides the movies, sailboats, and drinking, there were three other activities they had there to stave off boredom: snorkeling, mountain ball, and bowling."

"What's mountain ball?"

"It's a strange form of softball that you play with a ball that's a little bigger than a normal softball. It's also *very* soft. It sort of *gives* when you squeeze it. Home plate is a big square piece of wood set in the ground. The pitcher has to lob the ball so that it has an arc of greater than three feet from where it leaves his hand. If it lands on the plate, it's a strike. Forget going for the home run ball. Chief Younger could hit that ball as hard as he possibly could, and it would probably just clear the infield. You basically had to just punch it to wherever there was a hole in the defense and then leg it out to first. And you could overrun every base."

"Not just first?"

"Not just first. The field was strips of sod layered on top of coral. If you slid, it would peel up like winding back the top on a tin of sardines leaving the coral exposed. You'd shred the hell out of your leg or arm, or whatever else made contact with the coral. That's all the island was: coral and sand just a foot or two above sea level. The only other thing there besides military buildings was a clump of six pathetic palm trees we called 'The National Forest.'"

Jason laughed at the memory, then continued. "The snorkeling was great there. Pristine. Huge clumps of table coral that were about a foot deep at the top, but the sides dropped sharply away to a sandy bottom, maybe twenty to thirty feet deep. It's where I saw my first shark. A whitetip about eight feet long. I had just lowered myself over the side of our boat. I stuck my head in the water, looked down, and there it was directly below me. I was back in the boat so fast I didn't even have time to get wet."

Ed laughed. "Sounds like a line in a weird country song. 'The Ballad of Ole Whitetip.'"

"We saw a lot of them after that, but they didn't pay any attention to us. They were very well fed because the base would dump the day's garbage at the leeward end of the island and the sharks would scarf it down."

Ed was shaking his head. "Still, a shark's a shark."

"Well said. Anyway, our main activity at night, besides drinking, was bowling. We did a lot of bowling. Every night. Five games with beer frames. So, I guess we actually combined our two favorite activities."

"Yeah, they're not mutually exclusive. Were you any good?"

"Got my average up to between one eighty and one ninety and had a high score of two twenty-six. The third set of games were always the best. By that time, you were warmed up and in a groove, but after that you got a little tired and the beer would make its presence felt. After bowling, my friend Sid would take me as a guest to the enlisted club, where we'd bowl some more on a table-top machine."

"You mean sort of like a shuffleboard table but with pins?"

"No, in this one you actually rolled a wooden ball about the size of a softball. A normal softball, not a mountain ball. The 'pins' hung down from an overhead compartment and they would fold back up against the top if they were electronically 'hit.' You could put spin on the ball and everything. Sid and I never lost. After we got tired of the challenges, we would relinquish the table to some of the other guys." Jason paused. "Fuck, we drank a lot of beer."

"But I'm guessing you didn't pay for much of it."

"Right. We didn't. There was one drawback to all this; the captain was pissed that I spent so much time with the enlisted guys. He didn't know that we were all in a band together and that I hung out with them in Waikiki all the time. But on the small atoll, everybody knew everybody's business. It didn't come across well on my personnel records." Jason paused. "Well, that's all behind me now. Being with you and Joe and the rest of the guys on the *Everett* has been great."

"With the exception that we're in the South China Sea and getting shot at."

"Yeah. It would be much better if we were cruising around Hawaiʻi, making ports of call at the other islands."

"Dream on."

"The best part of Johnston Atoll was the food. It was out-fuckin'-standing. When I was in NROTC, I spent three weeks at Corpus Christi Naval Air Station. They had award-winning mess halls there. Navy bases around the world have an annual mess hall competition and Corpus comes in first just about every year. Johnston Atoll was just as good. Between the beer and food, I put on more than a few pounds there."

"Well, now you're on the WestPac diet."

"It's working wonders. Speaking of which, I wonder what's for mid-rats? Hope it's chili."

"C'mon. Let's check it out."

When they arrived in the wardroom, they were surprised to see Lt. Cmdr. Archie Burns there, along with Joe.

Jason asked, "XO! What brings you to the wardroom at this time of night?"

"I've been in CIC communicating with Seventh Fleet about arranging a rendezvous with the *Flint* tomorrow morning. In fact, Conley, I believe you have the watch then."

"Why are we hooking up with the *Flint*, sir? We just left port a few days ago."

"Funny you should mention that because having been in port has everything to do with why we need to VERTREP with the *Flint*. We need antibiotics."

Ed looked puzzled, at first. "Antibiotics, sir? Why would we . . . ohhhh."

Jason said, "Ah, the gift you can't declare at customs. I believe we may have a plumbing problem."

The XO shot him a look. "You're correct, Conley. About half of the crew that stayed overnight at the Harbor Hotel have 'the drip.'"

"Hmmm, certainly nothing to *clap* about."

"Hey, didn't you and Ed here stay over? Everything okay 'below decks?'"

"Yes, sir. Clean as a whistle. In fact, she didn't even blow my whistle."

"Thanks for sharing. How about you, Snyder?"

"Got everything wrapped up and under control. No problemo."

"Anyway, Conley. We won't need to come alongside as though we're doing a full UNREP. About one hundred feet will be more than close enough."

"Aye, sir."

"By the way, not only will we be taking on the antibiotics, but we'll be sending over something of our own."

Ed was curious. "What could we possibly need to send over to the *Flint*?"

The XO paused before he answered. "Not a 'what.' A 'who.'"

"Is it Horton? The *Flint's* making a port call in Whoville?" Jason could not resist.

"What?"

"Never mind, sir."

"Are you ever serious, Conley?"

Everyone wisely did not answer.

"Anyway," Archie continued, "the *Flint* is headed back into Subic as soon as we break away."

"Who gets to take a chopper ride?" Joe broke the silence.

"It's confidential. It's a medical condition."

Jason said, "Well, we'll all know tomorrow who it is when they're waiting on the flight deck."

"You're right, I suppose. It's Seaman Recruit Horowitz."

"What's wrong with him?"

"I believe I said it's confidential." The XO stared at Jason. "Let's just say that he has a serious eye problem."

A full minute passed before Jason said, "Don't tell me. He has clap of the eye?"

"I didn't tell you. You guessed."

"Clap of the eye! I don't believe it. How the hell does that happen?"

Ed said, "Sounds like he 'snorkeled' below the waterline."

"He obviously forgot his mask," Jason said.

Joe was shaking his head. "Considering how much, shall we say, *traffic* passes through that tunnel, I can't imagine chowing down."

Ed said, "Maybe she gave him a blow job and he thought he should reciprocate?"

The XO finally said, "Are you guys done?"

"Um, yes sir. I believe we are. Snyder? DiLorenzo? Are we good?" They both nodded.

The XO said, "Okay. I'm hitting the rack. Conley, I'll see you on the bridge tomorrow morning. Our rendezvous is set for zero nine hundred hours."

"Aye, sir."

"DiLorenzo. You're taking on the mid coming up, right?"

"Aye, sir."

The captain and I have amended the standing orders. There's a new course and speed to get us close to the *Flint*."

"Aye, sir."

"And by the way, if you hear any scuttlebutt about this situation with Horowitz, tell whoever it is that's spreading it to knock it off."

Jason said, "I'll keep an eye out for it, sir."

The XO sighed, turned, and left the wardroom.

Ed said, "Well, I hope Horowitz learned his lesson."

"I understand he's one good pupil," Jason said.

"I wouldn't talk about Horowitz to anyone. He could lash out at you," Joe said.

"Okay. I'll keep a lid on it."

The next morning, at precisely nine o'clock, the chopper from the *Flint* delivered the much-needed medication and poor Seaman Recruit Horowitz was airlifted off the *Everett* along with all his belongings, whisked away, never to be heard from again.

Many of the men would be out of commission for the next port of call: Hong Kong. While the symptoms of gonorrhea may disappear relatively quickly, it can sometimes be up to a month or more before an individual can be declared cured and noninfective.

However, before Hong Kong, the *Everett* would have a few more weeks on the gunline. They spent most of their time off the coast of Quang Tri in the South China Sea perfecting the use of the infrared sensor and camera and the laser-ranging capabilities of the new fire control system. When the whole setup was finally deemed a success, Jordan Kleiser and Sam Lee were air-lifted to the *Providence*, which was set to make one last visit to Subic before heading home to San Diego via Yokosuka, Japan.

The small boats stopped coming out of the river all-together, and the sightings of supply trucks dwindled to a trickle.

TWENTY-ONE

South China Sea and Hong Kong

FEBRUARY 1973

The day before setting sail for Hong Kong, Jason, Clarke, Stainton, and Seaman Recruit Jefferson made one last boat trip into the base at Da Nang to pick up mail and movies to distribute to the other ships on the gunline. It was Jefferson's first time going ashore in Nam, and his nerves were showing as he unhooked the boat from the davits.

Clarke was watching him carefully. "Don't worry, Jefferson. We'll be in and out of there in no time."

Jefferson didn't look consoled. "Actually, I'm more worried about coming alongside all those ships in these choppy seas we have today."

Jason said, "How many times have you been in the whale boat, Jefferson? Twice? Three times"

"Twice, sir. But that was in Kaohsiung Harbor hauling the guys back from having a good time. The most difficult thing on that duty was watching guys puke over the side."

Jason laughed. "You'll be fine. We approach all the ships on their leeward side. Smooths things out a lot."

They docked the boat and made their way to a Quonset hut at the end of the pier where a sailor in dungarees and a grimy white T-shirt sat sweating behind a large desk.

Jason said, "We're from the *Everett* to pick up mail and movies for the ships on the gunline."

The man looked up and simply nodded his head toward the corner of the office area where canvas bags were stacked in a pile. It took them several trips to haul all the sacks back to the whale boat. As Stainton and Jefferson cast off, Jason said to Clarke, "Sociable guy, wasn't he?"

"He looked pretty burned out, sir. Not much on military protocol, either."

"I'm guessing that's not all that unusual here, Clarke." Jason looked back toward the hut. "This is probably our last time here, and that's fine by me."

"I'm with you, sir."

They made their deliveries and movie trades to five other ships without incident, then returned to the *Everett* for a much-welcomed mail call.

Joe, Ed, and several other officers sat around the wardroom table as the mail was distributed. Ed, in particular, had a healthy stack of envelopes. Jason had four: one each from Lori, his parents, Sparrow, and again from his old girlfriend at Villanova.

Jason nodded to the stack in front of Ed. "Those all from Chelsea?"

Ed grinned. "Yeah, for the most part."

Jason looked wistful. "Must be nice." He opened the one from Lori first. In the letter, she tried to rationalize her decision about dropping him and going with her old boyfriend. It all sounded pretty lame to Jason and just pissed him off. He finished it, crumpled it up into a ball and made a nice toss across the wardroom into the trash can.

Joe was watching him. "Not good, huh?"

"Not good."

"Nice shot, though."

"Thanks."

Sparrow's letter cheered him somewhat. She was still at the hoagie shop, but was getting set for her first full semester at U of H. He hoped she would stick with it this time. The letter from his old girlfriend filled him in on some news about friends they had in common, but certainly didn't sound like there would ever be a reunion such as the one Lori was having with her ex.

He opened the one from his parents last. It was a response to the letter he had written to them after seeing the Bob Hope Christmas Special in Subic back in December. *Bob Hope! You actually got to see Bob Hope in person!* This made Jason smile. He thought back to all the times he had watched the Bob Hope specials on TV with his parents. They were big fans of Hope, Crosby, Benny, and all the other greats from their era. Seeing him in person had been so much better.

It was a hot and humid sunny day when Hope and his troupe were to play before the sailors and marines. Jason, Joe, and Ed had ventured over to the ball field where a stage had been set up. They were in civvies, so they had to sit in the bleachers out of view from the cameras that were there to capture images of all the men in uniform in the area directly in front of the stage. It felt almost surreal seeing Hope in person, on stage trading one-liners with Jill St. John, who looked particularly impressive in person, after having watched her so many times on the tube. Jim Nabors ambled out to trade a few lines in his goofy Southern drawl and then burst into song with his incredible, deep baritone voice. Talk about surreal. Lola Falana shook things up, literally, and the men went crazy. Finally, Redd Foxx took the stage with a set of jokes considerably more risqué, and funnier, Jason thought, than Hope's. They'd be on the cutting room floor after they edited the film for the TV special.

His parents wrote that this was Hope's last trip to the Vietnam war zone since things were winding down and there were fewer troops to entertain. They were trying to remember how many times Hope had ventured into the war zone to perform, bringing a huge cast of singers, dancers, comedians, and of course, Les Brown and his Band of Renown. Jason knew it was his ninth trip. He was glad that it would be Hope's last.

Jason was on the bridge early on a bright sunny morning to witness their entry into Hong Kong harbor. He was astounded at all the polished, high-rise buildings lining the water in the harbor, yet on the hillsides just a short distance behind them, terraced fields and run-down shacks climbed their way up the steep slopes. An odd juxtaposition of wealth and poverty. He would discover this to be a recurring theme.

Their arrival in Hong Kong was a special event in another way. Since the ceasefire agreement from the Paris talks had been signed on January 27, it appeared that the *Everett*'s combat role was over. They were to complete their WestPac assignment simply as a presence in the South China Sea. No one really believed it was the end of all hostilities. There were already reports of combat occurring on a regular basis between the North and South Vietnamese. However, the United States was taking a much less active role. The *Everett* would be spending most of its time making observations with their special sensory array, similar to what they had been doing along the coast near Quang Tri.

As navigator in training, Jason watched how Ed coordinated all his men to take the sightings needed for navigating the extremely congested body of water. Since it was a formal visit, and the beginning of February, the entire crew, except for those integrally involved in the sea and anchor detail, was in service dress blues standing at attention along the lifelines. Jason was unaware that Hong Kong would be the only place in his entire Navy career where he would be decked out in this dress uniform. They knew this stop was on their itinerary before they left Pearl, so they had packed away their formal gear for this one-time event.

Captain Ziegler and Lt. Cmdr. Archie Burns were on the bridge wing taking it all in. Jason, Joe, and Ed Ziegler stood next to them, also enjoying the view. As he scanned the harbor, Ziegler said, "This seems like déjà vu since I just did this same trip with the *Providence* a short time ago, right before I came on board the *Everett*. It's a different feeling, though, when you're in command of the ship."

"I'm sure it is, sir. We're glad to have you aboard," Archie replied.

"Do you have your introductory speech and warnings ready to deliver to the crew before we turn them loose?"

"Yes, sir," Archie confirmed. "All set. As you know, it's mainly a list of all the places that are off-limits, primarily shops run by the Red Chinese."

Ziegler looked at him, grinning. "You know, and I know, that a lot of these men are actually going to be taking notes. I wouldn't be surprised if some of the officers make a run for the shops selling Cuban cigars."

"Yes, sir. There are a few that come to mind," Archie said, giving Jason, Joe, and Ed a pointed look. "Three, in particular."

The three men kept quiet, their eyes innocently staring out across the harbor.

"On a different subject, when the *Providence* was in, we had the whole ship painted out by Hong Kong Harbor Mary. Saved the men in First Division a lot of work, not to mention they did a great job."

"I believe Mr. Conley and Petty Officer Clarke are on that, sir."

Jason confirmed, saying "Yes, sir. We'll get that done."

The *Everett* anchored in the middle of the harbor, in sight of the Kai Tak International Airport, known for its runway that jutted out into the harbor so that when passengers were landing, they had the feeling they were actually coming down to land on the water of the harbor itself. Once the quarterdeck was established, visitors were welcome, with an escort, to board the ship.

The first guest was there on official business: Hong Kong Harbor Mary.

Mary's painting barge came alongside, and the diminutive Mary, dressed in paint-splattered coveralls that seemed two sizes too large for her, scampered up the ladder. Waiting at the top of the ladder were Jason and Petty Officer First Class Clarke.

Jason bowed slightly. "Welcome aboard, Mary. May I call you 'Mary?'"

"Yes. Yes, please. Mary my name."

Jason nodded. "This is Petty Officer Clarke. He'll be making the trade arrangements with you regarding the paint-out of the ship."

Clarke, following Jason's lead, bowed slightly and said, "Nice to meet you, Mary. Would you like to go below to see what we have to offer you for your services?"

"Yes. Would like very much to do that."

Clarke looked at Jason. "If you'll excuse us, sir, I'll take Mary forward to the line locker to see what we can arrange. We've been saving our old line for this moment for a long time."

"Very good, Clarke. When you're finished, call me to the quarterdeck and we can finalize the deal. If it works out as we hoped, First Division will be on extended liberty to make up for the time they had to put in while we were in Kaohsiung."

"Aye, sir."

"And Clarke. Let's keep this deal as legal as possible, as in no retrograde."

"Shell casings, sir?" Clarke looked offended. "Not from us, sir."

"Uh, huh. Carry on."

"Yes, sir."

Jason watched them as they made their way forward. He was pretty sure Clarke was going to use some retrograde, anyway. He just didn't want to know about it. Officially.

About an hour later, Jason was called to the quarterdeck. Clarke and Mary were there waiting for him.

Jason said, "Good news, Clarke?"

"Yes, sir. The entire hull, including the numbers, will be painted out by Mary's crews on their barges. If for any reason they have to come on deck, escorts will be provided, although it's very unlikely they'll need to. Her barge crews are pretty amazing. Back when I was a third class I saw them work here."

Mary bowed. "It is an honor to work here. Mr. Conley. Clarke is very nice man. Drive a hard bargain."

Clarke was shaking his head. "She's been at this too long for anyone like me to 'drive a hard bargain.'"

Mary said, "I go now. Get crews ready for work." They watched her as she scampered down the ladder.

"Okay, Clarke. Let's give the men the news that, unless they have some other duty, such as a quarterdeck watch, they are free to be on liberty for the four days we're here in Hong Kong."

Clarke said, "I know they'll be glad to hear the news, sir."

Jason made his way back to the wardroom to see if Joe and Ed were hanging out there, waiting for the XO's announcement. He heard the 1MC crackle to life as he opened the door. Ed and Joe were seated at the table. Joe had a pen and paper in front of him.

Jason smiled. "I see you're ready to be the secretary for today's little tour guide speech."

"All set. Cuban cigars, here we come."

"Sounds good. I'm ready to do some shopping. Looking for another lens for the Nikon."

Joe said, "I'm looking to buy a jade and marble carved chess set."

Ed looked at him quizzically. "I didn't know you played chess."

"I don't. I just thought it would look good sitting on my coffee table at home."

Ed looked at Jason, then back to Joe. "Okay. Whatever floats your boat."

The three of them listened to the XO drone on for about fifteen minutes, making notes on some particular shops and areas they did not want to miss. When he was finished talking, Ed said, "It was really nice of him to compile all those off-limit places for us."

Jason said, "Very considerate. Just don't thank him for doing it. Let's get in our civvies. I think this is going to be very different from everything else we've seen so far."

TWENTY-TWO

Hong Kong Liberty

EARLY FEBRUARY 1973

The water taxi delivered Jason, Joe, and Ed to a dock that was within walking distance of the shops they were interested in visiting. As they walked along the streets in the shadows of tall business buildings and hotels, they were struck by the incongruity of the extremes that existed between the "haves" and the "have nots." Many of the office buildings and shops had recessed entryways that were draped with tarps and other makeshift shelters, homes for the homeless directly in the face of the affluent. For Jason, it was the most extreme division of wealth he had ever seen. Just about every other building had one to three people huddled under tarps, either looking for handouts or curled up in what had to be a fitful sleep.

Given what they were witnessing, they all felt a bit guilty about entering a tailor shop that had been recommended by the water taxi pilot. Buying a custom-made suit seemed like an extreme luxury as compared to what many of the street people were wearing. Once inside, they were confronted by walls that were stacked with bolts of what seemed to be every cloth available to the human race. An Asian man in a short-sleeved white shirt and nicely tailored black pants with a tape measure draped around his neck greeted them.

"Welcome! You come to buy suit? I custom fit and make in two days. Fraction of price in US."

Jason continued to look around in awe as he responded, "Yes, each of us would like a suit, but I don't know where to begin."

"No problem. I help. You want worsted wool? Tweed? You name it, we have it."

Jason, under his breath to Joe and Ed said, "Seems crazy buying a suit when I'm going back to Hawai'i where NO ONE wears a suit."

Ed said, "Don't forget; you probably won't be in Hawai'i forever. Can't pass up prices this low."

Jason turned back to the tailor. "Perhaps a light, wool dark gray or dark blue with a faint pinstripe?"

The tailor gave a slight bow and headed around a broad wooden worktable toward the stacks of fabric. He brought out several bolts and partially unrolled them on the table for Jason to look at. As Jason looked over and felt the material, the tailor did the same for Ed and Joe. Jason finally selected a bolt of dark gray, almost black fabric with a thin cream-colored pinstripe.

"Excellent choice," said the tailor. Jason thought, *Anything I picked would have been an "excellent choice," I'm sure. No matter.*

"Single breasted or double-breasted?"

Jason thought for a minute. "Let's go with double-breasted."

"Cuff, no cuff?"

"No cuff."

"Okay. I take measurements."

The tailor measured around Jason's waist, across the back of his shoulders, and then his inseam. With the end of the tape still up in Jason's crotch held by one hand, the tailor stretched it down to his shoe.

"How much break?"

"Just a slight break."

"You dress left or right?"

"What?"

"You dress left or right?"

"I have no idea what you mean."

Joe said, helpfully, "He wants to know which way you 'hang' so he can add a little extra room there."

"You can skip that part with Jason," Ed said. "There won't be much difference either way he hangs."

Joe added, "Yeah. Save the material."

The tailor, kneeling on the floor, looked up at Jason. "You friends very funny."

Looking up in the air, Jason said, "Yeah, they're a fucking comedy riot." Looking back down, "Anyway—right."

"Good, good. We all set." Looking at Ed and Joe. "You guys next. Pick material."

After about an hour, they left the shop with their tickets to pick up the suits in just two days. In the street, Jason said, "I hope I don't go to a wedding someday and have the sleeves fall off when I'm dancing at the reception."

Ed laughed. "Even worse, you could be dancing to something like 'Shake a Tailfeather' and the crotch of your pants could unravel."

"Always a popular move at a wedding reception. Well, too late now. Next stop, custom shoes."

The routine at the cobbler's was similar to the one at the tailor shop. Jason picked out some soft dark-brown leather for his custom-made "Beatle Boots." Again, not something he would be wearing much in Hawai'i, but it was very likely that he would be moving back to the East Coast at some point.

They wandered around the streets after leaving the cobbler, taking in the sights and smells. At a farmers' market they were immersed in a bustling crowd of people picking out vegetables and fruits, carrying live chickens back to their homes in clear plastic bags, tanks with live fish and lobsters, and small stands selling grilled meats and fried dumplings. Many of the shops had ducks hanging in the windows either dressed and ready for cooking or still with feathers. They bought some skewers of chicken and pork at one of the stands, confident that it was not the "monkey meat" of Olongapo, along with dumplings served in an aromatic broth in a cardboard bowl.

They rounded a corner at the far edge of the market and encountered a street that reminded Jason of Jewelers' Row on Sansom Street in Philadelphia. Watches of every make and model were on display in windows of many shops, while others exhibited necklaces, rings, and earrings featuring diamonds, rubies, emeralds, and other exotic gemstones.

Joe said, "I've always wanted a Rolex Submariner, and there's one here in the window for two hundred bucks—way cheaper than any I've ever seen back home."

"Look closely. You sure that doesn't say 'Rodex?'" Ed was skeptical.

"It doesn't say 'Rodex.' Let's go in and see if they'll bargain. I've heard you never pay the tag price in Hong Kong."

They went in and a man with a jeweler's loop in his right eye turned to them from his workbench. Small gears, minuscule screws, an uncoiled spring, and the opened body of a watch lay before him.

"You want to buy?" He turned, gesturing with his hand, "I do repairs too. One, maybe two day."

Joe said, "I'm interested in the Rolex Submariner in your window display. Can you give me a price you might accept?"

"Tag say two hundred dollar."

"No discount?"

"No discount on Rolex."

"Okay. Thank you for your time." Joe turned and started to walk out the door.

"Wait. You from Navy ship in harbor today? For you, one eighty."

"Okay. Thanks. I'm going to look around some more. We might be back." Jason and Ed followed him out the door.

Once outside, Joe said, "I noticed a sign for a watch shop about three doors down. Let's check it out."

They stood outside the window of the store down the street, and just like the first store, there was a Rolex Submariner in the window. Two hundred dollars.

As they walked in, it felt like déjà vu. A similar man sat behind a similar workbench, watch parts scattered in front of him on the bench surface or in shallow glass dishes.

"Yes? Can I help you?"

Joe said, "I'm interested in the Rolex Submariner in the window display. Can you quote me a price on it, please?"

"Tag say two hundred dollar."

"Is there possibly a discount?"

"No discount on Rolex."

Jason and Ed gave each other a look; we've heard *that* before.

Joe said, "Well, the jeweler three doors down"—he pointed in the direction of the previous store—"said he'd sell me one for one eighty."

The man mumbled something to himself in Chinese. Jason figured it had something to do with the other jeweler's character or his mother's marital status at his birth. In any event, he did not look particularly happy.

"Okay. One seventy-five—no lower."

Joe nodded. "Okay. We'll be back." Without giving the man a chance to reduce the price further, he left and went back to the first store. Before entering he turned to Ed and Jason and said, "Now *this* is how you barter."

Again, Jason and Ed gave each other a look and followed Joe in. The man was back at his workbench. He turned as they entered and said, "Ah! You back. I told you good price."

Joe was shaking his head slightly. "Well, the jeweler three doors up the street quoted me one hundred seventy-five dollars for the same watch."

If the jeweler had been in a Looney Tunes cartoon, steam would have been coming out of his ears. But, after some mumbling in Chinese, which was probably very similar to what they heard in the last store, he said through gritted teeth, "Hundred seventy dollar, final offer."

Joe nodded. "Okay let me think about it." He turned to leave.

"You leave, you no come back. Final offer."

Joe nodded, turned, and walked out the door and down to the other jeweler, Ed and Jason in tow. As they walked in, the jeweler looked up and said nothing.

Joe said, "Now the man three doors down says one seventy.'"

The watchmaker sat quietly for about thirty seconds, looking at all three men. Suddenly, he leaped up from the chair at his bench, waving his hands and screaming in Chinese. Joe backed away and Ed and Jason skittered to the side. When he finally managed to get words out in English he said, "GET OUT! You GET OUT my store! You no want to buy watch. You play games. I no sell you watch for *three hundred*! Go! Leave." More yelling in Chinese followed, an invisible force field shoving Joe out of the shop.

Joe backed away and departed quickly. Ed and Jason had to dodge their way around the jeweler to get out and felt very relieved when they made it to the sidewalk.

Jason looked at Joe. "Going back to the other store?"

Joe, staring off into space, slowly shook his head.

Ed said, sarcastically, "So *that's* how to barter in Hong Kong."

Joe glared at him, then started laughing. "Well, at least now I have a baseline price."

Ed and Jason looked at each other, shaking their heads. Ed said, "C'mon. Let's break the law and find a shop selling Cuban cigars."

Jason agreed. "Sounds like a plan."

They walked to the end of the street housing the jewelry stores and turned right, only to be confronted by a building that was under construction, not something unusual in a busy urban environment. What was unusual to them was the construction of the scaffolding. Instead of steel pipes screwing into fittings to form ninety-degree angles, the structure was made of heavy sections of bamboo, lashed together at each corner by heavy, fibrous rope. They crossed the street to get a better view and were astounded to see that it went up at least fifteen floors. There were men working on just about every floor on platforms that were connected by ladders, also made of bamboo.

Jason shook his head in wonder. "I don't think I would trust that to hold me, let alone all those men."

Ed said, "They better hope a herd of pandas doesn't get loose here."

Joe and Jason looked at him quizzically.

"You know; pandas eat bamboo."

Joe said, "Everybody knows that. It's just that I don't think there are many herds of inner-city pandas."

"A herd of pandas?" Jason was shaking his head. "I don't think that's the right group name for a large number of pandas."

"Well, I'm sure it's not 'flock' of pandas."

Joe agreed. "How about a 'bevy of bears?'"

"That would work if they were bears. They're more closely related to raccoons than bears," Jason explained. "How about a 'preponderance of pandas?' At least there's some alliteration there."

Joe and Ed nodded. Ed said, "That works for me. Back to our cigar search."

Years later, Jason discovered that the group name for pandas was an "embarrassment" of pandas. Thinking back to his time in Hong Kong, he thought, *I still like 'preponderance' better.*

After walking a few more blocks they came to a little hole-in-the-wall shop that, according to the sign, was selling Habana cigars, and the address matched one of the ones announced by the XO a few hours earlier in the day. After a few furtive looks to totally uninterested passersby, they entered the store and were surrounded by display cases and fancy humidors all loaded with cigars, seemingly infinite in shape and size. Jason guessed some of the humidors held over one thousand cigars.

A small Asian man dressed in what looked to be a black silk long-sleeved shirt came from behind a curtain at the back of the store. He took a long look at them and smiled. "You are from the new ship in the harbor, yes?"

Joe looked at Jason and Ed, and said, "Let's just say that's a possibility."

The man laughed. "No worry. Your money good here. What kind you want?"

Jason said, "Well, obviously, Cuban, but if you mean by size, we're all kind of into panetelas. By brand, we're not sure. Never had Cubans."

"I see." He went behind the counter and opened a small humidor. "These high-rated and very popular."

The label on the box said *Cohiba*. He opened the box and passed it around for the three men to smell. "These are Loguito #2 Panetela. Twenty-five per box. Five packs of five in each box. Twenty dollars American."

They looked at each other and Ed said, "I think we'd like at least one box of those. Could we see another variety?"

"Sure." The man went to another humidor and brought out a box labeled *Montecristo*.

Jason said, "I've actually heard of this brand. Probably from a movie, or something."

The salesman nodded. "Very famous. These are Especiales #2. Similar size to first box."

This box had a distinctly different aroma; not necessarily better, but they could tell the difference.

Joe said, "Wow! The Dutch Masters we've been smoking smell positively stale compared to these."

Jason and Ed nodded.

"How about a cigar for a special occasion?" Joe asked. "One you probably won't smoke every day. One that tastes and looks special."

The man smiled. "You like this one. Named after story and famous politician." He went behind the counter and opened one of the large humidors near the back of the store. He carried the box to them reverently, the way a Catholic priest carries the Eucharist. He opened the box and inside were layers of aluminum tubes.

Ed said, "Looks like a torpedo locker in a sub."

The man opened one of the tubes. It was substantially longer than the panetelas. "This brand Romeo y Julieta. Famous story, yes? Lovers die at end. And this is a #2 Churchill. Box of twenty-five. Thirty dollars American."

Jason eyed it almost hungrily. "Now, *that's* a cigar! To quote Kipling, 'A woman is only a woman, but a good cigar is a smoke.'"

Joe laughed. "Look at you! I thought that was an Ernie Kovacs line, speaking of Dutch Masters. By the way, I hear that he only smoked Cubans when off-camera."

They talked quietly among themselves, came to a decision, and told the man they would take two boxes each of the first two brands and one box of the Churchills.

"Very good. I package carefully. Plain brown wrapper, yes?" He smiled.

"Yes, thank you," said Ed.

The man handed them their packages; he bowed slightly, and they returned the gesture.

As they were leaving the store, the man said, "Enjoy Hong Kong."

Outside the store, Joe said, "You know, he wasn't so bad for a commie."

Ed laughed. "That's because he liked our American money."

They walked down the street looking for a camera shop. Jason had said he wanted to buy a wide-angle lens for all the city-scape type scenes they would be encountering here and when they pulled into Yokosuka, Japan, on their way home.

Jason bought his lens, with just a bit of bartering, and without being thrown out of the store. They flagged down a cab, Joe and Ed scrambled into the back leaving Jason, once again, to sit up front: the Death Seat. Jason said, "We'd like to go to Aberdeen."

The cabbie nodded. "Okay. Can do." As in Guam, the acceleration pushed Jason back into the seat. Weaving through traffic on crowded streets, climbing hills that reminded Jason of scenes from *Bullitt* in San Francisco, then plummeting down the other side to the bustling waterfront of Aberdeen had Jason laughing hysterically, the same reaction he typically had on the Wild Mouse ride back at the amusement park in San Diego. They screeched to a stop with a view across the harbor of the Tai Pak floating restaurant where they planned to have dinner later that day. However, at the moment, Jason was not all that hungry.

They paid the cabbie and piled out of the car as quickly as possible. Jason said, "I never thought I'd have a cab ride as hair-raising as the one in Guam. This guy absolutely killed it."

Ed was shaking his head. "Shit. He almost absolutely killed everyone. I wonder what the life expectancy of a Hong Kong cab driver is."

As they walked along the waterfront, they were astounded by the sampans and other boats rafted out five or six deep. It was obvious that the boats were their livelihood, primarily fishing, but they were also where they lived. Many had lines hanging from bow to stern with fish attached, drying in the sun. The aromatic mixture of food cooking on small charcoal grills, fish being cured, and human waste was incredibly cloying. As they looked at the water between the boats, it was obvious that there were probably many public health issues here, most likely untreated. However, to get a closer look, they decided to risk their health and rent a sampan for a boat tour of Aberdeen.

For one Hong Kong dollar, worth about thirty cents American, the three got to board a sampan and travel the waters of Aberdeen, stopping on occasion to buy a piece of fish or some dumplings. As they suspected from their waterfront walk, each boat was a floating house. Many had clothes drying on lines after being washed in the waters of the harbor. This made Jason shudder just a bit. He would never complain about having to go to the laundromat again.

At the end of the tour, they were deposited at the Tai Pak restaurant for dinner. They were seated at a small table with chopsticks for utensils. The waiter asked if they would like a knife and fork, and Ed said, "No, we're good."

He bowed and said the dim sum cart would come by and they each could select four dishes from the cart as part of their meal. The cart came by in short order and contained many of the foods they were familiar with from Hawai'i: dumplings, mini-egg rolls, small pieces of barbecued pork, and fried wontons. One item bothered Joe.

Joe looked from the cart to the server, then back to the cart, and finally back to the server. He said, "I'm not sure I've seen these before."

The server replied, "Chicken feet."

Joe looked surprised, "You said 'chicken feet.'"

"Yes, sir."

"As in, feet that chickens walk on."

"Yes, sir."

"But"—he looked at Ed and Jason—"there's no *meat* on feet."

Jason said to Ed, "Sounds like a Dr. Seuss book. 'I will not eat feet when there's no meat to eat. When there is no meat, I will not eat feet.'"

The waiter looked a little puzzled and tried to explain. "Is like tendon, not meat."

"It's fried, correct?"

"Yes, sir."

Joe said, "You know, my family used to raise chickens and I never, ever thought about eating their feet." He looked at Ed and Jason. "You know what chickens walk around in, right?"

Ed nodded. "I have a basic idea."

After a moment, Joe said, "What the hell, I'm going to try them."

The server smiled and doled some feet out onto a small plate and placed it in front of Joe. He watched, in anticipation.

"Finger food?"

"More like 'toe food,'" Jason said.

The waiter nodded. Joe picked one up and turned it every which way possible looking for a good entry point; the claws were still on it. Finally, using just his front teeth, he bit into the edge of one of the toes. There wasn't much there. He chewed thoughtfully, almost daintily.

"Ah, it has a delicate nuanced flavor, something between cardboard and a barnyard." He chewed a bit. "Very crunchy. Really, more of a waste of time than anything."

The server asked, "You like?"

Joe said, "It's fine, but I think I'd like a bottle of Tsingtao beer, just to wash it down."

Ed and Jason joined in his request for Tsingtaos. When the waiter returned, they ordered several dishes to share and went back to the ship full and tired after a long day of buying, bartering, sightseeing, and eating.

The next morning, Jason was having some scrambled eggs for breakfast in the wardroom with Joe and Ed. He looked up from his dish, and said, "We have to see Tiger Balm Gardens."

"Where do you hear about this shit?" Joe asked.

"I read. I got a little travel guide in the camera store yesterday."

"So, what is this 'Tiger Balm Gardens?'"

And from Ed, "And how do you get the balm on a tiger's lips?"

Jason ignored Ed. "From what I understand, there are two of these places, one in Hong Kong and I think the other is in Singapore. The owners of Tiger Balm commissioned some elaborate buildings that have some pretty far-out designs and artwork, a little erotica, and some scenes about how people are punished as they try to transition into the afterlife."

"Sounds like a fun place; too bad we can't take the kids," said Joe. "Can we walk there?"

"What? No, we can't walk there. We have to take a—"

"Death cab," Ed finished.

"C'mon, Joe. What's a little cab ride?"

"Okay, I'll go. But if I die, I'll be the first to say, 'I told you so.'"

The cab ride was mild compared to the one they'd taken the day before. However, it dropped them off at a rickety-looking tram that appeared to climb straight up to the sky. They stood at the base of the steep hill leading to Victoria Peak wondering if all modes of transportation in Hong Kong involved risking your life. Little did they know that another cab ride faced them to get to the gardens after the tram ride.

They paid for their tickets and climbed into the tram, finding seats in the back where a rear window would provide a panoramic view of the harbor and, at the top, most of Hong Kong itself. The tram started with a lurch as the cable engaged, followed by a loud grinding sound as the tram car slowly winched its way up the hillside. The view back down the track was both terrifying and spectacular. The pitch of the rails seemed to defy physics. Soon, the *Everett* floating in the harbor looked like one of the small plastic ships found in a Cracker Jack box. Jason had been on many ski lifts and the cable cars in San Francisco, but none of those rides could compare with this tram.

In addition to the view back down the hillside, the side views offered glimpses of ornate pagodas, office buildings, terraced farms tended by farmers in broad, conical, straw hats, and ramshackle buildings stacked on top of each other clinging to the hillside as if they were immune to the forces of gravity.

The tram lurched to a stop with a loud clank, and they climbed out. They took in the incredible views and used up a fair amount of film in the new cameras that they all had. No one wanted to leave because, as they now discovered, it meant getting back into another death cab.

The cab dropped them off near the garden entrance without any major casualties, and they were greeted by a large, ornately painted, tiger. Past the tiger, large figurines of mythical creatures, some half human and half dragon, rose up to greet them. Several statues were of creatures with human bodies and the head of a horse or an ox. Other figures depicted totally naked women bowing in supplication. There seemed to be no rhyme or reason to where or how things were displayed.

In one area, human-like figures, some with green or blue skin and elaborately painted faces, passed judgment on those who had died and were sent to hell. Punishment was meted out to suit the crimes committed during their lives. The disembowelments, amputations, and tongue-removals were all displayed in gory detail. Some bodies were cast into volcano craters filled with hot lava or crushed under boulders. The Ten Courts of Hell was not for the fainthearted. It was hard to look at, but at the same time, hard to look away. Jason admitted to himself that he preferred the naked women over scenes of dismemberment.

As they left hell behind, Joe said, "Really? This is what you wanted to see?"

Jason shrugged. "I must admit, it's not exactly Disneyland or a beautiful botanical garden. But you gotta admit; it's interesting. Years from now you'll be able to tell your kids all about it."

Ed said, "I doubt it. Anyway, is it time for dinner?"

Captain Ziegler had reserved the back section of the Spring Moon Cantonese dining room at the Peninsula Hotel, one of the most exclusive destinations in Hong Kong, for an officers' dinner. The menu selected by him featured seven courses of dishes representing longevity to celebrate the Chinese New Year. All the officers who were not on duty the final day in Hong Kong were invited. Their service dress blues was the uniform of the day for this special occasion.

The officers shuttled over to the docks in Kowloon in water taxis and the captain's gig, a covered version of the motor whale boat. The Peninsula, as its name suggested, was perched on a point of land that projects out into the harbor. The officers were gathering in an area of the restaurant aptly named The Bar, a room with polished rosewood paneling and a long rosewood bar with a dark-green leather upholstered bolster that ran the length of it to serve as an armrest. The stools were fronted with the same leather. Jason thought, *This is what the word* posh *is for*.

Joe, Ed, and Jason all ordered Canadian Club and Schweppes Ginger Ale with lime wedges as their predinner cocktails and then made their way around the bar talking with the other officers as they arrived. Doug Kimos was getting serious about his drinking with an Old Grandad bourbon on the rocks. He toasted them as they made their way over to where Jack Culpepper was standing along with Billy Weston. In his hand, Jack held a tall, thin glass with an opaque white fluid in it that resembled milk mixed with water.

"What the hell is that?" Jason asked.

"It's Pernod on an ice cube with some water. It's the reaction with water that turns it this weird color. Pernod is a brand name. The generic form is *pastis*, an aperitif."

"It's weird all right. How the hell did you end up ordering that?"

"Well, this place looks pretty sophisticated, and I thought back to the semester I spent in France as an exchange student, so I asked them if they had it. Of course, they had it! There's actually a French restaurant here in the Peninsula." He raised his glass to toast them. "Tchin-tchin!"

Jason returned the toast with "Sláinte!"

Billy started to say, in his Southern drawl, "Through the teeth and over the gums—" Their glares stopped him mid-sentence.

Joe snickered. "Now *that's* sophisticated."

They all sipped from their drinks.

Joe said, "I hope "tchin-tchin" doesn't mean 'up yours' in French."

Jack shook his head. "No, it's actually very appropriate here since its origins are Chinese. French soldiers brought the phrase back after fighting in the Second Opium War."

Ed said, "I'm impressed, Culpepper. Wasn't expecting that out of you. What's it taste like?"

"Sort of a licorice or anise flavor. Hardly ever see it in the US, but it's everywhere in France. Maybe an acquired taste." He looked at the glass as if in doubt that it really did taste good.

"Could I have a sip?" Ed asked.

"Sure."

Ed sipped it. "Wow. It is like licorice. Takes me back to when I was a kid eating Twizzlers. It's good, but I don't think I could take a lot of it."

Just then Captain Ziegler and the XO arrived. Anyone who was sitting stood, and everyone applauded. Ziegler just smiled and sort of waved them off. "Instead of applause, someone can get me a bourbon on the rocks."

Kimos said, "On it, sir."

After Kimos delivered the bourbon, Captain Ziegler said, "We have about a half hour before our table is ready. Just a heads up in case you wanted a traveler to take with you to the table." He then made his rounds, chatting with each of the men.

Jason said to Joe and Ed, "What a thoughtful man!"

Ed said, "Truly, an officer and a gentleman."

That phrase set Jason thinking about Sparrow and when they met at Sid's apartment. *I guess I'll look her up when I get home. Not like I'm entertaining a lot of other options.*

They secured a second round of whiskey and ginger and went back to chat with Jack and Billy. Billy was downing his third Pabst Blue Ribbon.

Ed watched him, then said, "Pretty amazing, Billy. Look behind that bar." Billy glanced over at the grandiose display of liquors behind the bartender. "You have all that to choose from and here you are drinking a PBR. I'm surprised they even have it here."

"Well, they didn't have any Jax. That's what everyone from the panhandle drank when I was growing up. This was about as close as I could get. I was feeling homesick."

Ed shook his head. "You drink enough of those, and you can forget the 'home' part. Must admit, never had a Jax. Guess it was a local thing, like Genny Cream in New York."

Jason nodded. "That was the beer of choice in the Adirondacks. I've pounded down a few of those. Good stuff!"

Joe noticed people starting to drift toward the dining room. "Looks like the table is ready."

A large round table covered in white linen sat in a private corner of the dining room with fourteen chairs comfortably arranged around it. The walls at the corner featured ornate Asian tapestries, beautifully illuminated by recessed lighting in the ceiling. Captain Ziegler and the XO maneuvered themselves into the back corner seats. Jason grabbed a chair and found himself seated directly across from Ziegler. He was flanked by Joe to his left and Ed to his right. Several waiters hovered around the table asking if people were comfortable with chopsticks or not. Everyone went with chopsticks except Billy.

While they were finishing the drinks they brought over from The Bar, several appetizers were served family style. Cha Guo savory rice cakes, a dish Jason was not familiar with from eating in Hawai'i, spring rolls, pork and fish dumplings, and some very interesting and spicy shrimp cakes, something else he had not tasted in Hawai'i. As the bar drinks were finished, the appetizers were followed by a very traditional egg drop soup. It was easily the best Jason had ever tasted.

As people started to order beer, the waiters suggested a few they should try, other than Tsingtao, that are not commonly exported to the United States. Two popular beers in China they mentioned were Snow Beer and Zhujiang Beer, both lagers typical of the style found most often in China. They also recommended a Tsingtao dark, which Jason thought sounded interesting, so he ordered it. It was excellent.

The next course featured poultry dishes that were similar to those Jason had enjoyed in Hawai'i, but with interesting twists. The duck was with a sour plum sauce that married perfectly with the richness of the duck and the chicken was similar to teriyaki chicken, but a hoisin sauce was used, and it was served with snow peas.

Jason, Joe, and Ed ordered more beers for the pork course. Jason had never seen anything like the Lions Head meatballs and couldn't quite figure out what was in them besides ground pork. The braised pork belly was incredibly tender and served with a side of stir-fried broccoli. The tangerine beef dish that followed was similar to the orange beef he was used to in Hawai'i, but the tangerine flavor gave it an extra tang. Jason hated to use the word "tang" to describe something that tasted so good, nothing at all like the putrid powdered drink the astronauts supposedly drank. Long Life Noodles accompanied the dish, imparting good fortune to everyone who was taking part in this meal.

By the time the fish course was served, the volume of the conversations around the table had picked up considerably, perhaps because yet another round of beers miraculously appeared. When Jason looked around to see who had ordered the round, he noticed Archie Burns across the table raising his glass. The XO shouted across to him, "I thought you guys looked thirsty." Jason raised his glass back at him.

When Jason tasted the ginger scallion lobster, he thought it might be the best thing he'd ever had in his mouth. At the same time, several serving dishes of whole steamed black sea bass were placed around the table. The amount of food was overwhelming, and yet it was disappearing at an incredible rate. Jason decided to skip the walnut cookies and sesame balls served for dessert. He pushed back from the table a bit as he finished his last bite of sea bass, quite full and with a pleasant buzz from the drinks. Directly in front of him was the skeletal remains of one of the sea bass, the head uneaten. *Sid would have eaten the eyes*, he thought. Without giving it much thought, he picked up the head, stuck his index and middle finger in the top behind the eyes, and stuck his thumb in the lower jaw. The mouth flexed like a ventriloquist's dummy.

Jason, using his best Henny Youngman-sounding voice made the fish head say, "Hey, Ed. Thanks for letting me get a *head* in this world. Being successful is no *fluke* because someone is always trying to put you in your *plaice*."

Ed turned to look at Jack Culpepper as if to say, "Can we make this stop?" However, Jack appeared mesmerized. Too much Pernod, probably.

The fish continued. "Take my *alewife*, please." A few boos mixed with some giggles rippled around the table. "Hey, hey, this is my best stuff. I'm not *floundering* around here." Now, some groans joined the chorus. Even Ziegler and the XO were now watching, perhaps in disbelief. The fish said, "If someone could tip me a *fin* here, it would help. This is a union shop and I'm working for *scale*."

The XO said, "Get the hook!"

"Oh, sure, threaten me, a dead fish, with a hook. Someone beat you to it." The fish looked around the table. "And for my finale . . ."

Most of the people at the table clapped or cheered.

"I'd like to sing you a song just for the *halibut*." The fish looked around the table. "Where's Les Brown when you need him?"

Joe said, "You're going to need more than Les Brown."

"And now, from *South Pacific*, '*Salmon-chanted* evening, you may meet a stranger . . .'"

The XO shouted out over the chorus of boos, "There's nothing stranger than this!"

The fish took several bows and then returned to his home on the plate. Everyone clapped.

Captain Ziegler said, "Well, now that the floor show's over, I'd say it's time for some after-dinner drinks. Shall we adjourn back to The Bar?"

A little over half the officers went to the bar, including Ziegler and Burns. When Jason came in, Ziegler came over to him and offered him a brandy snifter with some Courvoisier. "Here, maybe this will wash the bad jokes out of your mouth."

Joe chimed in. "I'm afraid it won't, sir. He's like this all the time—and I have to bunk with him!"

Ziegler smiled. "Then I'd say you're due some hazardous duty pay."

"Thank you, sir. Much appreciated."

Ziegler turned back to Jason. "Seriously, because in all honesty I can't say 'comically,' those were some of the worst puns I've ever heard, and yet they just kept coming out of your mouth."

Jason shook his head. "It wasn't me, sir. It was the fish."

Captain Ziegler smiled, patted him on the shoulder, and went off to find some more-scintillating conversation.

TWENTY-THREE

South China Sea and Yokosuka

FEBRUARY 1973

The *Everett* was back on the gunline, a destination now more appropriately called the "watch and see what happens" line. Jason was on the bridge wing by a pelorus taking some visual navigational fixes with his quartermasters to make sure the ship was in the right location off the coast of Quang Tri. There would be no firing coordinates coming in; they were there strictly to observe. Jason glanced up at the TV monitor mounted over the front windows of the bridge that received its signal from the infrared camera installed just a couple of months earlier. With the Paris Peace Accord in place, at least for the Americans, the glowing images of trucks moving south on the beach were no longer targets. However, the *Everett* was documenting the activities of the North Vietnamese as they continued their push south of the DMZ.

Jason looked over at Joe, who was OOD for this mid-watch.

"Pretty busy out there."

"Yeah. It's getting so they could use a traffic cop."

"At least those damn boats with the mines aren't around anymore."

Joe nodded. "Is all this getting recorded down in CIC?"

"That's what I've been told," Jason said.

Joe looked back out toward the beach, as if he could see what was happening a little over a mile away.

"Have you plotted our course out of here for Yokosuka yet?"

"Nah. But it won't be long now. Scuttlebutt is we'll be moving out next week."

Joe smiled. "Just be sure you have Ed check your work before we go. Don't want to get lost on the way home."

The helmsman snickered.

Jason gave him a look, then laughed to himself. "Yeah, I'd have a lot of guys really pissed off at me if I fucked that up." He walked out on the bridge wing, lit up one of the Cubans, and looked out over the South China Sea. The calm surface created a rippling pathway for the full moon that was low on the horizon. It was so bright that the Milky Way was barely visible. The bright "star" that was actually Jupiter was visible just to the right and slightly higher than the moon.

As Jason gazed at the view, he began to wonder what was in store for him upon his return to Pearl. Most of the guys had family or a special someone anxious for their return. He didn't. Even his friends from the *Engage* might be gone. They were scheduled to deploy in early March. They might be in for a rough time of it on their arrival in Nam. They would be working right on shore, clearing damaged vessels off the beaches and towing them to a repair facility in an attempt to get them reactivated in time to fight off the expected onslaught from the North Vietnamese. Everyone knew it was coming; it was just a matter of time. He was worried for them and for what they were about to face.

Jason had received a letter from Sid at their last mail call. He had told them the guys were getting ready to give up the apartment on Paoakalani. He wanted to know if Jason wanted to rent it. While he had fond memories of the jam sessions, parties, and meeting Sparrow there, it was not for him. The street noise was too much, and the high rises made it feel too closed-in to feel comfortable as a permanent residence. Jason figured he was making enough to find a little bungalow in the Manoa Valley, or maybe even over on the windward side where rates were lower and the scenery was spectacular. He told Sid that if they deployed before his return to just leave the Firebird in the main lot on the base. It would be at most a day or two.

Of course, finding a place to live would be his number one priority upon arrival. He definitely did not want to live on the ship and didn't like the option of life in the BOQ. Getting away from the ship and the base at the end of the workday was very important for him to maintain his sanity.

Things would be different. He was scheduled to go to navigation school on Ford Island for two weeks, but he wouldn't get to use his newly acquired skills for several months. The *Everett* would be in the shipyard for its scheduled three-year, post-deployment overhaul. *It's pretty easy to pinpoint where you are when you're tied up at a dock*, he thought.

He could imagine all the wives and families flocking around the gangway as everyone left the ship after they arrived in Pearl. Hugs. Kisses. Tears. The departure had been a somber affair; this would be far more joyous—for most. Jason figured since he didn't have a wife or family, he would be stuck with duty on board the first night in. That was okay. One more day on board wouldn't hurt. That's the way it usually worked. It was fair. When he had been on the *Engage*, he had volunteered for duty Christmas Eve and Christmas Day. Same for Easter Sunday.

Lori should have been there waiting for him to arrive. Boy, had that one gone sideways. There had been no letter from her at the last mail call. That was just fine with him at this point. The "what ifs" had used to hijack his brain, but now even those thoughts were beginning to be far less frequent. Just as well.

How to meet that special someone? *Hell, I had more luck meeting girls in the O' Club at Subic Bay than I did in Hawai'i*, he thought. *Well, with my bandmates deployed, maybe it's time to try to find a solo gig at a small bar.* He thought back to when he was a kid reading comic books that had ads like, "Be popular! Learn to play the guitar! Impress the girls." He laughed to himself; there was a similar ad for learning to play the banjo. Probably not the best pathway to getting a date.

His rambling brain was brought back to reality when Joe came out on the bridge wing.

"What are you still doing up here? Hit the bunk. We're not going anywhere."

"Yeah, I probably should. Just thinking about what it will be like getting back to Pearl."

"Well, as you know, I'll be leaving the ship, but not the islands. Got my orders for shore duty. Reporting to the Human Resource Management Center two weeks after we get back, then going to six weeks of training at the Memphis Naval Air Station."

"Say hi to Elvis for me."

"Don't think he's there anymore. Got too big."

"He's getting too big for anywhere, literally."

"We're more likely to see him in Hawai'i than Memphis. He's still trying to tour."

"I was never a fan. Buddy Holly? Yes. Richie Valens? Yes. Duane Eddy? Yes. First record I ever bought. "Have Twangy Guitar Will Travel."

"Why am I not surprised?"

"Okay. I guess I'll turn in. Enjoy the rest of this scintillating watch." He went back inside the bridge, snuffed out the stub of his cigar in the ashtray, and headed below.

The *Everett* steamed away from the gunline exactly one week after his conversation with Joe on the bridge wing. Jason was on the bridge watching the departure. Good riddance. The sun had already set, and he watched the few lights that were visible wink off as they sank below the horizon. Next stop, Yokosuka, Japan. The Navy had a huge base there, but Jason had plans to try Japan's famous rail system to get away to a small town or see some of Japan's famous temples, shrines, and gardens. There was one more Nikkor lens on his list too. The exchange rates were still good but creeping slowly up. The motorcycle buyers were getting nervous.

Jason didn't need a star shoot since he just had a visual fix upon departure. Morning would find them well out to sea. They would be passing through the Luzon Strait and out into open ocean. The pace of activity on the ship would slow to a standard pattern of watches and routine maintenance. No UNREPs, VERTREPs, gunline assignments, or visits to Da Nang for mail and movies. Jason was kind of looking forward to it. *Maybe I'll be able to finish the John Fowles novel I started two weeks ago*, he thought.

It was a cloudy morning as the *Everett* sailed into Yokosuka. The sea was calm; the water of the harbor was like glass. They were accompanied by two tugs as they made the approach to the docks. There was very little room to maneuver, certainly for a large ship with one screw, and the tugs would have to provide enough assistance to make sure the *Everett* was snugged up to its narrow berth. The tug captains had done this many times, so the *Everett* soon found itself securely against the pier.

As with Kaohsiung, the harbor was bustling with activity. Besides the military presence, Yokosuka was a primary port for ships delivering goods to Tokyo. And while he had heard great things about Tokyo, Jason had no intention of taking the train all the way into the huge city; he wanted something with a less urban flavor.

Jason had duty the first day in port and was on the quarterdeck as liberty was called. Joe and Ed were headed to the O' Club for some lunch, and then to the base exchange to see what it had to offer. Last chance for cheap, duty-free goods. He stopped Jack Culpepper as he was about to go down the gangway.

"Let me guess. Heading to buy that Yamaha motorcycle."

"Almost got that right. I might go for the Honda CB750 4-cyclinder. It's a beast from what I hear. Exchange rates aren't going to get any lower while we're here, so I need to get my ass in gear."

The quarterdeck was an interesting place for duty, especially on a ship's first day in port. Lots of excitement and anticipation. Jason was thinking that it was way better to be on the quarterdeck now than it would be when everyone staggered back from liberty after that first night in town after weeks at sea.

The next morning, Jason, Ed, and Joe caught the train that goes to Kamakura, a small city but a very popular destination. They had heard about this town because it boasts some incredible shrines and temples and is home to Japan's second-largest statue of Buddha. Also, Komachi dori Street was known for its many shops and excellent restaurants. The train stop was within easy walking distance to the shopping area and several of the shrines and temples.

They caught another train for a short ride to the Kita Kamakura station. They were surprised to find plenty of signage in English that made it easy to get around. The first temple was Engakuji Temple completed in AD 1282. It was a Zen temple dedicated to the fallen soldiers who died during the second invasion attempt by the Mongols. Jason thought it pretty stunning to be visiting a building that was erected long before Europeans arrived in America. The next Zen temple was even older. The Kenchoji Temple is the oldest Zen training monastery, dating back to AD 1253.

Another train transported them to Hase-Dera. The Hase-Dera temple features hundreds of small statues of Jizo Bodhisattva lining the walkways through the gardens leading to the main building. A few months later, a vivid memory of this visit would come to Jason when Steely Dan's *Countdown to Ecstasy* album was released. The lead track was "Bodhisattva," featuring a great guitar solo by Jeff "Skunk" Baxter. Finally, after a short walk from the temple, they arrived at the Great Buddha located outside of the Kotokuin Temple. Tourists could go inside, for a fee, but the group was content simply to view the exterior. No need to go creeping around inside Buddha's guts. Jason didn't think it would be as fun as going through the giant, pulsing heart at the Franklin Institute in Philadelphia.

Joe was looking at him. "What are you smiling about?"

"Just thinking about this giant heart you could go through at a museum in Philly. On a junior high field trip, my friends and I went through the heart backward, going against the flow of 'blood.'"

"You mean the people who were trying to take the heart seriously."

"Yeah. We created a human clot somewhere in the atria. The guards performed some 'closed heart' surgery; came in and threw us out."

Joe said, "So if you were in a heart, did you take a beating?"

Jason smiled. "Nah, they just hauled our asses out of there. Getting thrown out of the heart was almost like a badge of honor."

They caught a train back to the center of Kamakura and walked to Komachi dori Street, visiting many of the shops and marketplaces. It was there that Jason completed his camera collection with a purchase of a 200mm Nikkor lens. With hunger setting in, they began to check out the restaurants. Many of the places had plastic models of the food that was served inside on display in the front windows. Not very appetizing.

They started going down some of the side streets and found one small restaurant that just had what looked like a hibachi with a hot plate in the window. They decided a good teppanyaki-style meal would be perfect. They went inside, walked down a short hallway, and found themselves looking at a locked door. It was then they realized the restaurant was actually upstairs on the second floor. They went back down the hall and went up the narrow stairway. At the top they were greeted by a pretty Japanese girl in a kimono. She bowed and pointed at their shoes.

Ed said, "I think she wants us to take off our shoes."

Jason said, "Very astute of you."

The Japanese girl smiled as they took off their shoes and then led them to an area in the restaurant with a bamboo mat laid out on the floor. She motioned to the mat that had several serving dishes and chopsticks arranged on it. As they seated themselves cross-legged on the floor, they noticed that they were the only customers in the small dining area. There were only three other place settings that they could see, each partially separated from each other by rice paper screens, each one with paintings of trees and birds. After they were seated, she bowed to them, said something in Japanese, and then disappeared through a door in the back that was probably to a kitchen area.

Joe looked at Jason and Ed. "I get the feeling she doesn't speak any English."

Ed said, "I get the feeling you're right."

"Should make it interesting," Jason said, "since we don't speak Japanese."

She came back with a tray, which she set down in front of them. She kneeled and started to set out the bowls that were on the tray. One large bowl had what appeared to be uncooked, beaten eggs. Another contained small, greenish-gray sticks that were cut like a carrot would be cut for a delicate crudité platter. Finally, she set out three bowls, one in front of each of them, that they recognized as *sunomono*, a vinegar-based cucumber salad, something that was very commonly served in Hawai'i. This particular version also featured seaweed and very finely sliced onion. She stood, bowed, and said something in Japanese. Jason motioned for her to wait. He stood, pointed at himself, and said, "Jason." He then pointed to Joe and Ed, giving her their names as he did so. He then pointed at her and then opened his hands as if asking a question.

Pointing at herself, she said, "Tamiko."

Jason repeated, "Tamiko."

She smiled and said, "Hai." Jason understood that to mean "yes."

Tamiko bowed and left for the kitchen.

Jason sat back down. Using their chopsticks, they started in on the sunomono. It had a nice sweet, vinegary tang to it, and it was not long before their bowls were empty. That left the greenish-gray sticks and egg.

Jason picked up one and gave it a sniff. "Has a bit of a fishy aroma to it."

Joe did the same. "Reminds me of low tide in Annapolis."

Ed shook his head. "That's not much of a recommendation." He sniffed one. "What we have here is a bowlful of 'things-from-the-sea.'"

All three of them shifted their gazes to the egg. Then, they looked at each other.

"Whaddaya think? Do we dip these in that?" Jason motioned toward the egg bowl. Joe and Ed shrugged.

"I'll try it." Joe and Ed watched him as he made the dip and put the stick in his mouth. "Not bad. Not really that fishy."

Joe and Ed each selected a stick and dipped it in the egg. As they were putting them in their mouths, Tamiko came out carrying a hibachi. She stopped, looked at them eating the things-from-the-sea-dipped-in-egg and started to giggle. She came over to the mat and set the hibachi down. Still giggling slightly, she pointed at the sticks, then at the egg, and wagged her finger. Tamiko held up her hand, telling them to stop. She stood, made the motion with her hand again, then scurried into the kitchen.

Joe, Ed, and Jason looked at each other and then burst out laughing.

"I guess we had a slight misinterpretation of the meal plan," Ed said.

Tamiko hurried back out carrying a tray with plates of shrimp, slices of beef and chicken, and a small wok containing stir-fried julienned carrot, zucchini, and cabbage. She set the tray down and knelt before them. She picked up a piece of beef with chopsticks, held it over the hot plate hibachi, turning it back and forth, and then she motioned as if to dip the beef in the egg quickly.

Jason nodded. "I get it. She cooks the beef and while it's still hot, it gets dipped in the egg to coat it."

Joe and Ed looked at Tamiko and nodded too.

Tamiko put a wooden trivet on the mat and then placed the wok with the vegetables on it and covered it with a lid. She then held her hand over the hot plate hibachi, nodded, and then using a small spatula spread pieces of beef and chicken on to the surface. They sizzled. She looked at the three men and smiled. Joe gave her a "thumbs up," which by her expression, she seemed to understand.

She flipped pieces of beef onto their plates, which they picked up with their chopsticks, dipped in the egg, and popped into their mouths. Tamiko smiled and gave them a thumbs-up.

Jason said, "I think we're beginning to communicate."

They served themselves some of the vegetables while Tamiko, who they now referred to as "Chef Tamiko," continued to dole out the grilled meat and shrimp. Another girl came out of the kitchen carrying a tray with porcelain flasks and several cups. She bowed to the men, then to Tamiko, set the tray down, bowed again, and left.

Tamiko motioned to the newly placed tray and said, "Sake?" Joe, Ed, and Jason nodded vigorously. She pointed at the porcelain flasks and said, "Tokkuri." They all repeated it back. Tamiko pointed to the cups and said, "Choko." They repeated, "Choko."

She nodded back at them and poured sake into the three cups and then handed a cup to each man. Jason surprised them all by saying, "Domo." Tamiko smiled and clapped her hands together.

The three men raised their cups to her and sipped from them.

The rest of the meal was an exchange of words, hand signals, and head nods. All in all, it was an extremely satisfying and enjoyable meal.

Tamiko cleared away all the serving pieces and the hibachi. Jason, Ed, and Joe stood when she returned, and they bowed to each other. She pulled a piece of paper from a pocket in her kimono and handed it to Jason. The bill. The description of what they had eaten was written in Japanese, but the numbers were easy to read. Jason paid her and added what he hoped would be considered to be a generous tip since she had been server, chef, and language instructor. She looked at the amount with an astonished look and then tried to hand some of the money back to Jason.

He shook his head and pushed her hand back to her and smiled. "Domo!"

She watched them put on their shoes and escorted them to the top of the stairs. As they started down the stairs, she shouted to them, "Domo arigatou gozaimasu!" They turned on the steps, waved back at her, and then went out to the street. The incredible evening was all they could talk about on the train as they headed back to the base.

On their last night in Yokosuka, Jason, Ed, and Joe were joined by Doug Kimos, Jack Culpepper, and Norm Shapiro for a final dinner at the O' Club. It would take them eight days to get back to Pearl, with just one brief stop on the appropriately named Midway Island. While the food on board was good, none of it could be accompanied by cocktails, wine, and some after dinner whiskey.

The Yokosuka club had a fine restaurant on the first floor, with a bar and gaming room, including a full-sized pool table, on the second floor. They started upstairs for some drinks and a few rounds of pool. Jason and Doug teamed up against Ed and Joe for some Eight Ball. Steak was at stake. As the game started, Jason began to realize he was lucky to have been paired with Doug as a teammate. Not only could he sink his shots, but he also left the cue ball in horrible positions for whoever followed him; in this case, it was Ed.

Halfway through the game, Ed said to Jason, "Did you know how good he was before we started?"

"Honestly—I hadn't a clue."

Kimos sipped his Old Granddad throughout the whole game. After each shot, he would take a drink and say to Ed and Joe, "I like my steak medium rare."

Joe looked at Ed halfway through and said, "Does he have to say that after each shot?"

Jason said, "Just a little gamesmanship, guys."

The best-of-three match didn't make it to a third game. Doug, proving himself to be a good sport, bought Joe, Ed, and Jason another round of drinks before they went down to eat.

Like many O' Clubs, the restaurant section tended to be quite formal, with white linen tablecloths and waiters with black jackets and bow ties, and the Yokosuka club was no exception. However, unlike Subic, there were no live bands. The recorded music, big band swing, stayed in the background.

As usual, most of the guys got either strip steak or prime rib. Jason broke with tradition and got a broiled mahi mahi dish that came with gratin potatoes and asparagus. Again, breaking with tradition, he ordered a bottle of Pouilly-Fuissé, which got a big thumbs-up from former French exchange student Jack Culpepper, who was working on his second glass of Touraine.

After everyone was served and had a glass of wine in hand, Doug raised his glass and said, "Here's to a safe passage home. And, it was a pleasure serving with you men."

Jason had to admit to himself that he was going to miss Doug and many of the others seated around the table with him at the dinner. Most of them would be transferred within a month after their arrival home. It made him, once again, reflect on what might await him back in Pearl. It would be far different from what it had been like a little less than a year before.

TWENTY-FOUR

Midway/Pearl Harbor

MARCH 1973

Jason had become an expert at taking evening and morning star fixes by the time the *Everett* reached Midway Island. He was also comfortable with using LORAN for radio navigation if clouds obscured the stars, and if the ship was within range of LORAN C stations. Midway Atoll consists of two main islands, Sand Island and Eastern Island, along with a spit of land called Spit Island. They are part of the long Hawaiian Archipelago in the middle of the Pacific Ocean, and Jason thought that whoever had named the dots of land was not particularly imaginative or creative.

There was one air strip on Sand Island and a facility for refueling ships, and this is what constituted the Naval Air Station. The *Everett* wasn't going to stay in port overnight and was there just long enough to take on fuel. However, the men were allowed to leave the ship, visit the base, and explore the wildlife that was part of this remote atoll.

Jason was aware that several rare species of animals used Midway as a breeding ground, including the endangered monk seal and Laysan albatross. Albatross were still nesting when the *Everett* came into port, and Jason wanted to get some pictures of the chicks in their ground nests. He figured the 200 mm lens would be particularly effective. As it turned out, it wasn't needed.

One of the main nesting areas was within walking distance of the ship. Jason lugged his camera bag with all the lenses to some trees, perhaps Australian pines, that were near the beach. Albatross were everywhere and really couldn't have cared less about Jason being there. He spotted several nests with chicks and a parent standing guard at each. The downy feathers of the chicks were puffed way out, making them look at least 50 percent bigger than the parent. As Jason took some shots at the base of a pine tree with the 100 mm portrait lens, the parent bird waggled its head at him and clacked its bill open and shut but showed no real signs of being concerned about the intrusion. He assumed the other parent was out over the ocean catching fish to bring back to feed the baby in the nest, at which point the other parent would take off to do some fishing while the chick was being fed.

Jason walked out onto the beach and watched the birds as they soared gracefully over the water and the beach. Upon landing, however, that gracefulness totally disappeared, reduced to an awkward waddle. An interesting bird. Over half of the world's breeding population was confined to this island. The idea of not having all your eggs in one basket, in this case literally, popped into his head.

He returned to the ship, once again hoping that the pictures would come out. It was a once in a lifetime opportunity. He seriously doubted that he would ever be back to Midway again.

Not long after Midway, they entered Hawaiian waters. Jason, having just spoken with BM1 Bennie Clarke about the preparations for their arrival in port, walked aft from the forecastle toward the wardroom. He had congratulated Clarke on the paint job First Division had given the *Everett*'s superstructure to match the work Hong Kong Mary's people had done on the ship's hull. Everyone wanted the ship to look its best coming back to home port. Before going in, he took a look toward the stern, checking out Kauai as it faded in the distance off the port side. As usual, the mountainous center of the island had captured its daily ration of clouds. Next stop: Pearl Harbor. They were due to arrive at three o'clock. Now, it was time for some lunch.

He entered the wardroom to find most of the guys already seated. In fact, the only one missing was Captain Ziegler. As he was taking his seat, he looked at the XO. "Captain won't be joining us?"

"No, he's tied up with some radio communications with Seventh Fleet. He'll grab something later."

Bautista brought out a bowl of tomato soup and placed it in front of the XO. Jason said, "Well, lookee here! The same meal as when we left for WestPac."

The XO grinned. "Gotta love the symmetry."

All the conversations concerned what everyone had planned for the first night back in Pearl. Jason didn't have a lot to say since he was going to be stuck on board for another night after volunteering to take the duty first night in.

The XO was watching him and guessed what he was thinking. "Conley, on behalf of everyone here, I'd like to thank you for volunteering to stay on board."

Ed raised his glass of water. "Here, here!"

Joe countered, "There, there!"

The XO looked at the two of them and said, "You know, there are some things I am *not* going to miss." He looked over at Barnaby. "Just so everyone knows, Mr. Barnaby here will have the deck and the conn as we enter port. It'll be his last time to do so. Gonna miss it, David?"

Barnaby shook his head. "Not really. I'm ready for something new. What I'm really thinking about is flying over to the Big Island tomorrow for some leave time. My wife and I are booked into the Mauna Kea Beach Hotel for the week."

Norm Shapiro whistled. "You must not've spent much while you were gone. That's gonna cost a pretty penny."

Barnaby nodded. "It's costing us *a lot* of pretty pennies, but it'll be worth it."

Without a lot to contribute, Jason remained fairly quiet for the rest of the lunch.

Joe, Ed, and Jason stayed in the wardroom while the stewards cleaned up after everyone had finished lunch.

Joe asked Jason, "Do you have the albums?"

Jason nodded toward the sofa. "They're over there in a brown paper bag behind the sofa."

Joe nodded. "Good. I brought a roll of duct tape from engineering."

Jason asked, "Do you really think customs is going to care if we have a dozen bootleg albums?"

Ed shrugged. "Not sure, but that's what the XO warned us about. I mean, I have no idea if they're going to search the ship or not. They'll probably be busy checking out all the booty in the hangar bay. But why take chances?"

Jason stood up and reached behind the sofa for the bag of bootlegs that they hadn't gotten around to recording. Joe and Ed crawled under the wardroom dining table. Joe said, "Okay, give me the bag."

While Joe held it in place against the bottom of the table, Ed secured it with an excessive amount of tape. Joe said, "I think that's more than enough."

"Hey, you don't want this contraband hitting the floor while we sit around the table with the customs officials going over the declaration forms with the XO," Ed said.

As Joe crawled out from under the table, he said, "Good point."

Jason, in dress whites, was on the forecastle with part of his crew. They had already passed Barber's Point Naval Air Station where the P3 Orions that he would someday be controlling were based, and the distinctive pink of the Tripler Army Hospital was visible, nestled on the hillside overlooking the harbor. Besides being a hospital, it was a landmark that was easy to take a fix on when approaching the mouth of the harbor.

As the *Everett* swung around to port, Jason knew they were home by the odor coming from the Dole cannery. They slipped past the first set of buoys. "Red right returning" popped into his head.

When they were just about even with the ARS docks, a motor whaleboat came alongside and tossed a line up to his men on the forecastle. The second class petty officer at the helm of the boat shouted up to Clarke, "Here's a little gift from headquarters for your arrival."

Clarke hauled in on the line and a huge bag was yanked out of the whaleboat and brought on board. Clarke opened it up and began to pull out the world's largest lei in all its rainbow-colored glory.

Jason went to the lifeline and shouted down to the boat, "Mahalo!"

The helmsman shouted back, "De nada! Everybody needs to get 'lei-ed' their first day back home!"

The irony of the double entendre was not lost on Jason. *Not necessarily everyone*, he thought, as he made his way forward to see how his men were going to secure the lei so that it draped over the bow. As his men maneuvered the lei in place, he glanced to starboard and noted that the *Engage* was in port. Apparently, they hadn't deployed on their WestPac, at least not yet. He figured he would have at least one person to say hi to since Sid was supposed to bring him his car keys.

Halfway through the channel, a tug came alongside to escort them to their berth. Jason could feel the change in engine speed as Barnaby slowed the ship to make a sharp turn to starboard on the final approach to the shipyard pier. The engine reversed briefly, and the tug moved to the starboard side of the stern to give the *Everett* a little nudge to get it lined up with where it was going to be docked.

Jason could now see that the pier was totally filled with women and children waiting for their loved ones. They were waving, shouting, laughing, and crying, awash in their emotions. All the men on the ship not directly involved with sea and anchor detail stood at attention along the lifelines, looking for their wives, girlfriends, and children. The men on the pier were having a tough time getting the crowds to move back so the *Everett*'s men could safely heave their monkey-fisted lines. With one last shudder in reverse from the prop as the lines slid over and secured the ship to the dock, WestPac was officially over.

As Clarke and his men secured the forward lines, another contingent from First Division near the stern slid the gangway over to establish the in-port quarterdeck where Jason would spend the remainder of the afternoon. Once in place, an announcement came over the 1 MC.

"Now, secure from sea and anchor detail. Liberty will commence for all authorized personnel at sixteen hundred hours. Escorted visitors will be permitted on board."

Jason made his way aft to take his place on the quarterdeck. He was joined there by Petty Officer Second Class Liston.

"Well, this is a surprise, Liston. You were here when I first came aboard. How'd you get stuck with duty today?"

"Well, sir, I really don't have family here and a lot of the guys do. I figured, what the hell, what's one more day."

"Sounds familiar. I'm in the same boat, literally and figuratively. I imagine it's going to be pretty damn hectic here for the next couple of hours."

"I'm sure you're right, sir. Do you know when they're going to start unloading all that shit from the hangar bay? Hope it's not now."

"No, that'll start tomorrow after the dust settles."

At four o'clock, men with their duffels started pouring down across the gangway and into the arms of their loved ones. Jason had to admit it was an awesome and touching sight. As he surveyed the crowd, he noticed one person who stood out like a sore thumb: Sid. Jason waved to him and motioned him to come aboard.

Sid was still in his work uniform, having come directly over from the *Engage*. He had to wait for a break in the exodus before he made it to the quarterdeck. "Permission to come aboard, sir."

"Permission granted." Jason gave Sid a quick hug. "I thought you guys might be gone by now."

"Almost. We leave tomorrow."

"Shit, no time to get a jam in."

"There's no place to jam, anyway. Remember, we gave up Paoakalani."

"Yeah, I'm gonna miss that place. Well, as you probably guessed, I'm stuck on here for the night, then I have to start the apartment search tomorrow. Fun times."

"Well, you'll need your car for that. Here's the keys. It's over in Parking Lot F. Full tank of gas. Thanks for letting me use it while you were gone. JJ's over there waiting for me in my car. We're spending the night on the ship. We leave at zero six hundred hours."

"Wait. Who's taking care of your car?"

Without answering the question, Sid grinned and said, "Be right back. I've got a surprise for you." He turned, saluted the ensign, and left.

Jason watched as Sid scurried across the gangway. He lost sight of him momentarily as he merged into the throng of people but then saw him pop out on the back side of the crowd. He disappeared behind a small building, and after a few seconds, emerged with another person in tow.

Sparrow.

Jason was stunned. His heart raced a bit as Sid and Sparrow crossed the gangway. Sparrow had a brown paper bag in her hand. When they hit the quarterdeck, she shoved the bag at Sid and said, "Here. Hold this, please!"

She turned back to Jason, gave him a big hug, pulled back a bit and then kissed him hard on the lips. Liston applauded. Grinning, he said, "I thought you didn't have anyone waiting for you."

Jason hugged her and said in her ear, "Boy, am I glad to see you." As they disengaged, Sparrow took the bag from Sid and handed it to Jason.

"I figured you were probably tired of ship food, so I made you a hoagie."

Jason was shaking his head. "Get the fuck out of here! A hoagie." He opened the bag, and that wonderful deli aroma wafted up to him. He noticed a bag of chips accompanied the sandwich. "You're the best!"

Sparrow said, "I know you have duty and work to do now. I have to drive Sid and JJ back to their ship."

"Wait, you're taking care of Sid's car?"

"Uh-huh. I can drive, you know."

"No, I didn't know, but that's great." He gave her a long look. "I'm off tomorrow. Want an exciting day of apartment hunting with me?"

"Wow. You really know a way to a girl's heart."

Liston was watching all this and just shaking his head. "Real smooth, sir."

"Liston, don't you have something better to do?"

"I do, sir, but this is more entertaining."

Sparrow said, "Anyway, about apartment hunting, you can take your time, if you want."

"Well, I sure don't want to stay on board here or in the BOQ."

"Look, you goof, you can stay with me."

Jason looked over at Liston, who was still grinning but now nodding his head. "Oh, right, sir, something better to do coming right up." He left them to greet some visitors coming across the gangway.

"Are you sure?"

"Never more sure of anything. So, look, I've gotta get the guys back to the *Engage*. I have a class in the morning, but you can come over anytime. Here's the key. You were in 3B before. I'm in 3C. It'll look familiar, except that mine is better furnished than yours was. Beer's in the fridge."

Jason was shaking his head. He looked over at Sid, who gave him a thumbs-up. He looked back to Sparrow, then gave her another hug. "Best surprise *ever*. Thank you. And yes, I'll see you tomorrow."

He went over to Sid and shook his hand. "Thanks, Sid. You guys be safe over there. The band'll get back together when you return. Sorry you all have to go."

"Not as sorry as we are! We'll be fine. C'mon, Sparrow, you get to play chauffeur now."

Sparrow gave Jason a quick kiss, and she and Sid departed the ship. Jason watched them until they were out of sight at the end of the pier. All his worries had evaporated. He walked back over to Liston.

"Well, sir, it looks like you're sittin' pretty, and I do mean pretty."

"Yeah, she's pretty amazing. Quite a character."

"I just have one question, sir."

"What's that, Liston?"

"What's a hoagie?"

TWENTY-FIVE

Deep Water Off Kailua-Kona

AUGUST 1973

Pushing the limits. That's what the high-speed run was all about. Come out of the shipyard and let 'er rip. Of course, this ship was originally supposed to have twin screws and hit thirty-six knots to be able to play with the underwater nukes, but those pesky budgetary limitations had cut off one screw and the *Everett* ended up with a top speed of twenty-eight knots. This extended run off the coast of the Big Island was just part of the shakedown cruise every ship goes through after an extended shipyard stay. Fleet Training Group (FTG) personnel were crawling all over the ship from the bilge to the flying bridge.

Jason stood on the port bridge wing looking out at the sparkling lights surrounding the harbor of Kailua-Kona a few hours before midnight. To the right of the harbor lights and fifteen hundred feet above them were the lesser lights of the town of Captain Cook, a marker for the famous Kona coffee belt. Far down the coast was a solitary light perched at South Point, the southernmost piece of land in the United States. All of this coastline was fair game for Jason and his quartermasters, targets for fixes as they kept track of where the *Everett* had been and at what time it had been there in order to calculate the actual speed over water.

Inside the bridge, Lt.j.g. Jack Culpepper had the deck and a new officer, Ensign George Watson, had the conn. It was a beautiful, clear night with no moon visible. There was very little boat traffic out on the water, especially since the area in which the *Everett* was cruising was a dedicated Naval Operations Area. It was their second night out of port, and all seemed calm, significantly different from the inauspicious beginning less than forty-eight hours earlier.

Jason had left the two-bedroom bungalow he shared with Sparrow Gatling in Waimanalo at oh-dark-thirty to get to Pearl in time to get underway at six o'clock. The bungalow, surrounded by orchid farms on a small road named Orchid Row, used to be rented by Ed and his girlfriend, Chelsea, who were now back on the West Coast in San Francisco. The owner of the bungalow was glad to have another couple move in rather than rent to several Navy men, like Sid and his friends at Paoakalani Avenue, or a group of marines from the air station at Kaneohe.

Upon his arrival at the ship, Jason was shocked to hear that the new XO, Lt. Cmdr. Louis Rossitter, was going to be taking the ship out, rather than one of the more experienced officers. Rossitter had never been underway on the *Everett*. It would be really bad to have any screw-ups while under the scrutiny of FTG. To the XO's credit, he had been an ops officer on a DE that was the same class as the *Everett*, but all his experience was back on the East Coast. He had never taken a ship out of Pearl Harbor.

The sky over Pearl was just beginning to lighten. As Jason prepared his men on the bridge to get underway, he noticed that the XO had taken his position on the flying bridge, which meant all of Jason's recommendations for speed and rudder changes had to be relayed through the sound-powered phone operators. He didn't like the way this was shaping up. The lines were cast off and the *Everett*'s speed was set at back two-thirds. The *Everett* backed into the main channel of the harbor, and Jason recommended coming to back one-third.

No response. He continued to plot the ship's positions as information from his quartermasters filtered in from the bridge wings. He recommended coming to engine stop.

No response. Jason asked the sound-powered phone operator if he was being acknowledged. "That's affirmative, sir."

Jason recommended ahead one-third to put the brakes on and told the quartermaster at the ship's log to make sure all his recommendations were being recorded. Conley had no intention of going up before the "long green table" of review officers for being a fuck-up if something went wrong. Finally, the order for "engine stop" was relayed from the flying bridge to the helm, but by then, it was too late.

The stern of the *Everett* had the Arizona Memorial squarely in its sights. Jason leaned over the starboard bridge wing and looked at the memorial. A small Asian man carrying a bucket and a mop was walking out on the landing area to swab the deck down before the first round of tourists arrived. The first shuttle would be arriving at any minute. The man looked up and a horrified look registered on his face as he saw the ass end of the destroyer escort bearing down on him. He dropped the mop and bucket and began waving his arms over his head.

Even in the severity of the moment, Jason couldn't keep from laughing. He looked at the quartermaster on the starboard pelorus and said, "Like we can't see the whole fucking memorial, but we'll notice him waving his arms. Well, I don't know about you, but I don't want to be known as the person who sank the *Arizona* a second time." He waited just a few seconds to see if anything more was coming down from the flying bridge. He turned to the sound-powered phone operator and said, "Get the forecastle. Tell them to drop anchor."

"Drop anchor, sir?"

"Yes, drop anchor *now!*"

Several seconds later, the same order came from the flying bridge, issued by Captain Ziegler.

Everyone on the bridge could feel the chain clanking out of the chain locker as the anchor headed for the muddy bottom of the harbor. With a slight lurch, they all felt the anchor grab and the ship began to slowly swing, pivoting on the chain. Mud swirled around the stern; the screw was that close to the bottom.

Signals began to flash at them from other ships around the harbor. Jason asked the signalman what they were saying.

"Oh, they just want to know things like, 'Do we all have our tickets for our visit to the memorial,' or 'Do you know you can catch a shuttle to the memorial for free,' or 'Why aren't you at ramming speed?' You know, sir, funny stuff like that."

Jason sighed. He went into the bridge and asked the quartermaster if he got that whole exchange between his recommendations and the orders from the flying bridge.

"Yes, sir. You're good."

Captain Ziegler, the XO, and an agitated FTG observer made their way down to the bridge. Ziegler looked at Jason. Quietly, he said, "I assume you have recommendations to get us out of this, er, situation."

"Yes, sir."

He turned to the XO. "Haul anchor and let's get the hell out of here. Mr. Conley will give you a course and recommended speed."

"Aye, Captain."

Compared to yesterday morning, this high-speed run is a walk in the park, Jason thought. Data concerning the performance of the twelve-hundred-pound steam plant during the scheduled high-speed run had been collected, and the ship prepared to drop to a lower speed. Jason went out on the bridge wing where QM3 Patterson was manning the pelorus. They were gazing out at the coast when what appeared to be a huge ball of fire zoomed directly over the ship and disappeared over the horizon.

Jason and Patterson looked at each other. Simultaneously, they said, "Did you see that?"

Jason said, "Mr. Culpepper. Can you come out here for a moment?"

Jack Culpepper came out on the wing and said, "Nice night. I guess we passed the high-speed test."

"Did you notice anything on the radar?"

"No, why?"

"Can you call down to CIC and see if they had anything on the air search radar just a minute ago?"

"Sure." Culpepper got the sound-powered phone operator to make Jason's request. Jason could hear the reply.

Culpepper said, "Nope, they got nothing. What's this all about?"

Jason and Patterson explained what they saw.

Culpepper said, "Meteor?"

Jason shook his head. "I've seen lots of meteors but never saw one move like that. It seemed to originate near South Point, go right over us, and then continue out to sea west of Oahu."

As they were gazing up at the sky, another fireball was seen coming from the horizon near South Point. It followed the exact same track as the first and went directly over the *Everett*.

"Son of a bitch," whispered Culpepper. He said to the man on sound-powered phones, "Ask CIC again if they got anything."

A minute later, "No, sir. Nothing."

Jason said to Culpepper, "We'll have to really check this out when we get back in port. Testing some new aircraft? Was it meteors? Anyway, for now, they're UFOs. I think we should log the observations."

"I agree," said Culpepper. "What's the worst they can do? Slap us in the looney bin?"

"Well, we have at least three people who saw them. What I can't figure out is how they didn't register on surface or air search radars. Anyway, I'm about to hit my bunk. I think I'll just hang here on the bridge wing for a minute." Jason pulled out a cigar. "Well, maybe more than a minute. You know what's on tap for tomorrow?"

Culpepper said, "Yeah. We're going to test our new Basic Point Defense Missile System. We'll shoot some surface-to-air missiles at a couple of drones, and then we head in. Oh, you'll like this; the missile is called a Sea Sparrow."

"I think I'll just neglect to tell Miss Gatling that she shares her name with a missile."

After Culpepper went back inside the bridge, Jason was left alone with his thoughts as he stared at the silhouette of the Big Island. Being back out at sea made him think about all the time they'd spent in WestPac and what they did there. A lot had changed in just a year's time. He thought about how different life had been aboard the *Everett* as compared to the *Engage* and how it had changed him. He was immeasurably more self-confident in terms of his interactions with the men on the ship and how he carried out his duties. But at a deeper level, particularly when interacting with civilians off the base, some of that self-confidence was missing.

Jason rarely spoke to Sparrow about what had happened during his time off the coast of Vietnam, and for that matter, he never spoke about it to anyone unless he was asked directly about it. He never knew how they would react if he said he had served in the controversial conflict. Even in a place like Hawai'i that was steeped in military history, the Vietnam War was a divisive issue. Jason would come to understand that even many years later, it would still be a topic that he would keep close. Nothing to share, and certainly nothing to brag about.

Jason was due to leave the *Everett* in a couple of months, and while he would miss being out at sea, he was ready for a change. Like Joe, he would be heading to the Human Resource Management Center at Pearl. His main job there would be as a management consultant to commands in Hawai'i and Whidbey Island Naval Air Station in the Puget Sound. He would be trained to remediate communications and race relations problems in commands that were identified through a process called Survey-Guided Development. What really intrigued him was that one other duty he would have would be as an International Relations Specialist, conducting workshops so that Navy personnel about to be stationed in foreign countries wouldn't come across as ugly Americans. He was looking forward to that.

The HRMC assignment nearly didn't happen. Jason had been expecting orders for a transfer to a new post. He had spoken to his detailer about it, and had given him several preferences, including the Human Resource Management Center at Pearl. He had already spoken with the commanding officer there who said they had a position coming open. He figured it was a shoo-in.

Not so.

When his orders had arrived, they were for an unaccompanied tour of duty as officer in charge of a naval detachment on a Sea Lift Command ocean-going tug in the North Atlantic, a ship slightly smaller than the *Engage*. Jason was furious. The unaccompanied tour part he could almost understand; the Navy certainly didn't recognize his living arrangements with Sparrow as a family member who needed to be taken into consideration.

However, after spending three years on sea duty, including a WestPac/Vietnam deployment, he thought it was time for something a little better. Once again, he felt like he was on that runaway train with no control over its destination.

Well, he had thought, *it's time for me to be the engineer of the train.*

Jason had prepared a message for Admiral Zumwalt, chief of naval operations. Zumwalt had been very attentive to the needs of the enlisted men and officers in the Navy since taking over as CNO. He listened. He also had expressed concerns about the lack of junior officer retention, especially those officers coming back from WestPac. In his message, Jason explained that it was no wonder junior officers were leaving the Navy's ranks if the thanks they got for doing three years of sea duty, including a WestPac/Vietnam deployment, was more sea duty, unaccompanied, in one of the world's harshest environments, the North Atlantic. Additionally, he reasoned, why would the Navy go to the expense of shipping an officer and all his goods halfway around the world when a command at his current base requested his presence.

Of course, it was worded very carefully and included an endorsement from Captain Zeigler and an endorsement from the commanding officer of the HRMC, who also sent a separate message requesting that Jason be assigned to his command.

The messages were sent. He never would have had the nerve to make those moves three years ago.

Then, Jason had waited. He didn't have to wait long.

Four days after sending his message, Jason received message orders to report to the Pearl Harbor HRMC, message orders promulgated by Admiral Zumwalt himself. Jason had to admit that he was in total disbelief that it worked. He had switched the tracks the train was on and then stopped the train. He liked the station at which it stopped.

Even now, standing on the bridge wing, looking out at the Big Island, he couldn't believe he would be at the HRMC, working again with Joe, and living with Sparrow in Waimanalo. What a change from when he first came out to Hawai'i and reported to the *Engage*. He was genuinely excited about what he would be doing now, actually helping people to work effectively in commands and to be successful if they were assigned to a base in a foreign country. Yes, a far cry from what he had been engaged in over the past year, or so. Quite a change. A very welcome change.

Jason took a last puff on one of his remaining Cubans, took one last look at the Big Island, and headed for his stateroom.

When they arrived back in port the following day, Jason phoned Sparrow.

"We just got in, so I'll be home for dinner. Want me to pick up anything?"

"No, I'm all set here. Hope you're hungry."

"I am. What've you got?"

"It's a surprise."

Jason paused. He never thought he would say this. "Okay. Surprise me. Just anything but a hoagie."

There was a long pause at the other end. "Um..."

ACKNOWLEDGMENTS

As always, this book has benefited from comments made by my friend and colleague, Jane McFann, author of many wonderful young adult novels and cozy mysteries. Jane has had the dubious honor of getting to read everything I have ever written, going back over thirty years to my newspaper columns in *The Newark Post*. Her insights and critiques are invaluable. Susan Bartley, my very supportive wife, also was an early reader of the manuscript. Her comments were virtually identical to those made by Jane. I think they were in collusion. Susan also has a very good eye for detail, a skill that often eludes me.

Many other friends took the time to read early drafts of this novel and offer suggestions including Erin Tanner, Eileen Voltz, Geoff Franklin, John Pollard, Jasey Schnarz, Marsha Middleton, Christine Savage, and Maya Paul. My heartfelt thanks to all of you!

Everyone at Köehler Books has been a pleasure to work with, starting with John Köehler. His support and guidance, especially in marketing, have been invaluable. Lauren Sheldon created several outstanding covers after working with me to ascertain the kind of design I found attractive. The poll created by her to narrow the choices down to one was particularly constructive. Finally, Becky Hilliker, executive editor at Köehler Books, took my manuscript and made it much more readable. The improvements were dramatic. I am in your debt, Becky! Mahalo!

One technical point—the USS *Everett* is a Knox-class destroyer escort. A ship with this name was never commissioned. To maintain the ship's fictional status, I didn't want to use a ship that had actually existed. There were a lot of Knox-class destroyer escorts, forty-six to be exact, and none of them lasted in the US Navy for more than twenty-three years. They were also known as "McNamara's Folly" since they were scaled down from their original anti-submarine configuration due to budget constraints.

While this is a work of fiction, many of the events actually happened, in one way or another. The stories are based on my experiences in the US Navy, my life in Hawai'i, and my interactions with the many outstanding men with whom I served, friends I continue to be in touch with today—Ed Armijo, Tom Baker, Tom Kauffman, Richard Studley, Jerry Gallion, and Jackie Crowther. Knowing them has been an honor and a privilege.

ABOUT THE AUTHOR

Jack Bartley lived on Oahu for almost five years while serving as an officer in the US Navy in the 1970s, completing a WestPac/Vietnam tour on a Knox-class destroyer escort during that time. He returned to the East Coast to earn his PhD in ecology and was an associate professor at the University of Delaware. He is now retired and devotes his time to writing and music.

Jack's column "Educational Perspectives" appeared monthly in the *Newark Post* for ten years. He published the romantic comedy *Public Ed—A Novel* in 2005 and e-versions are still available through Amazon and Barnes and Noble. The first book of his young adult novel series, *Hilo Dome*, is scheduled for release through Histria Books on May 20, 2025, to be followed by *The Seekers* and *The World Awakens*. His children's chapter book, *Dinsdale*, is under review for publication by Histria Books. Jack has just completed the adult novel, *Incoming*, based on a real-life incident concerning an imminent missile attack on Oahu in 2018.

Jack has released two CDs of Celtic folk music with his former band, So's Your Mom, and is nearing the completion of a double-CD of Americana Music with his duo Whiskey Creek.

Jack is a volunteer docent at the James Farm Ecological Preserve and an instructor at the Osher Lifelong Learning Institute (OLLI) near his home in Ocean View, Delaware, where he lives with his wife, Susan, Jesse the dog, and Clementine the cat.

www.ingramcontent.com/pod-product-compliance
Lightning Source LLC
LaVergne TN
LVHW041746060526
838201LV00046B/925